PURE SWEET HELL

Bishop worked for the FBI and it was his job to investigate the cocaine smugglers who were now operating from a coastal town in Spain. Disguised as a sailor on shore-leave—and with two small packets of cocaine to flush out the dealers—he found Brad, his contact, and everything was going just fine. Then he ran into a blonde American tourist, Banjo Kelly, who wouldn't leave him alone... and a young pimp named Pablo, very helpful, very persistent, who introduced him to Pepita, a black-haired gypsy who only wanted to take him to bed.

Then Brad turned up dead and everything hit the fan. Now the cops are after him, his packets have gone missing, he's being followed by a couple of local thugs, and it's become a challenge just to stay alive, much less track down the drug dealers. It's going to be a long night, a back alley and rooftop race from one bar (and bed) to the next. In fact, it's going to be hell—pure sweet hell.

CATCH A FALLEN STARLET

Alan Dufferin had been married to Clare, Hollywood's girl-next-door. He had been one of Hollywood's hottest scriptwriters. But that was before the accident—when Clare was still alive—before Dufferin dried out and moved to New York. But now Dufferin is back, talking to Clare's old agent, Bertha Tweedy, and being offered a deal from has-been star Barry Kevin to script his big comeback production of *Cellini*.

That night he discovers Kevin beaten to death. And now a couple of heavies are coming around his sister's house, asking not-too-politely for a document that Dufferin doesn't have. Kevin's wife isn't any help, but her sister Gloria suddenly takes an interest. A strong, personal interest. Dufferin doesn't have what they want, but when a single page of a confession is mailed to him in Clare's handwriting, he knows he better find the rest of it fast, before someone else ends up dead—himself.

DOUGLAS SANDERSON BIBLIOGRAPHY

Dark Passions Subdue (US, 1952)

Final Run (UK, 1956) aka *Flee from Terror* (US, 1957) as by Martin Brett and *Un bouquet de chardons* (Fr, 1957)

Night of the Horns (UK, 1958) aka *Murder Comes Calling* (US, 1958) as by Malcolm Douglas

Cry Wolfram (UK, 1959) aka *Mark it for Murder* (US, 1959) and *La semaine de bonté* (Fr, 1958)

Catch a Fallen Starlet (US, 1960) aka *The Stubborn Unlaid* and *Cinémaléfices* (Fr, 1960)

Lam to Slaughter (UK, 1964) aka *As-tu vu Carcassone?* (Fr, 1963)

Black Reprieve (UK, 1965) aka *White Man Dead* and *Couper cabèche* (Fr, 1964)

No Charge for Framing (UK, 1969)

A Dead Bullfighter (UK, 1975)

As by Martin Brett

Exit in Green (US, 1953) re-written as *Murder Came Tumbling* (UK, 1959)

*Hot Freeze** (US/UK, 1954) aka *Mon cadavre au Canada* (Fr, 1955)

*Darker Traffic** (US, 1954) aka *Blondes are My Trouble* (US, 1955) and *Salmigonzesses* (Fr, 1956)

Flee from Terror (US, 1957) aka *Final Run* (UK, 1956) and *Un bouquet de chardons* (Fr, 1957) as by Douglas Sanderson

The Shreds published as *Sables-d'or-les-pains!* (Fr, 1958)

The Dead Connection published as *La came á papa* (Fr, 1961)

*A Dum-Dum for the President** (UK, 1961) aka *Estocade au Canada* (Fr, 1961)

Score for Two Dead published as *Le moîne connait la musique* (Fr, 1964)

*Mike Garfin series

As by Malcolm Douglas

Prey by Night (US, 1955) aka *A boulets Rouges* (Fr, 1956)

Rain of Terror (US, 1955) aka *And All Flesh Died* and *Le Fête a la grenouille* (Fr, 1956)

The Deadly Dames (US, 1956) aka *Du Rebecca chez les femmes* (Fr, 1956)

Pure Sweet Hell (US, 1957)

Murder Comes Calling (US, 1958) aka *Night of the Horns* (UK, 1958) as by Douglas Sanderson

Shout for a Killer published as *Chabanais chez les pachas* (Fr, 1963)

Pure Sweet Hell
Catch a Fallen Starlet

Douglas Sanderson

STARK
HOUSE

Stark House Press • Eureka California

PURE SWEET HELL / CATCH A FALLEN STARLET

Published by Stark House Press
1315 H Street
Eureka, CA 95501, USA
griffinskye3@sbcglobal.net
www.starkhousepress.com

PURE SWEET HELL
Originally published as by "Malcolm Douglas" by Gold Medal Books, Greenwich, and copyright © 1957 by Fawcett Publications, Inc. Copyright © renewed Dec. 26, 1985 by Douglas Sanderson.

CATCH A FALLEN STARLET
Originally published by Avon Books, New York, and copyright © 1960 by Douglas Sanderson. Copyright © renewed Dec. 23, 1988 by Douglas Sanderson

Reprinted by permission of John D. Sanderson for the Estate of Douglas Sanderson.

"Hold On: The Dark Wild Fiction of Ronald Douglas Sanderson" copyright © 2004 by Kevin Burton Smith

"Introduction" copyright © 2004 by John Douglas Sanderson

All rights reserved.

ISBN: 0-9749438-2-7
ISBN-13: 978-0-9749438-2-4

Book design by Mark Shepard, shepgraphics.com
Cover art by Marina Iborra

The publishers would like to thank John Douglas Sanderson and Marina Iborra for all their help in the production of this book.

PUBLISHER'S NOTE
This is a work of fiction. Names, characters, places and incidents are either the products of the author's imagination or used fictitiously, and any resemblance to actual persons, living or dead, events or locales, is entirely coincidental.
Without limiting the rights under copyright reserved above, no part of this publication may be reproduced, stored, or introduced into a a retrieval system or transmitted in any form or by any means (electronic, mechanical, photocopying, recording or otherwise) without the prior written permission of both the copyright owner and the above publisher of this book.

First Stark House Press Edition: September 2004

TABLE OF CONTENTS

Hold On: The Dark Wild Fiction
of Ronald Douglas Sanderson
by Kevin Burton Smith 7

Introduction
by John D. Sanderson 11

Pure Sweet Hell 15

Catch a Fallen Starlet 127

Hold On:
The Dark Wild Fiction of Ronald Douglas Sanderson
by Kevin Burton Smith

The operative words here are "Hold on."

In one of the most famous bits of plotting advice ever given to aspiring mystery writers, Raymond Chandler once cracked, "When in doubt have a man come through the door with a gun in his hand."

Were Ronald Douglas Sanderson asked for similar advice, he probably would have offered something along the lines of, "When in doubt have a bleeding man come crashing through the window with a gun in his hand, followed by a crooked cop, a dope fiend of dubious sexual orientation and ethnicity, and a chaste young white girl unaware that her twin sister is an alcoholic nymphomaniac laying dead in the closet."

Sanderson was born in 1922 in Kent, England, and passed away in 2002 in Alicante, Spain, where he had lived for many decades. He served in the RAF during WWII, and later emigrated to Canada with the intention of studying at Montreal's McGill University. He worked as a waiter, a clerk in a jewelry store and a nightclub singer, which lead to his employment as a presenter of musical radio programs for the Canadian Broadcasting Corporation. He soon began writing radio plays and documentaries for them, as well.

If he's remembered at all by the reading public, it's among paperback and crime fiction aficionados, for the two dozen or so hard, fast novels he wrote as, alternately, Malcolm Douglas, Douglas Sanderson and Martin Brett. Nobody would ever mistake him for a long lost literary giant, and most of his books have lapsed into obscurity (an error this volume hopes to begin to correct), but his twisted and often nasty tales of obsession stand up amazingly well, even forty or fifty years later, and still pack a visceral wallop that's hard to deny.

Sanderson's specialty was a sort of baroque noir. His books were twitchy, neurotic pulp fiction; jacked-up kaleidoscopic whirls of desperate, gloriously flawed characters, audacious coincidence and almost impressionistic action scenes punctuated by jarring explosions of violence and sex that would only finally make sense at the very end. And sometimes not even then.

For Sanderson's heroes, invariably damaged young men searching for some sort of salvation, redemption or at least the chance to live another day, there was never going to be any easy solution or any real refuge—not in the elegiac romanticism of Chandler nor in the terse, clean hardboiled heroics of Dashiell Hammett. The books were definitely downers, electro-shock therapy for the Cold War era's numerous psychoses and obsessions. The plots read like a shotgun marriage between Jim Thompson and Mickey Spillane—on speed.

Nor were they particularly enlightened reads. Sanderson, along with many of his contemporaries, was clearly working out major issues. Some of the attitudes expressed are way past their expiry date and jaw-droppingly politically incorrect: racial and homophobic slurs abound, and women are seldom depicted in their best light. Yet there's a vibrancy and heady energy to these tomes of violence and barely articulated anger that hold their own even now.

□ □ □

In 1952, while living in Montreal, Sanderson published his first novel, *Dark Passions Subdue*, a literary novel he claimed was "a puritan ode to repressed homosexuality." It didn't exactly set the world on fire, selling only a few thousand copies, so he went searching for a more profitable genre. Keenly aware of the nearby American market, where Mickey Spillane's Mike Hammer books were selling millions, Sanderson decided to take a stab at crime fiction.

The story goes that he visited a local drugstore, scanned the back cover blurbs of a few Spillane paperbacks on the rack and went home to see if he could write one. His first effort, *Exit in Green* (1953), a thriller set in a small Québecois village in the Laurentians met with some success, and was soon followed by several other noirish thrillers, including *Hot Freeze* (1954), which introduced Montreal private eye Mike Garfin. Garfin would be Sanderson's only series character, but he was typical of most of Sanderson's protagonists—not so much a Chandleresque white knight as a *bête noire*. He was, perhaps unsurprisingly, far closer to Hammer: obsessive, driven, angry, capable of great brutality and violence if provoked, but also capable of great loyalty. But these characters lacked the unflappable macho indestructibility of Spillane's detective/avenger—it's not uncommon for a Sanderson hero, in the midst of everything, to faint. From exhaustion, hunger, from too much drink… this odd vulnerability added a much needed human touch to the action which, in a Sanderson book, was always perilously close to going completely off the rails.

□ □ □

His work sold well enough in North America, but it was the Europeans, particularly the French, who really took him to heart. There, critics praised his work for its Existential bleakness, reveling in what they saw as his unflinching depiction of the noir underbelly of American Puritanism. Fifteen of his novels were eventually translated and published as part of the prestigious *Série Noire*.

Pure Sweet Hell, first published in 1957 by Fawcett Gold Medal, was written under the Malcolm Douglas pen name, and it's a real trip, literally. The action, which takes places in a series of bars, back alleys and bordellos in a hot, humid Spanish port town, reaches almost-surrealistic, nightmarish dimensions. The protagonist is Bishop, an "agency man" going undercover as a small-time cocaine smuggler to nab the mysterious Mr. Big of the local drug trade. But things go real wrong real fast, and soon Bishop is out in the cold, his only local contact murdered, on the run from both the police and rival gangs—not to mention Banjo Kelly, a spunky American photojournalist, and Pepita, an amorous Spanish whore, both of whom have designs on the handsome G-man. Along the way there are numerous killings, betrayals, a little genital mutilation and some prime evidence that frequently, inconveniently disappears. It's an almost perfect example of Sanderson's M.O.

❑ ❑ ❑

And 1960's *Catch a Fallen Starlet* by Douglas Sanderson and published by Avon, bears the same hallmark. Like a master jazz man or Jerry Lee Lewis playing Great Balls of Fire, Sanderson could rework the same motifs over and over again, and always make it seem fresh and new. Once again, Sanderson follows an ostensibly good (but far from perfect) man into a colorful setting and once again he flips that world over, exposing the place where the dark and nasty things thrive. The setting, as the title may suggest, is Hollywood itself, and Sanderson seems to take special delight in transforming the dream factory into a hell of ego and naked ambition fueled by greed, alcohol and narcotics, a virtue-free zone where wet-mouthed actresses chase "the gangster scum of the country" and actors "flout the Mann Act and import their own underage protegees." Into this maelstrom wanders Al Dufferin, a disgraced and despised alcoholic screenwriter once married to "America's sweetheart" and largely blamed by the public at large for the circumstances which led to her tragic death. Returned to his hometown after a few years of self-imposed exile in New York, working for the then-new television industry, Al's not back long before Barry Kevin, the washed-up actor who lured him back to town with promises of a job is discovered beaten to death. It doesn't take long before Al is dodging a murder frame-up, pursued by the law, assorted murderous thugs and the usual cast of Sanderson deviants, the violence mounting to Grand Guignol proportions. It's enough to make a guy jump off the wagon.

☐ ☐ ☐

And that's the thing with Sanderson's characters, even his "heroes"—they may be unsavory and unsympathetic, deserving victims of their own worst instincts and base weaknesses. You may not like them or even understand them, but you'll sure want to know what happens to them.

And you'll keep reading because, like Sanderson's protagonists, once you're caught in that nightmare world, it's damn hard to get out.

But don't take my word for it—see for yourself. Pour yourself a stiff one, and grab hold of this volume with both hands. You'll need a good solid grip—it's going to be a hell of a ride.

>   Kevin Burton Smith
>   The Thrilling Detective Web Site
>   http://www.thrillingdetective.com
>   California, June 2004

Introduction
by John D. Sanderson

These two novels, written by my father at two important moments in his life, have stirred up memories and other unexpected feelings in me when I have read them hardly a year after his death. *Pure Sweet Hell* was originally published back in March 1957, three months before he married my mother in Alicante, Spain. *Catch a Fallen Starlet* in 1960, when the three of us had just settled down in Montreal, Canada, where we would live for a long period of time. Over the years we never got to speak about these novels, these times, or so many other things either. Many questions now remain unanswered, so being able to delve into his work for this volume has been revealing in many ways.

I cannot help hearing my father's voice in their first person narrators. Bishop, an alien in Spanish territory, and Dufferin, a writer, are for me obviously his *alter-ego*. That *Pure Sweet Hell* of a town in southern Spain is clearly Alicante, where I live now, and Dufferin's struggle with the adaptations to the screen of his writing, as portrayed in *Catch a Fallen Starlet*, was present throughout the late fifties and early sixties in my father's life. To my knowledge, there has only been one production based on his work, a TV play of *The Night of the Horns*, which was premiered by BBC Television in May 1964. But something else might have happened in France, where he became very popular after meeting Marcel Duhamel, executive of *Editorial Gallimard*, who had fallen in love with his early thrillers set in Canada and eventually published fifteen of my father's novels in his *Serie Noire*. I have heard of a French television adaptation of *Lam to Slaughter* made in the early 70's, but have not been able to confirm its existence.

The two novels that make up this volume introduce easily recognisable features of his writing. The lead male character has just arrived at the location where the plot will develop (Alicante and Hollywood), looks around and tells us what he sees and how he feels in that environment. He is very aware of his appearance, and his self-deprecating irony is present right from the very beginning: "I felt like an unemployed samba dancer" (first paragraph in *Pure Sweet Hell*), "I looked like the Sultan's favourite" (second paragraph in *Catch a Fallen Starlet*). There are a whole lot of things going on by the time the narration gets started, and our hero updates us with his knowledge. But he does not know as much as he would like to, so the plot gets more and more entangled with seemingly secondary characters acquiring unexpected relevance.

He is not that physically strong either, so he gets most of the beating, which is assumed with sarcastic one-liners. I find that his sense of humour plays a far more important part in his novels than the gory details, even though some critics have claimed that the violence in them is "unbearable." And the hero's constant references to music, especially to opera, are only a logical literary consequence of what I heard played at home during my upbringing.

I have also come across some private family jokes and matters which have been fun to read after so many years. We used to find hilarious the way English names and words were pronounced in Spain at a time when hardly anybody learnt foreign languages (General Franco's dictatorship had isolated the country in many ways). *Esmitt* and *Meesta* are widespread in *Pure Sweet Hell*, where only the policeman who wanted to arrest Bishop and Pepita the gipsy for kissing in the street manages to put together a few words without much success: "Waat ees rahng, (...) I onnerstahn. I estoddy English tree years." Actually, my father told me in his later years that this episode was a real life experience of his. He had seen Pepita, a local whore, the day she won the lottery in Alicante, and they went on an all-night-boozing tour of the city; she paid. As they were kissing goodbye, a policeman stopped them and threatened to take them to *comisaría*. She blew up, screaming he was one of her customers and she had the right to make a living. The policeman let them go. However, the border between fact and fiction blurs with age, so whatever happened with the so-called Pepita is yet another question that will remain unanswered.

Some of the places described in the novel still survive in Alicante, such as *La Goleta*, a restaurant mentioned in the first chapter, and *Rincón Bohemio*, now a disco-bar. *Socorro Street* is evidently *Calle Virgen del Socorro*, where my father was living when he wrote *Pure Sweet Hell*. Actually, the excellent cover art of Marina Iborra, an Alicantina artist, portrays Bishop and Pepita running up *Calle Villavieja*, which leads from a square at the back of the Town Hall to *Virgen del Socorro*, which they are about to enter. I suppose my father simplified its name because an English-speaking reader would have had trouble linking the racket which was going on there with the name of a virgin. Officially, though, bordellos and other such places did not exist in Spain: whoever said otherwise was obviously an infiltrated communist. And cocaine?! As a Spanish friend was recently telling me, this novel was fortunately written and published in English. If it had been written in Spanish, my father would have ended up in jail, and he would never have had it published.

Sadly, places such as the old harbour gate and the Hotel Palas, also mentioned in the novel, no longer exist after having fallen victim to the longstanding obsession of the current local authorities with "architectural modernisation," achieved by pulling down ancient buildings and replacing them with blocks of flats. Lottery sellers chanting their numbers, guitarists playing spontaneously in bars and even irrelevant objects such as wax paper matches are also past remembrances now conjured up by reading *Pure Sweet Hell*.

As for *Catch a Fallen Starlet*, it reflects mainly the common passion my father shared with me for films (by the way, Dufferin, the male lead in the novel, has a young son called, yes, Johnny). In it you can find references to *Citizen Kane*, Cecil B. De Mille, Walt Disney and the cooperation between Graham Greene and Carol Reed in *The Third Man*, perhaps something he would have liked to achieve in those days when some film offers started trickling in. He never did. Interestingly enough, there are also references, some ironic, to several actors such as James Dean, Marlon Brando, Fredric March, Gary Cooper, Cary Grant *et al*, but not to the one actor I was brought up to believe was the best in the History of Cinema (and perhaps he was): James Cagney. Just by sheer coincidence, as I am writing these lines there is a James Cagney season on at the British Film Institute in London. And the other day I was watching *Footlight Parade* (Busby Berkeley, 1933) on video here in Alicante. There is something about that short, lively, chattering actor which does remind me of my father.

He loved films, but he did experience his own nightmarish experience with the world of cinema. It was with his personal favourite novel, *Prey by Night* (1955), the first one set in Spain, where he had arrived after his first seven-year period in Canada. The film rights had been bought by someone linked to Marion Gering, the director who had worked with the likes of George Brent and Carole Lombard back in the 30's and was now attempting a comeback in Europe. He actually travelled to Spain to meet my father and the head of a Spanish film company, Suevia Films, who, after numerous meetings and letters, eventually turned down the proposal saying that only a Spaniard could write about his country. Gering ended up directing what would be his last film, *Violated Paradise* (1963), in another exotic location, Japan, and *Prey by Night* never got made. I remember my father referring to this episode over the years, and perhaps his mixed feelings of excitement and rancour are present in Dufferin, since it was at the time he was writing *Catch a Fallen Starlet* when these negotiations were still going on.

I can also find in Dufferin his spite for television, which he considered a threat to cinema at a time when it only seemed to be able to release productions such as the *I Was a Wean Age Tear Wolf* which he mentions in Chapter 2. As a matter of fact, once we got back to Spain he did not allow a television set in the house, seemingly to keep us away from the Francoist propaganda blurting out of the screen. Therefore, I could only watch films at movie theatres and spend my free time at home reading books. That might have had something to do with the fact that I ended up teaching Film and Literature at the University of Alicante and professionally translating Shakespeare into Spanish.

On the whole it has been an extremely gratifying experience for me, with the occasional pang of pain, to go through these two novels and still discover new things about my father's writing and how it relates to our life. Therefore I would like to end this brief introduction expressing my gratitude to Stark House Press, and above all to Greg Shepard, for opening up a possibility to a new generation of readers who will have access to Douglas Sanderson's writing and, hopefully, will enjoy it as much as I have.

                      John D. Sanderson
                      Alicante, Spain. July 2004
                      sanderson@ua.es

Pure Sweet Hell

by Douglas Sanderson

A mi amigo
Zacharias Garcia,
truly a friend in need

Chapter One

I was waiting at the bottom of the gangplank wearing a white shirt, a thin tie, a pair of Spanish shoes that weighed an ounce each, and an electric-blue tropic-weight Spanish-cut suit with pants legs like tubes. I felt like an unemployed samba dancer.

The evening was roasting. I was sweating like a clay bottle. About one quart in every three was caused by nerves.

The sun wasn't down yet and the accumulated swelter of a day's heat wrapped everything like a blanket. The tall palms on the other side of the small harbor were motionless as the strokes of a paintbrush. The two other American merchant ships, the derricks, the glaring white mock-Arab architecture on the water front dropped into the water deep reflections that made me wish I were swimming. A band was playing somewhere.

The other guys came along the deck. They looked freshly scrubbed and slightly awkward as sailors do when they're going ashore. There were seven altogether—Bromfield, who shared the cabin with me; Bellington, the bosun; Lennox, the chief steward; and four others. We'd been a week coming from Italy and everyone had a head of steam for the first night ashore. Lennox, who looked fat and pink like a newly unpoulticed thumb, was being kidded about the stomach trouble he was going to have loving the girls. There were other jokes more or less on the same line.

We walked in a bunch from the bottom of the gangplank and I dropped back and started a pointless conversation with Bromfield. He looked instantly gratified. He was one of those guys who believe in sentimental friendships. Nobody had said anything about my suit and I was beginning to feel confident. We rounded a corner and my mouth turned into an old dry sock.

A soldier was standing on either side of the harbor gate.

They were short men with brown faces. The one on the left had a big grin and the one on the right a fixed bayonet. He jerked. He banged the butt on the ground and clacked his heels and made a fierce face at Lennox. We all halted. It was one of my less gay moments. An individual trickle of sweat walked all the way down the hollow of my spine.

Lennox lifted a hand. He said expansively in Spanish, "Hello, boys. How's the baby these days, Antonio?"

The grinning soldier grinned wider. "Fattest you ever saw. If he goes on like this you'll have competition."

The three of them laughed. The other sailors looked at Lennox in admiration because he was speaking Spanish so fluently. I kept a blank face as if I didn't understand. I was waiting for the ax to fall.

It did.

"Anything to declare, Senor Lennox?"

"Nothing."

"The others?"

The chief steward turned to us. "Shell out the liquors, the perfumes, and the precious stones."

It got a laugh. There were jokes about sailors' pay. The soldiers didn't understand but they got caught up in the general good humor. The bayonet one said, "We must search someone for appearance' sake."

"Me," Lennox offered.

"One of the others."

It happened with the inevitability of fate. Lennox looked around impartially, shrugged, grinned, and said, "Let him see what you got, Bish."

My stomach made two clear outside loops. I couldn't hesitate. "Couple packets of cigarettes," I said brightly. I reached into my inside pocket, fumbled, and withdrew the two decks of Lucky Strikes.

The soldier reached. He looked smart. He need to be only halfway smart to know at once by the weight. I could almost hear the tumbrils rumbling. Me for the guillotine.

His hand halted.

He gazed into my eyes. I grinned. Then he grinned. He slapped Lennox on the back, laughed again for no apparent reason, and waved us all on. I wasn't breathing yet. We went through the gate and along a narrow-gauge railroad track. We emerged through another, bigger gate, and then we were on the city's main esplanade. I exhaled slowly.

Thousands of people were taking the evening promenade. They strolled arm in arm under tall palm trees. They talked and laughed and made a great big noise. Over in a round bandstand an orchestra of men broiled slowly to death in bright green uniforms and huffed out *"La ci darem la mano"* from *Don Giovanni,* which in Spain struck me as odd. Beyond them the sea had the shimmer of trapped quicksilver. The sun hung an inch over the horizon like an overfried doughnut about to drop sizzling. The air was full of the scent of magnolias and the paradise tree.

On the other side of the wide esplanade was the café I'd been told about.

The eight of us from the ship stood uncertainly in a cluster. The passing people broke around us like water round a rock. The girls wore thin summer dresses, bright-colored and tasteful. The men had tight waists, pencil pants legs, correspondent's shoes in black and white, brown and white, and blue and white, and brothel creepers in yellow and green basketwork weave. All in all they were a pretty elegant crowd.

There were groups of girls, couples looking into one another's eyes, men with their arms around each other's necks in the approved Latin manner. Bellington, the bosun, made a crack about the men. It wasn't funny. Nobody laughed. Nobody liked Bellington. The conversation veered back to the night's plans.

Sailor's whoopee and girls.

Bromfield looked at me expectantly, awaiting a suggestion. I didn't make one. The guys had covered me through the gate. That was enough. I had to be rid of them. I waited while they decided where to go. The evening was getting slightly flat and nervous, as it always does when sailors first get ashore. They never know where to head for first.

Someone mentioned a place called La Goleta. He'd been there before. He made it sound like a paradise of wine, music, and houris, and everyone went Mohammedan and got enthusiastic. They started to move off. I thought I was free.

Bromfield called happily, "Come on, Bish."

"Sure," I said. "In a while. I'll see you there."

The group ground to a halt.

Bellington said, "What's this?" A faint air of resentment rose up. I wasn't doing so well. Sailors don't like stand-offs. I tried to think of a dodge. I couldn't. Then I was saved.

Lennox chortled, "Me too. I never did hunt in packs."

It made everything all right because he was popular and fat. The others moved off laughing again, Bromfield calling over his shoulder for me to be sure to get there soon because it sounded like really a place. I waved a hand and started across the wide esplanade.

Lennox fell in beside me.

He had the faintly ripening smell of the fat man who eats too much. But he was amiable. I grinned at him. It wouldn't be difficult getting rid of him alone. I said, "Looks like a nice town."

"Best in Spain. Been coming here nearly eight years." He mopped his moon face. "Hell of a hot place this time of year though."

"Yeah."

We threaded our way through the promenading hordes. They were spread all over the road. I was trying to check the men who sat crowded at the tables outside the café. There were too many.

"Show you round if you like," Lennox said. We reached the opposite sidewalk. "I know this town like the back of my hand."

"Well," I said. I saw Brad.

He was sitting alone at an outside table near the café entrance. He knew I was there but didn't look at me.

"Well," I said again, "how about a drink, Lennox, sir?"

"Swell."

He plumped into a vacant chair with a small gasp. I sat beside him. Across the way Brad slowly stirred a cup of coffee and put down the spoon with the handle pointing into the café. I said, "Gin and juice?"

"Swell." Lennox nodded cheerfully. He glanced up. Annoyance flitted over his fat features and he looked as irritated as his good-tempered face would allow.

Bellington appeared from behind me. He draped his long flabby frame uninvited into the only other chair. He said, "You guys got something special on, or what?"

Nobody rushed to answer him. Lennox said finally, "We're having a drink."

"Me too."

I could see everything Brad did by looking at a guy two tables from him. The other man wore a gray suit, had a slight potbelly and poached eyes. He was so inconspicuous you wouldn't have noticed him in a crowd of three. I glazed my eyes as if I were daydreaming and caught up with the conversation.

Lennox said, "You been in this town before, Bosun. Go find your own enjoyment."

"What's eating you?"

A waiter advanced. Brad left the table and entered the café. I got to my feet. I said, "Lavatory. Order that gin." I walked inside.

It was hot and noisy and more elegant than I'd expected. People stood three deep at a long mirrored bar and a man played bad cocktail music at a small Bechstein raised on a platform. The door marked *Caballeros* was at the far end of the room, partially hidden by a potted palm. I ducked the greenery and pushed open the door. That Continental lavatory smell is not ammonia.

Brad was alone.

He was always cautious. He didn't even look round. I checked the cubicles to see they were empty and stood at the stall next to him. He was grinning.

He said softly, "The Bishop himself. Come to save the day."

He hadn't a trace of envy or resentment in his voice. I couldn't have been so generous. I said, "Where from here, Sir Bradley?"

"Not far. We'll do it easy. They still follow me occasionally. I've changed addresses for extra precaution. Come in three quarters of an hour to Number One Calle Madrid. Back way. It'll be dark. Be sure no one sees you."

"Discovered anything?"

"Nothing on the Big Boy's transhipments, but there's a lot of small stuff peddled on Socorro Street. Who's the fatso with you?"

"Chief steward from the ship. We'll be unloading six days. I got two packets of stuff from Rossi before I left Naples, but nothing happens to him until we're clear at this end. We don't want a tip-off."

"Got it with you?"

"Smuggled it through the gate. I try free-lance peddling to start. I stay under cover till the job's over."

"Good. They won't be able to leak your identity. Bring a gun?"

"It would have been too much smuggling."

"You may need one. They're tough. I got a spare."

"One Calle Madrid. Three quarters of an hour."

"I'll spend half of it shaking any tail." He grinned again. "This is like three years ago in New Mexico."

"We'll get drunk after this, too."

"You bet." He chuckled deep. The door opened. He winked and went out and another man entered. I remained standing at the stall.

The other guy went to the mirror, carefully combed his hair, opened his shirt, wiped very hairy armpits with a red-bordered handkerchief, then mopped his face with the same rag. He took the two edges of his jacket and fanned at himself. He said, "Hot."

"Be cooler when the sun's gone."

"Wasn't last night."

I was pleased he hadn't noticed I was not Spanish. I'd been picked for that, and because I was not tall and because I was dark. They're thorough. They even got me the electric-blue suit from a Spanish tailor.

I nodded to the man and went out.

There was no other exit from the cafe. I couldn't avoid Lennox and Bellington. I had to go back down the room and out into the heat of the esplanade. Brad was gone. The other two looked expectantly in my direction. There were three drinks on the table. I went across.

The band had lowered its cultural standards and was ripping through "Nights of Gladness." The people chattered and laughed. There was a lot of noise. I still heard the Cellophane crackle as I sat down. The two faked-up packets of Lucky Strikes were deep in my inside pocket.

They contained cocaine.

Bellington said, "All right, you bastards, where do we go from here?"

Chapter Two

The bosun was big, blond, and sloppy, a tawny type with a permanently peeled red nose and an overaggressive manner that irked everyone. Some other time I'd have knocked the resident chip off his shoulder. I couldn't afford it now. I resumed my glazed stare at the respectable Spanish citizen in the neat gray suit.

"So what we gonna do?"

"Drink more gin and stay cool," Lennox said. "Why?"

"We been a week at sea. Don't we get some women, or are you two a couple of fairies?"

"You visited this town before. You know your way around. Go find your own women."

"I don't speak the language."

"You won't need it for what you'll be doing."

"You're not so goddamn different."

"No, slower is all. After a while Bish and me's going out to Casa Rebecca. Strongest wine and women in Spain. What say, Bish?"

They both looked at me. I said, "No, I got somewhere else to go."

"Where?" Bellington snarled truculently. "You never been in Spain before. Where do you know to go?"

I looked across at the citizen. "My mother's half Spanish. She thinks we have relatives in town. I'm supposed to look them up."

"Yeah. You look like a short-assed dago."

It would have been nice to mash the peeled nose. I refrained. Lennox said, "Spaniards are nice people. Like me to come and help with the language, Bish?"

"I'll manage."

In the bandstand the music stopped. The sun plopped into the sea and a saffron light fell over everything. I was sweating like Barney's bull. I had one of those churning premonitions where you think everything is about to go wrong. I said, "I'll be going."

"Where do these so-called relatives live?"

I stood up. I put a fifty-peseta bill on the table. "Drinks on me, Lennox. See you at this Casa Rebecca in a while."

"Be waiting, kid."

Before anything else could be added I stepped to the sidewalk and merged with the crowd.

The band started again, one of those gritty Spanish marches with the trumpets smeared in unison. I made my way among the strollers not too fast, listening to what they said, relieved I could understand their accents. I stood aside to let some girls pass. Someone pulled at my sleeve. I looked down.

He was a dirty-faced, button-eyed boy of about eight with a big box under his arm. He was hopping around like a little flea, asking if I wanted a shoe shine. It seemed a good opportunity to appear casual if the others were still watching from the table. I nodded. The kid split his head in a pure-white grin. He dropped to his haunches amid all the passing feet, pulled one of my shoes on his wooden box, and set to work.

He was about three minutes. The shoes glowed like patent leather. He gave a final cavalier flourish, stood up, and held out his hand. He was a cute kid.

I reached for the Spanish money and pulled off two bills. They added up to ten pesetas, less than twenty-five American cents. I thrust them at the kid and said, "Thanks." I made my first mistake of the evening.

In a country where wages run to five bucks a week, you don't give quarters to shoeblacks. The kid goggled at me for two hypnotized seconds. He gulped. He snatched up his box, and bolted into the crowd as if training for track.

I'd done wrong. I couldn't rectify it.

I glanced over my shoulder. Back at the table Lennox and Bellington seemed to be having an argument. The waiter was bearing down with more drinks. A line of colored lights came on like a string of costume beads along the esplanade. The dusk intensified. I started off again.

The band was now playing a jiggy little Latin waltz. Some of the couples hummed it together as they went along, At the fifth corner I asked a man the way to Calle Madrid, memorized his instructions, and walked in the opposite direction on the off chance that I too had a tail. It wasn't likely.

I went through several open streets. I took a last-minute short ride on a streetcar straight out of Toonerville. Twenty minutes later I was at an empty café in a small back street sipping black coffee out of a small clean cup. The vague disquiet had stayed with me.

I'll bore you a couple of minutes. The situation was this:

In Naples, a place I dislike, is a guy I dislike. You don't like him either, and neither do the world's police. The guy lives well. He is head of one of the biggest and most cast-iron monopolies in the world. His firm's two specialties are two bitter white crystalline alkaloids with similar chemical formulas- $C_{17}H_{19}O_3N$ and $C_{17}H_{21}O_4N$. Boiled down to everyday language, they mean morphine and cocaine.

The guy sells a great deal of both. He makes millions of dollars. He more than likely causes more physical and moral damage than any other single person alive.

Not that he looks sinister, or even bad. He seems very ordinary. His manner is mild. He wears spectacles. You know who he is, so do I, so do the world's police, I don't mention his name because nothing can be proved against him. The cops keep trying and he keeps ducking. The contest has reached the proportions of an international fencing match. The guy is all-time master of the parrying thrust. And he's lucky.

The Italian police do what they can. They make his life uncomfortable and complicate his business. Because of continual personal scrutiny, he has to have contacts who have other contacts who have yet more contacts. Commerce is conducted at four stages removed, an arrangement that cuts down efficiency and minimizes his personal influence. When he had direct control, in years past, none of his employees dared talk. These days the organization is looser and the fear filtered. Once in a while someone conceives a grudge. A grudge-carrier is always likely to talk.

The Italian police are like any other in the world. The odd cop has a line in corruption, the majority are hard-working and honest. There are intramural differences, but the entire force possesses one emotion that unites it solidly. It hates the guy in Naples. It considers him a disgrace to the country. Italian cops are more than willing to collaborate with anyone after the same quarry. This makes them some of the best co-workers the Department has ever known.

I know it all sounds like a setup for Interpol, the international police organization. Membership consists of fifty-three nations. The U.S. is not one of them. We resigned a few years back when Interpol became active in searching those Czech refugees who were seeking political asylum in the States. The political got mixed up with the criminal. Nobody could tell A from a bull's foot.

Whatever the rights or wrongs of the matter, we backed out of the organization. The result has been to make our job ten times as tough because we lost a lot of automatic cooperation and facilities.

Be that as it may.

I spoke the language too badly to work the Italian campaign, but I checked the reports in preparation for the Spanish assignment. It took five long years to run the guy in a hole. At the finish all illegal bulk shipments of narcotics from Italy to the United States were virtually at an end. The Italians and the Department were pleased with themselves. They exchanged congratulatory telegrams. Then it all came unstuck. The guy made his countermove.

It has the simplicity of most of his actions. He knew the scrutiny suffered by all ships leaving Italy for the U.S., so he merely took a side step. He ferried the stuff across the Mediterranean to Spain. He moved it from one vessel to another while they were still in harbor and transhipped it too America that way. It took a little managing, but he pulled it off. He always does. We were in as bad a position as when we started.

The Spanish authorities were willing to help. They had a drug problem of their own and figured it might tie in with ours. They were particularly nervous because of increased shipping for the American bases in Spain. A pilot plan was worked out. Everything was set. Everything fell flatter than a cold flapjack.

Brad was sent over. He had promises of full collaboration. He reported secretly to the local authorities. That was as far as the secrecy went. Somebody immediately leaked.

Within four days Brad's identity was known everywhere. He knew it by instinct. On the fifth day they began to tail him. His usefulness was finished before it started. He suggested the alternative himself.

We did it again with the consent of Spain. This time they didn't know who I was, where I'd land, or when. My orders were to stay under cover till something material turned up. Absolute secrecy. I started by shipping from the U.S. to Italy as a sailor.

In Naples there was some neat contriving. I met Rossi through apparently natural circumstances. The Italian police had him marked as one of the lesser four-times-removed operators and as a weak link in the chain because he liked extra money. Which I had. I told him I was shipping to Spain. He sold me the two packets of Lucky Strikes. That was the start.

It seems a long way round. It was the only way round. That's how I came to be sitting at a table in an empty Spanish café, drinking black coffee with too much sugar and feeling nervous.

I'd started. Now I had to continue.

I didn't have Spanish blood, but Bellington was right about how I looked. I exchanged a few remarks about the heat with the solitary waiter. He noticed nothing foreign. I finished the coffee, didn't make the same mistake twice, tipped him the equivalent of one American cent, which pleased him, said *ardiós,* and went off into the gathered darkness. Night had fallen with a bang. Long shadows lay along the narrow cobbled streets, giving an illusion of coolness that was completely false. It was stewing.

I knew the direction. I went two straggling blocks with one dim street light between them, crossed an open space with a litter heap in the middle, and found myself at the end of an unlit, unpaved road lined with tiny bungalows set well apart.

The sign said Calle Madrid. I peered at the first house. Number Forty-three. Wrong end. I started down. The architectural style was pseudo-California-Spanish. Time was when California used to imitate old Spain. New Spain now imitates old California's imitation. The result is not so good.

None of the bungalows showed light. They looked like week-end residences. It was opaquely dark and I stumbled over ruts in the baked road. I thought I saw the darker shadows of mountains against the starless sky. I passed each wide-apart house and ticked off an odd number. The heat was intense. At the end of the street there was no semblance of surface left underfoot.

Brad's place seemed to be standing in a dark field. I cleared a wire fence enclosing a small garden and wondered how anything could grow here. I paused a second and wiped my face.

There was a dimly defined pathway. I catfooted to the back door and found it open. My hand was at my pocket reaching for a gun before I realized that this time I didn't have anything more than a box of matches. I stepped over the threshold. A window was open somewhere. A suggestion of breeze eddied between it and the door. There was no sound.

I said softly, "Brad."

A long minute went by.

"Brad."

Somewhere not far away a car pulled up. The brakes squealed preternaturally loud in the hot stillness. The silence poured in again. My ears started to sing. My shirt was sticking to me. I made a move.

I gripped the matches, turned sideways to take anything that came with the point of my shoulder, and edged across the few feet of flooring and through the next doorway. I knew it was a small room by the position of the open window. I took a step forward.

My foot kicked something soft.

I froze. There was no point. Anyone in the tiny space would hear my breathing. I waited again, smelling a thick sweet odor on the air. Nothing came. I pulled out a match and struck it. I stopped.

He was lying face downward. He'd been caught by surprise, maybe by someone hiding behind the door. His legs were slightly drawn up, his arms flung forward. The knife was buried to the hilt in his back and the heavy-smelling blood no longer flowed.

We'd been in the same class at law school. We'd joined the Department together. Now Arthur Bradley, my friend, was dead.

The match burned my fingers and went out. I struck another. It was a Spanish waxed-paper match and bent almost double before it sputtered into flame. I knew I had to examine Brad, go through his pockets, turn on the light. I wondered about the gun he'd mentioned. I looked around the room, still crouched. There was no sign of a struggle. He hadn't had a chance.

You're not supposed to allow personal feelings. Sometimes you can't help it. The sickness in my stomach tightened to a knot. At first it was grief. Then the knot gave a couple of more twists and double-reefed. I saw it all at once. I was forked on a dilemma.

Forked is nearly the right word.

My orders were to stay under cover. That was no longer possible. If I kept quiet the murderer would escape. I had to report immediately to police headquarters and make myself known.

But that wasn't possible, either. What happened to Brad could happen to me. Leaked identity. One FBI man was possibly routine. Two meant the heat was on. Whoever handled Spanish traffic would be warned. The guy in Naples would know tomorrow. He'd make another feint. Next time we might not be so lucky tracing it.

There was one solution. I had to phone Italy for fresh orders before I did anything at all. I struck a fresh match, half turned, started to get up. A man was standing at the door.

He was looking down at me without moving. I couldn't see him distinctly. The matchlight gleamed dully on the gun in his hand. He said softly in Spanish, "That will be all."

I dug in my toes and jumped. The match went out.

Chapter Three

The first was instinct. The rest was training. I slammed him low with my shoulder under his arm. The gun jerked upward. His body hit the doorframe. I straightened up and rammed for his face with my head. He moved. I got his wrist and the gun was waving, and then he couldn't fire for fear of shooting himself.

We panted at each other in the dark. I butted again. I heard him grunt. I smashed the back of his hand against the doorframe, the gun went flying, I heard it land somewhere soft, and he was unarmed. I tried to work on him.

He was too tough. He knew what he was doing. He got his hands to my throat and made a quick twist and was away from the wall. He was choking me. We stumbled two steps in a dance. I kicked Brad's legs and nearly fell over. A corner of furniture hit my hip. I wrenched the hands from my throat, grabbed the man's hair, and jerked his face down to my fist. My sleeve button snagged an instant on the front of his coat. I hit him and didn't stop.

He wouldn't go under. The darkness was black glue. I couldn't see to punch him scientifically. I scuffled with my foot. It was no time for ethics. I scuffled some more and kicked sharply at his groin and made contact. He gave a great sigh and it wasn't of admiration.

He seemed to disappear. He fell draggingly down my chest. He hit the floor and lay still. I fumbled for the matches.

The sweat was pouring out of me in rivulets, flooding my eyes. I wanted the gun. My hands were shaking. The wax match was soft with heat. I scratched it against the box, but it wouldn't light. The man moaned at my feet and stirred slightly and a lot of things happened at once.

The match sputtered. I heard footsteps coming round the outside of the house. The flame leaped. The whole room turned bright orange. I stared down at the man on the floor. His eyes were open.

He was holding himself with one hand. He looked dazedly at me. He was a thin, fair, clean-shaven man with a narrow face. He was in his early thirties. He was groping for the fallen gun. I registered everything about him. It meant nothing compared with the main fact. He wore a uniform. There was a badge on his chest. He was a Spanish cop.

I couldn't tell whether he saw me or not. He made another movement and suddenly gave a shout. The footsteps outside came faster. The match went out. Someone blundered in the darkness against the back door. I had a vision of being shot out of hand, and maybe what I did was another mistake.

I dived through the open window. I dragged myself from the ground and fled up the road like a gingered hare.

I stumbled for maybe a hundred yards. I realized I was running toward what must be the police car. There could be other cops waiting. That unhorned me from the dilemma. I no longer had a choice. I had to identify myself. It was all clear as crystal, twice as simple.

The realization hit me.

In my pockets was some money, a handkerchief, two packets of cocaine, and not a card, a scrap of paper, nothing to prove what I said was true. My run turned to a zigzag. If two ordinary cops pulled me in for murder, the town would buzz. My identity wouldn't be leaked, it'd be blazoned. To establish it the cops would have to phone the boss in Italy. If there really was a paid man in local headquarters, he'd know not only me but the whole setup. The Spanish venture would be at an end. The boss's name would be spread. The entire organization even in Italy might suffer.

I couldn't quit. I had to make the phone call myself. I kept running.

The car was empty, engine idling, headlights dim because the battery was low. I fumbled at the handle. I fell inside and slammed the door. The engine roared.

I swung in a half circle and belted down the rutted road. Somebody fired a shot.

The car was in lousy condition. I couldn't figure which way was back to town. The corner came up. I got a hoist on the wheel, took a guess, and heard another shot. The near-side rear tire went off like an H-bomb.

I bucketed. I went in six directions. I skidded over a concrete pavement and then I was barreling down a tree-lined street with the dead tire thwacking and the wheel rim shrieking like a meeting of the Sabine Ladies' Morning Marathon Club. I was as conspicuous as a tea-drinker in a speak. A bunch of walking people stopped to see me coming. The glare of the town was showing over nearby roofs and I had to dump the car as soon as possible. I swung into another street.

It had one light at the far end. I squealed to the curb and leaped out and ran into an alley. I'm great on running. Another car roared to a stop nearby. Somebody shouted. I pounded.

I could see the people moving in the cross street at the far end. There were no side exits. If the crowd turned and someone was behind me, I was bottled. I hugged the wall and got on my toes. I practiced hard for the three-minute mile. I swung into the street and hit a blonde smack in the chest.

She went, "Ooof!"

"Sorry."

She tottered against the wall and tried to hang on to a large handbag. It fell to the ground. I noted the chest wasn't a bad one, that she had short blonde hair and big eyes. I noted nothing else. There wasn't time. I kicked to the far side of the road, swung around another corner, and braked.

A cop was in front of me.

The street was jammed. The cop seemed not to be noticing anything in particular. He was on his evening beat. I walked past him. My nerves jangled and every pore opened. My eyes skinned both sides of the street for a sign indicating telephones. There wasn't one. I broke into a small lope.

I got halfway down the street. A group of people spread in front of me, filling the sidewalk, entering a building. I glanced back. The fair, thin-faced cop was talking to the guy on the beat. There was another policeman with them. They were all looking in the other direction. I tried to move again.

Part of the sidewalk group was a fat woman. She blocked my way. She had black hair, an enormous Edwardian choker of pearls, and a crisp little black mustache. We dodged one way. We dodged the other way. We halted a moment and did a small minuet. She smiled at me helplessly. From the other side of the street the little boot-black shouted:

"There he is! There's the American!"

I grasped the fat woman by the elbow, smiled back at her just as helplessly, and escorted her into the building. Another crowd swept in behind us.

We all swished gracefully across an entrance hall and through another door. The fat woman looked bewildered, but pleased. I released her arm. I bowed. I took out a handkerchief and mopped my face. A man with politely raised eyebrows advanced on me and said, "Your invitation, senor."

I looked around. There was no retreat. It was a medium-sized salon with nasty little gilt chairs set out in rows facing a platform, ornate rococo fittings, hairy great chandeliers, and one solitary door on the far side. There were thirty-five or forty people present wearing complacently superior looks that marked them as intellectuals whetting up for a cultural feast.

I said, "My invitation?"

The guy's shirt was dazzling white. He nodded. Sometimes it fails. I tried anyway. "Oh, I'm a friend of Mr. Umuuuh—"

We looked at each other. "Plosch?"

I'd never have hit on that one. I said, "Plosch."

"This way."

I smiled again at the fat woman. She beamed. I followed the man across to the door at the far side of the platform and hoped there'd be another exit beyond. He hesitated. We were at the threshold. He looked into the room and said, "A friend of yours, Senor Plosch." Then he stepped aside. I entered.

No exit. Only a window. The door clicked shut behind me.

It was a small room. It seemed very full. A swarthy guy weighing some three-hundred-odd pounds leaned again the closed door and made the wood creak. He wasn't much bigger than a boxcar. His hands dangled very low at his sides. He stared fixedly at nothing over my head and there wasn't a glimmer of intelligence in his eyes. I turned my attention to the other man.

He was garbed in a beautifully cut English blue suit of what looked like a fine Glen Urquhart check. He was sitting before a mirror fixing his impeccably bleached bright-blond hair with a mauve comb. He put the comb down, turned slowly, stood up, and smiled. He delicately rubbed the palms of his hands together. His eyes were long and green like a tiger's. He was tall, lean, had a large aquiline nose, and moved very precisely like a machine with all the moving parts well oiled. His lips were vivid as butcher's meat and his skin glowed more fine and transparent than a very young girl's.

He had all the presence of a Roman proconsul. He had about as much human warmth as a proconsul's statue. I couldn't begin to guess his age.

"Senor Plosch?" I bleated.

His eyes traveled slowly over me from head to foot. He smiled slightly, tilting his elegance at me. He said, "And what may I do for you, my young friend?" His English was as perfect as the rest of him. It was much too good to be his native tongue. I groped for an exit line.

I said in Spanish, *"Discúlpeme.* I was shown in by mistake."

Senor Plosch continued to smile. His eyebrows went slightly up. Laughing Boy against the door didn't move.

"Interesting. You address me in Spanish. Your facial muscles, the shape of your mouth, indicate a more frequent usage of English. Every language leaves its mark upon the face."

"Really?"

"I assure you. It explains the pinched nostrils of the English, the lower lip of the Frenchman, and the prudently adenoidal expression of Scandinavians. By the slackness of certain consonant-forming muscles I judge you to be an American." He paused thoughtfully. "The subject would make a future lecture."

"What are you discussing tonight?" I brayed.

"The mysticism of Saint John of the Cross. A Spaniard, you know, very dear these days to his fellow countrymen. They gave him a terrible time when he was alive, with floggings and persecutions and religious prisons. All that is now happily forgotten. It would be impolitic even to mention it publicly. You will stay to listen?"

"I can't."

"I feared not. A disappointment." He paused again. He was a weirdie. He said, "To return to your face. How interesting and honest it is! Honorable I think is more the word. There will be a reception at my house after the lecture. I do wish you'd come."

He turned to the Ape. "The gentleman is invited. Remember that!"

I was trying to think of something in connection with the unblemished complexion. I was in no condition for academic recall. I nodded to him. He puckered his brows at me. He said, "Well, sir, you have run very hard to avoid someone, so I suppose you wish to be on your way."

A man stopped talking out in the main salon. There was a ripple of applause. The kitty-cat eyes suddenly seemed to slant and the languidness dropped away. He said, "I recommend the window. Wait until I commence speaking." He nodded at the Ape and the door opened. He went out.

The applause burst louder. The huge man and I stared. He was a better starer than I. There was no expression on his face to indicate he even saw me. He closed the door again.

The clapping died away. In the other room a throat was cleared daintily. Plosch's fruity Spanish rolled forth as flawless as his English, and just as foreign to him.

"Y adonde no hay amor, ponga amor y sacará amor."

I bet it was going to be a pip of a lecture. "Where there is no love, put love and you will get back love." I raised the window and hoisted myself to the sill.

The Ape slowly turned his head. I didn't know whether to say anything or not. I decided not. I swung my legs, smiled like La Gioconda, dropped from the sill, and felt the hot night close around me.

I took it slowly. I went cautiously up the wide alley to the other main street. I waited. I got on my toes. I peeped right and left. The sign was over the way.

The crowd surged. There were no cops in sight. I dodged a car that was dodging the people and got to the other side of the street. The notice over the double swing doors said *"Teléfonos."* The people inside were sitting on wooden benches. There was a double line of phone booths.

The third on the left was empty. I squeezed inside.

I checked the Lucky Strike packs, wiped my face, and took a minute off to readjust my breathing. I thought of Brad. I got an onrush of feeling like needing to cry. For a few seconds it grew to fury. I didn't want to make the call in case they took me off the job.

They train us too well. I picked up the receiver.

Chapter Four

The operator had a wonderful time exercising her small authority. "The traffic between here and Italy is very heavy. I'm very sorry. The call will be booked for three hours' time. Be very prompt!"

I said desperately, "Person to person."

"I heard you the first time." She hung up.

That was it. The matter was out of my hands. All I could do was lose myself for three hours, find a quiet bar, go to a movie. I wondered if the thin-faced policeman had seen me well enough in the matchlight to issue a description. I glanced into the mirror above the phone. I'd stopped sweating. I looked unruffled. It was a good start.

I turned to leave the booth and nearly jumped clear off the floor.

A face was pressed hard against the glass door, the nose flattened white. The guy drew back to let me out. He smiled.

He was about twenty years old, of average height, and really pretty. He had dark curly hair, eyes like newly unhusked chestnuts, a golden-tan skin, and a build that tapered from shoulders to waist like a peg. He wore a torn shirt and too-long pants with concertina legs. He had highly polished shoes and the ingratiating air of a tout. In fact, he was a tout. He smiled with dazzling professionalism as I came from the door. He was something more than a fox and less than a wolf.

He talked with head and hands. "You like a guide, Meesta Americano?"

I shook my head.

He wasn't that easily detached. He touched my arm. "I show all good places. Plenty girls. Whisky."

On the wooden benches the waiting people looked up at the sound of a foreign language. I unclasped the hand, pushed open the main door, and hit the street.

His accomplice was waiting. The little bootblack. They closed in on either side. They were going to cling like crabs. One of the lesser joys of foreign travel.

The kid smiled up like a dirty little angel. The other one said, "Very good girls. Very cheap. You get wunnerful time. Good places for filthy things."

"No," I said in Spanish. "Beat it! I got no money."

He shook his head. He assumed the brass face of the born tout. "You give this *niño* ten pesetas. It means you *americano*. Only *americanos* do that. *Americanos* have money alla time."

"No," I said.

"I take you all good places. You don't pay much to me. I take you all dirty filthy joints on Socorro Street. You like them."

I bit. Socorro Street was the only information I'd got from Brad. I didn't want to make more mistakes, but the temptation was strong. I had three hours. I said, "Where is it?"

His face lit like the rising moon. He withdrew a distance and pulled the bootblack with him. The child whispered, "Ten per cent for me."

"Five."

"I showed him to you. I'll never show another."

"You'll never see another. Five."

"Ten. The fig of your mother!"

"The *culo* of your father!"

"*Cabrón!*"

The rejoinder was anatomically unprintable. They glared, then shrugged simultaneously. The little boy gave one tragic backward glance and trudged dispiritedly into the crowd. The pretty one came back.

"I am Pablo. You?"

"Smith."

The crowd was as thick as ever. I studied it for cops. There were none.

"You speak very good Spanish."

"Let's go," I said. We pushed through the mob.

He stayed very close. Maybe he thought someone else would steal me. He said, "You have lost a button from your sleeve. I get another to replace it. All little services." He was nauseating.

"Never mind." I figured I'd lost the button when my sleeve snagged the cop. I said, "Let's hit Socorro Street."

"We march."

He exaggerated. We sauntered like everyone else. We threaded through the talking, laughing people and I was submerging the thought of Brad by concentrating on the town. It wasn't bad.

It had cobbled streets and sidewalks made of small smooth blocks. The houses were tall and cool with iron balconies at the higher windows, and all over the place were tall date palms and orange trees in bitter fruit. At several corners I saw offshooting squares, fountains in the middle, color rioting with roses and red hibiscus and bouganvillea draped in purple slashes. A lot of good-looking children jumped rope, played ball, and made noise. There were a lot of women.

Some ran to fat. They were a minority. The majority had form, feature, and everything else a man might want and usually does. The night was hot. I'd been a week at sea. I let my gaze rove. Pablo watched from the corners of his eyes and he wasn't missing a thing.

He gave the tout's small lascivious smile. He was almost too revolting to be true. He said, "Soon, Esmitt. Very soon." I decided I didn't like him. I'd get rid of him when I found Socorro Street.

We went about half a mile. We were reaching a darker part of town. The locale was altering, the crowd's appearance changing, the noise becoming fiercer. A blind seller of lottery tickets tapped past, led by a small boy, both howling. The other voices came from chestnut sellers, candy sellers, cigarette women, knife-grinders with small flutes, and a tarter in a side street beating a mule.

I was still sizing up the surroundings. I glanced ahead.

The blonde was sitting at the outside table of a café not ten yards away. I recognized her hair and her chest, I don't know what she recognized about me, but she jerked and started to get up. I pulled Pablo and said "Over the road."

We steered to the far sidewalk. He pointed to a narrow side street, shooting off at a right angle. I tried to go faster. The crowd was getting in the way. I could hear the clacking of the girl's heels. We swerved.

The narrow street was quiet and dark. The sudden tall buildings sliced off the noise behind. The following heels went clickety-clack and sprinted. The hand grasped my elbow.

I stopped and turned round.

She was pretty. The blonde hair was urchin cut, but saved from the usual scruffiness by small loose curls. The big eyes were blue as two spoonfuls of deep water. She was wearing a thin summer dress that hadn't been made in Spain. Her breasts rose and fell from running.

She looked capable, efficient, and modern, but not the sort of modern that knows its way unguided into too many men's apartments. She was clutching the big handbag.

I waited without speaking.

She relaxed. She smiled confidently. "My name's Kelly. No relation to Her Serene Highness."

I continued waiting.

"I had a whimsical, music-loving father with a passion for minstrel shows, so my full name's Banjo Kelly. We'll laugh and get it over with right away."

This time she waited.

The smile faded. She became brisk and efficient. "It's not my usual custom to importune strange men. Not in foreign countries. I was just wondering if you could help me."

I said in Spanish, "I don't understand."

Pablo frowned slightly. The girl said, "I speak some Spanish. Not enough. Talk English."

"I don't understand."

She said, "Look, son, it's a good gag, but quit. When you knocked me for a homer a while back you said, 'Sorry.' You said it like an American. You look like a Californian. Now why do I think that?"

I said in English, "What do you want?"

"Better," she said. She relaxed again. She settled down for a chummy chat. "You here to work on the new base?"

"No."

The blue eyes flashed angrily. She fought the emotion down. She was a girl used to getting what she went after. She said, "It's this way. I have only one more night in town. I want to see the fabulous Socorro Street. It's not safe for a woman alone. I'm tough, but not that tough. You're obviously going there."

"So?"

"Take me."

"Sorry."

Her jaw hardened. "I pay all expenses."

"No."

I started to walk away. She grabbed my arm. I had a bright idea to get rid of both of them. I turned to Pablo. "How about—"

He wasn't the same guy. His shoulders were back. His head was up, eyes stern, face glowing with righteousness. He was the incarnation of noble Spanish youth.

"Quite right, Esmitt. To save my life I wouldn't take a respectable woman there. A disgusting place."

"That's it," I said.

"That's not it. I shall follow you."

"Into a brothel?"

I thought she was going to clout me. She made a great effort and kept the anger in check. "Give me a few minutes. I'll explain how important it is."

"Good-by." I unlatched her hand.

She stamped her foot. She turned into a little girl. "I wouldn't have come anyway. You're too short."

"You should've sent a telegram. I'd have worn my stilts." I left her standing against the wall.

Pablo trotted along beside me. We reached the second corner away from the boulevard. He said admiringly, "What a truck!" He meant she was well built. It's a high compliment in Spanish slang. He was right. He said musingly, "Funny name for a girl—Pancho."

Socorro Street burst on us.

The lines of lighted bars stretched out on either side. It sounded like a fairground, a dozen tunes from as many different instruments. Groups of men ambled along and sang at the tops of their voices. A lottery seller whined his unheeded way down the street's center. The uproar was enormous. There wasn't a woman in sight.

I glanced back over my shoulder.

The Banjo dame straightened from the wall. She started after us at a quick trot with determination in every line of her. I grabbed Pablo's arm and headed diagonally across the road for the nearest bar. The sign said "Club Bolero."

A man was out cold against the wall. I stepped over his legs. Pablo said brightly, "Yes, we'll go here first and drink wine. You'll like it."

He pushed the door open and we went inside. The lights failed.

I clamped my arms hard against my jacket so no hands could get at the packets. Pablo said something, but I couldn't hear because the noise was going on exactly as before. Talking, laughing, a guitar, a woman singing in a loud strident voice about waking up in the morning and hearing the birds.

The lights came on again.

I said, "What was that?"

He still had to speak loud because ordinary conversation in the joint was conducted at a shout. He waved a careless hand at the double electric fitting. "The apparatus. It happens here all the time. Not in your country?"

"Sometimes."

He nodded. He leaned on the bar and shouted, *"Dos tintos."*

Two big glasses of dark-red wine came skidding along the counter. I cased the setup.

I saw why no women came to the district. There were enough in residence. They sat in various attitudes around the room, in a line along the wall, and they looked like a convention of professional wet nurses. In the corner a girl was having a mammary indifferently squeezed by the guy next to her. They were proving the case of whoever it was that said vice was boring. They were stiff with ennui. Pablo nudged me.

"María Teresa. Very good. Thirty pesetas." He chopped a hand suggestively through the air. *"Mucha carne."*

He was right about that. She was very much meat. About a nickel for twenty pounds at the quoted price. The whole line-up was generally plump. The only thin one sat alone on a high stool at the far end of the bar, still trilling her song about waking up and hearing the birds.

She was fine-looking in a fang, claw, and whipcord sort of way. She had a vivid orange dress, long green earrings, a bottle of champagne at each elbow, and a glass in front of her. Her hands were clasped around one raised knee. She leaned back precariously on the stool and turned in my direction. Our glances met.

Only for a second. I shifted my gaze and looked at the man beyond her. He was talking to the bartender.

I thought I saw a flicker of recognition. He was the inconspicuous, gray-suited, poached-eyed guy who'd been sitting at the café down on the esplanade. He put his drink on the bar and studied his shoes. The girl in front of him stared at me.

She straightened up. She pulled at her dress and stopped singing. She shouted, "All right. What you looking at?" Her voice was full of broken bottles.

I turned back to the bar. Pablo called, "Pepita!"

She got off the stool. She came undulating down the bar like an uncoiling spring. Up close she was different from the rest of them—darker skin, coarser hair, black eyes more brilliant, a lean gypsy. Better-looking than I'd thought, and drunker. Basically as tough as a shoe sole.

Pablo said, "Esmitt, this is my friend Pepita. She is a *puta*. She has much enthusiasm and is not expensive. You will like her." He smiled at her. He was fond of her.

She reached out and pushed his nose with the flat of her hand. A big rook-scaring laugh tumbled from her mouth. "Wrong! Tonight I'm an ordinary señorita like everyone else. Didn't you hear?"

"Tell me."

She laughed again. "I won the lottery. Eight hundred pesetas. Tonight I take a holiday. I drink champagne and make it the big night of my life and I don't go home with no man. A holiday." She looked at me with insolent black eyes. I suspected from the sparkle that within herself she somehow kept a constant holiday. She said, "Drink champagne with me. It costs you nothing."

I shook my head.

"Something wrong with it?"

Pablo said, "Esmitt is American sailor."

"Then we drink my champagne and smoke his real American cigarettes."

I had only two packs in my pocket and they weren't cigarettes. I said, "I don't smoke."

"American sailors have plenty of cigarettes."

"Not me."

"I love real American cigarettes."

"That's tough."

She forgave me. "Drink my champagne."

"No."

Maybe her sense of occupation was outraged. Maybe she took the coolness as a challenge. She reached out a hand. She put it caressingly on the back of my neck. She lowered her eyelids and went flaringly feminine. She said "But you'd like to come home with me, yes? I know you would."

The bartender was bringing her bottles of champagne along the bar. He was smiling. I lifted the hand from my neck. I felt like a fugitive from Sunday school. "No," I said.

Her upper lip curled. She looked cruel, dishonest, dangerous, drunk, and handsome. "And you won't drink the champagne?"

I didn't want trouble. I said, "Well." I noticed two things. The man in the gray suit had disappeared. The barman still smiled.

His lips twitched. His mouth widened further. The side of his face twitched. He took another step forward and his head trembled as if not properly set on his neck. His eyelids batted.

I said, "Sure I'll drink with you." The barman laughed. We all laughed. It was more than friendly. Pepita flung both arms around my neck.

Pablo said, "Here comes that Pancho girl."

Chapter Five

I pressed Pepita against me. She was as firm as a newly inflated tire. There was frangipani in her hair, and champagne and garlic on her breath. I watched the bartender over her shoulder.

He had long eyelashes. He put down the bottles and smiled at me. I winked. He twitched. He lowered his fringed lids and walked off down the bar with head tossing gaily and hips rotating on universal joints. Not to put too fine a point on it, he was a faggot.

Banjo Kelly said, "Can I get a picture?"

Pepita was clamped to me with her knees pressing my legs. She showed no sign of letting go. I gently pried her off, kept an arm around her shoulders, and grinned at Banjo. Then I was a little sorry for her. She was scared of the surroundings.

She said defiantly, "Didn't I say I'd follow you?"

Every guy in the place was looking at her. The girls didn't like it. She wasn't that much better-looking than the rest, but she was different. The men liked the change.

There were comments on her hair. There were other comments. If she understood them, it was her own fault. She shouldn't have come.

I said. "What's the aim?"

A guy sitting at a table called to her and patted his pants and grinned. Pablo said something in a dialect I didn't understand. The man shrugged good-naturedly and turned back to the annoyed girl at his side. Some of the other guys continued watching hungrily.

Pepita looked slowly and carefully at Kelly's hair, face, dress, and shoes. She said in a silkily disbelieving voice, "Is it true, like Pablo says, that you are not whore?"

"What's that?" Banjo Kelly asked me.

"She wants to know if you're a tart."

"All women are in one way or another. Tell her we're sisters under the skin."

Pepita said, "You like her, Esmitt?"

"Yes."

"And me?"

There were immediate reasons for keeping the peace. "More."

"Then we all drink my champagne. Even her. Four glasses!"

I'd been waiting. "I'll get them," I said, and move quickly down the bar. The bartender was reaching under the counter.

The noise had restarted. Someone plucked a guitar lazily. The atmosphere was thick with smoke. The woman with the chest moved to a more interested client. The bartender melted at me.

He didn't swish like California, or agonize like Greenwich Village. He just pooled his eyes like molten velvet and handed me the glasses. His lashes fluttered so violent I wondered if he was just that way and nothing else. Then his mouth gave two more uncontrollable twitches. The movement writhed over one side of his face.

I said, "Thanks. Nice night."

"Ever so warm." His lashes swept his checks.

I leaned intimately across the bar. "Where can I get some stuff?"

The eyelids were vibrating like hummingbirds. He gave a demure downward smile. "I don't know what you mean, I'm sure."

I didn't want him to think I meant that. I waited till he looked up to see why I hadn't answered. I shaped one noiseless word.

"Cocaine."

He stayed unruffled. He went on smiling as if we were discussing the weather, but all the velvet went from his eyes. He was nobody's pushover. He murmured, "None in town."

"Certain?"

"Secure."

"Good. I'm not buying. I'm selling."

The avidity on his face made me almost sorry for him. I said, "No. In bulk. You don't have that sort of dough. Who does? You may get a cut."

"I don't even understand you." He tossed his shoulders.

"I want cash. American."

He spread his hands. He shrugged and walked wiltingly away. I went back down the bar with the four glasses in my hands and my heart in the base of my throat. The others were standing in a knot. I put the glasses on the bar.

Pepita snatched a bottle and began pouring. She was in one of those lightning bad tempers that come to drunks. She filled only three glasses.

I said, "Looks like you don't get any, Miss Kelly."

"Banjo," she said. "You're Smitty. She thinks I'm trying to steal you, Smitty. I am, in a way, but only because I still need an escort." She fumbled with the large handbag. "I'll tell you about it."

She could stick closer than glue to a blanket. I said, "Don't bother. I've arranged to go home with Pepita."

The gypsy girl turned at the sound of her name. Pablo grinned. "The man is going home to bed with you."

"Tonight I go home with nobody." A slow smile spread over her face. She looked like a black panther baring its fangs for a nice juicy meal. "Nobody except Esmitt." She turned back with a flourish and started filling the fourth glass.

We were all smiling, Banjo Kelly as well. Her heart wasn't in it. She said,

"Well, I can't offer that. Not in cold blood, I mean. But who knows?"

The smile vanished at my lack of response. She flushed.

"What do I have to do? Fill out a form?"

"Nothing," I said, and wondered why Pablo was watching me so closely.

Pepita thrust forward the glasses, tipsily slopping the contents. She flung an arm around my neck. We all sipped. The champagne was Spanish and strong and tasted like boiled wood chips. Banjo Kelly crossed her eyes.

She said, "Can't say I blame you. She's about the only genuine local color in the place. Everything else is New Orleans in a different language. Maybe you could just dump me at a more interesting joint. You wouldn't have to stay."

"I know your game." Pepita tightened her arm around my neck. "Stop talking to him. We're going to sing, aren't we, Esmitt?"

I nodded. I was willing for anything. I was waiting for the bartender to make up his mind.

The arm slid down to my waist. Pepita vibrated. She shouted something to the guitar player. He changed key, banged the first bars of a waltz, and she burst into song. Her voice was harsh and strident and alive. It was the same song as before, about waking in the morning and hearing the birds. I suddenly thought that Brad would never wake again. I quit. It was the wrong season to get maudlin. The girl was swaying against me like plucked rubber.

It was a catchy little tune. She sang it, everyone sang it, another guy sang it, the company took it up again, they all wound up together with bang-up bar-parlor harmony and a culminating flurry on the guitar. There were shouts of *"Olé!"* as if we had just done the sextet from *Lucia*. Pepita bounced up and down with every muscle moving and the arm still around me. The blonde was fumbling with her handbag.

I suddenly got horribly wary. I said, "What you doing?"

"You give me a real American cigarette now, Esmitt?" Pepita asked.

"I don't have any."

She put both hands to my cheeks, dragged me to her, and clamped a great smacking kiss on my mouth. I didn't taste the garlic this time. It was all right. She said, "Then I buy you more champagne," and whirled around and beat her fist on the counter for the barman.

He wasn't there.

Perhaps they do it by telepathy. She shouted again, clapped her hands to call his attention. Someone at the other side of the room yelled, *"Olé!"* She clapped more rhythmically. The guitarist plunked his instrument at the same tempo. She took two proud prancing steps to the middle of the floor, clicked her fingers, tossed up her skirts, and beat a tattoo with her heels. Everyone else immediately joined the clapping. She began dancing. She was a beautiful, desirable, passionate animal.

Banjo Kelly's face came alive with excitement. She swiveled to a different position and dug at the handbag. She said, "God! I must get this."

"How?"

"Pictures."

My stomach fell away. The bartender touched me lightly on the elbow. "You called?"

He moved a little way down the counter. I followed. All I needed was photographs taken. I said, "More champagne."

"As you wish." He smiled his queerest smile. "It costs you nothing."

"For how long?"

"Twenty minutes. Afterward go to the lavatory. There is another door opposite. A gentleman will be waiting with American money."

"No."

"It's arranged."

"No. No little doors, dark rooms, or gentlemen with blackjacks. Something else."

"You're ever so difficult."

"I'm ever so wise."

"I'll ask the gentleman to meet you in the street."

"Good. But not this street. I have no friends here. You do. Choose another."

"Not possible."

"I have to pick up the stuff. I don't carry that much about with me."

The guitar thrummed deep and ringing. The *olés* were louder. Pepita's heels drummed like machine-gun fire.

The bartender gave a great patient sigh and leaned closer. "One hour. The outskirts of town. Rivera Street. Under the light." He languidly passed a bottle of champagne and I took it along the bar. Banjo Kelly had slid farther away, was gazing intently into the handbag. Pablo watched me with eyes like a prowling cat.

"What?" he said.

"What what?" I said. "Nothing."

He stared a second longer and spoke rapidly. "It's good for both of us. I take Pepita and you have the blonde. She wants you. I can see it. I want Pepita. I like Pepita. I know a place we can all go together. You pay."

The only place for me was Rivera Street. We'd go there together because I didn't know where it was and didn't want to inquire from strangers while the local cops were looking for me. I said softly, "We get out. Alone."

He stiffened. "Why?"

Banjo Kelly edged closer, her voice a moan. "Oh, God, I hope the light's strong enough. She's fantastic."

"You're taking photographs?"

"I hope so."

"Of me?"

"You're finally interested. Such vanity!"

"Look," I said. "We'll leave immediately. I'll take you to the main part of town. We have to talk."

"I want more shots of her."

"I'll wait."

In the center of the floor Pepita whirled her skirts into umbrellas. The guitarist's hand fluttered like a pigeon's wing. The noise must have been the loudest in the street. Maybe that's what attracted the guys. They came in. Three of them. They all wore civilian clothes.

The first two I didn't know. The last had bruises on his face. He was the thin cop from Brad's place.

I turned away. He didn't see me. He walked with his companions to the far end of the bar. The impulse to enlist his aid died as soon as it came. I couldn't chance it. There was a leak at local headquarters. Possibly paid. Possibly him. He'd come to Brad's place apparently unbidden. He now turned up in a joint where I'd made my first contact. If I wanted to co-operate, there'd be the tangle of identifying myself. The Rivera Street date would be gone.

I nudged Pablo. "Out."

"Why?" His face was dark with suspicion. "The girls. They like you. We stay with them."

"I'll pay you."

"For what?"

I had to do it alone. I nodded and started for the door. Banjo Kelly saw me going. She let out a yell and grabbed me and tried to spin me round. She said loudly, "Where are you off to?"

"I'm going," I said frantically.

"Abandoning me in a joint like this?"

"I didn't bring you here."

I got the door open. The music whanged. Something pushed me in the back and I was outside. The door closed. Pablo was beside me. Then I thought it had misfired.

A man was leaning against the opposite wall. He straightened suddenly. His face was in shadow. I figured he was a cop. Then I saw his white cloth slippers. I started to move again. On the other side of the door the music stopped.

Pepita yelled, "Esmitt! Esmitt!"

Her voice carried like a siren. There was a burst of conversation. The man on the other side of the street slouched again. Heels clattered for the door.

I dragged Pablo with me and ran.

Chapter Six

We cut through two deserted streets. The noise of Socorro was shut off behind us. We turned left into a third street and slowed to a walk and there was no sound of anyone following.

I reached in my pocket. I was rattled. I said, "We're going to Rivera Street. Got a cigarette?"

Pablo had said nothing during the running. His voice was flat and guarded when he spoke. "We'll buy some." He hadn't the ingratiating air any more.

The streets were dark. We turned two more corners. Under a street light a little old woman was sitting on a box with a big tray on her knees. She was wrapped from head to foot in heavy black, despite the heat. She had a wrinkled face like a withered lemon and long fingers gnarled with rheumatoid arthritis. Pablo grunted at her. She lifted the lid of her tray.

There were Spanish cigarettes in varicolored packages, plus Chesterfields, Camels, Luckies, Philip Morris, almost every other American cigarette I knew, and some I didn't. I thought of the two packets in my pocket. I had an idea.

I picked up two Lucky Strikes and one Chesterfield. The Chesterfields were for smoking. I said, "How much?"

Pablo shook his head. "Don't. They're bad."

"I'm used to them."

"Not these. They're *falsos*. Imitations. Made in the Canary Islands. They're horrible."

The old woman opened her lemon face and screeched, "They're good!"

He said witheringly, "You're an old liar."

"And you're *a chulo!*"

He moved his shoulders disdainfully and turned aristocratically away from her. She began shouting at him like a top sergeant.

I held the packets to the light. They looked all right. "How much?"

She screamed, "Eleven pesetas each!" and went back to abusing Pablo without a break. I dropped money onto her tray. I said, "Let's go." I put an arm around his shoulder and he flinched. He backed a couple of steps to disengage himself.

The old woman shouted on about the goodness of her cigarettes. Pablo said cautiously, "Where?"

His mouth was a thin line. I didn't know what was the matter with him. I didn't care. I said, "Come on," and began walking away. He stayed. I kept going and turned a corner. The street was empty. I stopped and lit a cigarette.

He followed as I dropped the match. The old woman was still praising her wares in an outraged shriek, but she was wrong. I guess she didn't smoke herself. The cigarette in my mouth tasted like camel dung. I said to Pablo, "Want one?"

"I bought some myself." He had a green packet in his hand. I took another draw, couldn't manage any more, dropped the butt in the gutter, and threw the pack of Chesterfields after it. *Falsos,* right enough. The imitation Luckies were in my left-hand pocket.

"I'll have one of yours," I said.

I felt for another match. The first puff of the Spanish cigarette nearly took the top of my head off. Around the corner the old woman raved on unabated. She couldn't have known we were still within hearing distance and I wondered if she was nuts. She paused for breath. In a voice near normal she said, "My cigarettes are not filthy, are they?"

She was talking to someone.

They teach you to check everything as a rookie. I ducked a look and checked. They teach you to register people at a snap. You lump them in groups like an aircraft spotter.

The man opposite the Club Bolero had been thin and had worn white cloth slippers. The man talking to the cigarette woman was thin and was wearing white cloth slippers. I'd thought he was a cop. He still could be. I had to keep the appointment in Rivera Street.

I dodged back. "Move!"

Pablo puffed idly on his cigarette.

"Fast! Anywhere!"

The calculation glinted in his eyes. I gave him a shove. Around the corner the woman was subsiding.

We went twenty soft-footed yards and into an alley. There was another street, another alley, then a reticulation of alleys. I felt like a guy on his first day in the Pentagon. I needed Pablo to get me out again.

We turned a last corner. He grabbed my arm. We stopped at the high door of a plain and respectable-looking house. He glinted calculation at me again and said, "You said anywhere." He pushed open the door and we walked in. I ached for a gun.

It still looked respectable inside. There was a carpeted entrance hall, a fat middle-aged woman sitting at a table, a staircase behind her, a landing at the top, a door and more carpeting. The woman flicked an appraising eye. She wished us good evening. It was the only preliminary. She snapped right to business.

"How long?"

"One turn," Pablo said.

"One hundred pesetas." She raised eyebrows at me. "Price all right?"

"I guess so," I said.

Her eyes slitted. She swore a stream of terrible oaths. "My God! A foreigner. I could have cooked you for three hundred. Why didn't you speak, Pablo?"

"Because I want no misunderstandings."

"What does that mean?"

"Tonight I also go myself."

She relaxed. She beamed all over her fat face. "Son! It's not often we have the pleasure when you bring the customers. Good! Two hundred pesetas the two."

Pablo watched me guardedly. "Is it too much? There are cheaper places."

"Sure, at ten pesetas," the woman snapped. "Go round to Alvarez Street and you'll get them in the cribs for five. What else you going to get? What do you want? A season ticket to the doctor?"

I looked at my watch. There was a lot of time. All in the line of duty. I wanted to keep Pablo with me, and he seemed determined. I dropped two bills to the table. "For me and him."

She dissolved again. "English?"

"American sailor," Pablo said.

"The best there are." She waved a ham arm at the stairs. "Have a good time. You deserve it." She smiled again, picked up a pencil, and began writing in a notebook.

Pablo was already halfway up the stairs. I couldn't figure what was wrong with him. I followed along the carpeted landing and we entered the room.

It wasn't the first time. Line of duty, of course. In Italy the legal licensed places have stone floors, white-tiled walls, and an anaphrodisiac accent on speed. Someone shrieks at you to get a move on the moment you enter and the other guys form a line behind. This was different. In fact, it was decorous.

There was a big crystal chandelier, semireligious pictures on the walls, and a lot of furniture. The chairs had antimacassars and some of the pictures were framed in pink sea shells. Nine girls sat on plush chairs with knees very properly together, holding a polite conversation with three men. They were discussing the weather.

They broke off as we came in. The girls smiled. The men greeted us like old fellow members of the same club. I sat down next to Pablo on an overstuffed Victorian sofa with rolled ends. He widened the distance between us.

A silence fell.

The women examined us politely. A great canary blonde leaned against the mantelpiece wearing a tight full-length gown of green velvet embossed with a complicated design of black ribbing. It made her look like a newly upholstered piece of furniture. She had a prodigious chest and eyelids like a pair of egg cups. I glanced at the time again.

Pablo's tone was cold. His watchful look remained. "It is not polite to check the time here. These are not cheap whores, like at the Bolero." Two of the babes nodded agreement. A Moorish girl wearing only a skirt and a line of black tattooing that ran from the center of her lower lip, over her chin, and down between her breasts gave Pablo an encouraging smile.

He said, "Hot."

"Very hot," she agreed.

There was a lull.

Two of the men began discussing a bullfighter called El Tino. A girl with streakily dyed hair went over and sat on the third man's lap. He grunted happily, held her close, and put a hand in her dress. Two other girls lit cigarettes.

I said, "We'd better move."

"Why?" Pablo looked at me stonily. "We've paid."

The bullfight men stopped talking. I saw them give no sign of making a choice, but they stood up and went with their girls through a second door on the other side of the room. I had a glimpse of a staircase.

Another lull fell. A quiet night. It was all about as sexual as the Chicago stockyards or a horse show at Madison Square Garden.

The lap-sitting girl hiked her skirt above her knees. The canary blonde batted her eyelids at me as if she were raising and lowering a pair of Venetian blinds. Pablo curled his lip. He was going to show off. He said in his terrible English, "Ooweech oowan you want?"

The effect was electric.

"He's French?"

"*Americano.*"

Seven girls were suddenly like a squealing seventy, clustering around, waving their hands, drowning each other out with pidgin English, suggesting various types of diversion, and asking if I had any real American cigarettes. They laid on hands and chittered like starlings. The lap-sitter dashed over to swell the throng. There was only one way to clear it.

I stood up. I nodded to the velvet-clad canary. "You."

The others fell back. The remaining man nodded approval, and absent-mindedly slapped her backside. She took my arm. I said, "Where?"

She pointed to where the others had disappeared. She said, "There."

The other man watched in incurious silence. Pablo stared at me intently. I said, "Let's go."

Downstairs the street door opened and shut. A voice began speaking. It had good Spanish but a foreign accent. It said softly, "You got an American sailor upstairs?"

The fat woman muttered an answer. I couldn't catch it. I smiled reassuringly at the blonde, took two steps to the open door, and looked through the banisters.

There were three men. I could see the face of only one. He was talking fluent Spanish. He was describing me. He was even using my name.

He was Bellington, the bosun.

The fat woman glanced up. She looked directly into my eyes. I shook my head at her and backed into the room. I closed the door.

Chapter Seven

I took the big blonde's arm and steered her rapidly across to the stairs. She went on up. I stuck my head back around the door.

"Pablo. It's important."

He sat like a dummy. "What?"

"Come here!" My mouth writhed with anxiety. He got to his feet and came after me, his face as blank as a clay mask. I backed a little. He came through the door. I shut it swiftly, heaved at him, and bundled all three of us up the stairs together.

He tried to resist. He was off balance. The blonde made slow squawking sounds to ask what was happening. We hit a dimly lit landing and there were doors all over the place. The blonde stared at me with her mouth open. I said, "We get out."

"What for?" the blonde asked. "Don't you like me?"

Pablo's eyes narrowed. He flicked a disdainful hand and hit me on the shoulder. His jaw jutted slightly. A contemptuous tough-guy, man-of-the-world smile played around his mouth. He said amusedly, "He doesn't like any woman. He had the chance of Pepita the Gypsy and a blonde American. He preferred to whisper to chichi in the Bolero. He's *a florita, a maricón*. He won't go with you because he wants to go with me because I'm pretty. He has made a very large mistake."

He rolled his shoulders, inviting trouble, confidently masculine. The guy was a switcher, a human chameleon, ready to throw himself with complete conviction into any part he thought the circumstances demanded. Before he'd been a tout. Now he was the dominant and unassailable male. He said loftily, "These foreigners. They bore me. Last week two Germans, the week before a Frenchman and a Dutchman, this week—"

I hit him. The blonde winced. He looked at me in utter shock. I said, "Get us out!"

He was blinking in astonishment. His hands lowered. He said, "You want us to run like before?"

I nodded. The door opened at the foot of the stairs. A shaft of light came up.

He galvanized himself into action. He dragged at the girl's sleeve and we all ran along the landing and through a door. He pushed her onto a bed. She was protesting it wasn't her room. There was a bedside table, a washbasin, a bidet, and a skylight. I closed the door behind us.

The girl was saying one of us ought to go back downstairs. Her co-workers would think she wasn't respectable if she entertained two men at once. She said something else. By that time I was up on the table with the skylight open. I floated a bill down to her.

She reached for it and smiled beatifically. She started to put it reverently in her bosom. I gave a great heave and was on the roof. Pablo shot up behind me like a jack-in-the-box. We scooted.

Spanish roofs are flat. They're on different levels. We dropped one, climbed two, dropped another. Music sounded around us. Voices eddied up from the narrow streets. A few stars shed a dim light in the indigo darkness of the sky. Ahead of us was the outline of a chimney funnel.

I whispered, "Here." I pulled him close. He didn't resist. I edged around the corner of the chimney and thrust him behind me. We waited. The heat was a slow boil.

We were a few feet from the edge. A man far below was singing the song about birds. There was a half-formed idea about Bellington jammed in the back of my head, but I couldn't force it out. There were other things more immediate.

I didn't want to meet him at this stage. But I had to know whether and why he was following me. I'd been taught to check all channels the hard way.

If the other guys had sent him—Lennox or Bromfield—he'd shrug when he found me gone and return to wherever they were. If he followed me this far on the roof, it meant he had other motives. I wanted to know them.

In the street the man stopped singing. There was a high peal of laughter from a woman who sounded drunk. The heat rose stiflingly. The silence felt blank and hot and utterly still.

A faint shuffling came softly over the roof. Behind me Pablo stiffened. I held my breath.

The man crept cautiously past the elbow of the chimney. He went the few paces to the edge and peered over. His face was visible in the faint rising light from the street below. He was not Bellington. He wore white cloth slippers and he was thin.

Pablo said, "Paloma!"

The guy wheeled and leaped all in one movement like a bridegroom going to bed. I think he didn't see Pablo. He came straight at me. The knife in his hand gleamed in a swinging arc. I tried to side-step. My ankle turned. The wall was at my back. I did the only thing I could do. I went straight down and rolled.

The guy fell on me.

He meant to finish it in one jab. I made an up-and-outward lunge and got his forearm and the knife point strained over my face. My other hand was pinned under me. I tried to roll again. He made a wriggle and got astride my hips. He fixed both his hands on the knife and pushed down and I wasn't going to he able to hold him.

His teeth showed. His eyes were stretched wide with strain. He groaned with effort and the sweat fell from him onto my face and the laugh of the drunken woman rose again. A man shouted something obscene to her. The laughter went higher. The man was appallingly strong and my wrist trembled and I couldn't hold him any longer.

I gasped, "Pablo!" I thought he had run away. I was wrong.

His shiny shoe flashed. It hit the man in the face with a single squashy thud. All the weight went off me. The knife clattered to the roof. The man stood half upright and staggered and started to topple. He made a moaning noise. It turned to a scream.

He screamed fadingly all the way down to the street. I heard him splash. The laughter stopped and there was silence, and then the woman howled. A dozen others joined her. I forced myself to my feet and snatched up the knife.

Pablo was standing with his back to the chimney. The emotions dissolved all over his face. He said formally, "I'm sorry I thought you were a homosexual." He was trying desperately to find a suitable part to play. There wasn't one.

His mouth opened wide. His eyes stared. He said, "What I did." Then he giggled hysterically. "What I did. I killed him." A babble of voices started down in the street. He gave a great gulp and started to cry.

I'd left Brad. I had no compunction about any guy in white slippers. I was sorry for the local cops, but the situation could be cleared afterward. I had to get to Rivera Street. I said, "Let's go."

Pablo needed no urging.

He knew the town like his own face. He didn't falter even when we jumped a narrow alley and the cobbles were a thin strip a long way down. The voices faded behind us. New ones arose. Snatches of music. Everything changed but the heat. I was drenched. I was confounded. I couldn't make sense of anything.

We came to the final roof.

There was a covered doorway. He stopped. He was no longer crying. He seemed recovered until he spoke; then his voice trembled and changed levels.

"You will report me to the police."

I shook my head. "Thanks for what you did." I put the knife in my pocket. It had a blade that fitted into the handle. I said, "Was Paloma a policeman?"

"No."

"I thought not. How well did you know him?"

"Only that they called him Paloma. He was a *chulo.*" Pablo suddenly started sobbing again. "He was a no-good *chulo* like me. He was always with the foreign sailors. He took them to the bars and the houses because he got a commission. Like me. I've killed him."

"Maybe he's not dead." The kid was suffering badly. I wanted to help him. There wasn't a thing I could do. I said, "It's all right. Trust me."

He stopped sobbing and looked at me dully. "You will report me to the police if I don't."

"Stick with me till we've been to Rivera Street. Let's get off this roof before they start searching."

He pulled open the door. He said, "There's a back way. No one will see us." He started a running descent. I followed. The music poured up.

There were five flights of stairs. The music stopped at the third, then started again—a guitar and a woman singing.

I went empty. I hissed, "This the Bolero?"

"The Nido." He kept going. The strident voice rang loud. I thought of the pansy bartender and his possible friends. I was getting the reaction of what had just happened. I was trying to make a connection between Brad, the cop, Bellington, the bartender, and the man in white slippers. Nothing came. We reached the bottom of the last flight.

It was the same song, the same voice, coming amid a buzz of noise from the other side of a closed door. There was a second door opposite. Pablo seized the handle and started to yank on it.

He pulled. Then the panic got him. He jerked furiously. He turned a white face to me and said, "The back way's locked. We have to go through the bar."

"It's not the Bolero?"

"No."

"Come on." I jerked my head, pushed open the other door, and walked in. It couldn't have been worse.

A roar went up. Banjo Kelly was over by the bar, working the fake handbag that was really a camera. Bromfield waved a hand and howled a greeting. The boys from the ship were all sitting together around a large table with drinks in front of them and girls on their laps. Except Lennox.

His eyes were closed. He was jigging his fatness around the floor in what looked like a dance interpretation of one of the remoter aspects of the Kinsey Report. Pepita was clasped in his arms.

She was drunker than ever, and singing the bird song in his ear. The other couples bumped against them. They didn't notice. The place was a joint with all the Spanish trimmings and it wasn't the Bolero. There was no immediate way out.

I waved back to Bromfield. I had to. I said I'd be there in a minute and walked to the long bar with Pablo at my heels. My first concern was Banjo Kelly. I had to know more about her photographs. One published picture might possibly mean ruin for present chances, future prospects, and a large section of the whole Department. I said, "Hello."

She looked up and refocused her eyes. She gave me one of those looks with which wives numb their beery husbands at two in the morning. Then her face cleared. She said, "But you're not drunk," and she smiled. She said, "O.K., Smitty, I don't hold it against you. You ditched Pepita too. That saves my face. And everything was all right directly afterward. The little fat man over there turned up and rescued me, then all the other boys arrived and made me one of the gang. The little man was asking after you."

I said, "Getting more pictures?"

"Hope so, but you never can tell with this available-light stuff until it's developed. You told anybody?"

"No."

"Don't. They'll freeze up and go phony. This series has to be something special."

"You professional?"

"Oh," she said, "spit in the other eye. Let that be a lesson to me. The price of fame. Ever hear of Weegee?"

"No."

"That makes it better." She grinned. She was nice. She said, "It's the new base they're building here. In a while there'll be lots of little fresh-faced American servicemen coursing through the streets. Our boys. My editor has a great big warm pulsating heart. He wants to show all the moms back home what Junior will be getting into. I'm photographing everything. There's noncommercial competition stuff here as well. Good for my reputation. Seen the guitarist?"

I looked. He sat on a stiff-backed chair. His hairless head was the exact size, color, and shape of a bowling ball, except that it had no thumb hole in the top. The hand plucking the strings had only two fingers.

"Somewhere in profile against a white wall," she said. "I want everything in the joint."

"We'll talk about that," I said. "Stick around. I hope to be back soon."

She gave me a long searching look. "So you're off again. What sort of professional are you, Smitty?"

I was going to stall. Lennox chose that moment to open his eyes. He let out a whoop and came waddling his pink beaming way to the bar. Pepita remained in the center of the floor, still singing. She didn't care. She was very drunk. Lennox beat on my shoulder enthusiastically. "Bishop! Where the hell did you go?"

Banjo Kelly opened her eyes. "Bishop?"

"Went visiting," I said. "What happened to Bellington?"

"He was here a while back. Bromfield got to worrying where you were. Bellington volunteered to go look."

"That doesn't sound very characteristic."

"Christ! Stop using fancy words. Didn't you see him?"

"No." Bromfield was still beckoning. I grinned across.

Lennox said, "Well, now you're here we can all settle down for a good time." He nodded at Pablo. "Who's the kid?"

"One of the relatives. A cousin."

"He looks sick."

"He is. I gave him some gin. I'm taking him home." Banjo flicked me a quick, calculating look. Lennox said, "Hell, Bish, don't run off again right away. You'll be all right again in a while, won't you, son?"

Pablo didn't answer.

Lennox waited. "Bish, if you don't speak Spanish, how do you make the guy understand?"

Banjo Kelly opened her mouth and shut it again so quickly her teeth clicked.

"Who, Pablo?" I said. I knew about Bellington. Back on the esplanade when first we came ashore he claimed he didn't speak the language. He'd been speaking it in the brothel. I said, "Pablo gets what you're saying if you speak slow."

"I don't know his linguistic abilities," Banjo Kelly said, "but he's delicious. I wish he were a few years older. However..."

She fumbled with her handbag. I knew what was coming, I leaned across the bar to block the lens. I said, "How's your Spanish dame, Lennox?"

"Jeez, what a handful! You can have her. She followed us from the place where I met Kelly, here. Now I can't get rid of her. She's stiffer than anything you can think of that's stiff."

He looked across to where she was still singing. He shouted, "Hey!" She turned and noticed me for the first time. The song stopped. Her lips curled back.

She advanced in a sort of long-legged prowl. She said, "Son-of-a-bitch. You promised to come home with me and then you ran away. Just because you don't want to give me real American cigarettes. You stink. So does Pablo."

She got a good look at him. Her voice changed. She put an arm around his shoulders and peered with boozy anxiety into his face. "What is it, *chico?* Tell Pepita what's the matter." She was a different woman. I suddenly liked her.

Lennox said, "His cousin's been feeding him gin."

The guitar thrummed.

"Cousin? What cousin? Pablo doesn't have any family. He's an orphan."

I wasn't supposed to understand Spanish. I said in English, "Dance, honey?" and whipped her to the middle of the floor. At the bar Lennox bent to ask Pablo a question. Banjo Kelly was working the handbag. Pablo's face was pale and his eyes were wide with shock and you could see how young he was.

Pepita's body was stiff against me. She had turned mean. She didn't want to dance. She said in a slurred voice, "You made me like you. Then you ran away. You're trying to spoil the big night of my life. I won the lottery."

"I was making a phone call. I returned and you were gone."

"What a dirty rotten filthy liar," she said. "What an entire son-of-a-bitch. Why do I like you?"

I tried to steer her into position to keep an eye on Pablo. She resisted. I put an arm around her neck and all at once she relaxed and moved very close. Her arms came up under my jacket and went completely around me. I felt her hot fingers through my shirt. She said, "O.K., I forgive you if you give me real American cigarettes."

I caught Pablo's look. I gave a faint nod toward the door and he started to move. I whirled Pepita into a spin. From the table Bromfield called, "You're doing all right there, Bish." Pepita laughed softly.

The hot fingers were playing erotic little tunes on my ribs. She slowed down until we were just standing and swaying and her writhing body was lithe and animal and vibrant with life. Suddenly I wanted her. She knew.

She looked up with eyes gone liquid, hands stroking all over my chest. I checked the public. Banjo Kelly was watching with what looked like mockery. Pablo disappeared. I had the sudden idea that he might panic and run away.

My desire went stone dead. I snatched a glance at my watch.

"Come home with me." Pepita took my wrist and looked at my sleeve. "I will sew on your missing button."

The lights went out.

I felt her grab at me. The music and talking and dancing continued. I lurched into one couple, teetered, hit a wall, and then I was outside the door. The street was black as pitch.

I took two steps and smacked into someone. We clutched. We held tight and danced together. The voice said half laughing, "Wait." A match was struck. The flame guttered.

He was the guy in the inconspicuous gray suit. The smile slipped completely from his face. He said stiffly, *"Perdone,"* and dropped the match. The darkness fell again.

From across the street Pablo called urgently, "Esmitt."

I stumbled for what I hoped was his direction. My toe stubbed the curb. I got to the sidewalk and said softly, "Where are you?" A hand reached out and held me. The street lights came on.

We were directly under a lamp. He had my arm and was looking into my face. Another man was a few feet behind him, standing against a wall. Our eyes locked.

He was the fair-haired cop.

I waited for him to shout, leap, do something. He remained unmoving, the bruises on his face like shadows. Pablo said, "We go," turned, and saw the cop. He froze.

The cop said, "Hello, Pablo."

He was no longer looking at me. He wasn't interested. He didn't recognize me. The relief was so intense my knees nearly gave way.

Pablo whispered, *"Buenas noches, Señor Torres."*

I nudged his arm. We walked slowly down the street. We turned a corner and took a few more paces and he said, "I killed a man."

He began crying again.

Chapter Eight

If White Slippers and the bartender were connected, I could expect trouble. If the bartender had set White Slippers to follow me he'd certainly have someone waiting for me at Rivera Street. I crossed my fingers and went anyway. I had to. There wasn't much else to do while I waited to make the phone call.

We walked a long way. Our feet fell soundlessly in piled dust. There were no sidewalks, no lights, the streets had degenerated into rutted earth, the straggling houses were little more than shanties. We were right on the outskirts of town. I didn't like it a bit. Everything lay too quiet and dark. The heat was intense and the country smelled like the inside of a kiln.

Pablo moved softly beside me and drew close. He was nervous. So was I. I couldn't see ahead of me. I was late. I had the vague premonition again that everything was going wrong. I wanted to strike a match and look at my watch.

Pablo nudged me. "What?" I whispered.

He took me by the elbow, drew me deep into the shadows, came to a halt, and pointed. "Round the next corner."

The whole idea suddenly seemed foolhardy. I almost backed out. I patted his arm and hissed, "Wait."

I flattened myself against the wall, did the last few yards with my shoulder brushing a facade of crumbling plaster. The sweat ran off me. My heart was thudding so hard I could feel it in the soles of my feet. I eased my head round the corner a quarter inch at a time and looked up the next street.

A hundred yards away a solitary light glimmered dim above the doorway of what might be a warehouse. A man was waiting. He wore a hat. It was an indication. In Spain you don't wear a hat at night unless you want to hide your features. He'd hidden his pretty well.

I strained to look at my watch and nearly broke my neck. I was fifteen minutes late. He'd wait two minutes longer. I slid back to where Pablo was a gleaming of eyes against the wall and I pulled the two Lucky Strike packets of cocaine from my inside pocket and thrust them into his hand. I don't know why I trusted him. Probably because there was no one else.

I whispered, "Hold them till I get back. If anything happens to me, run straight to the police station. Give these to anyone but Torres, the fair guy you spoke to. See the head man. Tell him these names: Arthur Bradley. The bartender at the Bolero. Bellington. Bellington is on a ship called the *Sea Rover*. Got that?"

He made a protesting sound, something like a half sob. I though he was going to argue. I didn't give him a chance. I went sharply around the corner and shuffled my feet in the dust and the man under the light turned toward me.

He kept his hands free. He wanted to show he meant well. He called softly, "Hello," and stayed where he was, head down. My feet made little puffing sounds. My jacket swung unbuttoned. The two decks of Luckies from the old woman were still in my left-hand pocket. My hand was thrust deep into the right, holding the knife with the blade out. I'd have given my eyeteeth for a gun. I said, "Hello."

His head lifted. I saw his plump waxy face, his little mustache. I recognized the type. I'd met it in a dozen different places. Everything was going to be difficult or useless unless it was handled properly. He was the boss's errand boy.

"I've been waiting, señor," he said softly. He had a singsong voice.

"Sorry, *amigo*."

"It does not matter." He spread wide his small plump hands in a shiny display of friendship. "I believe you have something to sell me, señor, something well worth waiting for. Where is it?"

"Where's the money for it?" I sang back.

"Oh, I have it." The warehouse behind him was a dark nothing. I couldn't tell if the door was open. "Naturally I have it." His teeth glinted gold. "But first the merchandise, señor. Show me!"

He was a pipsqueak, a third string, useless to me as an individual. He could make the deal and disappear. If I pinched him he'd probably prove as useless as a cut corn. I had to contact the organization, move in on it as with Rossi in Naples. I said, "No dice, *amigo*. This isn't a one-shot. I want to make arrangements for further deliveries. I can't do it with you. No insult meant, *amigo*, but you wouldn't know mice from crocodiles till one of them bit you. Who else is around? Tell them to come out."

His smile got bigger. His chest swelled. He looked like a tenor in a television opera. "You misunderstand me, señor. I am the boss." He gave a great humorous sigh and shrugged. His hand went to his pocket. "The money. Look!"

I looked. I watched his face. His mouth twitched and he wasn't reaching for money. I slugged at him with all I had.

He was too quick, I missed.

The blow glanced off him. His feet slid in the dust. His knife came out. So did mine. I retreated two fast steps. I wanted information, and if he got close enough one of us was going to get killed and that would be the end of everything. He circled me and I waited. I pivoted.

He made a rush. He was professional. He took a swift pace to the right and came in sideways with the knife at arm's length and his wrist bent for an upward thrust. He was a smaller man than I. He didn't have time to change the direction of his hand. I kicked hard. It was getting to be a habit. My foot smashed into his crotch. He hung for a split second in mid-air and his face writhed.

Then it was over.

Footsteps whispered behind me. I tried to move. My weight was wrong. The little man hit the dust and something smacked the back of my head and my legs scissored and I fell on top of him. My knife hurtled into the darkness.

The other one was under me. I tried to throw it a long way down the street. It didn't get far because all my strength was gone. Someone was sitting astride me and sapping at the back of my head and knocking me into the ground as if I were a stake. I couldn't move a finger. I sank deep. There was a spectacular display of colors, then everything was terrifically speeded up.

Bellington's voice said, "Get the cigarette packets." The pressure went from my back. Two men dragged the gasping little bloke from under me and the hands went through my pockets and took the packets and nothing else. It all lasted less than half a second. The same voice said, "Finish him, Manuel!" The little man was feeling all around my head and underneath me and trying to find his knife and still gasping. Bellington snapped, "Finish him!"

Somebody kicked my head. I went "Aaaaah."

The hands continued groping. I wanted to go out because I didn't want to feel myself being carved. I willed myself to unconsciousness and nearly made it. I almost reached the bottom of the blackness.

Down the road a woman started screaming.

Her voice was penetrating and loud. She went on and on like Yma Sumac. I heard her even when I was out. There were a lot of faces hanging in front of me. Half of them said in Spanish, "Finish him, Manuel," and the rest scowled and said, "I don't speak the language." They were all Bellington. Down the road the woman continued her long unending note, howling for the police.

A car engine got mixed up in it. I'd arrived at the stage where I couldn't sort it out. I quit trying after a while and just lay in the darkness and listened to the cantata for buzz saws in my head. Then there was not even darkness. I swam in a negative nothing. Everything dissolved.

A pressure crammed hard against my stomach. I felt sick. I bounced again, my eyes flew open, and the dark ground was close to my face. That cinched it. I was dead and being buried. I felt pretty brave about it and opened my eyes again for a better look.

My dangling arms were swinging against a pair of baggy pants. I was hanging bouncing over Pablo's shoulder. He was running like a streak through the darkness with his legs bowed under the weight of me. I didn't feel so brave any more. I figured we were being chased.

I whimpered, "Put me down."

I thought he didn't hear. He ran another hundred yards, stumbled into a narrow alley, and came to a panting stop. He tried to set me on my feet. The walls of the alley opened and shut and my legs gave way. He bent over me, pulled me up. He was groaning like a dying horse, eyes showing white all around the irises. He gasped, "You are not dead, Esmitt. Good!"

I wasn't so sure. I put a steadying hand against the wall and opened and shut my mouth several times to no effect. I wheezed, "Let's get away."

"Where?"

"Anywhere. Back to town."

He slid an arm under my shoulders and dragged me almost trotting. My head sloshed like a half-full basin of mush. I sucked down deep gulps of air, tried to think. There wasn't much pattern.

White Slippers and the bartender. Connected. And Bellington. He'd known how the cocaine was packed. He'd told the other to get cigarette packets, nothing else. He must have been wise to the stuff even before I landed. Hadn't stolen it at sea because he didn't want the risk of carrying it ashore. I was another sailor.

But who killed Brad? Friends of the pansy bartender. Contradiction. Bellington must also be a friend of the pansy bartender. One had steered me to the other. They didn't want only the stuff, they wanted to kill me. The same as with

Brad. Which indicated they suspected my connection with him, my identity.

That idea was nuts. Only three people knew what I was doing—the boss in Italy, Brad, and myself. Brad was dead, so there was only the boss and myself. The cover-up was foolproof. I was sure of it. To everyone else I was a sailor. Unless the fair-haired cop had really seen me at Brad's place and was playing a complicated game and—

I gave it up.

I released myself from Pablo's arm. I said, "I'm all right now." I didn't know how to phrase it so I put it into good strong dirty Spanish. I said, "Thanks for what you did. It took *cojones*."

He glanced at me, mouth all awry. He looked about thirteen. "To go to the police station like you said would have needed *cojones* like cathedrals. They will be looking for me about Paloma."

"You saw Torres. He said nothing."

"The whores in the house will have talked by this time."

"Maybe not. Don't worry. It'll be cleared up."

He said, "Your friends were too far away. I didn't recognize them. They drove off in a fast car. I couldn't see the number."

He waited for comment. There wasn't one to make. He said, "Yes, well," and stopped walking, feeling for one of his green-packed cigarettes. We were under a light.

"I make a good woman," he said. "I screamed like a raped young girl and the men ran like rabbits. I was very convincing."

"That was you?"

He nodded coolly. "Have a cigarette?"

I took one. It had brown paper. I patted my pockets for a match. I said, "Where's the stuff I gave you to hold?"

"Right here." He fished into the pocket again. The light was directly above us. His hand came out holding the two packets and the cellophane glittered brightly in the lamplight like glass.

I nearly lost my stomach.

I said in a sick voice, "Wait."

"What?" He stood looking at me.

A big pain went through my head. I didn't want to believe what confronted me. All I wanted to do was lie down and die.

On the flat of his palm was a brand-new packet of Philip Morris. The other was Lucky Strike, as it should have been, but that was wrong too. I knew it. I could see.

I closed my hand on it. It began to squash. I looked at Pablo and tried to speak. I couldn't. I went slightly nuts and ripped at the Lucky Strike packet and it was a sight.

The cigarettes went tumbling all over the street.

Chapter Nine

My head was an egg beater. Blame the knocks. I was thinking, Left-hand pocket, right-hand pocket, inside pocket, I couldn't have made so complete a mistake, but Bellington's got the junk after all. I said, "Pablo, where is it?"

"Where is what?"

His eyes opened questioningly. He grinned. I couldn't take it. I bashed him in the teeth and he ran backward clear across the street and hit the wall.

He started to slide. I went after him before he could recover. I clamped a hand on his throat and slammed his head against the wall and I was crazy. I gibbered, "Give them to me! The real ones. Where are they? Give them to me!"

His mouth opened. His eyes were bolting. He started to choke. He shook his head feebly, but he wasn't attempting to struggle. He gasped, "The men hurt you. You're sick."

I was. I had red lights in front of my eyes. I was trying to pound his head against the wall. Then he moved. He resisted. His fist came up with all his strength and hit me in the solar plexus. I let go of him. I lay down on the ground and sobbed a few times and retched.

He took to his heels.

I thought that was the last of him. He ran about twenty yards. I heard him turn. He came back and knelt beside me on the ground and clamped his hands to my shoulders to hold me down. He said, "Be quiet, Esmitt! You're sick. In a little while you'll be better. Be quiet or I hit you again."

I gulped for air. I was sick, but with shame. He didn't need to run. He could have walked off at leisure when the guys were pounding the life out of me and the sobbing little guy was feeling for his knife. I let my hands go limp in the dust.

I waited for breath. I said, "Give me that cigarette."

The others were strewn all over the street, white against the dark dust. He gathered them together, trampling some. I tried to get up.

He returned and squatted again, holding the unopened Philip Morris packet to the light. He said, *"Falsos.* The seal is always wrong. I thought you didn't like them, Esmitt." He ripped it across and pulled out a cigarette. I struggled to my feet. He said, "You are feeling good now?"

"Yeah. I'm sorry."

"My unlucky night. You'll be better if you walk. Come."

We went slowly down the street. Someone was driving a hot rod around my skull. I said, "What are the rules in Spain for picking pockets?"

Fifty yards later he answered, his voice like a cutthroat razor. "What now?"

"Not you," I said. "Somebody stole two cigarette packets from me tonight. They substituted two others."

"Sure. In case you realized your own were gone." He rubbed the back of his head and laughed nervously. "You must be crazy for your real American cigarettes. Like Pepita."

"Like her," I said, and light broke. Her fingers running all over my ribs. Into my pockets. I said, "They weren't cigarettes she stole. We have to find her."

"As you say." He flicked me a look. "She will still be in the Nido with the sailors. Listen. She's a good girl, but she's drunk. Don't be too angry with her." He giggled again. He licked his lips. "Funny if she tries to smoke a cigarette that isn't a cigarette."

My head hurt worse than ever. We went faster.

The street was as noisy as ever, and every bar except the Nido. I pushed open the door. My heart sank. The joint was almost empty.

No sailors, no Banjo Kelly, no Pepita, not even the ball-headed guitarist. A few bored-looking couples sat making desultory preliminaries to commercial love. Two small dark men like brothers stood at the bar spooning bicarbonate of soda into tumblers of water.

They stirred it, drank it off, waited to see who'd be first to belch. The man on the right gave a violent roar. The other was a split second behind. They both grinned delightedly. The bartender put the soda jar back under the counter and said, "The national drink of Spain."

I hadn't noticed him before. He was a big man, thirty-five to forty, and running to fat. His hair was a dark curly mass that he'd tried unsuccessfully to flatten and his teeth were good. He smiled. He said, "Hello, Pablo." A blowsy girl at a nearby table was telling her temporary boy friend of something that had happened earlier.

"I was just standing there—" she said.

"Where is Pepita?" Pablo asked.

The bartender shook his head, widened his smile. "That girl! She finished by swearing at the American, the little fat one with the pink face. She says she doesn't like Americans because they run away and leave her. She's right. She swears so much finally they all run away and leave her. All the sailors."

"She go with them?"

"Man, they were afraid of her. The little fat one buys her a drink and gives her one of his American cigarettes. Then he runs away too. She has another bottle of champagne all by herself, and off she goes."

"Where?"

"Who knows? She won the lottery."

I got a sudden stab of worry, unexpected and unwelcome as an aching tooth. I said, "How about the blonde American?"

"The truck? Gone too."

"Where?"

The voice of the blowsy girl at the table became more zestful. "And then it happens. We hear this scream and down he comes like a meatball and hits the sidewalk. Splosh! Blood like fountains. I fainted."

"Dead?"

"Minced."

The bartender said, "Still talking about Paloma. It'll last her for years. You knew him, Pablo?"

The kid was the color of putty.

"No."

"You did. You used to talk to him in here."

"No."

"To me it's the same. What do you drink?"

"Nothing." Pablo plunged for the door.

The bartender looked surprised and shrugged at me. I shrugged back and grinned. "Probably to vomit," I said, and lifted a hand and went quickly outside. My watch stood at three quarters of an hour to the phone call. If ever I needed instructions from the boss, it was now.

The drunks passed in singing procession. Pablo was leaning against the wall. I said, "Try to forget it for a while. We have to find Pepita."

He nodded. "I know a few places."

"Not the Bolero."

"No." He moved a beckoning arm. We set off.

He knew more than a few places. He knew every place. I quit counting after the first eight. I quit thinking about the time. The phone call was now secondary. A lot of people could be ruined by two Lucky Strike packets full of junk. I had to get them back.

We went along streets, down streets, up broad stone steps, into networks of alleys and more streets—into bars, houses, cafes, and joints. It was a tour I could have done without.

I saw the sort of girl you get for five pesetas. Walt Disney out of Goya with matching surroundings. There were dim and esoteric rooms with nothing but slow-moving shadows around the walls. There was one room not nearly dim enough with geese and knives, the smell of blood, and men only. A Moroccan importation. Someone once told me it was funny. It's not.

They all knew Pepita. They hadn't seen her. She didn't come to houses like these. She'd been at one of the bars fifteen minutes before. They grinned when they spoke of her. We didn't wait to hear the story. We kept going. My watch said fifteen minutes to the phone call and I was sickened at the size of the failure I must report.

I gave up and slowed to a normal walk.

"One of your cigarettes, Pablo."

He thrust a hand into his baggy pants. He said, "We're not going to find her." He looked hot and beat and his flesh glistened through the torn shirt. He said, "The cigarettes are damp."

"It doesn't matter."

He held out the green packet. I reached a hand. It happened.

Over in the next street or the next she began singing. She was yowling, screeching drunk.

"Cuando me levanto par las mañanas... "

There was only one voice like it. I started to run, trying to guess where it came from. She changed the tune and got on a single note. It went higher and higher. She sang the single word *"pájaros."* She tried to cheep like a bird. There was a bubbling sound and she stopped short.

Pablo was loping beside me. He dragged me down an alley and clear through a house from front to back. It took forever. We slid down a street, up some steps, round a sharp turning, and fetched up on the verge of a deserted square.

It was a handsome little square, lit with globes in clusters of three. There were orange trees, flowers in profusion, and a single tall date palm throwing a shadow from one side to the other. There was a fountain. Steps led up to it and tinkling jets of water sprayed high. Pepita sprawled full length on the steps with a bottle in her hand, dead drunk and fast asleep, her coarse black hair spread all around her head like dark liquid. I sprinted across.

I yanked her to a sitting position. I shook her. I said, "Pepita!" and the bottle came loose from her hand and rolled slowly down the steps without breaking. Her head fell sideways against my chest.

"Pepita!" I snarled. I slapped her face. There was no excuse except that I was hot and sick and weary and my nerves were shot. I struck her with my clenched fist.

She was breathing heavily, purring in her throat. She was dead drunk and in for a long sleep. Ten minutes to the phone call and I had to get the cocaine. I propped her in the crook of my arm and searched her. I went all over her. I even felt at the back of her hair and took off her shoes.

Nothing.

She began to snore. I stretched her out and replaced the shoes. I looked up at Pablo.

"Anything?"

"No."

"Where are they?"

I didn't answer. My head was starting to split. I put my face in my hands. I said, "Get her out of my reach before I beat her to death."

Chapter Ten

His feet scuffled. I looked up. He had an arm under her shoulders, the other at the bend of her knees, and was carrying her without effort up the last three steps to the fountain. He swung her feet to the ground. She sagged against him and laughed gurglingly. He clamped an arm around her chest, gave a sudden jerk at the nape of her neck, and plunged her into the fountain. He held her there.

He held her so long I thought she would drown. I didn't much care. He dragged her up spitting and gasping with a hand in her hair. He shook her violently. She gave a piercing scream and he ducked her a second time.

Her hands beat the surface. Gouts of water spurted all over the steps. She came up again and he released her and she turned flounderingly around, not knowing where she was. He got an arm around her waist. He led her down the steps and pushed her. She plumped beside me. She began to swear.

Her profanity was endless and enormous and gypsy. She cursed everything from the birds in the air to the worms in the earth. The torrent poured forth without thought. She wasn't seeing me or anything else. She banged her hands together, shook her head. Her hair swung like a spattering nest of rat tails.

Pablo removed his shirt. He swaddled it over her and began to rub. The profanity got more jerky. She fell silent. He said, "Pepita, listen! You stole cigarettes from Esmitt."

She said nothing.

"Did you?" he shouted.

"Yes."

"Where are they?" He jerked the shirt away and put it back on himself, all patches of wet and sweat. He fished a comb from his hip pocket and sat down beside her. "Tell it!"

She was between us. She seized the comb and raked furiously until her wet hair was a shining black helmet. I said, "Pepita, where are they? The packets?"

She turned a dopey expression on me. She was still drunk. "You got a real American cigarette, buddy?"

Pablo said with awful gentleness, "Pepita, you don't want a cigarette. Only harlots smoke in the street."

"I am a harlot." She leaned wearily against him. "I'm drunk. I won the lottery. This is the big night of my life."

"Sure it is." I went to the bottom of the steps, picked up the bottle, and held it in front of her. I said, "I brought this to celebrate."

She didn't take it. She stared at me with recognition dawning. "You," she said. "Esmitt. You printless son-of-a-bitch."

"What did you do with the cigarettes?"

"Pretending to like me, then running away. Your father is a son-of-a-bitch. Your mother is a son-of-a-bitch. All the Esmitt family are sons-of-bitches. Your uncles and your aunts are sons—"

"Where are the cigarettes?"

"You son-of-a-bitch."

I hit her so hard she fell into Pablo's lap. She lay there a while. None of us moved. The water tinkled musically in the fountain and the night was silent and hot. She lifted herself up.

She had a hand at either side of her face, rubbing her cheeks. Her eyes shone with surprise and delight. "You hit me. You like me!"

I hated her.

"I knew it from the start," she said. "I was certain. I will do everything for you. I wanted to sew the button on your sleeve. The man wouldn't give it to me."

It was like riding a jet. I got symptoms of blackout. "What man?"

"Torres. The policeman. He was looking for you. I recognized the button. He wants to find you because there is a message from your ship."

"You told him who I am?"

"Yes. You're Esmitt. He wouldn't give me the button. Give me a drink."

My hands were trembling. I twisted the wire. There was a report like a pistol shot and the cork sailed into the air among the orange trees. The champagne fizzed over.

She snatched the bottle. She downed a third and passed it on to Pablo. "Big night," she said, and stood up and grinned down at me, feet wide apart, hands on hips. "Your packets are important, Esmitt?"

"Yes." I got beside her. I heard a faint echo of footsteps from the far side of the square.

"If you really like me I'll tell you where they are."

"I do like you."

"Prove it. Kiss me."

Pablo said urgently, "No."

"Kiss me."

It seemed a small price. I put my arms around her. I fastened my mouth on her parted lips. She clutched at me and began to writhe and her hands walked slowly up my back and over my neck and into my hair. She returned the kiss. I had an inkling why some men marry girls from the profession. I sagged a little.

A tremendous blow hit me on the shoulder and we were torn apart.

I thought it was Pablo. I swung around. I went rigid. A middle-aged cop had Pepita by the wrist. He put out a hand like a shovel and grabbed my shoulder. He said, "All right, now we all go to the police station."

The tuft of cotton from the missing button on my sleeve showed prominent as a bloodstain. Pablo's face froze with fear. "You don't understand, señor."

"Shut up! I saw it." The cop tightened his grip on me. "Let's move. You too, woman."

I tensed. He was a bright cop. He let go of my shoulder and reached for the gun at his hip. Pablo got between us like a flash.

"He doesn't know, señor. He's a foreigner."

Shoe-button eyes flicked at my face. "Liar!"

I didn't know what was going on. I put the sleeve tight against my side and wondered if Torres had circulated a description of me. "American," I said.

"Liar!"

I switched to slow English. "Pablo, what is wrong?"

He screwed up his eyes and made the effort. "The porleesmahn-"

The cop tapped my arm. "Repeat!"

"I asked," I said in English, "what is wrong."

"Yes." The cop frowned. He scowled. He chewed his lower lip. His expression slowly brightened. "Waat ees rahng," he mimicked painfully. "I onnerstahn." He nodded complacently. "I estoddy English tree years."

"Only three years? You understand well."

"Yes." Then he scowled again, but only because he was trying to think of something else to say. It was going to be an awfully drawn-out conversation. I said slowly, "What did I do wrong?"

"Yes. Bad thing. To kiss the girl in the street is not the law in Spain. There are penalties."

"I did not know. In my country everyone does it."

"Yes, is true?" He perked up with salacious curiosity. "I hear also," he said, as if we were about to share a dirty secret, "that in the States United the ladies they wear the trousers sometimes like the men."

"Yes."

"Bad women. Like this one."

I drew myself up. "My mother used to wear trousers."

He was silent. He patted my shoulder. He said with embarrassment, "Naturally you do not know to kiss not in the street. Goo nyee."

"Thank you," I said. "Good night." I took Pepita by the elbow and steered her quickly away. Pablo was on the other side of her. We reached the corner of the square and I turned round and the cop was waving.

"Goo nyee," he called.

"Goo nyee," I called. I wheeled Pepita into the shadows of an alley and stopped. She linked her arm with mine. She seemed concerned about something.

She said, "Really I look like your mother?"

I didn't know how she'd got it that way. It didn't matter. "Exactly," I said. "Where are the packets?"

She nodded. She said gravely, "You love her as my little baby loves me, yet you say I am like her. It is the first time I ever remind a man of his mother."

I thought she was going to cry. She pushed back her wet hair. "I thank you for this wonderful thing you have said. We'll send Pablo away and go home to my bed."

I looked at my watch. I got a strong desire to scream. "The packets," I said.

She was still canned. She had another lightning change of mood. "You!" She slapped my shoulder and giggled. "You played a joke on me. I take all the trouble to steal your cigarettes and substitute the *falsos,* and then when I open the packet there is nothing but powder. I don't want it. I give it to the man for his little girl."

"What man?"

She smiled. Then she shrugged helplessly. "The policeman with the button?"

"That was before."

"Lennox? The little fat American?"

"No. He smells." She plucked lazily at her lower lip. "I am remembering. The little American gave me a real American cigarette. All the sailors had gone away with the ugly American girl. The cigarette was very good. Wait!"

We waited. Pablo said, "I'm going to hit you, Pepita. I'm going to smash in your face."

"I told you to wait." She waved him to silence. "I was standing at the bar. I wanted another cigarette like the real one and I opened your packet. The man laughed. I gave them to him."

"Who?"

"The bartender," she said patiently, as if I ought to have known all along. "In the Nido."

Pablo and I leaped off like a couple of greyhounds from the slips.

We got round the corner and then she came sprinting barefooted beside me, a high-heeled shoe in either hand. She could run like a gazelle. She wasn't even panting. She must have had four lungs.

"I did something wrong?"

"Yes."

"To you?"

"Yes."

"I'll help you."

"For God's sake, no," I said. "No!"

We ran in silence, the same streets and alleys, the same stone steps. I hadn't realized how far it was. I was developing a stitch in my side and a lead weight of worry in my stomach. I snatched a look at the time. The phone call was overdue. I prayed the rasp-voiced operator would keep the line open.

We reached Socorro Street. The music was playing. We burst through the door of the Nido.

The place had filled again. The two-fingered guitarist with the head was back in position, picking out the bird song. I turned to the bar and it was too late to dodge. A pair of arms wrapped my neck.

Bromfield fell against me. He was drunk, sentimental, and pally. My dear old cabinmate. He beat my back and got roisterous. "Have a drink! Meet my best girl!" He gave a great flourish. Banjo Kelly was leaning against the bar and I was ridiculously glad to see her.

She said, "Quite an entrance. Return of the Three Bears. Had fun?"

I disengaged myself from Bromfield. I didn't want witnesses for what was coming. I leaned close to her and said quickly, "Get him away a minute. Dance with him."

"I did. He doesn't. I have the bruises to prove it. You dance with me."

I wiped my forehead. I was on the point of death from tension.

"Sidney," she said, and took Bromfield's arm, "let's go watch the guitarist. He fascinates me." She led him unprotesting away. I hadn't known before that his first name was Sidney. I put my elbows on the counter.

Pablo was sibilating to the bartender. Pepita cut stridently across all the noise and everyone in the joint must have heard her. "You got my two packets," she shouted.

The guitar seemed to jangle more violently. Someone sang. The bartender ran a hand through his thick curly hair and looked blank. "Your what?"

"Packets." She beat on the bar. "I want them back."

His face cleared. He smiled at her. "Oh, them. Sure. Your two cigarette packets. What you got in them? Stuff for your hair?"

"Give!"

He reached under the bar and withdrew a Lucky Strike deck in each hand. The one on the left was opened. It was still full. The powder glittered dully as he passed them to her. She handed them straight to me.

"All right, Esmitt?"

"Yes," I said, and thrust them carefully into my jacket pocket, folding the open top and keeping my hand on it. The music stopped. I glanced over my shoulder for Banjo Kelly. The dancers were returning to their tables. The guitarist was sauntering to the door. Bromfield had his arms around a girl who looked like the back end of a small percheron. Banjo was bearing down on me with her handbag swinging. I beat her to the punch.

"One more favor. Keep Pepita occupied while Pablo and I slip off to make a phone call. Don't go away. *Don't go away.* I have to talk about those pictures."

"Talk now. I hate mystery stories."

"You're a pretty girl, Banjo."

"O.K., I'm sold. You're not bad-looking yourself. And you used my first name without smirking." She turned. She put an arm around Pepita's shoulder and drew her a little apart. She said in slow Spanish, "Your hair is different. I like it. What did you do?"

"Got it wet."

I didn't wait for more. I gave Pablo the high sign and slid.

Out in the street the drunks went roaring by. The guitarist was re-entering and he treated us to a friendly nod. A man up the road a piece was being sick against the wall. I dragged Pablo round the nearest corner.

"What now?" He looked washed out. I was sorry for him. I was sorry for myself. I figured it wouldn't be for much longer. Italy was sure to instruct me to reveal myself.

"The telephone place," I said. "Where you first met me."

He nodded wearily. "It's not far. We'll take a short cut." He walked a little ahead. I followed him into an alley, making out a mental report. There wasn't much.

Bellington and the bartender at the Bolero. Small fry. Their arrest would probably make no difference to any organization—if they belonged to one. If they did, the arrests would tip off their bosses. My own boss wasn't going to be elated.

I reached in my pocket to check the open packet. Pablo got to the end of the alley, stepped into the street, then came back so violently he knocked me staggering a couple of steps. He flattened himself against the wall. His eyes were like small cartwheels. He whispered, "Torres is there. The cop."

The voice called, "Pablo!"

He turned and bolted back down the alley.

I hovered a second. Pepita said the cop had a message for me from the ship. A lie. He did have the button. He wanted me in connection with Brad. I had to talk to Italy. I heard the footsteps approaching. I ran after Pablo.

He had disappeared.

I shot through the alley and into the street and somewhere behind me the cop shouted again. Across the road the door of the Nido was opening. I couldn't return. I'd be holed up. I veered to the left and ran into another alley. There was no light. I ran hard.

It happened quickly. I saw nothing. Something brushed me and a hand grasped my arm and swung me round. For a split second I thought it was Pablo. There was no time to think anything else. Something hit me in the back of the neck.

I went out like a snuffed candle.

Chapter Eleven

I was on the phone to Italy and the boss had lost his temper. He was giving me a rehash of all the things they start drilling into you the moment you join up. You follow orders. You never allow personal inclination to overcome training. You are among the most individual of the world's policemen, but guard against too much individual initiative or you'll start fancying yourself a free lance. Don't talk. Say only what you have to say and never more or you're bound to give away information. Et cetera.

I repeated all the adages five times. His head emerged from the phone mouthpiece and he told me how wonderful I was. He said I was personable, agreeable, honorable, hard-working, had a razor-sharp intelligence, a flair for meeting emergencies, was certain to take over his position when he retired, and without doubt I'd eventually be President of the United States because I was that sort of guy. I smiled modestly.

I woke up.

I sat squashed between two bodies. There was a gun jammed in my ribs. Lights flickered over my eyelids and I heard a motor. I was in a car. We were traveling fast. I kept my eyes closed and waited for my head to clear. I opened my eyes a little, saw that the car was large and that I was in the back. A uniformed chauffeur was at the wheel on the other side of a glass panel. A passing car flashed its headlights and I lolled my head and looked to the side where the gun was. I'd never seen the guy before.

He was small, short-nosed, very Spanish-looking. He had a deep thumbnail-sized scar on his forehead as if a piece of flesh had been gouged out, and in his hand was a great big gun. I said, "Who are you?"

His voice was soft. He had a half lisp on his r's, but none on his s's. He said, "You wouldn't be intevested."

"Want anything special, or just passing time this way?"

"You're angvy," he said. "I understand. I apologize. We hit you because you stavted to put up a fight. Will you take a cigavette?"

"No."

Another car passed. The small man looked mildly worried. "I'd appveciate if you don't mention we used violence. We had instvuctions to handle you gently. It was veally the fault of my fviend. He's impulsive, like a child. Aven't you?"

There was no answer. I turned to look. The man on the other side shifted his bulk and fixed me with a simian gaze. He still didn't answer. He was Plosch's Ape. The hair on my head tried to stand to attention. I realized I was scared. "Nice to see you again," I croaked. That ended all conversation.

I leaned against the upholstery, stared at the chauffeur's neck, and tried to relax. We whizzed through the night. Neither man spoke a word. The gun didn't vary its position a fraction of an inch. We hit open country and picked up speed and the tires hummed louder. The windows were open, and the smell of brine came in, and the sound of the sea. I felt cool for the first time since coming ashore. In fact, I felt cold.

The house was surrounded by a high wall. We swept through the big open gates and every window in the place was lighted. The joint was as big as a small castle, a fine tribute to somebody's bankroll. There was statuary in the garden and fountains and about a dozen cars parked on a stretch of gravel. We swept right on past it all and went round to the back.

The chauffeur pulled up. The little man nudged with the gun. "Out!"

They stood close on either side of me. I was still tottery from the tap on the head. The big guy gripped my arm in a rock-pulverizing hand and we entered the house by a back door. There was a long empty corridor.

Somewhere at the front a piano rippled the clean cool notes of the Scarlatti sonata that sounds like a combination of the Spanish national anthem and "Diamonds Are a Girl's Best Friend." The corridor walls were paneled in oak. The light came from what were probably the only tasteful chandeliers in Spain, and the amethyst-colored carpet underneath had enough pile on it to drown a baby. The joint reeked of luxury and I might even have liked it had they brought me in by the front way and without a weapon.

The small guy opened a door. He gestured politely with the gun. The big guy got in the rear and gave me a shove. The door closed and all sound of music was cut off. I was sorry about that. I looked around.

The room looked as if Oscar Wilde had just set up house with J. K. Huysmans. It had brocaded furniture, an undue amount of colored silks draped over everything, and a carpet that was thick, pale green, and Bokhara. In the corner was a double-keyboard mid-eighteenth-century harpsichord. On the air was lingering perfume. On the walls hung a Daumier, a doubtful Ingres, a fake Daubigny, and something that may or may not have been a Gauguin—the usual naked Tahitian girl standing under a tree, stippled by shadows.

I sat on the brocaded settee. The big guy draped himself against the wall in what was apparently his characteristic pose and the little guy took a chair opposite me. He pointed the gun. He delicately crossed his feet. He had patent-leather shoes. He said, "Now we wait."

We did. I looked at my watch. I looked at the Tahitian girl. I was interested in the picture's authenticity and that was just as well because I had to look at it for twenty minutes before the door opened again.

The little guy leaped respectfully to his feet.

Plosch walked in.

He had changed to evening dress, and he was as immaculate as ever, teeth gleaming, not a blond hair out of place, long eyes glowing vivid green in the transparently smooth skin. He came forward smiling. It all went click and I knew about the skin. He was an arsenic eater.

I said, "This is a fine way to bring someone to a party."

He blinked. "But honestly, I did not know it would be you. How very agreeable that it is! I remarked before that I liked your honest face."

"I'm toasted all over for my beauty. Now what? We speak English or Spanish?"

"English. There is no longer cause for deception. We are going to be terribly honest with one another. Aren't we?"

"Yes."

"Good." He sat beside me on the settee. "Drink?"

"No."

"I am in accord. Drink only after business." He examined me as if I were a rare butterfly. "Now what have you to say for yourself?"

I pointed. "That picture a fake?"

"Indeed not. A genuine Gauguin, at Gauguin prices. Don't you adore his work? But I have no sympathy for the man himself. He almost deserved to get leprosy, don't you think? He had an attitude toward life with which I cannot for a moment agree."

"Yeah, but you've got it better than he had it."

"Well, yes." The green eyes glinted. "I haven't perhaps his genius, but in a practical way I'm infinitely more clever. There are good things in the world for all to take. I take them. I suppose that you sometimes think of doing so."

"Frequently."

He patted my knee. "We shall do marvelously together."

"When?" I said.

He drew a loose cigarette from his pocket. The little guy with the scar stepped forward hastily and struck a match. Plosch inhaled deeply, expelled two lingering plumes from his pale nostrils. He flicked the ash. He said, "A few questions. Your name?"

"Albert Smith."

"I am the Maharaja of Cooch-Behar."

"O.K. I'm Terence Anthony Kevin Bishop."

"I knew it. Irish-American. It explains your Spanish appearance. The men washed up on Ireland's shores from the wreck of the 1588 Armada stayed and bred—those who weren't eaten by the natives. Fascinating how the resemblance persists."

"Another subject for a lecture."

He nodded. "I shall call you Antonio. Have you always been a sailor?"

"Ten years."

"Visited Spain many times?"

"This is the first. I'll be coming again. I'm regular crew on the regular run from Naples."

"Naples," he said. He studied me silently. "You were running away when first we met this evening, Antonio."

"From other members of the crew. They wanted me to booze with them."

"And why not?"

"Other things on my mind."

"Private business?"

"Don't you know?"

"Ha-ha," he said. "Admirable cageyness." He put his fingertips together. "However, you've been careless tonight."

"Harassed," I said. "Your boys play too fast and rough."

"Rough?" The smile disappeared. He switched to Spanish. "These two?"

The little guy with the scar stiffened nervously. I said, "I get tired of being smacked on the head."

Plosch got up and walked over to where Scarface stood rigid. He said calmly, "I told you no violence," then he stubbed out his cigarette on the side of the little guy's neck. "More obedience in future." He turned back to me, eyebrows raised. "Satisfied?"

"I think it was the other guy. It's not important. They're pals."

From behind him Scarface fixed me with eyes gone snakelike. He hadn't even lifted a hand to his neck. The Ape stared vacantly ahead. Plosch went to the harpsichord, took another cigarette from a box, lit it himself, and smiled at me.

"Business," he said. "Show me the material."

I reached into my pocket. Scarface reached in his, but more quickly. I drew out the two Lucky Strike packets and his hand came away empty. I said,

"American money only."

"Naturally." He took both packs, stirred his finger in the crystals of the open one, tasted it, and shuddered fastidiously. "Filthy stuff." He held out the packet to Scarface. "Check it!"

The little guy shot out the door like a streak. The Ape took his turn at pocket reaching.

I said, "That first one got opened by mistake."

Plosch tossed the closed packet on top of the harpsichord. "The guitarist is an employee of mine. He saw the girl pick your pocket. Imagine his surprise when she tried to smoke a cigarette."

"Imagine hers."

"I understand she is stupid. You are wise to go with stupid women. They cause less trouble and are invariably better in bed."

I said, "Leave her. She did us both a good turn. You get the cocaine. I get the money."

"And I can find a more useful occupation for the guitar player."

"The roundhead without fingers?"

"You're observant. That's useful. There were rumors connecting the Nido bartender with the narcotics trade. My guitarist has been watching him. It will no longer be necessary. A man dealing in drugs would have recognized your cocaine and then, of course, not returned it to you."

I said nothing. He came over and sat down again beside me. He sat too close. He said, "Why do you deal in cocaine, Antonio?"

"Because I'm tired of walking around with nothing in my pocket except a bent nickel and a latch key."

"A salient reason. Only with money can we obtain those things that alleviate the recurring miseries of quotidian routine. And this is your first venture into extra-nautical activities?"

"My fourth. The others were in the States. It's getting too tough there. The cops have closed in."

"Here the matter is more simple. The police are underpaid. It makes the weak easy to deal with."

I wondered if his easy-dealer was Torres. I said, "Mr. Plosch, you're putting a lot of confidence in me. Why?"

"Because you are intelligent and honest and one must always trust associates to a certain degree. You have just been elected associate. You are going to work for me. You have no choice now. It will be pleasant. We are both men of honor. Aren't we?"

"You bet."

We shook hands with undue warmth. The door opened. Scarface came back in. He crossed the room, put the cocaine on the harpsichord, and waited for permission to speak.

"Well?"

"First quality, señor."

Plosch nodded thoughtfully. He crushed out his cigarette. Abruptly he reached into his inner pocket and pulled out a great wad of American notes. "We pay," he said, and riffled the bills and began counting them into my hand. He did it almost voluptuously.

He stopped at three thousand. I thought he was through. He carried on to four thousand, five thousand, more. He said, "I am grossly overpaying you, as you may know."

"I like it."

"I hoped you would. I mean it as encouragement to maximum effort. There'll be more in the future, though naturally you will work harder for it. Nothing in life is free."

"I've noticed." I ran a thumb along the notes and wondered if they were traceable. The smartest guys can fall down on bill numbers. I said, "So what's the plan?"

I started to thrust the dough in my pocket. I nearly swallowed my own throat.

A girl's protesting voice came down the corridor outside.

She said, "Get your hands off me, you boob. Find me someone who can speak English. I shall complain to the police about this."

Banjo Kelly.

She'd followed me. I knew it. She had only to reveal her occupation, or even the fact that she knew me, and we were in bad trouble. I could have strangled her for her foolishness. I swallowed the rest of my throat and jumped to my feet. Plosch was quicker. He flashed in front of me like a cat and reached the door. He opened it about a foot. The bluff had to be attempted before she started talking. I got behind him, yanked the door wide open, and looked over his shoulder.

She was struggling in the grasp of a short, blue-jowled hood type. Her big handbag dangled from her wrist. She looked up as the door opened. Recognition leaped to her eyes, her face cleared, and she started to smile. She said, "Hello."

I talked so fast I gabbled. I said, "Hello, hello, and who are you? Are you an American? What's the trouble? Any way I can help? I love to help unknown young ladies. Are you an American?"

The smile slowly vanished. She stood and stared at me.

Chapter Twelve

The money was still in my hand. She glanced at it, back to my face, then switched on the smile again, especially radiant. She said, "What a relief! Perhaps you can explain I meant no harm. You American too?"

"Yes," I said, and beamed frantic thoughts at her. "Sorry we can't exchange visiting cards. I'm fresh out. I'd still like to help if I can. Put me in the picture, as the English say."

Plosch turned with a polite smile and eyes as cold as green ice. "The young lady can as easily acquaint me with the facts, can you not, señorita?"

"Señorita Briggs," she said. "I think I do have a visiting card." She snapped open the clasp of her handbag, looked down, and started to fumble. Scarface moved in the room behind me. I swayed closer to Plosch, lifted the bills, scratched the side of my face. He began to turn. I jammed the money into my pocket, the handbag clicked shut, and she said, "No, I don't have one after all. Anyway, the full name is Carol Briggs. Do I owe the explanation to you?"

"No," I said, "to this gentleman."

We were standing in a little bunch at the door. She made as if to enter the room. Plosch barred the way. She said, "Well, I'm sorry, I appear to have trespassed on your property. I'm staying in town. I go away tomorrow and I thought tonight I'd take a walk in the country. I was passing your gate and all the cars came out and I saw the fountains and the statues and I thought it was a public park. We don't have private gardens back home as big and beautiful as these, so I came in to look around. The gentleman who needs a shave grabbed me. Here I am."

She gave Plosch a particularly concentrated smile. "I'm not really a burglar."

"I'm sure of that." He gave a faint flick of his fingers. Scarface moved into position, hand in pocket. Plosch went a little way down the corridor and took Blue Jowls with him. They murmured together. I didn't move. Neither did Banjo Kelly. Neither did Scarface. Plosch came back smiling.

"Miss Briggs, I have remonstrated with him for handling you roughly. I do not approve of violence in even the mildest form. My chauffeur will now drive you back to town, because it is late. If you care to return in the morning's light I shall personally show you my gardens with the greatest pleasure and pride." He held out his hand.

She said brightly, "How kind! Thank you." It was only because I'd seen her before that I knew how frightened she was. She flicked a nervous sideways glance at the blue-jowled guy. I couldn't do anything about it. "Goodby," she said, and nodded to us and turned down the corridor with the guy walking close. Plosch backed swiftly into the room and shut the door.

His eyes were emerald slits. He opened his mouth to speak. I beat him to it.

I said, "O.K., the deal's off."

He blinked. His mouth shut again. It was the first spontaneous emotion I'd seen him show. "Why is that?"

"We've been seen together. I can't take the risk. I work in absolute secrecy or not at all."

The Ape straightened. Scarface thrust the hand deep in his pocket and watched his boss's face. Plosch carefully lit a third cigarette and blew out a long lazy cloud.

"I appreciate your caution, Antonio. But there is no need at all for timidity. I also thought the girl's arrival rather too well timed. Later we shall know more. I have arranged that she be investigated. As for our future dealings, you will not see me again. The conditions are foolproof."

"It's off. Nothing is ever foolproof."

"I like your attitude," he said. "It augurs well." His long green eyes regarded me almost tenderly. "But let me explain that among my numerous negotiations is a fruit business. Bananas. It necessitates the use of a warehouse and office inside the harbor. There is an employee always on duty. You will deliver consignments to him without even passing through the gates. You will never see me." He paused.

I thought I had the entire Naples-Spain-U.S. setup. I said grudgingly, "Sounds all right."

"Foolproof!" He nodded briskly. He was pleased at the way he'd got back into the dominant position. "Antonio, are you certain of a regular supply from your source in Naples?"

"Sure. His name's Rossi."

I watched for a flicker of recognition at the name. There wasn't one. Plosch delicately tucked the fingertips of both hands into his jacket pockets.

Suddenly and irrelevantly he whistled a few bright bars of the Scarlatti, tonguing the trills like a bird. He gave a huge grin. His beautiful skin exploded into a mesh of wrinkles and he looked old as Methuselah. He said exultantly, "Antonio, we have launched ourselves. You are going to be rich. I richer. Isn't that a beautiful thought?'

He swayed lightly on his toes as if about to dance. "Your ship, I learn, returns in twenty-seven days. Take no unnecessary risks, but bring as much merchandise as can possibly be secreted during ship inspection. My employee will make contact as soon as you dock. All future arrangements and payments will be made through him unless you need to see me in an emergency. Agreed?"

"Agreed."

The huge grin was still wide on his face. We were two schoolboy pals sharing an adventure. "One thing, Antonio. I am a rich man already. My influence is great. I have an impeccable reputation, an unassailable position, and many strong friends in all countries. You will never try to deceive me. We have shaken hands, given our word, we are honorable men. I shall always look after you. But if ever you are unable to get to Spain, should you fall sick, for example, rest assured that some of my friends will call on you wherever you are. Even police friends."

"Warning taken," I said. "I've always enjoyed the best of health. That all?"

"Except for the celebratory drink."

"I never do. I want to get back to the ship with this money."

"The men will return you to where they found you."

"So long as they don't slam my head again."

He put a hand on my shoulder. He slid it down my arm, pausing briefly at the muscle. "Antonio, we shall do brilliantly. Your insouciance is perfect. Best of luck to us both and you may leave by the front door. My guests have departed."

"Good-by," I said.

"Good-by, dear Antonio. It hurts me to see you go."

I went out and down the passage, flanked by the Ape and Scarface. We passed through a great cool marble hall. It had blue mosaic tiles, sparse black furniture, and a painted ceiling. We emerged into the hot night. The same car was waiting in the driveway, the same uniformed chauffeur. We climbed in and the soft upholstery wrapped me. We headed for the gates. Back in the house all the lights went out.

I was a bright boy. I had the entire Naples-Spain-U.S. setup. Until I thought about it. Then I had nothing but a headache. I sat and tried to figure some sense into what had just happened. I looked at the back of the chauffeur's neck.

The saliva dried in my mouth.

I tapped Scarface. "How many chauffeurs has Plosch got?"

He lifted a hand to his blistered neck. "You can go to hell, you son of a whore."

There hadn't been time for the chauffeur to return from driving Banjo Kelly back to town. The ache of worry for her sprouted like a mushroom.

Chapter Thirteen

The car pulled up in the dark deserted street. I got out on the sidewalk, shut the door, and looked in at them. I said, "It was vevy nice meeting you and your fviend."

The Ape stared fixedly ahead. Scarface lifted a hand again to his neck. He gave me a parting look of hatred, leaned forward, and tapped on the panel, and the big car slid ahead and merged into the inky shadows down the street. I didn't move.

A school of cats was howling nearby. The smooth sound of the engine came back through the stillness.

It slowed at a corner. It went fadingly down another street and slowed again at what could have been a second corner. No door slammed, but I couldn't take risks. I'd seen the telephones three streets away. I didn't want to be tailed. I ran across the street and through a dark open gateway into what seemed some sort of inner courtyard. The place looked like a high-class block of apartments. There were magnolias somewhere and the smell hung heavy. I eased into position.

I could see most of the street by walling my eyes round an iron grille. I heard a noise. An old man shot by on a bicycle that jangled over the cobblestones. The cats nearby were still yowling. The other figure appeared again out of the shadows.

One hand was thrust deep in his pocket. He saw the street was empty, got on his toes, and ran. He must have been sweating in the heat. He halted momentarily opposite where I was hiding and looked at the shadows, and I thought he was coming across. He ran on. He passed under a light. It was Scarface. He disappeared around the next corner. I waited.

Three minutes later he reappeared. He lifted his head and turned from side to side as if trying to locate me by smell. Then he ran off again in the direction taken by the car. He vanished into the shadows. I waited another two minutes.

Then I ran hard across the road and scooted around the corner and down the next street. The lights of the main town were flinging an aura into the sky. I headed for them, made a zigzag, backed on my own tracks. I kept looking over my shoulder for Scarface.

Maybe he was following off his own bat, wanting to pay off the cigarette burn. I doubted it. Plosch wasn't the type to employ men who'd buck him. Which meant he himself had given the instructions, was double-checking on me. That was feasible. It explained why everything had gone so easily. It meant I'd probably be followed the rest of the night. It was pretty near funny.

No half measures for Bishop. I had three people on my tail—Scarface, Bellington, and Torres. I hoped the boss would appreciate the joke. I had an idea he wouldn't.

I halted at the corner and took stock. The *"Telefonos"* sign was across the way. It was almost one in the morning but many people were strolling, mostly men now and sweatier than before, but still cheerful. I envied them. A guy sat at a café opposite. He was so perfectly the plainclothes-cop type that no force in the world would have employed him. I wasn't so sure about any of the others. I wondered how good a description of me had been issued.

I sauntered across the road at the same pace as everyone else and went through the double door of the telephone building.

They looked like the same people on the benches, waiting for the same incoming calls. The third booth was empty again. I ducked inside. I lifted the receiver and said, "Operator Eight, please," and there must have been something about the booth that made me think of Brad. I was sure to be elected back in the States to visit his wife. They had a baby named after me. I stopped looking at myself in the mirror.

"Mr. Pastor," I said. "My call to Naples still open?"

"No, Mr. Pastor, it isn't." Her voice was loaded with silky delight. "The lines between here and Italy are very busy. You can hardly expect us—"

"When can I call again?"

"If this is not a joke, I can manage in two hours. If you are on time."

"No sooner?"

"Indeed not."

"I'll send a telegram right away."

There's one like her in every telephone and post-office building in the world. "Not from here, you won't," she meowed. "I'm a telephone operator, not a dispatcher. There's a desk for telegrams outside your booth."

"See you in two hours."

"Promptly," she purred. She'd had a delicious time. "Good-by, Mr. Pastor."

I quit the booth. I was so low I was traveling on my hipbones. The telegram desk was at the other end of the building with three girls behind it, two of them pretty. I picked the other one. They give you better service.

I scribbled out my form, handed it to her. A guy moved into line behind me, awaiting his turn.

The girl was ferociously ugly. She had horizontal teeth, a mandarin mustache, and a squint. I smiled. The guy behind me sighed with impatience. The girl seemed to be analyzing my handwriting.

Among her other attributes was a voice deep enough to sing the lead in *Boris Godounov*. She pointed the pencil and read the telegram aloud. All the nearby heads lifted in interested appreciation.

"Dear Uncle Luigi," she boomed. "Town too hot. Stop. Continue expecting call. Stop. Your solitary nephew repeat solitary Terence." She pronounced it "Terenthay." She read out the address.

She said, "Eighty-five pesetas. I know it's expensive but Naples is a long way. Do you really find it hot? This is nothing compared with last month. I thought Italians were used to heat. My brother was there once and—"

I thrust the money toward her and continued to smile. The man behind gave an exhausted snort and walked away. I said, "I'll collect the reply here. You mind?"

"Of course not." She was conscious of the other girls watching her. She gave me her teeth right back to the wisdoms. "Till later, then."

"Good-by." I turned away. The man from behind me was vanishing through the swing doors. He wore a tropical suit of the color Spaniards call "Ike" and pronounce "Eekay." I followed the same route and stepped outside and into the road. I got halfway across.

Torres appeared a hundred yards to the right, talking to two uniformed cops.

I turned my head and kept going. I expected a shout. I got to the opposite side street, walked a few fast steps, and flung myself running down an alley. I didn't get far.

A car squealed to a stop at the alley mouth. The footsteps came whispering. I dodged to the left and right, and then the alleys were a maze and I was back in the Pentagon with nothing but walls and darkness. The footsteps pattered behind me and the heat dripped.

I tried. I couldn't lose them. The Spanish assignment was up the spout, maybe the Italian setup endangered. I attempted to speed up. I hadn't the energy left. I ran into a last wide alley and there was a faint light high on the wall and two men were coming from the other end. The only thing I saw clearly was that each had a gun in his hand. I stopped stone still.

I was afraid. I didn't want to be left alone with the fair-haired cop. I figured he'd killed Brad. He might do the same with me. I stood beneath the light and lifted my hands.

I called, "Don't shoot. I'm unarmed." The two small plain-clothes men advanced slowly, hugging the wall on either side. The one on the left was smiling. I heard footsteps and turned and the other two were behind. The first one moved into the orbit of the light.

He wore an Eekay-colored tropical suit. He was the guy from the telegram desk. The one behind was bigger. I saw the gun first. I saw the fair hair. I waited for the bullet. He wasn't the cop.

He was Bellington.

He said, "Get away from that light, sailor." A gun rammed into my back. I took two paces forward. Bellington shoved and someone stuck out a foot and I staggered into the shadows and fell. They started kicking me.

I think it was all of them. I stopped a foot in the belly. I gasped and tried to roll and I was thinking it was great and glorious to work for the Department, but they didn't pay enough to put up with so goddamned much of the stuff. A toe slammed my kidneys. I went limp and played dead. It wasn't hard. They went on kicking a while.

Bellington said in Spanish, "He's out. Take him to the house. I'll go tell the boss."

His footsteps retreated. Two of the men grabbed me under the arms and ran back through the alleys at high speed. My toes dragged. I stayed limp. I was getting my breath back. The third man ran ahead and the two who were carrying me slowed and gave a hoist. Then I was upright with my arms around their shoulders.

An engine started. I opened my eyes and the street ahead was lighter. The car was at the curb. The man behind the wheel hissed, "Now!" The two guys dragged me across the narrow sidewalk. One of them pulled open the rear door.

A voice shouted, "Hey!"

Both men jumped with nerves and turned sideways. It all happened quickly. One of them said, "Torres!" They bent to fling me in the car. I slid my arms and clamped their necks and smashed their heads together.

It made a lovely sound. A gun clattered to the ground. I spun around and tripped and stumbled. Then I went back up the alley like a springbok.

A shot fired. Gears clashed. The car leaped away with a howl. I kept running.

A long while later, when I was nearly dead, I stopped and sat down and took my shoes and lined the inner soles with the money Plosch had paid me. It was the only evidence I had. I didn't want my pocket picked again.

Chapter Fourteen

The only place we had in common was Socorro Street. I headed for it. I went wringing wet from one alley to another and all of them seemed to be waiting for me.

Someone had brought a guitar into the street. A guy was howling flamenco and a lot of people clapped the offbeat rhythms. I slid through the shadows to the end of the alley and peered out.

The Nido bar was down the way. The guitarist and singer were standing against a wall surrounded by an encouraging semicircle. On my side of the street, sitting on the curb, was the vivid orange dress.

I said, "Pepita!"

She couldn't see me. She looked all around, then stood up and straightened her skirt. A cigarette dangled from the corner of her mouth. Her dried hair hung down one side of her face. She looked raw and stringy and tough. She said loudly, "Who is it?"

I showed myself briefly and beckoned. Her head went up. She sauntered over. I backed into the darkness of the alley and she came in beside me and stared up into my face. She had untanked somewhere and wasn't drunk.

She said softly, "Esmitt," and her voice was much more gentle than before. She leaned against the wall, standing close. I couldn't see her very well. I couldn't see anything very well. She said, "I waited for you. I knew you'd return. I knew you liked me."

"That's right," I said. "Look, I need your help. I have to find the blonde American girl."

There was a long silence. Pepita said contemptuously, "The ugly bitch has run away. She was afraid of the competition. All Americans run away. Maybe if I set off fireworks you'll run, too. Go on! Bang! Run!"

She turned disgustedly back toward the street. I laid a hand on her arm. "I have to talk to her on business, Pepita. Have you seen her?"

"No!" The answer was like spitting. I released the arm and moved from her. She hesitated. She turned toward me again.

"Esmitt, I am lying. The ugly girl was here ten minutes ago. She was seeking you. She said it was important. She didn't have a place to wait so I sent her to the Rincón Bohemio. You wish to go?"

"As quickly as possible."

Pepita moved in. Her hands slid from my shoulders and down my front. I hadn't the time or the inclination. I removed her by the wrist and linked her arm through mine. The journey took five minutes.

We heard the racket three minutes before we got there. It rose high above the rest of the din in the quarter. We arrived at the darkest of the streets and crossed the road and went through a great Moorish archway. There was no sign. They didn't need any advertisement. The noise sufficed.

A yellow-lighted room was at the end of what seemed like a long high tunnel. A small slim man danced on a table in an off-white shirt and black pants painted on his legs. There were fifty others present, all men, all beating their hands together, all singing. They looked like a bunch of brigands. The uproar was fantastic. I shouted, "You mean she's here?"

We were halfway down the tunnel. Pepita reached an arm around my neck and pointed to a wide, barely visible staircase winding upward. "I live up there," she yelled. "The ugly American is waiting in my room." The arm tightened. She almost dragged me. We went up the stairs.

The walls and floors must have been ten feet thick. The music and clapping were cut off almost immediately. Pepita breathed heavily beside me. The arm slid down my back. She said, "I've never got like this before, Esmitt."

"What?"

She gave no warning. She rammed me against the wall and her teeth nibbled all along the side of my face. She thrust with her body. She pulled tight with her hands.

Something slithered between our legs. A cat mewed.

She let go of me. She ripped out a string of oaths and kicked wildly into the darkness. The animal yowled to crescendo. Its body landed somewhere down the stairs. I heard it scamper. She said, "Goddamn it, now it'll sit outside all night and scream." She swore again. She took my arm, and drew me close, and we finished the stairs and went along a wide dark landing.

She said, "Here." She fiddled at the door and pushed it open and I stepped into what felt like a large room. There was an overpowering smell of perfume. A dim reflection of light shone through a window. A vague figure was outlined darkly against the whiteness of a bed.

I said, "Banjo."

The figure moved quickly.

A husky shape was silhouetted briefly against the window. The door closed behind me and the latch clicked. The man moved fast. I jumped. We hit the floor and began to struggle.

He shouted, "Mamma!"

The light snapped on.

I looked down into his face. I rolled off him and we got up. He resembled her strongly and was built like a full-grown man, but his voice hadn't broken yet. He stood scowling at me. He was very brown and had fluff on his chin. I guessed it was her baby. He was bigger than I'd anticipated.

She swooped on him and kissed his cheek and hooted with laughter. She put an arm proudly around his shoulders. "This is my Pepito," she said. "Isn't he good-looking? Isn't he strong for thirteen?"

"Strong as I am," I said. It was what the kid wanted. He softened up slightly and grinned at me. He was pleased with himself. His face was saved.

She said, "In a few years he'll be a bullfighter. We'll be rich. In Spain there's no other way for a poor boy to become rich."

She was completely different. Her eyes glowed. She was laughing. She appeared no older than her son. She said jubilantly, "Look at him!"

I did. My heart was aching for him. I eyed him from top to toe and said judiciously, "Yes, he has the shape for bullfighting. Legs for a *natural*, chest for *pasos por alto, la planta perfecta de un torero.*"

"*Olé!*" she cried excitedly.

The kid grinned with delight. He was going to put hand on my shoulder. She slapped him playfully across the backside.

"Get out, Pepito! I'm going to entertain Esmitt." She fished into the top of her stocking and handed him some money. "Down to the bar. Buy yourself a drink! Find yourself a girl!"

He nodded. He hesitated at the door, still grinning a me. "Good-by, Esmitt. I'll see you again."

"Sure," I said, and listened to his footsteps clatter down the dark stairs. Outside a cat wailed.

I looked around. The room was large and low with sloping ceilings and one small window. There were two single beds with spotless white quilts, one each for her and the boy. The strong smell came from at least a doze vases of fresh flowers standing around the room. There was a table and two chairs and one of them had some of her clothes draped over it. There were framed and inadequate photographs of a lot of very adequate-looking men. They'd have put me off if the boy hadn't.

The place was as clean as a hospital.

We stood in silence. She looked down at the dress she was wearing. It had a stain on the skirt where she had spilled some drink. She clucked her tongue and looked across at me and clucked again. She said, "You got dusty rolling on the floor," and she went across to a shelf and came back with a whisk brush.

She dusted me down the back. She moved in front of me and gazed fixedly into my face with brilliant black eyes. She began brushing the front of me with long uncleaning strokes. Her wrist moved slowly. Her eyes didn't waver. She said, "You like the flowers?"

I nodded.

"Fresh," she said. "I steal them every night from the parks."

"Don't get caught."

She shook her head. Her glance dropped. She turned aside and walked slowly to the window and dropped the brush on the sill. She looked into the night, running both hands through her coarse shining hair. The cat squalled again and was joined by two others. She turned around.

"I deceived you. The ugly American is not here. I have not seen her for hours."

"I know. It's all right."

She lowered her head and re-examined the drink stain on her skirt. "You don't want me now like on the stairs."

"No," I said.

"Because of my Pepito?"

"In a way."

"Yes. Now you have seen him, I appear too old. I'm not. I had him when I was thirteen. His father was also a gypsy."

She had the wrong slant. I decided to leave it. I said, "Fine-looking boy."

She nodded, playing with a button at the top of her dress. "Are all American men like you, Esmitt?"

"I don't know. I doubt it."

"It would be magnificent if they were. You are like no man I ever met. You're wonderful. You're different."

"Don't say that."

She nodded again, slowly. "You are right. It makes me sound like a harlot. Well, that's what I am." She went back to the window and held her face to the glass. "Would you like something to eat?"

"I have to find the ugly American girl."

She turned a smiling face. "Isn't she, though! Ugly as sin. I'll help you find her." She put her hand to her hair, glanced down again at her dress. "I'll change into something smart."

"Don't bother."

"For you. I want to do it."

It was a single operation. She flicked her fingers at the buttons. The dress opened at the shoulders, slid down her body to the floor, and she stepped out of it. She had been wearing nothing underneath. She was naked except for her high-heeled shoes and a medallion on a chain around her neck. Her face was lean, but her body was softly rounded and peach-colored and infinitely beautiful. She stood apart from me.

Pearls gleamed in the whites of her eyes. The public face was gone. She was grave and serious. She lifted her arms and her small firm breasts rose and desire hit me in the stomach like a physical blow.

She said, "You will like my other dress. It is new and very fine." We moved at the same moment. Our arms enwrapped each other and we pressed tight and the heavy smell of flowers was an intoxication. My hands slid over her satin skin. She gave a little sob. I lifted her against me and walked stiff-legged to the bed and sank to the whiteness of the quilt. Her shoes fell off.

The obliviating sense of isolation settled upon us. I crushed her beneath me. Her body was an arched suppleness. Her lips were soft. We didn't speak and the cats outside were howling and the world was warmth and delight.

The door opened.

They came in and halted just over the threshold. Pablo said in a voice of vast approval, "Very, very good!" I scrambled to my feet.

Chapter Fifteen

I hated most of all the fact that it was Banjo Kelly who had caught me. My worry for her went like ash in the wind. I was furious.

She pushed the door shut. She dusted her fingertips together. She said, "Button your gaiters, Bishop, your miter's showing." She giggled. "What would the See say if they saw?"

"Spare me the lousy puns." Despite the giggle, she wasn't amused. In back of her eyes was anger and something else. I said, "Wait downstairs. You'll get some fine photographs of men dancing on tables."

"I've got them. A hulking adolescent told Pablo you were up here. We came."

"Why?"

"To get pictures of men bouncing on beds," she snapped. "For my private collection. Why do you think I came? Correct me if I'm wrong. I thought you wanted to see me urgently."

Pablo still grinned. Pepita remained on the bed. She put her hands above her head, crossed her ankles, and gave a great feline stretch. She swung her feet to the floor, stood up, limbered her naked shoulders like an animal emerging from hibernation. She laughed maliciously. "Jealous," she sneered. "Poor little cold American girl."

"What's she saying about me?" Banjo stared Pepita in the face. She lowered her head and slowly raised it again. "No," she said soberly. "No, I don't blame you. She's beautiful. What a body! Think she'd let me take some pictures?"

"That reminds me—I want to talk to you about pictures."

"Ask her."

"I said I want to talk to you about pictures."

"Stop repeating yourself like Hemingway just because you're in Spain. Hemingway would have locked the door." She fumbled in her handbag. "I'll give her a business card. Maybe we can make an appointment for her to pose tomorrow."

Pablo nodded eagerly. "We've given several people cards. In many cafés. Señorita Pancho is also to take pictures of me. They will be published in all the big American magazines."

"What have you done?" I said. "What pictures did you get of me?"

"I got the point, you want to talk about them. I want to talk about you. You reek of news, maybe pictorial news. We'll go somewhere when you're ready."

Pablo turned to Pepita, grinning widely. "We're all going out."

"Sure we are. I was going to put on my new dress. It was all arranged." She danced like a naked bacchante over to a cupboard in the corner.

Banjo said, "So we all go together. This youth has ideas of seducing me. He's been sitting awful close. He'll be worse after the aphrodisiac effect of seeing you on the bed."

"We'll go alone."

"We won't!" Her anger surged back. "You don't have a girl flat on the bed and then leave her flat on her rear end."

The feminine sex was standing together. The conversation was getting screwy and formless. I tried to yank it back into line. "Did you get a picture of the guy with bleached hair?"

"Can't tell till the roll's developed." She was determined to be difficult. The rage smoldered deep in her eyes. "I saw a couple of guys putting you in a car. I knew you weren't drunk, so I hailed a cab and followed. The idea was a gallant rescue. I got to the house and you were a calm guest."

"Now you're being followed," I said.

"I am? Why?"

"I can't tell you."

"Pity. I can't tell you anything about photographs."

"Who brought you back to town?"

"I can't tell you."

"Stop being so damned feminine."

"You weren't complaining about females just now."

"Who brought you back?" I snarled.

"All right. The unshaven one."

"Then he'll be doing the following."

"Why?"

Pepita swirled over from the corner. She stood before me and pivoted on her heel. The dress was low cut, ankle length, a shiny white background with a pattern of flaming great crimson leaves vivid enough to pluck your eyes out. There was a carnation from one of the vases tucked in her hair. Her mouth was a smear of thick orange-colored lipstick.

I said, "Good God!"

You can never tell with women. Banjo Kelly vaulted clear to the other side of the fence. She snapped, "Leave her alone." She cocked her head on one side.

Pepita waited with beetling brows. Banjo Kelly joined thumb and middle finger, kissed the tips, flung the hand in the air, and cried, *"Olé!"* The women put their arms about each other and crowed with delight.

Pablo rubbed his hands and said, "To the Casino."

Everyone was suddenly in a wild and gusty mood. It struck me as theatrical. I snatched a look at my watch. Then the door was open and they were sweeping down the stairs like kids going to a school picnic. A reform-school picnic. I ran after them.

I had to talk to Banjo about the photographs. I didn't want to lose her again, and I didn't want to indicate to Plosch or his guys that I knew her. If she was being followed ...

Halfway down the stairs I caught up with Pepita. She took my arm. The boys in the bar were kicking up hell's delight and I had to shout. "Is there a back way out?"

I couldn't hear her answer. We got to the bottom and she pushed us all toward the room where the guy was still dancing on the table. Pandemonium reigned. A man with a voice like an outcast angel's was wailing flamenco about his mother. Flamenco songs are always about mothers. Two guitars thrummed, the dancer's feet thrashed the table. Everyone else stared hypnotized at his feet and clapped. Pepita's kid was sprawled over in a corner, tilting red wine down his throat. He waved. Any of the others could have been Plosch's employees.

I saw the door in the far corner and got in back and did some pushing of my own before the party settled. I steered them ahead through a high earth-floored room that smelled sweet and cool of wine, and then we were in the street with the back door closed behind us.

I'd thought that, since it was a back street, it would be empty. It had more bars than Socorro Street and was jammed with drunks. A 1930-vintage cab was trying to nudge its way through the press.

"The Casino," Pepita said, and put two fingers in her mouth and whistled like a Marine. The cab jarred to a halt. I wanted to keep out of sight. I dived for it. I pretty near sat on the floor.

"The Casino," Pablo cried. I was getting tired of hearing it.

We went through a meshwork of narrow streets. Pablo and Banjo Kelly were on the folding seats. Pepita and I slithered over cracked leather upholstery at the back. She leaned close with her head on my shoulder and her hand on my thigh and the perfume in her hair smelled good. We emerged onto a main boulevard.

It was very late. Mobs of people still strolled about, fanning themselves against the heat and with collars undone. Pepita sat very erect. The lights flickered over her face. I could see the faint superior smile hovering about her lips. She was being ladylike, haughtier than a duchess.

We turned into the esplanade and the crowd was thicker. She reached over Banjo Kelly's shoulders and snapped a switch. The light came on in the back of the cab. She wanted the peasants to see us. It was a very strong light. I said, "Turn it off!"

Banjo Kelly looked back maliciously. "Ashamed of us?"

I made a lunge. She got her shoulders in the way. I couldn't reach. She said, "Never roll a girl in the hay if you're ashamed to be seen with her afterward. Your sins always find you out." Pepita's arm came round my neck. The cab pulled up with a wincing of unlined brakes. The winking electric sign said "Casino."

We went through a large swanky door. There were tables, a band playing, people dancing, concealed lighting, and several waiters. A headwaiter in particular. He smiled. He clamped eyes on Pepita and Pablo and the smile faded. I thought he was going to fall over. I said, "Table in the corner."

He managed to jack his smile back into position and we followed him. The money in my shoes began to hurt my feet.

The table was really deep in the corner, next to two doors. One door said *"Damas"* and I could smell the camphor disinfectant, but it was at least an improvement on the pseudo ammonia of the *"Caballeros."* We all sat down. Pepita smoothed out her frock. She was causing a sensation.

Spaniards are snobs like everyone else. Maybe a little worse. The women on the dance floor steered their partners into position for a better look. Three dames at a nearby table whispered together and began giggling. I wanted suddenly to protect her against them. It wasn't necessary. She inclined herself elegantly across the table.

"They're talking about me."

"Jealous of your dress, dear," Banjo Kelly said in quicker Spanish than I thought she could manage.

Pepita nodded genteelly. "Because it's new. They'll be more jealous when we drink champagne. Order it, Esmitt! In high society it's always the gentleman who speaks to the waiter."

Banjo Kelly reached out and touched her hand. I said, "Where you staying, Banjo?"

"Hotel Palas. Why?"

Pablo got smartly to his feet, smiling with all his teeth. He thought I was cutting him out. He said, "Dance?"

"Love to." Banjo stood up. She was slightly taller than he. He put an arm around her waist and they glided out onto the floor. The snob element boiled right over and the other dancers drew aside. Pablo took advantage of the extra space. He could dance better than the music deserved.

The band was playing "In the Mood." Someone had been listening to a disc of the old Glenn Miller arrangement and they were trying to imitate. The result was as horrible as most Spanish attempts at the American idiom. The sass was all wrong, the ensemble stodgy, there was no jump. They thumped like someone hitting a wet tire with a small hammer.

"Good, huh?" Pepita jiggled her shoulders. "Dance with me, Esmitt."

The wads of money in my shoes had sweated into small brick. "In a while," I said.

On the floor Banjo was being held tight. Pablo's face appeared set and serious at her shoulder, eyes bugging with adolescent lust. I glanced at my watch. Still a lot of time till the phone call. The band was making what it fondly imagined to be American cries of enthusiasm. I looked around to find someone to bring the champagne.

Scarface and the Ape were talking to the headwaiter.

A serpent went slithering through my insides. My toes curled over the money. I didn't want to see them until I'd made the phone call. Above all I didn't want them to see me with Banjo Kelly. I lowered my head. I said, "I have to get out."

"Yes." Pepita nodded eagerly. "The ugly girl is nice, but it's time for us to leave her. She is going to bed with Pablo. We shall go back to my room." She stood up.

"Not that way."

"*Cómo?*" She flicked a glance around the room. Her head jerked back. She looked suddenly like an animal. She said. "Come on."

It was too late. Scarface and the Ape had seen me. They were advancing. I prayed they hadn't yet seen Banjo. A bunch of departing people rose at the next table and temporarily blocked the view. Pepita said, "This way!" and jerked my arm. We went through a door. She slipped the latch. A woman began screaming with shock.

We were in the *"Damas."* The first screamer could make more noise than all the rest together. She was nearly supersonic. Pepita cracked her hard across the face and it silenced the lot. I jumped on a washbasin and pushed at the frosted-glass window.

It swung open. I reached a hand, jerked Pepita up. She hung a moment. Someone pounded at the door and the women started to screech again, and then we were both out on the other side and through an alley and running down a narrow deserted street.

The sweat trickled down my legs. The heat was stifling. My feet hurt. We got to the second street and slowed to a walk. She clutched my arm. "You got trouble, my Esmitt?"

I didn't answer.

"One time when my little boy was a baby and I had no money I got into that window from the outside and stole something. God helps the fainting poor if they help themselves." She was chattering. She was frightened. I held her arm tighter. She said, "We'll go back to my room now, Esmitt."

"Yes," I said. I glanced back over my shoulder. Scarface and the Ape were fifty yards away and coming fast.

I swung her hard around the next corner. We were back in the meshwork. The streets seemed darker. I said, "Run, Pepita!"

She wouldn't let go of my arm. I ran with her. I was scared and sweating and the money hurt and my breath was strangling. We turned two corners more. The heat made a great silence. I heard them behind us and their shoes made an odd scuffing noise because they were right up on their toes. It scared me most because they weren't hesitating.

I realized why. They knew where we were going. They'd followed Banjo Kelly there. I couldn't let them catch me now. I felt sick because the girl running beside me had a tough enough life without my dropping more trouble on her head. I gasped, "Not home, Pepita. Somewhere else. Anywhere. Not your room."

She dragged at me. We ran diagonally across the road and up another street. All at once she started to cry, a shocking whimpering sound like an animal's. She was frightened. It wasn't for herself. She said, "They will hurt you, Esmitt. Run fast! Don't let them catch you."

Somewhere along the route she had kicked off her shoes. I'd have given an arm to do the same. Every time I put down my feet the money wrenched my ankles. The narrow pants rubbed my knees and the clothes were sticking to my back. We sprinted up some steps and she pulled me and we doubled on our tracks. My ears pounded. I couldn't hear the footsteps any more. Pepita was sobbing.

She broke away from me. I followed her into the last dim alley. It was too narrow. We couldn't run abreast. We got halfway down and the light in the adjoining street flickered. It went right out. The blackness fell on us.

My shoulder brushed a wall. I couldn't see anything. I hit a brick corner and there was something like a shadow. She said, "Esmitt!" and grabbed my arm and swung me around in an arc. She gave a little moan. We were abreast again, running down a wide street. She was hanging on to me. She was saying, "Not far, Esmitt. You will be all right, Esmitt." Her voice was gabbling and tight as if she were choking. Her whole weight suddenly dragged. She came to a dead halt.

She was up on her toes, unmoving. I couldn't see her. The sweat was soaking me and there were no footsteps and nothing else except the silence and darkness like thick black wool. She whispered, "Help me, Esmitt." She was exhausted. I got an arm around her. "Over here, Esmitt," she said. I wondered how she could see.

The back of her dress was wringing wet. She dragged her bare feet and stumbled with all her weight on me. We got to the sidewalk. She groped. I heard a door handle turn and hinges groaning. We went down two shallow steps.

We were in a house. I closed the door. We waited in blackness. A hot eternity passed. There was no sound of pursuit.

I whispered, "A moment," and let her go. I slapped my pocket and found the matches and struck one. The light sputtered. She was gone; I thought she'd run away. Then I saw her sitting on the floor with the back of her head against the wall. Her lips were moving. No words came.

I held the light higher. The shadows ran down the passage. A great fist seized hold of my heart and squeezed hard. I said, "What is it, Pepita?"

She moved her head slowly from side to side. "Those men hurt me, Esmitt," she said, and gave a deep sigh. I dropped to my knees beside her. I saw the color of my hand where I had held the wetness of her dress. The guttering match burned my fingers and went out with a hiss.

I was fumbling for another. The ceiling flickered and a dim light came on and went out and came on again. I reached for her. Her head was fallen forward on her knees. Her hair was spread like a dark fan. Her fingers scratched feebly at the floor as she tried to push herself upright. A knife was buried to the hilt high between her shoulder blades.

I didn't touch it. I said. "Pepita." I raised her gently and cradled her head on my chest. Then my nerves quit me and I started to weep.

She said faintly, "Don't cry, Esmitt." She moved against me and groaned. The light in the ceiling was growing brighter. She said, "It's a joke. They tried to kill you because you're an important officer on the ship, like Pablo says. They hurt only me."

"I'll get a doctor."

"What for?" She lifted a limp hand and clutched the medallion hanging around her neck. She said weakly, "We had a good night, Esmitt. I wore my new dress. All the other women were jealous because I looked elegant."

"You looked beautiful," I said.

"Because you loved me. I saw it from the start. You loved me. You treated me well. It was the best thing of the night that you loved me. No man was ever like that before. Will you kiss me, Esmitt?"

The light flickered. I lowered my head. The blood was coming from her mouth. Her lips moved. She said, "My Esmitt," very softly. I wanted to tell her my real name. It seemed suddenly very important that she know my real name. I said, "Pepita."

She writhed. She tore from my arms and her back arched. She screamed, "My poor little boy. My Pepito! My little Pepito. Oh, Christ! Oh, Christ!"

She fell to the floor. I touched her and the big night of her life was over. She was dead. The light went out.

I lowered her limp body. I stood a while. Then I went out and closed the door. I walked down the dark street.

There was a fountain in the middle of a square. I washed my red hands and got my sleeves wet and went on again. I passed the top of a cross street and thought I saw Lennox. I didn't call. I didn't want to talk to anybody. I knew where I was going and what I had to do.

I pretended to rationalize at first. I had practically nothing on Plosch. If I went again to his house I might find something solidly incriminating. The Department could blame me only for using too much individual initiative.

I quit the illusions. I told myself the truth. Right then I didn't give a damn for the Department. They train us well, but not that well. Nobody can be trained that well. I took the knife from my pocket.

In another street a man was whistling the waltz about the birds.

Chapter Sixteen

The lights of the city were far behind and there was no traffic on the road. The night was dark. I walked a while along a low cliff and everything seemed to brighten because of the faintly glimmering sea. Then the road curved. The darkness was complete again. I went between two vague horizons of tall cactus.

My feet gritted softly. I got off the road and went across what seemed part of a plowed field. I reached the high wall and stood a couple of minutes trying to collect myself. I was dying of thirst. It was so dark I couldn't see my own feet. I wiped a hand over my face.

I stood on my toes and reached upward. I touched nothing but more wall. I stretched higher until my back hurt, but it was useless so I settled on my heels again and kept my fingertips against the stone to guide me through the darkness and started to walk. The ground was hard and rutted. I kept tripping. My feet hurt like blue blazes.

I reached the corner and took a few more steps. Up ahead about thirty yards was the big heavy main gate. It was shut. A dim light gleamed on either side of it. I gauged the height of the wall, felt my way back around the corner, and returned stumbling to where I'd been before. I'd never known such heat.

Every pore was open. My clothes were plastered to me. I waited a while to gather up some energy, rubbed my wet hands together, wondered if there'd be any broken glass or spikes. I got a foothold in the loose earth and bent at the knees the way they train us to do. I put my hands high above my head and jumped.

My toes scrabbled at the wall. I slipped. My fingernails nearly tore out. I let go and landed with my knees still bent and leaped again on the rebound. My hands slapped the top. I hung there panting and pulling. My arms were coming from their sockets.

I scraped my knees, swung myself up, and cocked a leg. I sprawled flat on the top, panting my lungs out, with an arm hanging down on either side. I lay still and tried to get my breath. The lights over the gate seemed a long way off.

There was one other light, shining ahead of me from a second-floor window. I could see nothing that lay between. The darkness was Stygian. I sat up and took the knife from my pocket, gripped it hard, and flicked out the blade. I put a hand on either side of me. I jumped down into the garden.

A massive shape hurtled from the thicket.

I wanted to scream with fear. I tried to run. A vise of teeth clamped my leg. I went full length. The muzzle snarled around my neck and I was afraid for my throat and I heaved with my arm and the animal sprang away. I rolled. I was flat on my back. The vise closed over my ankle.

I kicked madly with the other foot and saw its red eyes coming. A growl tore from its throat. It leaped astride me. I got a hand over my neck and slashed upward. I pushed hard on the handle. The snarling stopped and the blood ran. The dog died without a whimper.

I thrust the body away. I kicked upright and got my back to the wall and waited.

There had to be one more. A guy who bleached his hair would want at least two big dogs to complete the picture. I stood panting. The other one gave a faint howl. I couldn't tell where it was.

Its footsteps padded. That was all. The silence fell. It was waiting for me somewhere. I had to move. I couldn't spend the night checkmated by a dog.

I shuffled my feet, brushed my shoulders against the wall. Nothing came. I waited again. There was a faint outline of shrubbery, an open space beyond. I got on my toes. I gripped the knife for an upward thrust, moved to the left, and ran for the space.

The dog leaped snarling from the bushes.

It was enormous. I stabbed blindly and its full weight hit me and its jaws clashed on the air. I staggered backward. It fell to the ground, gave a writhe, and got up. It made no sound. It stood perfectly motionless on its four feet and I waited for it to jump. I heard it sniff. I said softly, "Here, boy." I made a move.

It turned and ran silently toward the back of the house.

I knew it would return. I waited in the silence. Nothing more happened. No extra lights came on. The one on the second floor gleamed on flatly like a half-blinded eye, throwing no light into the surrounding night. I was terrified of the dog. I forced myself to calmness. I got my breathing almost to normal and started to creep forward.

Plosch was a rich man. In a sun-baked country he could afford a thick soft lawn complete with sprayer. I got near the spray and then I thought I heard the dog coming back. I panicked. I flung myself down on the cool grass. The water sprinkled over me. The dog, or another, gave a short bark somewhere at the back of the house. I went over the rest of the lawn in a jungle crawl.

I reached the wall of the house, stood up, tried a window. It was solid. I slid along in the shadows and looked down the drive and watched the lights above the gate. I was getting near the front door. There were two more windows close together, then a third, then French windows. I stopped and tried with my fingers. The frames didn't fully meet in the center.

I took the knife, jammed it in the crack, got it against the latch. I jimmied upward. The knife slipped. There was a tiny noise on the other side as the blade tip tinkled to the floor. I tried again, levered the knife against my wrist. It slipped a second time and nicked my arm. I got angry. I wrapped both hands tight on the handle and heaved with all my strength and the knife jerked high.

One side of the French window swung slightly open. I stepped inside.

Silence. I reached out and touched the inner curve of an archway. I took ten steps forward. My movement set up a soft echo. I got up on my toes and the money hurt me and the sweat ran off me and I was shivering. The echo turned to a faint long-drawn whisper like someone laughing at a bad joke. I stopped, then I took another two steps.

There was a faint click. Above my head all the glittering chandeliers burst into light.

Plosch said, "Hello, Antonio."

I turned right around once only, then stood still. I was in the middle of the big hall with black furniture and mosaic and a painted ceiling. Plosch stood at the top of a wide marble staircase, one hand on a gilt banister. He wore an elaborate dressing gown. His cigarette was in a long holder. He was posing. He said, "Nice of you to call again, Antonio."

Scarface emerged from one of the arches. He had a gun in his hand, a .32. My tongue grew very big and filled the inside of my mouth. Scarface smiled and I turned to meet him. It was a mistake.

The Grand Canyon closed on my neck, I tried to kick, I wanted to fall, but my knees wouldn't bend. I tried to do something with the knife. A pile driver hit my right arm and the pointless blade fluttered to the ground in slow motion like an autumn leaf.

I saw my feet rise. They swung. I dangled in the air a while and it was an interesting new experience, then the clamp opened from the back of my neck and the floor jumped up and hit me in the nose. I rolled. The Ape stood over me a thousand yards high. He bent down.

His hand closed on my throat. He lifted me clear into the air by my chin and I did more dangling. I grinned at him with all my teeth. I popped my tongue out at him. Everything was bright red and my ears rang and my eyeballs were falling out onto my cheekbones. I was thinking it all served me right, I should never have ill-treated an animal, a dog is man's best friend. Somewhere among the angels Plosch was chanting mellifluously, "Not too much, now, not too much, not too much."

I closed my eyes, practiced underwater swimming, and waited until the squeeze went off my neck and the weight off my feet.

A stag with wide-spread antlers stared down at me. I thought of a couple of jokes. There was the one about the man whose wife slept with the iceman and the other about the man whose wife slept with the insurance man. Neither seemed funny. The iceman joke was out of date. I wagged my head a little.

Two glass-eyed lion heads, a wildebeeste, a goat with cornucopean horns, no elephants. A glass case full of pistols, two racks of hunting guns. A long low room with dark paneling, cups, trophies, two large shields balanced on the top of the paneling.

My neck felt as if it had been through a mangle.

I was sitting in a straight-backed wooden chair, the Ape on one side of me,

Scarface on the other. Scarface was smoking. Plosch sat nonchalantly on a long narrow table, dressing gown removed, clad in jodhpurs, a hacking jacket with diagonal pockets and a flap at the back, and a knotted yellow silk scarf. He held a riding crop. He smelled of after-shave and brilliantine. He looked conversational.

Scarface took a deep drag at his cigarette. He took it from his mouth and brushed it against my neck. I jumped. Plosch leaned forward and tapped me on the chest with the riding crop. He said, "Apologies for the uncouth treatment. What can you expect when you make such an entrance? I'd have run down and answered the door myself had you rung the bell." He tapped again. "And you killed my dog. Not a very friendly act."

"Not a very friendly dog. The other one's a coward."

He stared at me intently. Lanterns glowed behind his pale-green eyes. He was trying to bore a way into my head. He said, "Explain, Antonio. You disconcert me. My men reported that you completely eluded them. Why have you come back? Driven by a troubled conscience?"

Scarface dragged deep again. The coal glowed bright. He put it on my neck. This time I managed not to flinch.

I said, "He should stick to murder and give up smoking. He'll get lung cancer. Hasn't he read the reports?"

"Murder?" Plosch smiled. "You anticipate a little. Are you by any chance mad, Antonio?"

I said, "I haven't started eating arsenic yet. Though it does give you a good skin. It did the same for my grandmother. She had to take it for her heart."

"I, too." His eyes went glassy and bright as imitation emeralds. He lifted his arm. He slashed me across the face with the riding crop. I nearly bit off my tongue.

He went across to a sideboard, poured himself a drink, came back with the glass in his hand. "Regrettable loss of temper." he said. "Very bad. The discipline of oneself is as important as the imposing of discipline on others." He sighed. "We are all human. Where is the money I paid you?"

"Back at the ship."

"Recoverable." He sipped the drink. "Tell me why you cheated me. What is it like to be a cheat? Do you feel spiritually septic? Do you have a physical desire for atonement by cleanliness, like, for example, wanting to change your socks?"

I said, "What are you talking about?"

"An answer in the best tradition. Refusing to betray your associates. You'll change. I am not a man of great patience. I am capable of much more terrible things when my temper is retained."

"Like murdering Pepita?"

"What? Who is Pepita?"

"Ask your playmates."

His eyes narrowed. He jerked his head at Scarface. "Who is this female?"

"A whore, sir. The pocket-picker. She was with him when he escaped us."

"They caught up with us. He killed her."

"Well?" Plosch asked.

Scarface and the Ape shook their heads.

A tiny pulse beat in Plosch's throat above the yellow silk scarf. "So. You killed my dog because you thought I'd killed your bitch. A pleasantry. A mistake. My men are permitted violence on direct instructions only. They do not flaunt me. Neglect in small things, perhaps; direct disobedience, never! You prevaricate, or you have been embroiled in a minor side issue that is none of my concern— a discarded pimp, a dissatisfied customer."

"They meant to kill me. She got in the way."

"They were ordered to bring you here alive under any pretext. Antonio, you are making counter-accusations merely to evade the main issue. The injured party is myself. You know it well."

"No."

"Yes. The deception was discovered ten minutes after you left. A clever trick, but painful to me. I trusted you, Antonio. I have prided myself always on my swift judgment of character. You will realize the blow to my self-esteem."

I looked into his face. There was a message for me. He was going to kill me sooner or later. I thought of the change-over. I thought of a second change-over. I said, "I guess I was fooled, too."

"You know what the unopened packet contained?"

"Cigarettes?"

"Try again."

The message was getting stronger. The killing was coming much sooner than later. I said, "I don't know."

The switch quivered in his hand. The sweat broke out on his fine skin and beaded his eyebrows. "The corner of the second pack," he said, "was sealed with wax. Clever! And what was inside, Antonio? What?"

"I don't know."

"Bicarbonate of soda."

He slashed. I dodged. I fell off the chair. He slashed again and I jumped him. I got about two inches.

The garrote clamped my neck. The Ape planted his feet behind me and squeezed and put his nose down on the top of my head. I totaled up the night's occurrences. I had run a thousand miles, been sapped twice, kicked in the ribs once, squeezed once. It didn't seem worth while hanging around for any more.

I fainted.

Chapter Seventeen

Another room. I was on a couch with a slithering pink silk cushion behind my shoulders. Plosch was holding me up by the bruise that used to be the back of my neck, trickling cognac down my throat. He said, "Better?"

I pushed the glass away.

The room was different, the atmosphere the same. Scarface and the Ape stood quietly against the wall like mortician and assistant. Plosch was finishing off the remains of the cognac left in the glass. I just lay.

"You realize," he said, "how your deception humiliated me. I trusted you. I admired you. As a man of honor, I thought I was dealing with another. A bitter pill to swallow. Why did you, Antonio?"

"I didn't."

"No more tiresome denials!" Scarface made a movement. He was smoking again. Plosch said, "Now, Antonio. From the very beginning. Who was it that told you about me?"

"Nobody."

He ran a hand over his beautiful blond hair. He looked at his fingertips. He said, "In this town there are several men who might have bought your cocaine. Dishonorable creatures all—unscrupulous criminals with trust for no one. You did not sell to them. And why? You knew they would immediately check the unopened packet. So you selected me."

"Don't you remember? It was you who picked me up."

"No, sir!" He shook his head emphatically. "Consider the facts. Your scheme becomes crystal-clear. You knew my name when you entered the lecture hall. You especially asked the attendant for me. You were going to approach me directly, but there was no time. I had to go out and speak."

"That put me in a hole," I said. "What did I do next?"

"Tried another method of approach. A clever one. You arranged that the courtesan pick your pocket and open the good pack in front of my guitarist. This is a matter of some significance. It indicates your accomplices are aware that the man is in my employ, or how could they advise you to proceed thus? If they knew that, if they knew the guitarist would tell me, if they knew I might purchase the cocaine, they know also that I am trying to enter this profitable business in competition with them. A disquieting realization with all the implications of an unpleasant trap. They know their enemy. I do not know mine. Until you tell me."

I said nothing.

"The only pleasing aspect is that the hinge of the trick was my sense of honor. They were certain I would trust you and not open the second packet. Who is it, Antonio, who knows me well enough to assure you I am a gentleman?"

"Look," I said. "I bought both packets in Naples. I saw Rossi fill them from the same box with the same scoop. If one was cocaine, the other was cocaine."

He leaned over and patted my cheek. He smiled. "I anticipate you. Antonio. Flimsy. You're going to say someone changed a packet when you weren't looking."

I was thinking it. Pablo or Pepita. She was dead. She'd have told me if she'd made another switch. She wouldn't have died like that without saying something. I was sure.

Then I saw it.

I said, "I could use a drink."

"Indeed not."

I had to be brisk and confident or he wasn't going to believe me. He was following a trail. So was I. A brand new superhighway had opened up in the last five minutes.

I had to follow it. I'd been steering wrong all night.

I went back to working for the Department. "Why was your ball-headed guitarist in the Nido?"

"I ask the questions," he said.

I stood up. The room rocked. Scarface and the Ape came two paces nearer. I said, "The tortuous Latin mind. You're so tied up in intrigue you can't see what's staring you in the face. The bartender was being watched. You'd heard rumors he was—"

"Antonio, I am not Latin. Or so tied up as to be deceived by having you retell me something I have already told you. No man in the bartender's rumored position—"

"No man dealing in narcotics," I snapped, "would have handed back the packets. You said it yourself. You were right. He didn't hand them back."

"You're beginning," Plosch said, "seriously to annoy me. Why did he not tamper with both packets?"

"Because one was open. I'd have recognized bicarbonate when I went back. He expected me back."

"Ingenious. Not convincing."

"Start with the bartender and you'll trace your rivals." He looked at me with contempt. "Like all cheats, you try to overpersuade."

"I'm not cheating." I thought I had an inspiration. I said. "My word of honor."

His fist lashed out. I sat down on the couch. I straightened up and he hit me again, and the pink cushion slithered to the floor with me. I lay there and reflected on my psychological error.

He stood over me. He said, "You soil that word with your filthy mouth." Then he kicked me. I let him do it. I was getting used to it. I had chosen the gambit and I was stuck with it.

He went over and poured himself another drink. I crawled to my feet. He came back with the glass in his hand and stood in front of me breathing heavily. He said, "What do you say now?"

"Word of honor."

He threw the drink in my face. He swung his foot and kneed me. I wanted to fall down again. I didn't dare. I staggered, kept my balance, and wheezed a bit. I got a Fearless Fosdick tilt to my jaw and some steel in my eyes. I was Jack Armstrong, All-American Boy.

I said, "My word of honor, Plosch. You and a thousand like you couldn't take it away."

His mouth firmed. He nodded without knowing. He liked the routine. We stared flintily at each other like two second leads in a Grade-Z movie. He narrowed his eyes. He grated, "I'll allow you this, Antonio. You're *cojonudo*. But even rats show courage in corners."

The dialogue stank. I wondered if he could keep it up. He couldn't. He flung a glance over his shoulder and snapped his fingers.

"Get the car to the front. We don't need the chauffeur. I'm handling this alone."

The Ape shot out of the room like something from a howitzer. Scarface stepped smartly forward and stood to attention.

"You know the Nido?"

A nod.

"It has a back entrance?"

Another nod.

"Enter that way. If the bar is still open, close it discreetly. Clear the premises of all but the bartender. Inform me. I shall be waiting in the car with this man of honor."

"Watch it," I said. "You're beginning to repeat yourself."

He turned to me, smiling with his mouth only. "I should like to be wrong about you, if only to justify my first impressions. To make an error of judgment is bad enough. To have one's instincts proved wrong is altogether too painful. If you are speaking the truth, why did you come back to this house?"

I said, "To kill you."

"For any particular reason?"

"Pepita."

He frowned. "No. You are playing the part too hard and pushing it too far. Perhaps she did some whorish thing to inflame your imagination. I've heard it happens, but in your case I fear not. I fear she is only a subterfuge. You would never have jeopardized all the money we could make together for the sake of a courtesan, inflammatory or not. Between us, what was the real reason for returning?"

I shrugged.

He crossed the room and refilled his empty glass. His third. He sipped. He said. "When we return from the bar—when you have been proved a liar—I shall make you pay for the exaggeration. I shall do exaggerated things to you."

"You're pretty tough," I said.

The door opened. The big guy stood respectfully on the threshold. Plosch put down his glass, fastidiously adjusted the yellow silk scarf, and smoothed his blond hair.

We all went through the door and across the big echoing hall.

He said, "But if this much does prove to be truth, we shall afterward check on the business of the girl."

"What girl?" I said.

"This Pepita."

I'd thought he meant Banjo Kelly. He hadn't even mentioned her. It was something.

Chapter Eighteen

My watch had stopped. I knew it must be late in the early morning, but there were no clocks anywhere and no trace yet of dawn. We were parked in a narrow side street. The car was dark with the shadows of tall stone houses.

A lone man went past. The sound of his footsteps bounced back from the confining walls. Somewhere far off a thin voice was singing a *jota* from Aragon, traveling like a steel shaft in the hot silence. Two scraggy cats flew at each other in the gutter and fought briefly. One fled with a twinkling of feet. Near at hand a clutch of other cats howled contrapuntal mating choruses.

Sitting still put me in a bad state. My face smarted, my back hurt, my neck was pulp and paper. I was sick over the mistakes I'd made all night, I was frightened enough to sweat like an open sluice gate. I glanced at Plosch. He hadn't moved or said a word in the five minutes since the other two went away.

He was studying me nonchalantly from the cushioned corner. A passer-by wouldn't notice the flat black automatic in his hand. His finger was curled over the trigger. He'd pull it if I sneezed.

I said, "What time is it?"

He didn't answer.

I took a breath, tried again. I wanted to bolster my sagging spirits. I said, "I liked that Scarlatti I heard at your place tonight. Always had a leaning toward the cleaner classics. Do you know that piece of Vivaldi that goes diddle-dee diddle-dee plink plank-plank?" I wasn't in my best voice.

"The hell with music," he said softly. "We have other preoccupations. Shut up!" His culture was slipping. He looked a bit rough.

The distant *jota* went to a high liquid note and died away. I curled my toes over the money in my shoes and wondered if I'd ever get my arches up again. A darker shadow fell.

Scarface came round the corner, hands in pockets. Plosch wound down the window. He didn't take eyes or gun off me.

"Everything ready?"

"The bar was closing. We've told him we want it for a pvivate pavty." Surface smiled thinly. "He is willing."

Plosch said, "Out!"

I opened the door and got on the strip of sidewalk. Scarface went ahead. Plosch walked six paces behind and I suddenly thought that if he was considering me one of his rivals, there was no reason why he shouldn't kill me right now. He'd still be able to question the bartender.

I got an impulse to run. I squeezed my fists and quieted down. I whistled a little of the Scarlatti between my teeth. It was the only sound. No one spoke.

We went into a slot between two houses, through another alley, and over a tiny yard. It was littered with wine kegs, wooden crates, and empty bottles. I stopped whistling. We passed through a door into a passage and the lighted bar was at the other end. The Ape was leaning relaxed against the counter.

A bright voice said, "Here are your friends." The big bartender with the shock of curly hair blocked the entrance and peered at us through the darkness. He said, "Welcome, gentlemen," and smiled at Scarface and stepped back. Scarface walked into the lighted bar. Then I did. The bartender's smile drooped at the comers and flickered. It grew bigger. He cried, *"Hombre!* You've come back. Like my wine, huh?"

He reached out to bang me chummily on the arm. He looked over my shoulder and saw Plosch. He took three backward paces and bowed so low his nose hit his knees. It must have been the blond hair that impressed him.

Plosch looked around with unconcealed disgust. He dusted a chair with his handkerchief, sat down, and stretched his legs carefully in order not to spoil the set of the jodhpurs. He acted as if he didn't know the bartender was there. He nodded at Scarface.

"Cognac! Fundador. Be sure the glass is clean."

The curly-haired guy was quicker. He scuttled behind his counter like an overeager beetle and came back with cognac, a jug of seltzer, and four glasses. They rattled on the tray as he put them down. His hands were shaking. He said, "The house is yours, señores." The polite Spanish formula never sounded so empty. "Anything is yours."

Plosch leisurely held a glass to the light, examined it thoroughly, wiped the rim, and poured himself a neat cognac. He took two slow sips, put down the glass. He said, "Anything? Good! Get me some cocaine."

The bartender went blank. There was a long silence. The sweat ran down my armpits to my chest. My heart floated to my throat. I thought I was in the middle of yet another mistake.

"Cocaine?"

I said, "The stuff you took from one of my packets."

I sounded pretty flat.

The bartender frowned slightly. He flickered his eyelids He smiled again and it was boyish and open and nice. "Packets? What packets?"

He was a tough egg. But I thought I'd won. The guitarist knew he'd handled the cocaine. So did Plosch.

Plosch said softly, "Don't you remember?"

The guy was tough and also smart. He ran a hand thoughtfully through his curly hair. "Oh, packets! The two belonging to Pepita." He looked around at us and laughed. "Is Pepita joining you later on?"

It sounded good. I was being quickly shifted to the losing side. I got nearer to him. I smiled. I slugged him and he went from one end of the bar to the other and fell over a table.

It was my night for mistakes. He picked himself up and Plosch had the gun out and the bartender saw it was covering both of us without discrimination. He was more than smart. He grasped immediately that he and I were in the same pot of stew, equals, him against me. I was the smaller and he wasn't even beginning to be afraid. He half grinned.

He swayed a couple of seconds, clenched his fists, and came on the run. I slugged him again. The Ape lurched between us. That finished it.

"Enough!" Plosch shouted. "Violence will come later if necessary. You are here to speak. One at a time. Antonio, you first!"

The bartender held the side of his jaw. His eyes went bright with relief. He radiated confidence, and it may have been that he was an honest man after all. I crossed to the table, poured myself some cognac. I never needed it more. I sat down.

"Pepita had two packets here tonight," I said stiff-lipped. "There was a big laugh when she opened them. She was drunk. She didn't know what the powder was. She gave them to this guy for his kids. He recognized cocaine, sifted the contents from the corner of one packet, and substituted bicarbonate of soda."

"Now you," Plosch said.

The bartender scratched his head. He looked humorous. "I'm not following this. The girl had two packets of stuff for her hair. I returned them to her. It was when they were all here together—him and Pepita and the American girl photographer."

"The what?" Plosch asked softly.

"A girl named Kelly, a blonde American." The bartender put a hand into his apron pocket. The hands of Scarface and the Ape moved in unison.

I said, "He's frothing around. He wants to put you off the subject. He's—"

Plosch leaned over the table and tapped me on the mouth with the gun. He said gently, "Shut up." The bartender looked pleased. His hand came from his apron pocket holding a card. Scarface and the Ape relaxed. Scarface was as pleased as the bartender. I wasn't among friends. I was getting to be outnumbered.

Plosch stared at the card. "Blonde?" he asked. "Short hair? Very blue eyes? A good figure?"

"Yes."

"Why did she leave this?"

"I was to give it to the man who comes here sometimes and plays the guitar. He didn't return. She wants him to pose tomorrow. A customer who knows about pictures says she was already taking photographs from a camera in her handbag."

"Isn't that interesting! And she was speaking to our friend here before you even returned the packets."

The bartender bobbed his head.

"So he knew her before she came to my house. And when she came to my house he didn't know her."

The bartender looked bewildered. My skin crawled. Plosch was smiling at me like a tiger at a tethered goat.

He said, "However, one thing at a time. We'll return to the subject later, and at length." He swiveled back to the bartender. "And the packets contained a hair preparation?"

"I thought so."

"They were not given you for your children?"

The guy spread his hands in good-humored bewilderment. He was riding the crest of the wave. "I have no children."

"Oh."

The silence in the room fell flat as a platitude. Plosch studied the gun and blew gently down the barrel. He looked at the ceiling. "No children. A report was submitted by the guitarist. Who remembers?"

Scarface said as if he was reading a timetable, "Ernesto Fuentes. He's thirty-eight. Bartender. Twenty-five pesetas a day plus tips. He vents the fourth floor of Twenty-eight Plaza Colon. Seven years mavvied. One child. A girl."

"Well done!" Plosch gave a deep sigh. "Men are such liars. I am so thorough. Aren't you relieved, Antonio?"

I was. Temporarily. He lowered his head and looked at me steadily. The lanterns were back behind his eyes. He was sitting there going swiftly off the rails with his own idea of himself.

He was nuts.

Chapter Nineteen

He sighed again. He lifted the automatic and sighted along the barrel at the bartender. "Overplaying your part. Everyone does if given enough leeway." He curled his hand, made the knuckles turn white, and patted softly with his finger. If it had been a hair trigger, the bartender would have been nesting three bullets. I felt almost sorry for the guy. His hair didn't look so curly any more.

He backed against the counter. His lips trembled. In the silence he tried to swallow.

"Forgive me. I lied. I didn't want to involve her, you understand. No man speaks of his children at a time like this." His voice was dry. He nearly gagged. He said, "I didn't take your narcotics."

"Not mine. Whose were they? Most important, for whom did you take them?"

"On my baby's head, I don't know what you're talking about."

"How unfortunate! We must try to clarify your mind."

Plosch got to his feet. He was having a good time. He glanced coolly from the other guy to me and back again. He said, "You're both lying, but one more than the other." He smiled into the bartender's face. "I'm not completely sure of Antonio's type, but your type I know like my own hand. Under certain circumstances I might trust Antonio. Indeed, I have done so already. But to you, my friend, under no conceivable circumstances could I extend the same courtesy. Therefore it is with you we commence."

The bartender flung up his arms. He ran about two yards. The Ape moved like a supercharged truck and swung a fist and the curly head hit the deck. I'd seen it happen before. To me. The Ape reached to the floor, the bartender whirled through the air and dangled a bit, then his back was clamped to the Ape's chest and there was an arm around his throat and a hand clamped over his mouth.

His eyes popped. He quit struggling.

I didn't move. Plosch was pointing the gun at me.

He came back to the table and sat down facing me. He poured another cognac. He sipped it, leaned back, and crossed his legs. He wasn't so careful any more with his jodhpurs. He said airily, "Search!"

There was a faint scuffle. The Ape dragged the purple-faced bartender a few paces to the rear and I couldn't see them any more. A chair scraped. A door closed. Plosch smiled.

"This Spanish cognac is the best in the world. Not so strong or fine as the French, but more to my taste. Join me?"

"Thanks."

It went down my throat like a stream of fire. My pores opened. The sweat gushed slowly forth. I couldn't let him see how scared I was; he would love it too much. He'd feed on it. He was getting nuttier by the minute. Behind me the bartender gave a strangled whimper. I didn't look.

"Nothing, señor," Scarface said.

"Search the place."

Plosch took a cigarette from a golden case and lit it with a golden lighter. He didn't offer me one. He said, You're not married, Antonio?"

"No."

"Better that way. Makes a man too vulnerable."

"I guess."

Scarface was behind the counter, bending and reaching. He'd had a lot of practice. He searched like a professional. The bottles chinked rhythmically.

"When you left my house the first time," Plosch said, pointing a finger at Scarface, "you gave him the slip. You knew in advance that he would follow."

"And did he?" I asked.

"You are most difficult. We shall manage nonetheless. I want to know very much about your friend Miss Briggs-Kelly, the photographer."

Scarface said respectfully, "Nothing at all, señor."

"I see." Plosch nodded. "He passed it on to his associates. Question him!"

Scarface nodded and smiled. He went behind me. There was a short scuffle, some cloth tore, a chair scraped. I poured myself another shot of cognac. I looked at the gun on the table.

Plosch's slim white hand was wrapped around it, his finger on the trigger. He wasn't looking at me. At that range he didn't need to. He gazed languidly over my shoulder. He sounded bored.

"Mr. Fuentes. There is a possibility you have information of value to me. If so, I shall extract it. Answer questions by nodding or shaking your head. You understand.?"

He waited questioningly. He nodded himself in approval. "Good! We begin simply with an elementary question. Did you tonight remove cocaine from a packet?"

There was a silence.

"Denies it," Plosch said sorrowfully.

"He's a liar."

"We shall see." Plosch snapped his fingers.

A match sputtered and struck. Nothing happened. The pause went on forever. The guy screamed.

He couldn't get it out properly. The result was horrible.

A faint whiff of burning meat drifted into my nostrils. I closed my hand tight around the glass and felt sick. It didn't help that I wanted information about the guy's associates as much as Plosch did. The strangled scream turned into a gargle.

Plosch smiled. "How absurd a man seems in only his shirt and shoes. Take a look!"

"It would bore me."

"It won't when it's happening to you." He nodded. Another match struck.

The screaming started again and this time it didn't stop. It curled around the room in spirals. The burning smell was foul.

"Ernesto," Plosch said severely. I doubted the guy could even hear against his own scream. "Ernesto Fuentes, you know the question. Give me a satisfactory answer."

The bartender was soprano. I couldn't take any more of it. I let go of the glass. I said, "How come he didn't take the stuff?"

"Are you recanting?"

"Yes."

The hand lifted. The screaming died into a muffled sobbing. I said, "Listen—"

Plosch smiled. He reached across the table and patted my shoulder. "Antonio, that was noble. It confirms my original opinion of you. The gesture, however, is useless. Mr. Fuentes has just admitted his guilt."

I took one look over my shoulder. I turned back to the table and I needed a drink badly. I picked up the bottle. It rattled against the glass like the hoofs of the Lone Ranger's horse. The bartender was gasping and sobbing something I couldn't hear.

"You understand?"

"Yes, sir." Scarface came nimbly into view, tucking the box of matches into his pocket. He went behind the bar, reached under the counter, and came back with the bicarbonate jar. He put it on the table, lifting the lid.

"I guessed it all along," Plosch said. "It wasn't very original, was it?" He stirred in his finger, licked the tip, and shuddered. He looked over my shoulder.

He said, "Well, then. End of stage one, Mr. Fuentes. Now comes stage two."

"Lay off him," I said.

He ignored me. He blew down the gun barrel and smiled thoughtfully. "Let us make a working, though not necessarily true, construction of the events leading to our present scene. Antonio brought cocaine ashore. The drunken girl stole it. Ernesto obtained temporary possession and substituted bicarbonate. These facts, except the last, were made known to me by my guitarist."

He twirled the gun on his finger. It was a good opportunity to jump, except that Scarface was an inch from my shoulder and for all I knew the Ape was breathing on my neck. The bartender sobbed quietly.

Plosch said, "There is also the alleged murder of the drunken girl and the mystery of the lady photographer. Was the girl murdered because she knew it was cocaine she stole? What pictures did the lady take with her magic handbag? We must momentarily ignore these speculations, interesting though they be, and return to the main current. Now! Antonio sold his packets to me. I discovered deception. Antonio protested his innocence and blamed Ernesto. The claim proves true. Leading to more immediate and vital speculations."

His expression altered subtly. My blood curdled. He said, "Ernesto recognized cocaine. Indicating he has seen it before. Indicating, as rumor said, that he traffics in it. Indicating that he has contact with whoever controls the traffic in this area. Ernesto must now tell us who the contacts are."

The sobbing stopped. I could hear the guy trying to get control of himself. He said faintly, "I took it because I'm an addict."

"Nonsense, dear man. You were watched. We should have known. Your countermove is poor. Tell me the contacts!"

There was a long silence. Plosch dropped his cigarette on the floor. Scarface stood on it.

"I understand your reluctance. Reveal their names and they will possibly kill you. Even injure this child of yours. But what is to prevent my doing the same?"

He waited. His green eyes grew rounded. He said, "Then we continue."

"Leave him!" I snapped.

"I think not. It is you who will leave. Stand up! Turn round!"

I did as he said. The bartender was clamped in the chair by the Ape, face sweating and congested, eyes filled with the anticipation of more pain. I saw the place and type of thing they'd committed on him. My stomach rose. He started to say something. The words were cut off by the Ape's great paw.

"You see why it is better not to be married." Plosch laughed. He was making a joke. "He'll be unable to marry again for some weeks, don't you think?"

I said, "You filthy, rotten bastard."

A gun burrowed into my back.

Plosch waved a hand. "Take him away. Keep him in the car. I don't want him to hear what is about to be said. Antonio has invention and imagination enough to improvise on it for his own use when he in turn is questioned. Already this evening he has quoted back to me something I had told him only an hour previously. He even whistled back to me my own Scarlatti. Take him off. I shall continue your work. I have a cigarette lighter."

Scarface giggled. The gun jabbed. I passed the bartender's despairing eyes and stepped into the dark passage.

"*Hasta leugo,*" Plosch called.

I made no answer. The gun eased me along. Back in the room a voice murmured, then the bartender began again his awful screaming.

The door closed.

Chapter Twenty

The few faint stars had gone. The junk-littered yard was dark as the inside of an ink bottle. Near at hand the cats were yowling. They sounded like a mockery of what was happening back in the bar.

I started to turn around. The gun stuck into my spine and displaced a pound or two of cartilage. I planted my feet resolutely. I said softly, "Amigo, we could make a deal. I have a lot of money."

He pushed harder. He said, "If you have, I shall take it all. Señor Plosch will permit me." His voice was gentle and light, his lisp more pronounced. "I shall also take your vist watch. It is a good one. Now you must march. If you vun I shall shoot you. If you stand still I shall cut you."

There was a click. The gun stayed hard in my back. His other hand came over my shoulder and laid the flat of a knife blade against my cheek. He wasn't playing games. I marched.

The squalling of cats grew louder. They were singing a funeral hymn. We turned into the alley leading to the car and my foot kicked an empty flattened can. There were scratchings, dim shadows. The animals scattered from a corner. A pair of eyes remained green and gleaming. I thought of Plosch.

"A cat," I said. "Look." I walked more slowly. I got on the balls of my feet. I was afraid it would run. "I like cats," I said fatuously.

He didn't answer. I could hear his breathing, measure and undisturbed. If he thought I was nuts, he made no sign. He was about ready.

"Cats," I said and loosened my shoulders. It was a gamble. There was no other remedy. I said sweetly, "Kitty-kitty-kit-kit-kit." The eyes moved. The cat came as a swift shadow.

It mewed. It rubbed my leg. Scarface jabbed me. I did it all in one movement. I snatched downward and scooped the furry shape under the belly and flung it back in his face. It hung there spitting.

His hands went up. He gave a little shout and I kicked him. He staggered, slumped. I dived at him and smashed his right hand against the wall. The gun dropped. I scraped at it with my foot and it went slithering into the darkness.

The cat was screaming its way along the alley. The guy was half down and trying to force his way up again. I slammed his shoulders, brought up my knee, hit his chin. His head smacked the wall. He was still getting up. I fell on him and squeezed his throat and grabbed for his left arm.

The hand came over. I sank my teeth in his wrist. He twisted his arm and nearly broke my jaw and the knife ripped into the shoulder padding of my jacket. I thought of Pepita. I went mad.

I didn't care then if he made hamburger of me. I butted with my head and his nose cracked and I flung away and kicked him in the face and kicked again. The knife clattered on the ground. I sprang upright. He moaned and tried to breathe through his blocked nose and fell full length.

I stood over him. He didn't move. I bent to pick up the knife, and then he squirmed. He grabbed at me. The knife went clean through his palm and out the back of his hand and stuck there. He gave a shriek. I struck his forehead and knocked his skull against the wall. I ran.

I ran out of the alley and past the car and I was sweating and my lungs burned and the money in my shoes was turning my feet to lumps of raw meat. I didn't know where I was going. The whole evening had blown up. Only one thing mattered now.

I ran through the deserted streets looking for a cop. I had to do something about the bartender.

There were alleys, arches, and steps, all looking alike, all deserted. There were tall houses on either side with not a light among them. I got the idea I was running in a circle. My face twitched with loony laughter because I'd spent the night dodging cops and now I couldn't find one. I ran for the next corner and hurtled around it with my head down.

We met like colliding planets. We held in a bearlike hug to save our balance. The lamp from the far end of the street shone dimly on the other guy's face.

That was the looniest moment of all, like a movie running backward. We broke apart. I stepped aside to let him pass. He took a look at me and the muscles of his face collapsed like seared wax. His jaw dropped. His eyes glared. A scream of pure fright tore from his throat and he flung me against the wall and ran down the road as if the hounds of hell were after him.

He was the paunchy man with poached eyes, the respectable citizen in the modest gray suit. He went like the wind.

I didn't follow him. I couldn't; I was too beat. It was easier after seeing someone else's panic. My own disappeared. I leaned against the wall a while. I started off again, tightening the hold on myself. Most of the streets were fairly straight. I picked a direction. When it ended in an alley or a flight of steps, I threaded left or right and stayed parallel. On the eighth street I saw a cop.

He was halfway down, walking away from me. I ran for him. I saw he had a gun and thought probably he also had a description of me. I was afraid he would haul me in without even listening to what I had to say. He heard my pounding footsteps and turned.

He looked about forty-five. He was alert and tough. His hand went to the holster and he waited with mouth slightly open as if already disbelieving me. He said, "What?"

I leaned panting against the wall. I said, "They're beating up a cop in the Nido. They've got him locked in. He's shouting his head off."

I didn't even get an answer. He turned on his heel and flashed down the nearest alley, loosening his gun. He looked once over his shoulder to see if I was following. I stayed where I was. He didn't stop. His footfalls echoed flatly away. The long silence descended again. I moved.

There were two immediate tasks: Phone the boss. Find Banjo Kelly.

I crossed a silent square. A sleeping ill-dressed man stirred in his sleep on a bench. The smell of jasmine was overwhelming and the palm fronds whispered high overhead in a faint breeze. It was suddenly cooler than it had been all night. I thought of taking the money from my shoes, but didn't have the initiative. I went down a narrow street, not sure where I was, and when I got to the far end it was like an unexpected birthday present. I emerged onto a main street. Across the road was the sign that said *"Teléfones."*

The door was locked.

A pale-yellow light burned over the telegram desk. There was no one in the building. I wondered what happened to Spaniards who wanted to telephone or telegraph at these hours. I turned away, knowing where I was now, heading toward the esplanade. Banjo Kelly had said she was stopping at the Hotel Palas.

The street was almost deserted, chairs and tables taken in from the sidewalk. I passed an empty café and another with five customers inside, sitting well apart, not talking, the sort of people you find in cafés at that hour in all parts of the world. A well-dressed man walked by, swinging a walking stick, leading a small dog. Maybe it belonged to his mistress. If so, he'd spent a better night than I. He was humming the waltz to himself. "When I get up in the morning and the birdies begin to sing..."

An old convertible Ford with English plates came around the corner, top down, back seat piled with luggage, the man and woman in front laughing like fools about something. I could have stood a joke right then. I was thinking of Pepito, who wanted to be a bullfighter. I wondered if they'd found his mother yet, if he knew about her. I couldn't even guess my way back to where she was lying.

I reached the esplanade.

The breeze blew faint and fresh off the sea. The water along the sands was sighing. The sea had a pearly glimmer in the creeping light of false dawn and the anchorage lights gleamed in the harbor. I crossed the broad street and went under the palms. I was back near the gate where I'd first started out. I looked from side to side and wondered where the Hotel Palas was. There wasn't a soul in sight.

The guy must have been hiding behind a tree. I didn't hear him until he spoke. He was right behind me. "Señor."

I almost sobbed with fright. I turned in a jump.

He was a small raddled old man not more than five feet tall. Crafty little eyes glittered in a seamed face the color of tobacco juice.

"You want a nice señorita?"

"No."

"Something else?" He mentioned it.

"No."

A whine crept into his voice. "You give a poor old man a *duro*? Five pesetas? Even two pesetas? *Limosna, por Dios*. I haven't eaten for three days. Nowhere to sleep."

"Take me to the Hotel Palas. I'll give you ten."

"Pay me now."

I fumbled in my pocket and pulled out the wad. He took the two bills. His little eyes flicked over me. He didn't move.

"A very small hotel, señor. In fact, it's only a pension. It's shut now. Even the *vigilante* has gone home."

He'd checked how much dough I had. He had something to tell me. I waited.

He looked at his two bills as if they might be forgeries. He squinted at me.

"Will you give me more?"

"Sure," I said, and felt around and couldn't find anything smaller than a hundred. I held it out.

He snatched it and tucked it in his filthy shirt. *"Dios se lo pague."*

"Now what?" I said.

"You are Esmitt, the sailor who was with Pablo. He has looked for you an hour. He wants you to go with him to find the girl."

"What girl?"

"The American girl. She has gone away."

"Where?"

"He didn't tell me. He only asked if I had seen you. An hour ago. He was very anxious."

"Where is he now?"

The little guy's mouth opened slightly. His teeth were jagged and bad. "I'll bring him to you if you give me more money."

"Take me to him. I'll pay you then."

"That's what you tell me." He made an obscene gesture. "I've heard it before. We'd find him and you'd tell me to —off."

It was a deadlock. We stood and stared. I peeled off a thin layer of bills and tore them in two. I handed him half.

"Bring him to me. You get the other parts of these when you return. You can stick them together with stamp paper."

His face exploded into a grin. It was a tout's grin and nauseating at that time of the morning. He pointed. "There is a seat under the trees at the end of the harbor. Wait. I know the places he'll be. I'll return in a few minutes."

He turned and ran. Everyone in the town had taken to running of late. There was too much of it altogether. I watched him out of sight and took the direction in which he had pointed. I went past a place where fishing boats were moored.

There were nets and a good smell of tarred rope. All the boats were deserted. The wall of the small harbor came to an end. The beach started. The whisper of the sea grew louder. The stone bench was over in the shadow of the palms.

Too shadowy. I looked around and descended three high stone steps from the esplanade to the sand. I sat down with my back to the wall, the sea in front of me. I couldn't be seen from the road, but the guys would probably be talking and I fancied I'd be able to hear anyone coming.

I wound my watch, held it to my ear to be sure it had restarted, squinted a look at the face to check the time. I decided to give them fifteen minutes. I didn't know what I'd do after that.

Toward the horizon the false dawn was fading fast, the darkness falling from the air again. The street lights behind me on the esplanade flickered and grew dim and came back a little brighter than before. I was dog tired. I slid my back down the wall and put my shoulder on the sand and curled into a sort of U. My back hurt. I closed my eyes. There was no danger of falling asleep the way I felt.

I tried to sort out ideas, separate facts from theories, organize a mental report in case I finally got through to Naples. A Department man is supposed always to keep his mind on the job in hand. I didn't do so well. I'd been knocked on the head twice. There were too many mental intrusions, like Brad face downward with a knife in his back, Pepita lying in my arms with the blood bubbling from between the orange lips. And Banjo Kelly.

I wondered about the cop I'd sent to the Nido. I worried about him. I worried about everything. In the movies Department men are unruffled, efficient, and infallible to everything except bullets. I worried because I wasn't like the guys in the movies.

I opened my eyes and looked toward the horizon. It had gone completely dark. I had no premonitions.

The guy must have taken lessons in a school for panthers. I didn't hear him coming. He leaped down from the esplanade, his feet hissed in the sand by my head, and he stood over me. He said, "Hi, Bish."

I couldn't see his face in the darkness, but I knew who he was.

He said, "Jeez, you're a hard guy to track down."

A car approached from the distance and purred to a halt.

He said, "Going back to the ship?"

I kept silent.

"The Old Man's pretty fussy about us reporting back on time."

"I'll get around to it."

The last time I'd been stretched like this he'd been telling someone to stick a knife in me. I rolled my eyes and the other shadowy figure came down the three steps and stood about five feet away.

"You drunk?" Bellington asked.

"Yeah."

"I'll help you."

"I'll do O.K.," I said.

The sea lapped. The slow sound of a small wave broke all the way along the beach. Near at hand the idling motor purred softly.

Bellington said, "Shall we quit stalling? I've been on to you for hours. I think you're on to me. I'm standing here with a gun in my hand. You ain't got a chance."

I knew it. I lay and wondered if I could roll out. Two of them were too many. I got slowly to my feet and closed my hands and thought of fistfuls of sand in the face. Two were too many, especially with one standing behind me.

I gave up. I said, "You're too late, Bellington. The packets have gone. I sold them."

"We know," he said. "We want to see you because you did sell them."

I turned around and the man in the gray suit was smiling. I said, "Hello, you son-of-a-bitch," and in case he didn't speak English I translated it into Spanish. He went right on smiling. A gun glinted in one hand. He was swinging something in the other.

"Poor old Lorca," Bellington said. "You scared the guts out of him back there on the street. He thought you were dead. So did I."

He nudged me. I started to move. The sand slipped under my feet. He said, "Matter of fact, I thought I'd killed you myself. What happened?"

I dived at him.

My reflexes were shot to hell. I didn't even touch him. He stepped aside and I went full length on the sand.

They moved in. I got to my hands and knees. I looked up and I was disgusted at the sound of my own voice. I whined, "You don't have to hit me. I'll come."

The guy in the gray suit swung his hand and hit me anyway.

Chapter Twenty-one

I had a dream in which Pablo, disguised in a not very convincing false beard, was opening a long line of steel-toothed man traps into which I would afterward put my feet. He was laughing at his own cunning. Then I dreamed that my head was an overripe tomato and I was trying to push it up through hard earth. The dream merged into reality.

My skull was pulsating like the skin on boiling porridge. The pink glow grew stronger, but I didn't raise my eyelids because any form of light was going to tear out my eyes. I remained limp and still and tried to adjust to the surroundings.

My head was back. I was flopped in an armchair. My hands were in my lap, the money was still in my shoes, and my feet were like hamburger. There was a murmur of voices. I couldn't understand what they said. I took it slowly.

My lids creaked a little as I forced them up. I stared at some fancy curlicues on a blinding white plaster ceiling, then at a cheap chandelier with four electric imitation candles. I lowered my head. A gaggle of minor devils slid around the inside of my skull on very sharp skates.

Bellington was opposite, grinning.

He said, "You don't look so good."

His chair was tilted against the wall. He held a drink in his hand and it wasn't his first of the evening. His eyes were red. He looked bigger, blonder, and sloppier than ever, but not sloppy enough. There was a table between us with his feet on it. Between his feet was a gun. It was a lot nearer to him than to me. I resigned myself.

He said, "How do you feel?"

I didn't want to discuss my health. It was nonexistent. I took stock of the setup.

The room was medium size, jerry-built, and had cracks in the white plaster walls. There was a half-open door leading to what looked like an adjoining bedroom. It was lighted. Two other doors were shut. There was not much furniture. A big frame window with thick net curtains was set in one wall. I couldn't tell whether or not there were shutters outside. If not, it was still dark.

I calculated the chances. There weren't any.

The armchair was deep. The gun would be firing two seconds before I was on my feet. I made a slight move to get my balance and Bellington thumped the chair down from its back legs, put his elbows on the table, looked in the direction of the lighted bedroom, and grinned. He called, "O.K., Boss. He's with us again."

One of the closed doors opened. A breeze blew into the room and the guy in the gray suit entered. There was darkness outside and the sound of the sea.

He closed the door and came right in. He smiled down at me, being pleased with himself. "Welcome to my humble seaside villa. This is your house."

The way I felt, I couldn't think of a snappy rejoinder.

Bellington finished his drink. Gray Suit said, "Everything is all right. I turned the car around. You'd better get back to the ship. Leave him with me."

"The boss wants to talk to him."

The Spaniard shrugged amiably and sat down on a chair, watching me with amusement. Bellington looked again at the half-open door. "Ain't got much time, Boss."

In the other room someone yawned. The leisurely footsteps approached. Maybe it was all the knocks on the head. Everything fitted suddenly. I sat waiting for Pablo to emerge.

He didn't.

The guy came into the room, still yawning. He smelled ripe and fat. "Hell, I'm tired," and shook his head and made his pink jowls quiver. The mangled remains of Banjo Kelly's big handbag dangled from his right hand.

Lennox.

He looked down at the handbag, walked across the room, dropped it into the drawer of a sideboard. He grunted, "Neat arrangement. Never have guessed it was a camera. One of those things might come in handy."

He scratched his fat neck and turned to me, blinking. He said without any preamble, "Who'd you sell the stuff to, Bish? Snap it up! We got to get back to the ship."

"Yeah." Bellington poured himself another drink. "Us and not him. This time for sure. Can't figure how I missed last time." He took a long swig. "Imagine me knocking off that dame."

Lennox chuckled. He quivered all over with mirth. He looked like the same guy who had come down the gangplank the previous evening, the jolly, amiable, everlasting uncle to all the world's children. He made my flesh crawl.

"Bish, where'd you get rid of the packets? Come on, pep it up!"

"Leave him here. He'll talk to me." The Spaniard reached into his nice gray jacket and pulled out a nasty great knife. "I know he'll talk to me. You don't have to worry."

They laughed. They were a genial bunch. Lennox said, "If I know before I leave, we can spend the day figuring counteractions." Three pairs of eyes swiveled to me.

I said. "Interesting. You're all knife boys."

"Rules. You'd never guess the trouble that guns lead to in these parts, what with ballistics experts and everything."

"Must be tough."

They waited. It was my turn to say something else. I couldn't think of any more stalls. I said, "O.K., how did you find out, Lennox? Go through my kit when I was on watch?"

"You're supposed to be professional." He chuckled again. "You acted like a rank amateur. Know what? I heard about the stuff less than an hour after you bought it. Sure. Rossi and me's got close ties. He wouldn't dare cross me."

I was finally near the guy in Naples. Nobody would give two hoots about crossing Lennox, but anybody would think ten times before displeasing the guy in Naples. Rossi wasn't the weak link we'd all thought. Or maybe he'd intended a cross until he found out where I was sailing. He'd have known the importance of the town. Maybe he got a bonus for his information.

I was near the guy in Naples and a fat lot of good it was doing me.

Bellington said, "We knew it was in your pockets before you even walked aboard."

It was my cue to keep playing sailor. "Then why didn't you do something about it?"

Lennox scratched. "You go slow to catch a monkey. Your two packets weren't going to make much difference to no one. You were just Bishop in those days, another crew member. If you see what I mean."

I did. I was sunk.

He looked at me, sucked his teeth, and stopped smiling. His eyes had as much expression as two newly opened oysters. I saw how anyone like the guy in Naples would find him the ideal employee. He said, "You see, I'm a simple, softhearted soul. I'd always sooner avoid trouble than make it. You were just another crooked sailor. There's hundreds of them. I could handle you easy. First off I wanted you to stay with us. I was going to slip you a mickey later on and lift the stuff from your pocket. Only you wouldn't play. You had to go see your relations." He made a sound in his throat that might have been laughing. "Pretty thin, Bish. You could have done better than that."

The Spaniard sat on the edge of the chair and skimmed his thumb back and forth over the blade of the knife. He said, "Yes, all very good. But find out where he sold it."

I'd tell them in the end. I had neither wish nor reason to protect Plosch. Maybe they'd take turns wiping each other out. After they'd wiped me out. But I just wanted to know.

I said, "I lost it."

The Spaniard stood up and smacked me hard across the face.

Lennox said, "Hold it, Lorca. We're getting to the part where you didn't do so good."

I said, "He did lousy. Was he supposed to be trailing me?"

"Not at first. He was looking after Bradley."

"Who?"

"My friend Lorca."

"Sounds like the name of a movie about a horse. I don't mean Egg Eyes. I mean Bradley. Who's he?"

"Your mate from the FBI," Bellington said.

It put us in the open. It put us so far in the open I had no cover except a hard face and a lot of bluff. I said sarcastically, "Sure. Coke-running sailors are always tied up with the FBI. There's a lot of them in town."

"Just two of you." Bellington sneered. "Just you and the girl. We've tracked every move you made tonight."

I said to Lennox, "Is only Bellington nuts, or all of you?"

"We're all smart," he said. "We're organized. We got leaks in the cop shop. We knew about Bradley as soon as he arrived. We tailed him. He was getting too close. I brought instructions from Naples last night that he was to be knocked off. He was. Lorca knew where he lived. He went to his house and waited. Exit Bradley. Meanwhile, Bellington and me was trying to follow you. You led us a barn dance."

"You should have let me know."

"It was all right except it got complicated. Lorca found you by accident when you were fixing up a date with the pansy bartender in the Bolero. He's one of our pushers. Lorca left a guy outside to watch you. Bellington thought he had you cornered in a warehouse. He sent one of the boys after you on the roof."

"Exit Paloma," I said. "Same guy."

"Luck of the game. A few minutes later Lorca told me about the appointment you'd made. Then you turn up in the Nido and start whispering to your blonde workmate. That's when I decided you were causing too much trouble, innocent sailor or not. You had to be knocked off."

"It was tried on the roof before then."

"Bellington's own idea. Personal animosity. He don't like you. He had another try in Rivera Street."

"When the bastard left us with two packs of cigarettes," Bellington said. "Some goddamned dame came screaming down the street before we could finish him."

"It turned out for the best," Lennox said calmly. "Everything does if you're well organized. A little later we heard from our leak that a guy was being sought for the murder of Bradley. That was a laugh. Then we heard the description. It was pretty detailed. It turned out to be you. You'd left a button near the body. Now, why would you do that? How would you even know about

Bradley?"

He nodded placidly and did some more scratching. "We thought it all over. Lorca remembered you'd gone inside to the lavatory at the same time as Bradley when we first came ashore. That cinched it. Tough luck we all picked the same café for our first contact."

"Well," I said, "it's a nice story. A little complicated, but complete. I sort of fancy being FBI."

"You won't when we start asking questions," Lennox said. "Neither will your girl stooge who takes photographs. I'll tell you something: That dame advertises too much. She left cards all over the joint."

"Where is she?"

He continued smiling. He said, "A lot of questions. This is big business. You don't realize how big it is. We're the same as any other big business. We don't mind tossing a few bodies in the sea to conserve our assets."

Lorca was getting irritable. He banged the knife on the table. He said, "That's your end of the business, Lennox. I'm only concerned with what happens in this town. This man tries to lay an FBI trap by selling cocaine. Nobody in my organization bought it. Somebody else did. Who? I have to know who's contemplating competition. If I don't keep the Spanish outlet clear I'm in trouble. You know that."

He looked hard at me. "Who bought it?"

I twisted a grin and beamed it to Lennox. I said, "You like complications. You'll relish this bit. Remember the switch I pulled? I'd already had it pulled on me. The gypsy girl in the Nido, the one you danced with, the one Bellington knocked off—she did it. She picked my pocket. I hear you bought her a drink and gave her a cigarette. You should have hung around. She was opening her own cigarettes just after you left. Only they were cocaine."

"Very good." The Spaniard sneered. "Leading to what?"

"The second switch. The girl was drunk. The bartender got hold of the packets and changed the contents to bicarbonate of soda."

Lennox' head jerked. "The Nido bartender? How about it, Lorca?"

"Nothing about it. He refers to Ernesto Fuentes, pusher, one of the least important members of my organization. Fuentes has no direct contact with me; he is not even aware of my existence. But had he thought Beeshop was carrying cocaine, he'd have informed his immediate superior at once. He'd have been afraid not to. I should have received the information within ten minutes."

"You were crossed up," I said. "He decided to trade on the side."

"Enough!" The Spaniard picked up the knife and touched his thumb on the point. "Who was your customer?"

"Who'd buy bicarbonate of soda?"

"Somebody did," Bellington said. "He went celebrating with the photograph girl and the whore and the little Spanish pimp. The bastard went driving down the esplanade with the tart sitting next to him and all the lights on like he was king of something."

My head ached. The night suddenly seemed wound up and done. I'd failed, I was in trouble, I wasn't going to get out, I'd had no satisfaction from anything.

I said, "Bellington, you're a dirty, gutless murdering son of a whoring bitch."

"Maybe." He liked it. He grinned with pleasure and poured himself another drink. "Don't get so sore, it was an accident. When you came running out of that dance place you went dodging round the streets and I thought I'd lost you for good. I had luck. I was listening for your footsteps and all of a sudden you come running up the alley with the dame in the lead. I thought I had you pegged. Even when the lights went out. I still don't see how it happened."

He tossed off his drink and poured another. He was getting drunk. "You were dead for sure," he said. "I told Lorca so. He nearly passed bricks in his pants when you ran into him on the corner. He's chicken, ain't you, Lorca?"

Somebody had to pay for it. Lorca smacked me hard across the mouth. He said, "Who bought the cocaine?" He grabbed a handful of my hair and pulled hard. I thought my scalp was split. "Who?"

Bellington went on guzzling. He said, "The luck held. A short-assed old guy with a yellow face finally fingered you on the esplanade. We gave him five hundred pesetas. He'll be drunk six months."

Lennox said, "Speed it up, Lorca. Show a little imagination. We gotta get back to the ship."

"Save him till tonight," Bellington said.

The Spaniard lifted a clenched fist. He said, "Who bought the cocaine?" I was going to answer. The fist hit me in the mouth. He drew back again and his temper went. He pounded me. He fell back exhausted. So did I. I got whorls in front of my eyes. I gasped, "Wait!"

He stood panting, glittering poachy eyes at me. He fingered the knife. I saw them all with unnatural clearness. They were ten times the size of life. The gun on the table was a cannon.

Lorca said, "Who?"

The door slammed open.

A cool breeze blew into the room. I heard the sound of the sea. I dragged myself painfully from the deep armchair and swung my fist from way back in the next province. I smashed Lorca in the middle of his face.

He rocketed back against the wall. He stayed there. His nose was broken. The blood streamed down over his chin. Temporarily I was almost happy.

I said, "He bought it. The elegant one in the rear."

They stood at the threshold like three newly dismounted horsemen of the apocalypse: the Ape on one side, the ball-headed guitarist on the other, Plosch behind them, smiling faintly. They all held guns.

Plosch stood perfectly still. He said, "Hands up high." The Ape and the guitarist began to move on opposite sides around the room.

Bellington snatched drunkenly at the gun on the table.

Chapter Twenty-two

He did pretty well. His hand closed and his finger squeezed all in one movement. There were too many directions. He could take only one of them He chose the guitarist.

The explosion nearly burst the walls. I had a blurred impression of Plosch's gun staying firm and Lorca and Lennox reaching for the ceiling, then the Ape went pass me like a greased streak and Bellington started to scream.

The guitarist was sitting down. His fingers curled around the edge of the table. His round brown polished head sank slowly from sight. It looked exactly like a bowling ball now. You could have put your thumb in the round red hole in the top. I watched with interest while the fingers uncurled again.

Bellington went on screaming. The Ape had a grip on an arm. He was bending it at a crazy angle backward and upward. It cracked and made a grinding noise. Bellington's voice went up like a coloratura singing the "Bell Song" from *Lakmé*. I think the Ape didn't like it. He put one paw around Bellington's throat and the other on the nape of his neck. Then there was no noise at all.

Bellington was big. The other guy made him look like a midget. The hands squeezed, the silence solidified, and we all stood quietly and waited to see if Bellington would breathe again. The reason for the quiet was that Plosch still stood at the door with the gun trained on us. The other guys kept their hands in the air. Mine were half lifted as if I were about to take a dive off a high board. I wished like hell it was even remotely possible. I was feeling drunk.

I watched the Ape. He displayed no emotion. Maybe it just looked that way in comparison with the victim. Bellington's neck was getting thinner. I wondered if eventually it would get like a pencil.

He put his tongue out and scuffed his feet and lolled his head at the same angle as his broken arm. He rolled his eyes appealingly at me in the way a dying animal does. I suppose I should have leaped to his defense, shouted a protest, done something. I didn't care about Bellington. I even got a certain amount of pleasure from it.

There was no nonsense about death rattles. He made no sound. His tongue emerged farther than I'd have thought possible and he changed color several times, getting deeper with each one. Then he stopped doing anything at all.

The Ape let him drop to the floor.

Lorca began weeping with fright. He looked pretty silly standing there sniveling. His quivering mouth was caked with blood from the blow in the nose.

Plosch moved inside and shut the door. In the artificial light he looked arrogant as Lucifer and pretty as Phoebus. His air was nonchalant; his bleached hair blazed. He still wore the phony riding gear and the yellow silk scarf was nicely ruffled at his neck. He sighed.

"How unpleasant and unnecessary." He nodded at the Ape. "Remove them."

The big guy slammed into the lighted bedroom from which Lennox had first emerged. I heard him bundling about. He returned more slowly, grabbed the bodies by their clothing, and dragged them both from sight.

Lennox said, "Who is this guy?"

Lorca made a great effort. He nearly recovered himself. He sniffled a thin trickle of blood back up his nose and you could almost see the thoughts working in his puffy eyes. He said quaveringly, "Señor Plosch, this is an honor for me."

"Who?" Lennox asked.

"In our city Señor Plosch is famous."

"Thank you." Plosch inclined his head. "I cannot return the compliment. I had never heard of you until less than an hour ago."

The Ape came back from the bedroom. He loaded his pockets with fallen guns, checked his own, pointed it in general fashion at the room, and leaned his weight against the cracked wall.

"The secrecy surrounding the name of Lorca," Plosch said, "was admirable. I had to question closely two men before it was even mentioned. A most difficult progression. The first was a bartender called Ernesto Fuentes. He knew only the second man. The second man was of a higher echelon. He was able to send me straight here."

Plosch looked grave. "Please! A prayer for the fallen. Both men succumbed under question. You have just seen how that might have happened."

I wondered about the cop I'd sent to the Nido. I kept my mouth shut.

Lennox said, "Can we put our hands down?"

"I think so. And tell me now who you are."

"A sailor, señor," Lorca interrupted. "I met him tonight for the first time."

"Of course. Your messenger from Naples."

"I don't understand."

"Come! Lies if you must, but not silly, tiresome lies. Your two men talked fluently. I learned that a great deal of money is being made in narcotics, none of it by me. I am grieved. You are conducting vast business in Spain and also transhipping to the United States. You are connected with Naples. You are members of the monopoly." He paused. He looked lazily from one to the other.

Lennox said calmly, "All right, you want to be cut in. It can be arranged."

"Can it? I think not. I know the workings of your cartel. I should want all of Spain. It has already been allocated to Mr. Lorca. In the past months, while I have been trying to enter this business, it has been demonstrated conclusively to me that there is room in this country for one person only. It appears that the only way I can take over from Mr. Lorca is to eliminate him."

Lennox smiled a little. "That could be arranged, too. I've got pull in Naples."

"Excellent. And what happens to Mr. Lorca?"

"Who cares? Who's in this business for love?"

"Or for honor?"

"I'm in it for money," Lennox said. "I can't afford things like honor."

Lorca was so frightened it became obscene. He tried to straighten from the wall. The Ape slammed him back into position.

Plosch said, "But I would be haunted by the fear, little fat man, that you would also betray me if the occasion arose."

"Not all the while I was getting good dough."

"Truly?"

"Certain."

Plosch said slowly, "It is possible that of all the little fat men I've met, you are the nastiest. I have no wish work with you or your cartel."

"You're just talking," Lennox said arrogantly. "They're too big to buck."

Lorca said in a high squeak, "He's going to kill us."

The light flickered in the four imitation candlesticks of the chandelier. Lennox' glance darted to the window. We had the same idea. We had an equally small chance of putting it into operation. Plosch's finger curled around the trigger. The Ape was up on his toes. The light fell dim for three long seconds, then glowed steady and bright again. The half chance was gone.

I edged two steps around the wall. The Ape made a slight movement of his gun and I came to a halt. Plosch looked directly at me for the first time. He smiled. He did it only with his lips.

He said, "Hello, *machote*. Hello, manly one. That was a disastrous mess you made of my other employee."

"This guy's an FBI man," Lennox said.

Plosch continued as if he hadn't heard. "Poor Paco, he crawled back from the alley as I began requesting our friend Ernesto Fuentes. His condition was really catastrophic. I thought it expedient to leave the Nido immediately and take Mr. Fuentes with us. It would have been foolish to stay."

I knew then that the cop had not found them. I said, "It was a pleasure to beat up Paco. I didn't like the way he lisped."

"But a good man," Plosch said judiciously. He turned to Lennox. "What did you tell me?"

"Bishop. He's an FBI man."

The Ape twitched again. I'd seen him do it the first time.

Plosch said, "You are trying to side-track me."

"He's FBI. There was another one sent over before. We found out about it. We've got someone in police headquarters."

"They are handy. Continue."

"The first one has been put out of the way. Bishop was planted on our ship and sent across with two packs of cocaine."

"I know about that. How do you know that Bishop is an agent of the FBI?"

"Let's make a deal."

"A little more slowly. This is very serious. If what you say is true, Bishop knows all about you."

"And now you," Lennox said.

Plosch twirled the gun once around his finger. The butt slammed hard into the palm of his hand. "You speak like a man with an ace up your sleeve."

"That's what I got."

Plosch said, "Make no mistakes, fat man. You're not in a bargaining position. If your ace has anything to do with Bishop, I can rob you of it at once."

He lifted his left hand lazily. He laid the muzzle on it and trained the gun on me. I stood there and started to tremble. The lights flickered. Lorca's eyes were huge with fear. He was about to faint.

"Please yourself about Bishop," Lennox said unrufffedly. I could see why the guy in Naples employed him. He said, "Matter of fact, I'd like to see him knocked off. I've got his partner stashed away. His partner's a woman. They're easier to work on."

Plosch said, "The woman takes photographs?"

"That's right."

"She is blonde and American? She carries a large hand bag?"

"A camera," Lennox said. "That's right."

"You don't stash her very far away," Plosch said. "She's over there behind that locked door. She's bound and gagged. She's tied to a bed. You should realize, silly little man, that I check everything. We entered that room before we entered this."

He smiled. Smiles come in types—maternal, friendly loving, charitable, humorous, sarcastic. The one he switched on me fitted none of the categories. I tremble a lot more at the back of the knees and the sweat ran out of ducts at my temples and poured down my cheeks. The time had come.

He said, "All the same, Bishop, I don't need you an more. You really are rather dirty and dishonorable. Good by."

"You couldn't justify this philosophically."

"I wouldn't attempt to. The spiritual pleasure must suffice."

I said, "The handbag is over in that drawer. The film is somewhere in this house."

He didn't hear me. His green eyes blazed like limelight. His knuckle went white around the trigger.

The lights snapped out without a flicker.

I hit the floor. The bullet pinged across the room and glass shattered and Plosch howled something I couldn't understand. The glass was still falling. There was a cracking of wood. Someone outside yelled, "Esmitt!" and the door slammed open against the wall. A rectangle of dim gray light invited me to run. I wasn't fast enough.

Lorca's scream went over the room like a smear of red on black. A shape shot past me, a foot trampled my hand, and a pudgy shape was silhouetted against the door. A gun started spitting.

Lennox rose on his toes like a ballet-dancing hippopotamus. His arms went up and he clutched at the doorframe and hung there and twitched as if he were crucified. The whines from his throat didn't sound human. He sagged. Lorca went on screaming. I got on my feet and put my arms across my face and jumped.

There were no shutters.

The glass went into my hands. The curtains snagged and the windowframe shattered. I got a whack on my pulpy skull. Then I was hanging head downward with my feet caught.

It was vague. I heard a wince of brakes, a confusion of voices. More of Plosch's men. Someone was running around the outside of the house toward me. I gave a kick and part of the frame fell on me and I sprawled to the sand. There were more brakes.

The feet still came. A voice in the grayness was saying, "Esmitt! Esmitt! Esmitt!" as if I were a dog. I threw myself upright. I slithered four steps and then I ran.

I saw a beach, an ocean, a cliff. There was sand under my shoes, pads of money under the soles of my feet.

I didn't stop.

Chapter Twenty-three

The beach shelved. I stumbled. The light was growing fast and the cliff face gleamed a dull yellow, as smooth as glass. I shot a look over my shoulder. There was nothing but dim dead rocks. The cliff ahead jutted into a promontory far across the beach and I ran toward it and rounded the corner. I came to a halt. I was making a fool of myself. I took a deep breath.

The horizon was a line of flame. The lower sky blazed with a mixture of pink and silver and green that colored the edges of wispy clouds. The sea lay translucent and without a ripple, like a great pale emerald. My feet were damp.

I looked down. The water was lapping at my shoes. The jutting rock had not been a promontory and there was no more beach. In front of me the sea washed the base of the cliff.

A voice above me shouted, "Esmitt!"

I looked up. The cliff beetled. I could see no one. I pulled myself back around the corner to the dimness of the other beach. It was very hard to see anything at all. A gun belched.

The bullet ricocheted from a rock behind me and whined into the air. I scuttled back around the corner like a turtle. The sea sucked at my feet. The money was probably useless as evidence, but I'd toted it all night and it was tangible. Salt water is bad for money. I tore at my shoes.

Two hundred yards away the cliff was lower. I thought maybe I could climb it. My shoes dropped upside down and the sea pulled and one of them began drifting. I clutched a wad of soggy money in my hand and ran again. The coolness of my feet was beer to a parched throat. I got twenty yards without trouble.

I went up to my ankles, over my calves, then the water began dragging at my legs. I lifted my knees high like a plunging horse. I must have looked pretty silly. I was thinking about Banjo Kelly. She was right about my being too short. I could have gone faster with extra inches.

My shoulder brushed the cliff face. I waded. The water reached my thighs, hips, waist. I could see ahead now clearly. On the face of the rock there wasn't a break, a ledge, a hand hold. I held the money high but it was pointless because soon I'd have to swim. Probably underwater. I wondered about the guys behind me, but I didn't look around. A rock spiked under my foot.

I tried to save myself. My ankle turned and I grunted and the water closed over my head. I began a graceful submarine pirouette. I tried nice and slowly to drink the sea. I completed the pirouette, turned right around, my toes curled over more rocks, and I was still holding one hand above water. I got a foot under me, slipped again, felt firm sand, and pushed up. I took a gasp of fresh air.

I weighed a ton. I shook my head and got my salt-burned eyes open. I was facing back in the other direction. Plosch was shin-deep in water twenty-five yards away with a gun leveled at my chest. We stood in silence and examined each other.

He wasn't the same immaculate Plosch. The dapper riding jacket was torn, the yellow scarf undone to disclose a scrawny hen's throat. His mouth was slightly open, the long blond hair hanging over his face in a brittle curtain that almost reached his chin. In the morning light he looked as if he needed a shave. He looked nuts.

He said, "I have to do this to vindicate my honor, to live with myself afterward. Who are you really?"

"A sailor."

"Of course. You're in it for money, like the rest of us. I watched you. That hand above the water."

There was no breeze. The sea was an unmoving transparency. Another baking day was coming. Not for me.

He waded slowly forward. The water reached his knees. He said, "The FBI would be offended. They are an honorable group, if one can believe the reports. I don't suppose one can. But I can understand how you would adopt their reputation. It gave you the appearance of higher motives."

"No," I said. "I did it to intimidate Lorca and his friends."

"It wouldn't succeed with me," he said almost querulously. "I can't see the sense of it."

He looked beyond the sense of anything. I said nothing.

His eyes flickered to the money. My hands were above my head. My balance was unsteady. I took a slow step backward and groped with my foot for a rock.

He said, "Don't move!" He started coming again. He was a taller man than I. The water washed his groin. The gun was high.

He was going to do it anyway. I didn't like the way he diverted himself by drawing it out. I said, "Plosch, get it over with."

He nodded. "We're all in it for money, but some more than others. You, I think, more than I."

"I'm less honorable."

"Yes. That hand above the water. Disgusting. You must adore money. My money, remember. With you it's a vice, with me no. Open your hand. Let it drift away."

"It's a nice gesture," I said. "It doesn't cost you much. You can afford it."

"Drop the money into the sea."

I said, "Plosch, go to hell!"

On the horizon a burst of glory heralded the coming sun. It was a nice world to be in. I didn't like looking at the gun. He took another step and light glinted off the barrel. The only sign of strain was in a slight tautening of his red mouth. He said, "Well, then, good-by, Bishop." His finger tightened.

A rock struck his elbow and the bullet went skimming away over the sea.

He fired again automatically. He hadn't time for proper aim. Pablo descended from heaven. His feet hit Plosch on the shoulder and they both went under.

The water boiled. They came up again. The gun was gone and Plosch was fighting like a woman, clawing at Pablo's face, trying to gouge with his thumbs. I stood with the money above my head like the Statue of Liberty. I made no move to interfere.

They went down again, rolling. They churned the sandy floor and muddied the clear green water. Plosch's head broke surface. He struggled upward. Pablo was clinging to him like a crab, legs around his waist, head crushed hard to the skinny chest. Plosch staggered.

Pablo fell back and flailed. It happened by accident. His hands met Plosch's throat, he dug in his nails, he pressed with his thumbs. He unlocked his legs. He made a sort of swinging movement. He stood firmly on the sea bed and squeezed with all his strength and thrust Plosch backward and downward.

In a small dark way he was magnificent. You'd have thought he was trolling fish except for his face. He walked slowly away to where the water was clearer, holding Plosch below the surface. I said, "Pablo!" He took no notice. His arms moved and he dragged Plosch up again.

The hacking jacket was half off. The blond hair, turned dark with water, was hanging around Plosch's ears. His silken shirt was plastered to his body and I could see all his ribs. He hung limp, mouth open, eyes bulging. Pablo bent over him.

He said, "Important Mr. Plosch, you spent all night trying to kill my friend

Esmitt. They have found Pepita in a passage and she is dead, but she was not important so nobody cares. Only me. I care. I'm not important, either. Neither will you be."

He pushed the choking face below the surface and started walking again. I shouted, "Pablo!" and started after him. Plosch's features were swelling. His eyes were rolled right up in his head, his mouth was wide open, the water was rushing in. All at once he seemed to merge with the sea.

I moved a little faster, not too much. It took me a while to catch up. I put a hand on Pablo's shoulder. I said, "Hey!"

He turned a face disfigured by adolescent cruelty. He grabbed a handful of hair and lifted the bloated head above the water and said, "Eeyuh! What an ugly thing!" He opened his hand.

Plosch settled down to the sandy bottom. For a second he drifted. He lay still. Pablo stared at me. He said, "He killed Pepita."

"Yes," I said. I couldn't tell him he had killed the wrong man. What did it matter, anyway? Bellington had already got his.

"Well ..." He rubbed his hands together. He shrugged and began to smile. He said, "You can make it all right. You're a policeman. That's why you told me not to worry about Paloma. You belong to the Effay Bay Ee."

I nodded. "The FBI. Let's get out of this water."

We started to wade slowly back to the promontory. He said matter-of-factly, "The fat man came up to Pancho and said he was going to take her back to the hotel. He told me to go away. I wanted to go to bed with her. I looked around the corner, and he and another man were pulling her into a car. They drove off. So I looked for you."

The water was down to my knees. I put the money carefully into my wet jacket pocket.

He said, "I saw old Alberto Lopez and he told me where you were. I ran down to the esplanade and this time some men were putting you in a car, holding you up as if you were drunk. This I knew was not true. You had things on your mind all night. You couldn't be drunk if you fell in a wine press. I was suspicious. The car started up and I ran from behind the palm tree and hung on the rack at the back. My God! My teeth!"

He was gradually assuming the part he must play. He began living it up. His eyes glowed with admiration at his own prowess. He looked like a very small boy.

His head jerked with excitement. His arms moved like semaphore flags. He said, "I rattled and bumped and the car slowed and I rolled off before it stopped. I hurt myself, but it meant nothing. I stole quietly to the window and tried to look in. The curtains were too thick. I couldn't see. But I could hear. And I heard your danger. I heard you are a member of the Effay Bay Ee. Then I knew that everything was all right and we could do anything we wanted. I ran down the road for several *kilómetros* until I found a house with a telephone. I called the police."

I was relieved about the telephone. I said, "Then what?"

"I came back to the chalet. Another car had arrived. The important Mr. Plosch was inside. The police were taking a long time to arrive and I thought I ought to go and look for them, but how could I leave my friend Esmitt in trouble? I couldn't. I waited. I thought of the light. They had to go out sometime soon. In this town they always go out sometime soon."

His face had grown vivid. He rubbed his hands. "I sneaked to the door and there was a crack of light underneath. I was about to listen. The light disappeared and there was a big pim-pam with guns, then people howled and somebody screamed and I smashed the door open. I shouted for my friend Esmitt. Pim! More guns. Pam! More screaming and shouting. My friend Esmitt dived through the window like a swallow, rolled on his face, picked himself up, and ran in the wrong direction. The police had arrived."

Pablo began to laugh. He laughed himself weak. The tears ran down his face. We scrambled around the promontory and stood on the beach.

His laughter subsided. He looked deep into my eyes.

"Pablo," I said, "you've saved me, you've helped me. What do you want?"

He shook his head. A spasm of pride crossed his face. I thought I had hurt him. The tears of laughter in his eyes were all at once tears of emotion. He said, "Nothing. I want nothing. You are my friend. It is enough. I had a good night."

We stood and looked at each other. Suddenly his emotion got the better of him. He took a step forward and put his arms around me and embraced me hard. He patted my back. He put his head on my shoulder for about two seconds, then stepped back and grinned wryly at me.

"One little thing, Esmitt. For an unimportant person, a boy in my position, it is not good to mix with the police. Not for anything. They'll get to know me, and then, just out of friendliness, they'll always be watching me and..."

He trailed off. I waited.

"Esmitt, you promise me? I can go now?"

"Yes," I said. "O.K."

"Thank you, Esmitt. We are friends for always." He held out a hand. "Goodby, Esmitt. Good-by, my friend."

"Good-by, Pablo."

I turned away and walked down the beach. When I looked back he was gone.

The day was beautiful. The water gleamed limpid green and the rocks on the shore were like roasted topaz. I thought that later on I'd take a swim. I began to feel good. I approached the chalet.

It was crawling with cops. There were three ambulances. Nobody saw me until I was about ten yards away, then Torres turned his head and hauled out a gun and came on the run.

He held himself very formally. He said, "Sir, you are wanted on suspicion of murder."

"I don't think so," I said.

Purely by accident my hand brushed my pocket. The top of the lining was hanging out slightly. I patted myself, not very hard, because Torres was a bit quivery with the gun. I said, "The boy, the one you spoke to when he was with me—Pablo. Could you do me a favor and have a couple of your men pick him up? I think he's probably trying to leave town."

Somewhere among the babble of voices Banjo Kelly was wailing, "Doesn't anyone have a camera? Can't somebody get me a camera from somewhere? Oh, hell, oh, hell, oh, hell!"

Chapter Twenty-four

"I guess I'm not the figuring type," I said. "I should have figured a lot of things."

"Such as?"

"Torres' appearing at Brad's place only because someone had reported me as a prowler."

"You were a little agitated at the time," she said.

"Agitation won't cover everything. I came running down from the roof into the Nido and you'd just been brought there by Lennox from the Bolero. You said he'd been asking after me. How did he know we even knew each other unless we'd been seen by one of his stooges—probably the pansy bartender? Why didn't I think of that?"

"More," she said. "Punish yourself."

"I thought they were all working together. Yet the guitarist wasn't able to tell Plosch about the cocaine until after Pepita had picked my pocket. The others knew before. And it was clear right from the start that Plosch had nothing to do with killing Brad."

She reached across and touched my hand. "Shorty, that's the night before. This is the following morning. Why not let me figure it all out for myself?"

"All right," I said.

We were sitting at a sidewalk table, shaded by a vivid umbrella. She was drinking a multicolored *pousse-café* very carefully, so as not to disturb the different layers of liqueur. I was gazing into her eyes. I liked her eyes.

There were a lot of gaily dressed people in the street. Every time the old man went by with the jasmine arranged like a parasol on the end of a long stick I bought her a sprig. She had five, one behind her ear and four on the table. The smell was good. The old man was edging back again for another killing, at less than a nickel a spray. There was another old man across the street with balloons that floated against the brilliant blue of the sky. When he came over to our side I'd buy her one of those, too. I wanted to buy something for everybody.

Torres had got through to Naples in seven minutes. It showed it could be done, even in Spain. There was checking, triple checking, and finally I talked to the boss. He was more pleased than I had expected. The rockets about too much individual initiative would come later. He gloomed about some aspects; that was his way. But he couldn't keep out of his voice the satisfaction that we'd chopped off the latest tentacle of the guy in Naples.

They were going right away to arrest Rossi. They couldn't arrest the big gun yet. Maybe we'll never arrest him. I don't know. We'll keep trying.

I bought the balloon and tied it to the back of her chair. It floated lazily over her head.

She said, "Anyway, the camera was insured."

"I'm glad."

"Don't you dare be so cool with me after what I went through on your account. I was lying bound and gagged on that bed in the other room. First time in my life a man ever silenced me."

"They thought you were connected with me."

"A nice idea."

"Not bad," I said. "I don't feel so cool about you."

"Now it's me that's glad."

I looked into her eyes again. She finished the *pousse-café*.

She said, "What about Lennox?"

"Bullets in shoulders, legs, and buttocks. Buried in fat. He'll live. They're taking extra-special care of him. He's being flown to Naples this afternoon for special treatment. Lorca stays here for special treatment. That way the Spanish police get one, the Italians the other."

"I didn't like Lorca. He was the hysterical type."

"The treatment for hysterics is to slap them. He's in a nice cool underground room and Torres is doing the slapping. Torres is eager for results. He's anxious to discover which of the boys are the headquarters leaks. Then there'll be more slapping. Torres is all right when you get to know him."

She tapped her glass. "I'd like another of these."

The waiter brought one. I had a beer. The old man edged near and stood patiently and that made six sprays of jasmine. I looked up the street. A large plain-clothes man was approaching with a hand on Pablo's shoulder.

They halted at the table. The plain-clothes man said, "Señor Torres reported you wanted to see this man."

"Thanks. You needn't wait."

Pablo sat down.

The waiter brought another beer and Pablo sipped it. He watched me foxily. He said, "Hello, Pancho."

"Banjo," she said.

We had a silence.

I said, "Still got it on you?"

He widened his eyes, then decided not to fight it. He nodded.

"Let's have another friendly embrace. I can steal it back."

He nodded again. He looked crestfallen, downcast, humble, submissive, repentant. He was pretty good. He muttered, "Forgive me. A sudden temptation. I thought they were one-dollar bills. I didn't realize—"

A tear stole from the corner of his eye. He brushed it away and set his lips bravely. "I don't blame you," he said. "You'll have to send me to prison even though I did save your life. You're a policeman. You have no alternative. It's only that my poor sick mother—"

With a great effort he prevented himself from breaking down completely. He didn't have a mother. He put a hand to his pocket and slowly held out the money. He said, "But whatever happens, you will always, always be my friend."

Banjo Kelly said, "Bishop, you're a swine."

He flashed her a look of gratitude. He was still holding out the money.

I took it. Then I handed it back.

"Half shares. Half for you, half for the son of Pepita. Go find him. Take him to the bank. Put the money in. I'm holding you responsible. I'll check on you tonight. Now get going."

"I shall be a brother to him. An elder brother." He put the money slowly back into his pocket and stood up. He sucked his lower lip, softened his eyes. He was going into rehearsal for the scene he would play with Pepita's son, preparing for the magnificent and magnanimous gesture. He turned to me with a stately smile.

"Then until tonight, Friend Esmitt. We shall meet in Socorro Street. Do you feel that we should get drunk?"

"I do indeed."

He turned away. He whipped back again. "I saw old Alberto Lopez. He's drunk. He said you owed him some halves of bills. I'll take them."

"Beat it!" I said. "And ten per cent of everything for the little bootblack from last night. I'll check that, too."

He winced slightly. He gave me an approving pat on the shoulder, gravely inclined his head, and walked solemnly away. We watched him go.

Banjo said, "Isn't what you did illegal?"

"The money was lost at sea. Want another *pousse-café?*"

"If we're all going to be drunk tonight, I'd better get back to the hotel and go to bed for a while."

"I'll go with you."

"Fine," she said.

We stood up and gathered all the jasmine sprays and walked down the street in the hot sunlight. It was a good day and everyone was glad to be alive. A man went by humming the bird song.

THE END

Catch a Fallen Starlet

by Douglas Sanderson

For

LOLIN & ENRIQUE in Australia

ONE

I parked the car in a lot and went on foot across Vine toward Western, trying to get the feel of the place again. The weather was warm, lunchtime had half cleared the streets and the springtime sun battled down through light smog—the same smog that some people claim killed the motion picture industry. It's as good an excuse as any, but still an excuse. Television and lousy films killed the motion picture industry.

I saw no one I knew. I passed a bar, a cool beery odor in a dim interior, but did not enter. It was a long time now since I had taken a drink. Temptation was no longer fierce, not in the daytime. I glanced in a store window and thought my face was improved, though I didn't like my clothes much. I had dressed for the occasion in a powder-blue suit and thick-soled suede shoes with heavy stitching. I looked like the Sultan's Favorite, but in Hollywood you are judged by appearances. This was the right appearance.

I turned left and looked up. Bertha was at her third-floor window with her elbows on the sill, gazing into space. I was too far off to see if her jaws were moving, but I guessed she was eating. She always lunched in her office at this hour, and I had come now because I wanted to catch her alone. We had never been especially friendly, but I respected her business abilities, and she had been a great pal of my wife and would maybe give me information for old times' sake. More likely she would give it to me for ten per cent.

I went into the building, past the cigar stand and up in the elevator.

The single oak door had TWEEDY on it in plain gold letters. Bertha was one of Hollywood's best and longest established agents, and that was all the publicity she needed. I took a breath, momentarily afraid; then I pushed open the door and walked into the waiting room. Twenty pairs of eyes jumped at me.

They were the usual crowd, mostly girls, kids from all over. I knew the type well. My wife had been like that. Facile glamour in dark movie houses had obsessed them with facile dreams. They were convinced, every one of them, that given only that chance, that lucky opportunity, they too could win fame and fortune and the love of the world and be like the stars. So here they were in the air-conditioned jungle, lining up for the casting couch, willing to sacrifice love, honor and a last ideal, if one remained, for the chance to walk onto a movie set.

It was sad.

They took my measure. I might be someone. A boy in jeans, T-shirt and fancy sandals squinted shortsightedly and gave me a slow burning look along his left shoulder. Brando type. I walked the length of the room and the switchboard girl on the other side of the barrier glanced up and raised her eyebrows.

"Yeeees?"

She was something special—tall, well-built and extraordinarily beautiful for

Hollywood. She had red hair, green fingernails, a skin like polished marble, but her hard, intelligent face was without emotion. The big man to the left of her looked up from his typewriter and regarded me with soft patience. He had pretty eyes, a low forehead and no lips. I opened my mouth to speak.

"Closed till three," the girl said. "Call back."

"Tell Miss Tweedy it's Mr. Dufferin."

"Or take a seat," the girl said. "But it'll be a long wait."

"Try her. Mr Dufferin."

The big man swiveled on his seat. Everyone was silent. The girl looked at her green fingernails, yawned, lowered fly-leg lashes to flawless cheeks, then suddenly opened her eyes wide and clapped a hand to the left bulge of her sweater. "Not *the* Mr. Dufferin! Not the one I never heard of!"

I grunted. They all get like that in a few months, especially the failures. They talk as they fancy the movies talk, and somehow it softens defeat for them. I saw she was prepared to keep it up for hours. I said, "Yes, *the Mr.* Dufferin," and pushed through the swing gate.

The big man came out of his seat, but slow, off the mark. I had the door open and was in the inner office.

TWO

Bertha spun her bulk from the window, took a quick step forward and came to a halt on the other side of the food-littered desk. "Al," she said. "Why, hello. I didn't even know you were in town."

"Hello, Bertha. Get this man off my back."

She said, "All right, Hymie, go back to your roost. This is a friend of mine."

We waited until the door closed. She looked at me blankly and said, "Sit down, Al. Eat something." She took a bottle of rye from the desk and poured two stiff jolts into paper cups. I shook my head.

"I don't any more."

"No?" She sat back studying me, and I studied her. She hadn't changed. Her badly dyed hair bushed out like a mauve crysanthemum, and her clothes looked as though she had walked backwards through a scrog bush. She still looked more like a stevedore than a woman. But she still had integrity in her eyes.

"So you quit it," she said. "That explains what happened to the sags, bags and red veins. Seems to me I heard a rumor of you modeling a strait jacket in Bellevue. Did New York run out of liquor?"

"It had too much. I finally wised up and realized I couldn't drink it all."

"That's good news," she said. "The cops know you're back?"

"Should they?"

She shrugged. "You know how popular you are around here. You might have been smarter to stay East. I heard you were doing all right writing for TV under another name. If you're looking for work, I'll do what I can, but you know your position in Hollywood. That hasn't changed, and everything else has. For the worse. Shakespeare, Dante and Hemingway couldn't get jobs now without a pull at the studio. Things are terrible."

I had heard it before. Closing studios. Independents shooting, for cheapness, in places like Spain. Folding movie houses; plummeting attendances; the Hollywood myth-flower withering fast in a financial frost. I made sounds of sympathy.

She said, "There's been a revolution. Time was when you could fill Cinemascope with a freak bosom, pack the cinema and send the customer away happy. But a bosom's no use now without a Monster gnawing at it under a title like I Was A Wean-Age Tear-Wolf. They make that junk for less than half a million a time. The writers get next to nothing, and the top actors two hundred a week. Imagine my position. Most of my clients are hangovers from the postwar boom and still want to make big pictures. They think it's my fault they can't. Hence Hymie. I need protection sometimes. This has turned into a rough, tough business."

"It was never anything else." I glanced around at the glossy pictures of the stars and near stars smiling down from the walls with all the retouched presumption of the good years. I said, "Hymie looks like a hood."

"Hymie's an ex-hood," she said. "Stop swiveling your eyes like a chameleon, Al. I took Clare's picture down."

"I see you did."

"Why not? She's dead. She was your wife, and you seem over it, and she was only my client. She wasn't big enough to start another Jimmy Dean cult."

"You mean it's forgotten?"

"It will be, but not yet. The splash was too big. They were firing her to stardom with all the guns. She was going to be the married mother all-American home-town girl. New style Mary Pickford. Shirley Temple grown up. She was going to bring back all the other home-town girls who sit watching TV instead. She was a bitch, we both know, but everyone else believed the publicity up to and including the boys who put it out. Everyone still remembers. You remember."

"Yes." I had been the all-American girl's all-American husband. I was a writer, but the flacks overcame that by proving that I was an extrovert writer, a nice normal guy with no intellectual eggheaded nonsense. I loved hot dogs, ball games and a good old glass of beer. I did, but not the way they made it sound. And the glass of beer was my undoing.

The public was enraged when they learned how much I really drank. I had betrayed them doubly because apparently I had betrayed Clare. The night she killed a man I had already been taken home stewed from the party. I was stewed at her trial. She emerged free, famous and triumphantly vindicated, and

I could have been forgiven in the great national wave of sympathy that gathered for her. But at six o'clock one morning, when the police sought me to say that Clare had been burned up in a car accident, I was out cold again in a bar.

I drove her to it, of course. She had died a martyr, an escapee from a drunken husband. I was the bastard who had deceived her and the entire American public.

Bertha said, "So why've you come back, Al?"

"I happen to be a local boy. I was born here."

"You could die here," she said. "Of starvation. Made any contacts yet?"

"None. I came just a week ago, on a visit. I'm out at Los Olmos with my sister. She's been looking after the kid for me."

"So is this just a social call?"

"No. I want to hear what you know about Barry Kevin."

"That's easy, I know nothing. He's a Salinger client, not mine."

"That's why I'm asking. I'll get a straight answer from you."

"All right, if you want one." She lit a cigarette and screwed up her eyes. "Barry Kevin made his last picture three years ago. It flopped so hard there were earthquake rumors in Persia. The one before that, a year before, was a great big turkey roasted slowly by the critics and stayed away from in millions by the public. Barry Kevin's out of sight now and out of mind. If anyone remembers him at all they think he worked with Pearl White and Mabel Normand."

I said, "He's going to make another picture."

"No." She shook her head. "He's not. You and fellow-drinker Kevin may have got plastered together, but there won't be another picture now or ever. He's no good for comedies, musicals or Method, and he thinks he's too good to play Monster. There's nothing else being made. He can't do an Independent because for that he needs a reputation and/or money. He has neither. There was a rumor that his new wife was loaded, but no one has seen any evidence. So no picture for Barry Kevin."

"He phoned yesterday," I said. "I'm going out this afternoon to discuss a script."

"You're crazy. What did he offer?"

"We didn't discuss it."

"Then finish your little visit, go back to New York and make more money at TV."

"Why?"

"The routine as before," she said. "Kevin's last stand. No one will touch him with a ten-foot broom, no one will touch you with a twenty-foot broom, so the two pariahs get together. He'll want an adaption, an original even, he'll try for a percentage deal or, failing that, offer up to a thousand on account. When you've done all the work of hand-tailoring him a part and you can't back out, he'll offer another five hundred for a six-month option, then he'll start hunting for backers. He won't find any. You'll be left with a star-part screenplay that fits no one else. For a lousy fifteen hundred."

"Nonsense. He knows what I used to get."

"So do I. It doesn't exist in Hollywood any more, except in the publicity handouts. Don't forget you're a writer, the guy even the starlets don't talk to in the commissariat—no rights, no publicity, the bottom of the Hollywood heap. After Clare you're at the bottom of the writers' heap. Forget Kevin. Go back to New York and TV and money."

"I'll visit him anyway."

"As you like," Bertha heaved from the chair and came around the desk. Her business eye was glittering hard. She said. "We'll work it this way. I'm your agent, and all contracts are signed through me. He'll fight, but fight back. If he has any real money, I might lay hands on some of it for you."

"Or he might get another writer."

"That, too." She looked me directly in the eyes, her face suddenly sober. She said, "Clare's photograph is put away, if you want it. It was signed Adoringly Yours."

"Yes, they all were. I don't want it. It's over."

"Bad?"

"At the beginning, yes. I was stroking ropes for a while. Fingering knives, looking at gas ovens."

"That so?" Bertha grinned. "Guns are best, son, or a good swift poison. But don't lose that last line. Barry Kevin will love it in his movie, the little ham." She patted my arm, still grinning, as plain and unattractive as a concrete casting. "Keep your chin up, Al. Phone me the moment anything happens."

"Good-by, Bertha."

I closed the door. Hymie regarded me blandly, and the redhead flicked her lashes again, but in a subtly different manner. Her face was resigned, beautiful, no softer, and her voice was low and throaty. "I'm Lona Forman, Mr. Dufferin. I want to apologize. I didn't know you were a friend of Miss Tweedy."

"It's all right," I said. Her eyes were sad. It was sad, too, that she did not have a face for pictures even if pictures still existed. I glanced around the room. Everything was sad.

I had come from the inner sanctum, which proved I was somebody. The girls cheesecaked at me. Three were on their feet in the careless carefree youth pose. The Brando boy was trying to fracture his neck.

I tasted the room's illusions in my mouth, and I thought of Clare. I wanted to tell them all to go home and get married and do honest things. I wanted to tell them to run and run fast.

I'd have been wasting my breath.

THREE

I was nearly to the gates when the gray Jaguar convertible leaped out with a roar. It turned almost at a right angle, nearly sideswiped me, hared off down toward Hollywood and left me still standing on the brake. I saw blonde hair and heard her shout, "Fool!" I sat while my pulse rate got back to normal, then went through the gate myself and up the drive.

There were two other cars on the gravel stretch, a Buick and a Thunderbird, neither of them this year's model. I rang the bell at the open front door, looked around and thought the setting was good. Wrought-iron gates in a high white stucco wall, fine tall trees and large grounds. But the flower beds had not been tended, and the lawn needed a shave. The swimming pool was too far off to tell if it was still in use.

I rang again.

The sky was clouding up for rain. My watch said four-thirty, which was the right time for the appointment. I listened to the silence a while longer, then stepped through the door into the main hall. I felt like a schoolboy in a museum.

Faint dust lay over everything. The hall was as high as the house and large enough for a tiger hunt. Chandeliers reflected dully in the parquet floor, and a wide staircase swept to an upper gallery. The walls were wood-paneled and covered with Winterhalter-type paintings that did not chime with the Spanish architecture. The place reminded me of its owner's past films—a lot of brio, no art and no taste.

I went back again and rang the bell.

A panel opened across the way, revealing itself as a door. An elderly wet-handed woman emerged, pulling herself into a maid's apron, obviously having come from another chore. She raised her eyebrows in the approved manner and wished me good afternoon. I said I had an appointment with Mr. Kevin. She told me to wait while she found out if he was awake.

She walked the length of the hall and disappeared through another panel, leaving it ajar. I tried to distinguish other doors from panels, and was reminded of an old Harold Lloyd horror-comedy with concealed exits and entrances. Anything is possible in California, and there may have been priest-holes. I studied a picture of cows in a cornfield.

"Good afternoon," a voice said. "Not good, is it?"

She was descending the wide staircase, a cool, hard woman dressed in pants and sweater, as though she had recently played golf or sawed logs. But she was too elegant for such boisterous pastimes, and her figure was not designed for masculine pursuits. She had dark blonde hair, topaz eyes and an aura of sex at first glance strong enough to send an anchorite howling back to the desert to fight more demons. Only at first glance. Close up her eyes were cold and disillusioned, her mouth discontented and, for want of a better word, prim.

She said, "I quite like the cross-eyed cow, though. I'm Karen Kevin."

"Alan Dufferin."

We shook hands, and she released her grip too quickly. "Dufferin?"

"Alan Dufferin."

"Oh. I once saw your wife in a film. She was lovely. She had a sweet personality."

I said, "I met some of your husband's other wives. They were nice, too."

I could have bitten out my tongue. But she had caught me unawares. We looked at each other a moment, and I said, "Sorry. That was unnecessary."

"It was. But perhaps I shouldn't have mentioned her."

The servant said, "Mr. Kevin will see you now."

I went alone across the parquet floor, ashamed of myself; it was bad that I had been needlessly rude, worse that I was still hypersensitive about Clare. I glanced back over my shoulder, and Mrs. Kevin was prowling off upstairs again. She stopped.

"Simmons," she called. "Simmons, if Miss Mason comes back or telephones tell her that I shall go to the Top Hat tonight." She looked down to where I was but, I think, did not see me, because I had stepped through the panel. A voice inside shrieked, "Sonofabitch! Sonofabitch!"

A gray African parrot with a red tail was chained by one leg to a portable perch in the corner of the room. Like a mad old man it muttered twice, "Polly wanna cracker," and straddled its perch and swayed its head irritably from side to side. "Sonofabitch!" it shrieked again, and was abruptly still and silent. It watched me with an eye full of evil, a lusterless gray bead.

Kevin was not in the room.

The furnishings were Spittoon School, a sofa and deep chairs covered with brown leather and with ashtrays attached to the cloths draped over their arms. Sun windows and French doors ran all along one wall, and there was a brown wood bar in a corner flanked by a bookcase that contained no books, but a mass of tattered old film scripts. Through an open door, in an adjoining room, were more sun windows.

I stood, waiting, looking from the windows at the untrimmed shrubs. The rain had begun spitting. I felt like a poor relation on a touch.

"That you, Dufferin? Make yourself at home. Pour yourself a drink. Come in here."

I took my pick. I went in there.

It was a bedroom furnished in Louis Quinze reproduction and carpeted in green. Barry Kevin was in front of a long, high, open wardrobe with his foot on a taboret stool and his chin pensive in one hand. I knew the pose. Napoleon at Elba. This was going to be a historical film.

He said, "Hello." He was wearing pinkish pants, a knotted silk scarf at his neck, a pale blue shirt and a corset. He pointed dramatically to two hundred hangers of clothes. He said, "Which jacket?"

It was nothing to me, and I was used to actors. I said, "Green."

"Right." He took it, shrugged it on with a single movement and came lightly around the bed. "That's a very smart suit," he said. "I don't like the shoes."

"No?" There was dust in the hall, untrimmed shrubs and unmowed lawn, and Bertha had said fifteen hundred. I've never needed that little money that bad. I said, "Pity. Next time I'll come barefoot."

"Oh God, your feelings are hurt." He took my arm and began leading me back to the other room, gazing into my face with a burning earnestness. "Listen," he said. "You and me, I hope, are about to begin a very intimate relationship. Unless we say from the start whatever comes into our heads, unless we give immediate reactions and then argue them out, we shall get nowhere. Complete collaboration, a meeting of the minds, Reed and Graham Greene, we have to practice. I don't like your shoes." He was at the bar now. "A drink?"

"Reed's a director," I said. "No drink."

He said amiably to the parrot, "Sonofabitch yourself, you old bastard," and began playing with bottles. I watched him.

He had been a movie idol back in the days when they made idols by giving intense publicity to a single marketable trait. Kevin's strong trait, his only one, had been sincerity. He was pouring it out now with the drink. He was a short man, and had stood on a few boxes in his time to make love to the taller actresses. He was quoted as saying that all great actors had been short, from Garrick and Edmund Kean down to Olivier and Brando. He was not quoted as saying that they could act and he could not.

"Sit down." I lowered myself into an overstuffed chair, and the leather creaked at me. The parrot turned its head and watched malevolently from the corner. Barry Kevin swished from the bar with an elegance that would have been pansy in anyone but an actor, but he was only rehearsing. A historical picture for sure. He was swashbuckling. At his age it was more buckle than swash. His face was the weakness. You can't put a corset on a face.

He was not very bad. He was Fredric March-Gary Cooper vintage, better preserved than either, though not so well as Cary Grant. He would not need his jowls strapped up, and the corset was good except for pouting his chest when he sat. But he'd never play juvenile again, no matter how they slathered him with plastic. His age gathered on him when he smiled, the way he was smiling now—earnestly, frankly, sincerely. I sat and made bets that he would want to play a juvenile.

"You're not permitted to drink?" he asked.

"Does it matter?"

"We're going to be honest, Dufferin, as I said. I heard about the psychopathic ward in Bellevue."

"You heard about the booze ward. Then no drink for a long time. Then the discovery that I could take it or leave it alone. I leave it alone. I was a drunk, not an alcoholic. There's a medical difference."

"Thanks for telling me," he said. "We're doing fine. Now direct to another point to clear everything right up. I never worked with your wife. I never met her. So far as I know she never worked at anything outside of a couple of B's. She may have been the most lovable thing since Minnie Mouse and you may have drunk enough to drive her to death. To me that's nothing. My only interest is that you write a good script. You're about the only writer on record who ever got an Academy nomination for a costume picture."

I remained silent. His eyes were full of man-to-man directness. Suddenly: "How's my voice?" he snapped.

I had the game by now. I snapped back, "Hoarse."

"Smoking too much. Brooding on the new part."

"Which is?"

It was all one movement. He got to his feet, rose to his toes, stuck one hand to his hip, the other in the air, flung back his head and grinned down his nose like a devil. He cried, "Benvenuto Sellini."

Ham.

"Well, man? Reaction? Don't you know the book?"

"Yes. There's a good picture in it."

"There was a bad one in it," he said. "Back in the thirties. March and Bennet. This will be different, Dufferin. This will be an epic."

"Could be. What incidents you propose using?"

"Incidents? Nothing incidents. We'll film the entire book. Cinemascope, Technicolor, *Gone With the Wind*, *Ten Commandments*, *Benvenuto Sellini*. An epic. They're the only things that make money these days. Anything against it?"

"How do we explain those boy apprentices?"

"What boy apprentices?"

"My turn to be honest," I said. "When did you read the book?"

He came down off his toes. "When the hell do I get time to read any great long book? I read an article somewhere—*Readers' Digest*. I got enough experience to know what constitutes good material. Sellini is a natural."

He plumped down, put hands between his knees and hunched forward in a ball of intensity. "Here's a rough idea," he said. "We get a kid for a prologue about Sellini's childhood. The bit about the scorpion that didn't sting. I play Sellini's father."

"Pronounced Chellini."

I thought he had not heard. He hunched further, aging himself, being the father for a moment. Then his face cleared, he straightened, he smiled with all the impish ingenuousness of youth. "From there," he said, "we jump to where the father is dead and the guy is twenty or twenty-one. I take over the part of Chellini himself. Get it? Two parts. The chance for some character acting."

A juvenile. I could have groaned.

His head was back again, eyes burning. "Art," he said. "A man of genius. Statues, fountains, beautiful gold and silverware, and all fashioned with my own hands. Lovely goblets to fondle. We emphasize my hands. I have a short black beard, curly hair and earrings—maybe only one earring. I womanize. Love scenes, swordplay, action. And then—and then I meet Lucrezia Borgia, the Pope's daughter."

I knew my period. I said, "You don't. She died when Cellini was nineteen."

"What the hell sort of writer are you?" he said irritably. "Poetic license. I meet Lucrezia Borgia. I need the Vatican absolutely—the pomp, the pageantry, the spectacle, the religion. Chellini leads an army to a war that saves Christian civilization. We get in a De Mille message about humanity and God and democracy. Lucrezia is beautiful. She waves me good-by from a turret."

"And you wave good-by to the Catholic customers."

"So what are you trying to do?" he snarled. "Make Borgia something else, some sort of Vatican high official. Metro once made Cardinal Richelieu a civilian, and nobody beefed."

"All right," I said. "We won't bring in the Pope until the end. You are putting on the cowl, entering the humble monastery, forsaking forever the tawdry glitter of secular life. A vast crowd of extras has gathered to bid you farewell. In the sad, empty silence a voice cries out, 'There goes a man!' But the Pope, lifting his hands in slow benediction, murmurs only to himself and the audience, 'No. There goes a saint.' Surge of music with heavenly choir. Close-up of your exalted face. Slow fade."

"Yes," he said. "You've got it."

For fifteen hundred bucks I didn't want it. I said, "The Tweedy agency draws up my contracts."

"Tweedy? Bertha Tweedy? That goddam sad old nymphomaniac?" He blinked at me once. "No agents. This is independent. We work together with no outside interference."

"What contract have you in mind?"

"Fifteen thousand down, fifteen thousand more the day shooting starts, plus a percentage. Yes?"

"Yes "

He pulled a sheet of paper from his pocket. He carried his cigarettes loose, and a fine shower of tobacco fell to the floor. He said, "Supporting cast list. Look it over. Build parts for them. Reaction?"

I was still Hollywood enough to bug my eyes. Most of the names were as big as Kevin had been and bigger than he was now. "Reaction?" he snapped at the top of my head. "Reaction? Anything? The handwriting?"

I went on gaping. He said, "We won't disagree on percentage. Don't sit there like a dummy. What do you think of the handwriting?"

I looked up. The game was on again. "Bad," I said. But he was waiting for more. I said, "You write like a woman."

"Do I? Yes. Well, all right. Are we in business?"

"You bet."

He sighed.

I said, "Who'll direct?"

"Me. Yes, and everyone else will be surprised. But I've got ideas. I can make this the most revolutionary thing to hit films since *Citizen Kate*. Not so hard to take, but revolutionary. They'll be on their knees begging me to direct afterwards. I shall retire from being an actor."

I knew now what he meant by his reference to Carol Reed. I said, "And who'll produce?"

"Co-produce. With me. Leo Holst."

I took that one slowly. I said, "Holst's a director. He's pretty nearly *the* director. He's tied up with Super."

"You've been away too long, Dufferin. Super shut down."

He suddenly walked to the window and stood looking out. The rain was falling steadily, and the evening sky had turned the ominous color of purple grapes. "Well," he said, "I've given you the idea. Run along now while you're warm and buy a copy of the book. Go through it tonight. Pick out themes, make a general framework. Come back tomorrow with what you've got, we'll talk things over, draw up the contract and maybe I'll be able to pay you the first money. All right?"

"Sure." I stood up, conscious of the parrot watching me. "Right," I said, and suddenly felt awkward and uncomfortable, as though I didn't know what was really going on. I said good-by and went out across the darkening paneled hall, out to the gravel.

The Thunderbird and Buick were still there. I looked around again at the garden, the uncut lawn, the untrimmed shrubs, the untended flower beds. Barry Kevin could have got a script for ten thousand. He knew it. He could have used some of the other money on wages for gardeners, housemaids, someone to dust the hall.

Perhaps he was crazy. Perhaps it was all a gag.

I drove down toward Hollywood, rain flooding the windshield and slicking the road. There was little traffic, but I went carefully. My mind was a thrown-up ragbag of all I had ever heard or read of the Renaissance period, the Borgias, Cellini. I was trying to sort them out and stitch them into a tailorable cloth.

A siren sounded behind me.

I pulled over slowly and wound down the window.

The prowl car drew alongside, the door opened and the cop sauntered over, taking his time, and stuck his head in the window. He said, "Know the speed limit around here, mister?"

"I was under it."

"Stay under it." He sniffed for afterglow. "Been drinking?"

"The nearest doctor can decide."

"You didn't change, did you?" He was a young, good-looking man, and he looked at me with implacable hostility. He said, "We heard you was back, Dufferin. We wanted to make you welcome. Watch your step while you're here, and don't stay too long. We'll be watching you. That's all." He went back to the car.

I sat until they were out of sight. Clare came back, as she always did, and roosted in my skull. I was thinking that police and public, they couldn't all be wrong—maybe I had really been responsible for her death. That thought had been with me since the day of her funeral. I wanted to weep, but I was long past that.

FOUR

I had a foot dangling over the arm of the chair and an unlighted cigarette between my fingers. My brother-in-law, Chester, grown nervous at the silence, was fiddling with the TV set. We could never think of anything to say to one another when alone, and we were both wishing that Fay would come downstairs again. We were not fond of one another.

I picked up the Cellini autobiography. It was illustrated, privately printed, had cost twenty dollars and I had found it in a de-luxe-edition bookshop off the Boulevard, where it was being sold as pornography. The man behind the counter also offered me art photographs. He must have been new to the game, because he blushed when I said no.

My stomach knotted at the thought of the work in front of me. Five hundred closely printed pages, and I did not know where to start. I could have used some encouragement. I thought of calling Bertha, but she had gone home from the office now and her private phone was not listed. I riffled pages.

Chester said nervously, "Not on yet."

"What's that?"

"Show I wanted to see. My watch must be fast." He looked at his wrist, glanced up, accidentally caught my eye and looked hurriedly away, embarrassed. A beer commercial appeared on the screen. Animated bottles poured frothing great glasses, and an enticing voice told of the joys of drink. In the lulls we heard the rain at the window.

Chester gulped.

"Bad night." His head jerked, his scalp flashed pink through thinning hair and folds appeared in his neck. He said, "No one'd want to go out on a night like this, I should think."

"No."

"Good book?"

"Not bad."

"It looks big." He cleared his throat. "Wish I had more time for reading, but I'm always bushed when I get home nights."

"I guess." Then uncomfortable silence again. Then music from the set and

Chester turning to it with relief.

I stood up, book in hand, conscious of his apprehensive glance, and walked out and upstairs to the bedroom. The door of the adjoining room opened softly and my sister came out.

She was still bright-eyed and pretty. She looked a lot younger than thirty-three, but that may have been because I was very fond of her and could not see the changes. She held her finger to her lips. "Not too much noise, Al. Johnny's asleep." Then her eyes opened wide. "Going out on a night like this?"

I put down the book. "Fay," I said, "I've had enough, and don't for God's sake you start. Chester's down there fidgeting around like an old goosed hen. Get it in his fat head that if I do go out and get drunk it'll be no disgrace to him."

"Oh Al, he's thinking of you and Johnny, not himself. He's perfectly sincere."

"Like an alarm clock," I said. "He doesn't want me here, Fay. I'll move."

"We've had all this before. It's not worth it for so short a time."

"It was a short time," I said. "I may be staying longer. There's breeze of a job. I've been asked to write a screenplay for Barry Kevin."

"What?" She paused a moment. She flung her arms around me. "Al! That's marvelous! Barry Kevin! He used to be one of my top favorites. All right, now you'll have to stay. We'll love having you with us."

"Will you?"

We had never kidded one another. "Well, near us," she said, and grinned. "You do make Chester uneasy. His nerves are not what they were."

"I'll rent an apartment."

"That might be best." She nodded. Something like alarm appeared in her eyes. "Will you take Johnny?"

"I don't know." We looked at one another, as fond and intimate as we had always been. I said, "Visited any doctors lately?"

"I ran out of them, so Chester finally went. We'll never have one of our own. Don't tell him I told you."

"Sure not. But I have to take Johnny some time."

"Why? I've been watching. You can't get near him. You don't even really like him. We've had him two years now, and he's like our own. Chester's crazy about him."

"I know," I said. "That's most of the trouble between us."

She looked away. I knew her well enough to know she was about to change the subject. She said, "School tells me the boy's awful bright. Maybe he'll take up writing, like his father."

I said, "Or acting, like his mother."

"Maybe," she said, and there was a rain-filled silence. She put a hand on my arm. "Stop torturing yourself, Al, for heaven's sake. You were innocent. Concentrate on it. Remember what Milton said about no stubborn, unlaid ghost having power over—"

"You stop it." I shook off her hand.

"I won't! Responsible or not, you deserved a medal. *De mortuis* and all that, but she was a first-grade category-one undiluted bitch, to you and everyone else. I've never told you before, but she once tried to get between me and Chester. She—"

"She's dead," I said. "Shut up. Go downstairs. Chester's watching a girlie show. He might need a restraining influence."

"As you say. Are we quarreling?"

"No."

"Good. I'll mix you a drink if you want one."

"Don't be so bloody patronizing, Fay. Get out." She grinned and went.

I knew it was useless, but I sat at the table. I arranged pencils and paper and listened to the rain, and finally opened the book. I skipped, going from highlight to highlight, making notes, only half my mind at it. It was a long time since I'd worked at a major project, and it came hard and empty. To reduce Cellini's life successfully to four hours running time would be like making a cartoon of the Bible.

And I wanted a success. Not for the bitch-goddess or for professional reasons, but because with a single hit the Hollywood ethos would forgive everything it imagined of me. And after Hollywood, the world. It was my main reason for taking on the job.

Useless. Clare came every night at this time. I gave up, closed the book and thought of her. In one way I could do it coldly now.

She had been a starlet. Even when most in love with her I knew that she was completely without talent. I thought she realized it, too. But that was before the party, the night when to defend herself she killed Phil Greco, the night the publicity started.

Publicity was inevitable. The setting was Hollywood. The story a film script in itself. A small fair-haired girl, abandoned by her drunken husband, struggling for her honor in a darkened room. Phil Greco, known mobster, West Coast vermin, as the papers called him. The swing of the heavy ornament, the groan, the skull-shattered body on the floor.

Reader-identification was complete.

Any American wife would have done the same, would have borne herself with equal dignity throughout the trial. American womanhood and all America cheered the acquittal. And Super Studios, realizing they had a national heroine under contract, cashed in and took up her option. They gave her the treatment.

Her face gleamed on a million shiny magazines. She had dancing lessons, a voice coach, the grooming was on, the big parts coming. She had always been a little hard, like most starlets, but she grew metallic now, contemptuous of me. I did not move in the same circles. I drank more, and one night I hit her. That same night, a few hours later, she crashed over a mountain side and died in a burning car.

There it was, as the public saw it. If I had stayed sober at the party she would not have killed Phil Greco. If I had not struck her a drunken blow—

As the public saw it and as I could not escape it.

I got to my feet, impelled, and went into the other room to see the boy. I felt no warmth. It was Clare's image there on the pillow. I stood looking down at him, and suddenly my guilt was insupportable. I returned quickly to the other room, snatched up my notes, skimmed through the book and looked at the cast list. But Clare was there with me, a multiplicity of her in all her aspects.

A loving bride, an indifferent mother, an ambitious bit-player growing harder. A contemptuous fury and a final complete fake. Publicity, fan mail, requests for photographs. All signed personally, Adoringly Yours, Clare. The hours she practiced the flourishes because her own handwriting was so bad.

I came to a standstill in the middle of the room. I looked at Barry Kevin's cast list.

Clare had never written me a letter. There were short notes left on tables, half glanced at, thrown away. A barbed hand, barely legible, falling, scrawled like this one. Exactly like this one.

Sweat sprang out on my forehead. I felt it trickle down to my eyebrows. The cast list was in my wife's handwriting.

I folded the paper carefully, put it in my pocket, went downstairs and took my raincoat from the peg in the hall. Fay appeared at the living room door, then Chester at her shoulder saying something about crazy of thinking of going out on a night like this. I did not hear properly. I said nothing. Then I was in the car and whining through the pelting night toward Beverly Hills.

I thought once of the police. Only because I was speeding. I was afraid of the police. Tires hummed, lights flicked, neons snaked across the road in wet reflection. The car climbed, driving itself, trees swished, the buildings thinned. Then I was through the open wrought-iron gates and crunching onto the gravel parking space.

Only the Thunderbird was there. It had not moved. I parked beside it, leaped out and ran for the front door. From the side of the house a window cast light across the drenched lawn, through rain falling like a bead curtain, hissing through the trees, gurgling in the gutters. I rang. I shivered. I put my finger to the button and held it there.

Nobody came.

I dodged off the porch and ran around to the side of the house. Earth squelched underfoot, and grass licked my ankles. Beyond the sun windows the room was empty, looking with the brown furniture like a bad film set. I fumbled at the handle of the French door, stepped inside and stood dripping on the carpet.

"Sonofabitch!" the parrot shrieked. It moved sideways and stiff-legged along the perch away from me, muttering to itself. I stood a moment then called, "Mr. Kevin." The rain hissed at me. "Mr. Kevin," I called, and shut the French door.

The sudden silence was an assault. "Mr. Kevin." I walked through the adjoining door and felt for the switch.

Light burst from the chandelier.

The room was empty.

I stood a moment listening to my ears pound. I looked all around the room and saw the piece of green jacket wedged in the closed wardrobe door, down near the floor. I thought detachedly, No, he's not a man to be careless with his clothes. I went across, slid the wardrobe wide open and looked down at him.

He was smaller than he had ever been. He was lying in a heap, on his back, his knees up and his neck at a strange angle. He had been beaten to death.

FIVE

I don't know how long I stood there. I reached inside the still-warm jacket for a heartbeat and felt the rubber corset ripple under my fingers. I sought a pulse in his wrist, in his neck, and I discovered why he was lying so strangely. His neck was broken. He was not long dead.

His gaping smashed face was making me feel sick. I wanted to turn away. I saw the tiny tobacco shreds on the shiny wardrobe floor where they should not have been, the others clinging to the jacket. I fought off the nausea and searched him.

The two side pockets contained only loose cigarettes. The breast and inside pockets were empty. I could not bring myself to feel into his pants. I patted. Nothing. I felt all over the body. Nothing. Either he had been carrying nothing or whoever was there before me had made a thorough job. I stood up and concentrated for a full minute on keeping my stomach down. I had my hand over my mouth.

"Sonofabitch!" the parrot shrieked in the other room.

There was a faint click. A door had shut.

"Sonofabitch!"

I jumped for the window. But it was too late for that. Whoever it was would see me before I got away. I was in bad enough as it was. Escape would bring further incrimination. I thought of police, of what lay ahead, and my stomach tied in a knot. I walked into the other room.

"Sonofabitch!"

Empty.

I looked at the French door. The cast list was in my pocket. Clare's handwriting. I changed my mind, ran across the room and flung open the door to the hall.

Darkness rushed down the wide staircase at me. "Anyone here?" I called, and began to walk forward. "Anyone here?"

I came to a halt in the middle of the floor and looked about me.

Light from the other room gleamed dully at the corners of the paneling. My mouth was dry; I was conscious of the wet raincoat collar about my neck. "Anyone here?" I called for the last time, and thought I saw one of the panels move. Panic hit me. I fought it down. I went on again, opened the front door, closed it behind me and walked slowly through the slashing rain to the car.

I drove away.

On the hill I began to shake. Sweat was running down behind my ears. I thought of the police again, fingerprints, they were validly excused by my having visited Kevin this afternoon. The wife could testify. So could Bertha. If the fingerprints were discovered and checked. I had no intention of going to the police voluntarily. I had had enough of police for one lifetime.

I would not think of Clare until after I had had a drink.

I pulled up at the first bar I came to. It was a long, ill-lit, dingy place with booths along the wall and tables in an open space at the far end. I sat at the bar and drank Scotch. I thought of nothing else but that. I concentrated on it. In a booth behind me were a bunch of beatniks talking loud in baggy sweaters and conceit. I concentrated on them.

They looked like tired old Orientals. They were discussing without emotion last night's experience with last night's chick on last night's borrowed pad. A bunch of little Huysmans without the sophistication. The semiconscious fabricating a self-conscious world to live in. Two were calling one another sweet and darling. One said, "My little marrowbone." Without emotion. I envied them.

Emotions were for people like me.

I had more Scotch.

She was dead. She was *dead*. The writing only looked like her writing. Dead in a car crash. I identified her. There was no error, burned as she was. It was her car, her wedding ring, her shoes with those buckles. I had killed her as she killed Phil Greco.

But no need to start all that again. Best to stay out of everything. Barry Kevin was nothing to me. I was merely on a visit. I did not get a job, but I did not come for one, I was not expecting one. No bones broken. Forget everything, especially that I had been there tonight. And forget that for reasons of his own Barry Kevin had most elaborately tricked me into saying that he wrote like a woman.

The writing only looked like her writing. She was dead.

Ted Wilson walked in the door.

"Al!" Arms flung open. "Al boy!" banging me on both shoulders. "Goddam you, you old sonofabitch, long time no see." Then pounding the bar. "Drinks, barman, drinks! The terrible twain are with you and happy days are heeahruhgain."

He looked drunk. I had never seen him any other way. We had been fellow-alcoholics working for the same studio when he was in public relations, one of the men who had built up Clare. He had liked her. He would talk about her in a few minutes.

The Scotch came up in my throat.

"You old bastard, what are you doing here? They said you were East." He was older than he acted by many years, but he was guilt-ridden by his drinking. He had to be overgenial to suppress his fears. "Boy, this really calls for a celebration." He banged my arm again. "You back to work for somebody?"

"Just a visit." My voice sounded peculiar. I had to say something more. "You still PR with Super?"

"What Super?" He downed his drink in a gulp and rapped for more, grinning all the time. "Lost your grip in New York there, boy? You're slowing up." He knocked off his second and smacked his lips. "Two more, barman." He said, "There's no Super any more. They shut down. Goddam TV on every lot. They tell me you been trying that stuff. Any luck ?"

I moved my head.

"Took a shot at it myself. Couldn't make it. I quit the business altogether. I'm a legman now on the *Gazette*. And don't tell me I'm too old for it."

Suddenly he was looking at me closely. I had to speak. I said, "Maybe Super will open up again."

"Never closed," he said triumphantly. "Things in this town are never what they seem. Super merged with Splendid. Super took over TV, and Splendid sticks to movies. Bigger than ever. Bigger bastards."

He drank again. I had not realized before how fast a drunkard will drink. He said brightly, "They took advantage of the shuffle to get rid of the mature guys who were pulling in the money. Guys like me. We got the cross. You never saw so many knife-flashes in the dark. Know who wound up on top? I'll tell you. Leo Holst. The same bad-tempered bastard Leo Holst that I nursed through his first pictures when he first got here from Chicago back in the forties. I can't even get near him now, he's so important. I don't want to get near him. So what the hell, let's have another drink on it."

"No," I said.

If he had not been drunk before, he was drunk now. Surprise chased across his face, then resentment. Then a thick sympathy. I knew what was coming.

"Sure," he said. "Tough being back, eh? It's bound to be like that at first. But all the brooding in the world won't bring Clare back, so I'm not going to let you brood at all. Barman! Two more!"

"A minute," I said, and slipped from the stool and went outside into the rain.

I stood a moment. I put a hand on the wing of the car and vomited the whisky into the running gutter. When I had finished I wiped my mouth with a handkerchief. One of the hipsters was leaning against the wall, watching me with a detached sadness.

I said, "Bud, could you tell me how I get to the Top Hat?"

"I guess maybe I could."

"A new joint, is it?"

"I kinda think so. Second left, fifth right, second left again and way out past the end of Laurel. Spew again, man. That's really living."

I was all right now. Stone sober. I got into the car and drove off.

SIX

The Top Hat was almost out in the country, a fair-sized place standing back from the highway and surrounded by trees. It had a man to park the cars, a foyer lined with pleated silk, a big doorman and a pretty hatcheck girl. The doorman looked like a tough.

I sat on a stool at the recessed bar, holding a cuba libre but not drinking it because the smell alone made me want to throw up. I was the only person at the bar; I had held the drink nearly half an hour now, and the barman resented that. In the big dimmed main room a discreet band was playing the *Handel's Largo* cha-cha and a few people were dancing on the special sprung floor. When the music stopped you could hear above all the other voices the shriek of a female TV star who wanted to call attention to herself and was drunk.

I never knew how much drinking went on until I had stopped.

The weather was keeping customers away. Those present were famous, recognizable and had money. People came and went, but none that I knew personally any more and none who wanted to know me. To placate the barman I held the glass to my mouth as though I were drinking.

The man came into the foyer.

He gave his wet black coat and white scarf to the hatcheck girl, who had come especially from her nook to take them. He smiled at her, patted her, came down the two steps to the main room and crossed to a plain door in the right-hand wall. The barman called, "Mr. Frascatti, sir." The man sauntered over.

He was young. With no sexual overtones, though he had those too, you could say he was beautiful. Overpoweringly good-looking. Medium height, well-built and moving with suppleness. But there was weakness in him somewhere.

"Hello, Mike," he said. "This all we got tonight?"

"Yes, sir. Weather, I guess."

"Give me a bourbon."

His voice was deep and caressing, smooth, soft. Falsely so. He was trying to fit it to his appearance. Everything about him was a little overdone—the shoulders of the expensive tuxedo a little too wide, the waist a little too narrow, the teeth gleaming a little too white in his too-brown face.

The Adonis features under the helmet of curls knew how good-looking they were. He seemed supremely confident. Until you saw his eyes. *A West Side Story* slum kid looked out of them, a still not fully-grown man neither convinced nor quietened by what his exterior was trying to be. That was where part of his weakness lay.

He and the barman moved to the other end of the bar. I heard the barman murmur something about "Lady waiting office, Mr. Frascatti," and they both lowered their heads. I watched them in the mirror on the back of the bar. Frascatti frowned.

"Yeah, I'll see to it." He straightened. "Keep everyone else out." He left his drink untasted on the bar, winked at the barman and disappeared through the plain door.

Music played. The TV star screeched with laughter and everyone stared at her, which was what she wanted. The barman looked at me from the corner of his eye.

"That was a nice-looking guy," I said. "Actor?"

"That's Mr. Frascatti, the owner. Can I put some ice in that drink for you, mister? It must be near boiling point."

"It's how I like it."

He grinned at me bleakly. His head jerked up and he called, "Hey, miss! Just a minute, miss! Miss!"

She came away from the plain door and over to the bar, a blonde child not more than seventeen years old, fragrant and innocent and very beautiful. She wore street clothes and a wet raincoat, and her big topaz-colored eyes shone with a clear candor. I had seen eyes like that once before today. I had seen her before. She was the girl who had been driving so fast in the Jaguar.

"I'm looking for Mr. Frascatti," she said.

"Yeah, well he's not in yet. I'm sorry. Can I serve you something?"

"Rum and Coke." She glanced at me without interest. She looked around and back to the barman and said, "You wicked man, you told me a lie." She turned away. Frascatti was emerging from the office.

His expression was blank. Mrs. Kevin was behind him, with glittering eyes and a flushed face. He made a half turn to say something to her and saw the other girl approaching. I did not watch any more. It would have been too obvious.

I took some money from my pocket, played around with it, then put five dollars on the bar in case I ever needed the barman again. I got off the stool. The others were back in the office now with the door shut. I went slow to the foyer, got my coat from the hatcheck girl, told her what lousy weather it was and made jokes about the Californian spring. I tried the same jokes on the doorman. He was not receptive. I said my car was the yellow Ford, and the man ran off to fetch it from the parking lot. I stood and looked at the rain.

I felt her behind me, and turned. I said, "Good evening, Mrs. Kevin. Bad night."

"What's that?" Then she recognized me. She made an effort and brought herself under control. "Mr. Dufferin. Fancy running into you again."

The man said, "Your car, sir."

"Is mine fixed yet?" she asked.

"About fifteen more minutes, ma'am."

"Then call me a cab."

I said, "Mrs. Kevin, can I drop you anywhere?"

She hesitated. "Can you take me home?"

My stomach lurched. "Glad to." I opened the door for her.

We drove in silence. Rain dashed at us, and droplets wriggled down the windows like transparent tadpoles in a race. I looked from the corner of my eye at her hard, handsome profile. She was leaning back, puffing too hard on a cigarette. I did not know where or how to start.

I said, "Nice place, the Top Hat."

"It's a sink."

Silence again, all the way through town. We began to climb. A car passed with a slash of headlights, and I saw how tight and thin her mouth was around the cigarette. I said, "I was rude to you this afternoon, Mrs. Kevin. I'm sorry."

"What? It was more than probably my fault. We can all get oversensitive about what happens to those we love."

She took a last deep drag at her cigarette, wound down the window and threw the butt out into the rain. She said, "Were you and my husband talking business this afternoon?"

"Yes," I said. "About a film. He wants to do Cellini."

"That's news. Who sent you to him?"

"The idea was his. He called me. I don't even know how he knew I was in town."

"You could ask him," she said. "Did he mention backers?"

"No."

The rain thudded on the roof. We swept through the gates and up the driveway to the gravel parking space. The Thunderbird was not there.

"Well, thank you, Mr. Dufferin," she said. "I can offer you a drink if you like."

"It doesn't matter."

"I'd prefer it. So would my husband. He likes to know with whom I come home."

"All right," I said, and switched off the engine. We ran for the front door.

"Maid's night off." She fumbled a key from her handbag and got the door open. I closed it behind us while she switched on the hall lights. She called, "Barry? Barry?"

Within the sound of rain the house was like a tomb.

"Barry?" A light shone from the open door of the sitting room. She crossed the hall with me at her heels, entered the room and went directly to the bar. "What will it be?" she asked, and turned to the parrot. "Shut up, you filthy animal. It is supposed to be amusing that this parrot swears. What was it you wanted? Don't mind if I don't join you, but I don't like the taste of alcohol."

"Scotch." The adjoining door was open, the bedroom beyond in darkness. She mixed one highball, came over from the bar and gave it to me. "Barry?" she called sharply. "Barry?" Then she walked past me and into the bedroom and switched on the light.

I looked at my glass. I saw my trembling hand and tossed down the whisky in one gulp. She came out of the bedroom and said, "Seems to me you really needed that drink. Have another." She removed the empty glass from my hand and went back to the bar. "Same again?"

"A little more ice," I said hoarsely.

She glanced at me strangely. I turned away, moved to the French door and gazed out at the drenching night. I saw the mud that I had previously brought in on the carpet. I moved slowly, automatically around the room until I came to the door of the lighted bedroom.

I looked in.

The wardrobe door was wide open, with all the clothes neatly in place. Everything was as it should have been—except the body of Barry Kevin.

There was no trace of it.

SEVEN

She said, "As my husband doesn't appear to be home, Mr. Dufferin, perhaps you had better drink this up and go."

I went over to where she stood with her back to the bar, her damp hair honey-colored in the light. She turned her topaz eyes on me, looking at me strangely again. "Mr. Dufferin, are you unwell?"

"Thanks. No. But I'll drink this one more slowly."

"Take any reasonable time you like. But one thing. Don't finish by making a pass at me or I shall be bored. Bored and nasty. If you will accept that fact, we can go on to the light conversation. Did you say Benvenuto Cellini?"

"Renaissance period," I said. "The Florentine artist."

"Yes, thank you, I was vaguely aware of it. I've read that lying autobiography twice. Ideal for my husband. Are you going to build it into a part for him?"

"I hope so. I'll have to work on the basis of how he goes about building a part for himself." I set down my drink and pulled one of the old film scripts from the bookcase.

The bold handwriting flowed on every page. "Blow cigarette here." "Slow to left profile narrow eyes." "Looking down with tragedy-mask mouth." "Close-up here essential for anguish."

Nothing like the handwriting on the cast list.

I said, "Did your husband write these comments, Mrs. Kevin?"

"All of them." Her lips curled faintly. "Years ago, of course, because he has not been working lately." She straightened. A car was coming up the drive.

"This will be him," she said. "You can have a third drink now if you like." She went out into the hall.

There were a few moments of silence. The front door opened and shut.

"Why oh why oh *why* did you have to go down there and interfere?" the girl shrilled.

"Be quiet, Gloria. Stop acting. We have company."

"What's that to me? I don't care. Why did you have to go down there and stick your nose in? He sent me home."

"He did? What a surprise. I didn't think he had that much decency."

"Stop sneering. He loves me. He's the finest man in the world."

"He's a cheap third-rate hoodlum with a fourth-grade education. He loves a great many females. It's his profession. Or do you consider him just a poor crazy mixed-up sexual maniac?"

"You don't understand and you never will," the girl said, suddenly calm and dignified. "He loves me deeply. He has proved it to me. And you can't stop me seeing him."

"I'm your legal guardian, and you're a minor. I shall call in the law."

"Just try it."

"Go to bed, Gloria."

"I shall not. I shall try to forget with drink."

Her heels came clicking across the parquet floor of the hall. She entered the sitting room and stopped dead, hostility in her eyes. "I've seen you before," she said accusingly. "You were at the Top Hat. Are you in on this with Karen?"

Mrs. Kevin appeared behind her. "My sister, Gloria Mason," she explained drily. "This is Mr. Alan Dufferin, the writer."

"Alan Dufferin?" The girls eyes widened. All at once she smiled and came forward with outstretched hand, her voice gone early Hepburn. "Awfully glad to meet you, Mr. Dufferin. Sorry you were let in on the family squabble. You heard, I suppose."

"I couldn't help it."

"Dear Karen means well, bless her, but she doesn't know what she's talking about. She thinks I need protection."

"She thinks Mr. Dufferin needn't be bothered with the details," Mrs. Kevin said.

"Why not? He's a writer. He'll be interested. I've nothing to be ashamed of. You see, Alan, I happen to be a friend of Frankie Frascatti. He used to be a hoodlum but now he's going straight for my sake, only my sister won't give him a second chance. She thinks he's after my money. Why, Frankie earns so much with the Top Hat he could retire now if he wanted."

She turned on her sister. "Today wasn't the first visit you paid him."

"Did he say that?"

"I guessed it. That's why he's always been so discreet about where he meets me."

"You little idiot," Karen Kevin said. "He's discreet because he doesn't want his lady customers to find out about you."

"Don't you dare say that."

"And don't you start again. Mr. Dufferin is not interested, and I am very tired. Mr. Dufferin, are you going to wait for my husband?"

"I don't think so. It's late now."

"Alan, don't go." The girl was mixing herself a stiff highball, stirring at it vigorously with a swizzle stick. "Stay and talk to me about movies," she said. "Your movies. You know, I think you're one of the greatest writers Hollywood has ever had. I saw *Love Veil* and *The Dark Night* and they were marvelous. Absolutely the most. Don't you want to make films again?"

"Yes," I said.

"Of course you do. Everyone wants to make films." Her eyes glowed. Suddenly her chin was up and her arms straight at her sides, palms spread downward, in the affected pose of every obsessed little girl who ever received applause in a high-school play. She said, "I would give my life to make a film. One will be enough to make me famous. I shall not change my name, Alan, because Gloria Mason has a ring to it, don't you think?"

"It's pretty," I said. She looked like any girl in Bertha Tweedy's waiting room. She looked like all of them when the fever gets them. She looked like my wife.

She said, "If I could only get the right part written for me—"

"Gloria, Mr. Dufferin has heard it before. We all have, and it bores us. Let's call it a night and off to bed."

"Aren't you going to wait up for Barry?"

"No. Mr. Dufferin, the rain seems to be slackening."

"Yes, I'll be on my way."

I moved without thinking toward the French door.

"You'll get your shoes muddy out there," Gloria Mason said, and glanced at my feet. "But they're muddy already, so it doesn't matter. When do we see you again, Alan?"

"Very soon, I expect," her sister said. "This gentleman and Barry are apparently discussing a film project."

"What that? What?" The girl pressed two hands to her bosom. "Oh Alan. Darling Alan. Will there be a part for me?"

"Mr. Kevin makes the decisions."

"So try and persuade him, Gloria. It might keep you home some of the time. Good night, Mr. Dufferin."

The girl saw me across the hall. "Good night, Alan."

"Good night."

The rain was tapering off. When I got down to Hollywood, it had stopped altogether. The time was after midnight, and I drove straight on out to Los Olmos, parking in the street because my brother-in-law's garage was only one-car.

I went into the house.

Chester was sitting in a chair with Johnny in his arms. The child was asleep. "Something up?" I said. "Is he sick?"

"Ssshhhh." My brother-in-law made a quieting face. "Bellyache or something," he whispered. "He was crying upstairs. I didn't want him to wake Fay."

"I'll take him," I said.

"He might wake up and start again. I'll sit a while longer. I'll take him into my bed."

I saw his arms tighten. We looked at one another across my sleeping son with a total lack of mutual sympathy. I said, "Please yourself. I'm going up."

I left them.

EIGHT

It was a bright morning full of warm sun and the fresh smell of earth after rain. The street on which my sister lived was on the outer edge of the suburbs and had houses on only one side. The other side was thickly wooded. This morning the trees were full of perfume and birds. Spring was advancing, and the jacarandas would soon be in bloom.

I went to the bathroom.

Below the open window Chester was getting his car from the garage, preparing to drop Johnny at school on his way to the office, as he did daily. His voice floated up, cheerful and bright and mock-ferocious. "Get in, you little bum, or I'll run you down."

The boy hooted with the ecstatic laughter of the very young being menaced. "Not going to."

"I'll use my machine gun on you. Tat-tat-tat-tat-tat. You're dead."

"I'm not. Come and catch me, Uncle Chet. Catch me."

Scuffling and laughter and a trajectory of sound as the child was swung through the air. "You dog, I love you."

I understood why my brother-in-law did not want me there.

Doors slammed, gears meshed, the car whined off into the warm distance. A smell of coffee and bacon drifted up from the kitchen, together with the voice of Fay singing *Sheep May Safely Graze,* tootling like a Disney sound track during the recorder rest bars. Fay had been a Bach addict ever since I could remember.

I finished shaving.

The kitchen table was set for two, the screen door was open and the sun shone a nice lemon color on the back porch. "How many eggs?" Fay said. "Brother, you look a bit gaunt this morning. The thought of this Kevin job getting you down?"

"No, it's because I wasn't drunk last night. Did Chester say?"

"Now, Al." She put the plates on the table, fetched the folded morning paper from the porch and sat opposite me. "Delicious. Smell that coffee. The only moment of the day I can kid myself I'm a lady of leisure. Work hasn't started yet and those two have gone."

"I heard them."

She flashed me a quick look and concentrated on her coffee. She said, "Wonder if the rain yesterday did much damage," put down her cup and opened the paper. She sucked in her breath. There was a palpable moment of pause.

"Oh God!" she said.

"Give it to me."

"Al, don't." She clutched the paper to her. "It'll make you feel terrible."

I reached over and took it.

Big banner headline. *BARRY KEVIN KILLED.* A black-bordered front page. A fifteen-year-old photograph of Kevin at his handsomest.

At the head of the lead paragraph was: *Mountain death spot claims second star victim.*

The picture of Clare was on the center page.

I folded the paper and numbly drank my coffee. Fay carried away both untouched plates and went into the other room, and I was grateful to her. I took up the paper again.

Both dead in the same manner. The paper could not make enough of it. Both had turned at the same corner, plunged over the mountain at almost the identical spot, gone hurtling down to be burned to death far below.

A flash picture of Karen Kevin surrounded by reporters at the door of the house. Stills from a selection of Kevin's past films. "And so one of our greatest dramatic actors has made his final exit, leaving us with only the precious memory..."

Separate features on other brilliant lights extinguished by violence. Dorothy Dell, Lupe Velez, Carole Landis, Robert Walker. James Dean, greatest of all. And lovable brave Clare Dufferin. A separate feature on Clare Dufferin. They couldn't resist it.

It was a Hollywood paper. There was nowhere a hint that Barry Kevin was a has-been or that pictures were on the skids. Kevin had been loved wherever pictures reached—everywhere. Messages were pouring in from admirers all over the world. His former wives had tried to express their unspeakable grief. The present widow was hiding her tears in the great and gracious house that had been his home.

Inquest that afternoon. May he rest in peace. Nothing that told me anything. I went into the hall and dialed a number. "Mrs. Kevin, please."

The answering voice was dark, fraught with tragedy, the voice of a bad dramatic actress. "I am sorry, but you will understand that she is speaking to no one. Would you care to leave a message?"

"Tell her Alan Dufferin called."

"Alan!" The voice changed. "Isn't this perfectly terrible! My poor sister. Why don't you come out?"

"Maybe later," I said. "Good-by."

I hung up.

Fay said behind me, "More coffee?"

"No, thanks."

"Al, you look awful."

"I expect so," I said, and went out to the car.

I drove downtown. I looked up occasionally, through the valley of the hills, out to the mountains beyond. The clearness of the day had gone. The streets were crowded, smoggy, full of exhaust fumes, of coaches advertising television tours. I waited for the light at Vine, went up toward Western, turned left. I pulled up beyond a No Parking sign and entered the building.

The elevator was down. I said, "Miss Tweedy in yet? Third floor?"

The colored operator shook his head. "She does not come in at all on Wednesdays, Sir. The office is shut all day."

"Thanks." I hovered. "Excuse me, do you know if she still lives on Wallace?"

"No, sir. She does not. She moved more than a year ago, sir." He took a little red book from the breast pocket of a uniform and turned the pages. "She is now at the Penon Apartments, sir, on Mortimer. The penthouse."

"Thanks." I proffered a dollar.

"No, sir, I was merely doing my job. I neither wanted nor earned an honorarium. Thank you all the same."

"Thank *you*." I went back to the car.

Mortimer was a recent development out beyond Edgewood, a long stretch of fifteen-story blocks divided from the sidewalk by soft emerald lawns as closely trimmed as pool tables. The apartments had been built with an eye on TV stars who commuted between the coasts and needed a pied-à-terre. They had ramped basement garages, figured façades, large windows. They looked as expensive as they were.

I passed through glass and gilt doors held open by an Armenian admiral, crossed a lobby lined with real marble, entered the elevator and pressed the button. A small tail-coated man shot from somewhere and waved his hands at me through the glass. Then he was out of sight as the elevator rose. It made no more noise than a purring cat.

I alighted. The walls of the upstairs private hall were padded in alternating triangles of red and black leather and made me think of Bellevue. I stabbed a buzzer. Chimes somewhere in the apartment played the first few notes of *The Bluebells of Scotland*. A phone began ringing. I played the tune three times more, the phone continued, the door burst open.

Bertha peered at me from under her wild blue hair with eyes like fried eggs.

She was dressed in a housecoat, and her feet were bare. She said, "What do you want?" and winced. "My head!" She stamped back into the room, tore the phone from its cradle on a small table and said, "What? Oh, it's you, Mr. Tribblestitch." Or it sounded like Tribblestitch. "No, no, he's a friend of mine, he won't do me any harm. Yes, well fire the doorman. And don't let anyone up again without an announcement or I'll move."

She slammed the phone back in place and turned on me. "I was going to invite you in anyway—you merely beat me to it," she said. "Wait till I get something on my feet." She went up a short flight of stairs to a gallery containing two closed doors—a bedroom and a bathroom, I supposed. She entered one of the doors and closed it behind her.

I examined the apartment.

It was a single enormous room built at two levels, with a kitchen door down at the far end under the gallery and a large picture window in one wall giving a cineramic view out to the mountains. On one level the carpet was smoke gray shot with red streaks, and on the other black. The chairs had thin iron legs, bucket seats and were upholstered in black and white fur. They looked as though no one sat in them. On the walls were a Braque, a Rouault, a Raoul Dufy of four men on a stage playing chamber music under a hammering orange light. All the pictures were genuine.

I took the cast list from my inside pocket, looked at it and put it away again. I sat down in one of the chairs and felt as though I'd fallen down the toilet. On the black-topped table in front of me were sticky circles, two dirty glasses and an ashtray brimming with stubs, some tipped with lipstick, others just brown from dried spit. I lit a cigarette of my own. Bertha emerged from the bedroom and closed the door.

She had run a comb through her hair and put on slippers, but she still looked rough. She came down the stairs drinking a bromo from the glass in her hand, so I guessed there was also a communicating door between bedroom and bathroom. "Better," she said, smacking her lips. "I needed that. Well, what's all the panic that gets me out of bed at this hour? How did you know where I lived? I'm not listed."

"Elevator boy at the office," I said.

"William? He shouldn't have done that. You must have been extra polite. He's a push-over for politeness."

"He struck me as pretty nice."

"He's all right." She put down the glass and suddenly transformed. Her eyes went hard and bright, and her hangover was gone. "Barry Kevin. What? Did he make a deal?"

"He wanted an adaption of the Cellini biography."

"Who cares what he wanted? What did he offer?"

"Money."

"Real money?" She was glittering. "Do we visit him, or does he come to the office?"

"Neither," I said. "He was killed last night."

"What?" She stared at me incredulously.

"It's on the front pages. Car accident. The inquest's at three this afternoon."

She moistened her lips. Suddenly she put the knuckle of her forefinger to the bridge of her nose and lowered her head. "Poor little has-been bastard," she said quietly. "Sometimes I hate this rotten business."

Then she was alive again. "Inquest? They may want you as witness. One of the last to see him alive, state of mind, that sort of thing. Do you want that?"

"No."

"You're probably right, the way the cops feel about you."

"And the public," I said.

"Yeah. You were smart to come here. Look. I've got a beach cottage out at La Playa, miles from anywhere. Hole up and pretend you didn't even know he was dead. You went there to work on the script directly after seeing him. Once the inquest is done you'll be safe."

"Thanks," I said, "but I'll stay in Hollywood. I'll keep circulating all day so they don't catch up with me."

She looked at me sharply. "Something else on your mind?"

"Yes." I hesitated. I looked at the Braque, the Dufy and up to the gallery. I looked again at the butts in the brimming ashtray. Someone up there had opened the bathroom door about six inches.

I said quietly, "You alone, Bertha?"

She went right on looking at me. Her face flushed a slow crimson that set her mauve hair to shrieking. "We're friends, Al. Don't presume on it."

I stood up. The chair sucked at me. "Sorry I intruded. I'll be going."

"Maybe that's better."

She walked with me to the door. She even opened the elevator for me. I got inside and stood a moment, unable to leave without asking the question. I said, "Bertha, you heard anything lately about Clare?"

"What's this? Should I have done?"

"I saw some of her handwriting yesterday."

"What does that mean?"

"I don't know exactly."

"Well, if it's important, come back later today when I'm alone," she said, went back into the apartment and shut the door.

I stood a moment longer, then pressed the button and went down.

Mr. Tribblestitch was waiting in the lobby, hands under his coattails and a little smile on his pink face. "Good morning, sir. You must forgive that I telephoned to check on you, but you will of course realize that with such important—"

"Of course," I said. "Miss Tweedy would like you to send up all the morning papers."

"Of course," he said. "Good morning, sir."

I sat in the car and thought about Bertha. Barry Kevin had called her an old nymphomaniac; she had a reputation in that direction, which might explain why she had hired someone like Hymie, who was pretty obviously no use in the office. It was all none of my business. I drove out to the mountains.

I'm no use at estimating the size of crowds, but this one ran to thousands. They had all come by car, and the block was a mile long. I couldn't get near the site of the accident. Everyone was pushing and shoving, crushed kids were crying, the ladies in black were out in force. One had stolen a march on her rivals by climbing to a vantage point where her sobs and wails could be better heard by the public. She was being pointed out as the widow by the man selling picture postcards of Barry Kevin.

I left.

Back at the outskirts I pulled up at a pay phone and got through to the *Gazette*. The voice at the other end told me Ted Wilson had not come in this morning, that he needn't come in any more at all and that he was fired. In the car again I saw a girl who looked a little like Clare. It wasn't Clare and I knew that immediately, but my heart skipped.

I went looking for Ted Wilson. It took hours.

NINE

I found him finally on one of those wide back streets off the end of Sycamore, sprawled across the table of a squalid little joint called Paco's. He was the only customer. At that bar, at that time of the afternoon, it was not surprising. The Mexican barman, who may have been Paco himself, told me Ted had been unconscious for five hours.

I lifted his gray-stubbled face from the sticky table and said, "Ted!" No response. I hoisted him by moist armpits and shook him until his sagging jaw jolted up and down. He grunted, briefly opened red-marbled eyes and shut them hard again. "Go away," he moaned. He snored.

I got a grip round his sagging shoulders and walked him half staggering down to the back of the bar and into a nasty little washroom. Both taps had worn washers and water ran continuously everywhere except in the cubicle, which was blocked up. I propped the body against the wall, turned the taps farther, filled my cupped hands and tossed the water into Ted's face. "Ted!" I said. "Wake up! I'll buy you a drink."

His bleary pink eyes opened wide, and he straightened. He ran a hand through his hair and said reproachfully, "Gee, you were gone a long time." Then he looked around. "When did I come to the john with you? Where are we?"

"A joint called Paco's. How do you feel?"

"Horrible. How do you expect I feel?"

The door burst open.

"You all right, Mr. Wilson?" the barman asked.

"He's not rolling me, if that's what you mean. I got nothing to be rolled for. Two shots of bourbon, amigo. Big ones. Come on, Al. Let's celebrate."

He pushed back into the bar. He saw the daylight at the far end. "Jesus, what time is it? I got to make a phone call."

"I made it," I said. "You're fired."

Despite the smell from the washroom, he sat down at the nearest table. "Second time this month," he said. "Means I can take the rest of the day off. They'll hire me again in the morning. There's no one else on the paper knows Hollywood like I do. They need me. Amigo, the bourbon."

"Before you was drinking wine," the barman said.

"A nightcap. This is morning. I need bourbon like other people need liver salts. Looks like we made a night of it, Al."

"You did," I said. "I just found you here." I smelled the bourbon and shuddered. I said, "Your paper's probably mad because news has broken. Barry Kevin was found dead last night."

"Amigo! Another! Bigger!" Ted had tossed down his first drink. His eyes were swinging from side to side in their sockets. "Barry Kevin? Who'd have thought the little guy had guts enough to kill himself? Most of the has-beens who can't make TV go on the bottle. Maybe he didn't have the dough. He's been broke for the last five years."

"No," I said. "He had influence. He was a pal of Leo Holst."

"What an idea." Ted knocked off his second drink direct from the tray. He nodded for another. "Pals, nothing. They didn't work together, they weren't even with the same studio. Leo Holst is too top-man on the totem for anyone to influence him, and he never had any pals. Let's sit at the bar, Al, for God's sake. It's too long between drinks."

"It's cosy here." I called for the barman to bring the whole bottle. When he was back again behind the counter, I said, "You know Kevin well, Ted?"

"I know everybody well. That's why the paper takes me back." He knocked off a jolt of bourbon that made my stomach cringe for him. "I see it all clearly," he said with increasing geniality. "They'll want follow-up features on Kevin, pretty little intimate things that only my vast knowledge and golden pen can supply. Nothing of course about how he used to swing right across country looking for suckers to finance another picture for him. That would be detrimental to the industry. The advertisers would object. I shall get an up-to-the-minute story by persuading an ex-wife to jump in a lake. I shall write heart-rendingly of the inquest."

"You won't," I said. "The inquest's on now."

"Well, do tell." Ted suddenly laughed. His voice was thickening quickly, and his eyes had become fixed. They looked like boiled tapioca. "On now," he said. "I smell fish. I smell that lavatory, but fish, too. Somebody's rushing."

"It might be your story."

"Oh go on," he said, "don't be so goddam fragrant. If a fish can exert that much influence, he's a big fish. The thing's already fixed from top to bottom. I couldn't get a story out of it, neither could you, neither could the President of the United States."

"By which you mean the fish has bribed whole departments. Nuts!"

"Where you been all your life?" Ted said. "He's bribed no one. He phoned some other top guy. 'Sammy boy, how's the wife, how's everything little thing? Say, that's a nasty business here about Kevin. Not the sort of thing to keep in front of the public, not doing the industry any good. Golf this weekend, Sam? We're having a little party to celebrate Junior's adenoids. Going to be mad as a rattlesnake, Sammy-boy, if you don't come.'"

Ted's face changed. He looked suddenly drunk, bitter, and venemous. "I was PR," he said. "I know Hollywood. The town of the big hush-up. One day I'll write a book about the consequences, about what goes on under this big gilded pie-crust. Actresses hobnobbing with the gangster scum of the country, boozing, supporting a narcotics industry, aborting every second year. Actors doing all that except abort, flouting the Mann Act, importing their own minors and giving boy-parties. Mary Astor's diaries got in the papers and so did Lana Turner's boy friend, but they were mistakes. The rest has been silence. The lid stays on, and people disappear and get beaten-up and murdered just to keep it on. It's on tighter than ever now because the industry's failing. They're all afraid of the final blow that'll knock 'em stone dead."

He stopped and filled his glass. He said, "You're not drinking."

"You're doing all right for two."

"Because you've come and depressed me. My poor old mother could be murdered in this town and I'd be helpless to do anything about it if it meant hurting the industry. I've sold myself, Al, like everyone else here. I'm a he-whore."

He paused. "He-whore. Hell's bells, I sound like a goddam donkey."

He put his head back against the wood of the cubicle, stone drunk as only an alcoholic can get in a few minutes. I did not try to persuade him to quit. I had been a drunk myself, and persuasion is useless. I said, "What have you got to lose, Ted? Start with Barry Kevin. Write your story."

"And lose my job," he said. "And be one of the guys who gets beat up. There's a long list of addresses in this town, pal, where they supply muscle when it's needed. Not officially on the studio payroll, but always on hand. So what do I stick my neck out for? The public interest? The public wants the glamorized Barry Kevin the papers will give. He'll have a lovely funeral, even better than Clare's."

He lowered his head. His eyes had gone out, and there was saliva at the corner of his mouth. "Sorry."

"Forget it." I picked up my glass and put it down again without drinking. "Someone said the other day they'd seen a girl around town who looks like Clare."

"Yeah?" he slurred. "Well, she was ordinary enough. Pretty and nice, but ordinary. I'm glad you're over it, pal. I had a bad time when the wife went. You've got the kid, at least. I just got the bottle."

He picked it up. I said, "What makes you think Kevin was a suicide?"

"What?" He leaned forward and tried to peer at me intently. Then his eyes rolled up in his head. The bottle slipped from his fingers, gurgled in his lap, fell with a hollow sound to the floor and rolled down the bar. He put his head to the table. Out cold.

I shook him. Nothing. I stood up. The barman came from behind the counter with a weary expression. "You going, mister? Can't you take Mr. Wilson with you?"

"I don't know where he lives."

"He pretty damn near lives here," the barman said. I paid and left.

Down the street I tried to phone Leo Holst. He wasn't listed at a private address, so in turn I called Super and Splendid. Both told me he was unavailable. One was shocked that I should expect to contact so great a man, the other amused.

I drove to the Penon Apartments, where Bertha lived, then changed my mind. I went on, bought some gas and idled around for about an hour, staying away from where the inquest was held; then I returned to Los Olmos.

Neither police nor reporters had tried to contact me, and there had been no phone calls of any kind.

TEN

Chester was not there for supper. Wednesday evenings he worked late at the office. When he got home he always made the same joke about fiddling the books, and Fay always laughed and asked couldn't he fiddle her up a mink coat. She didn't really want a mink coat. She wanted a baby.

Darkness had fallen. The night was calm and starlit, and a faint scent was coming through the open window from the coppice over the road. Fay had the child in her lap and was playing him the Brandenberg Number Three on the record player. I was reading the special editions again.

Scenes at inquest. Vast public. Medical evidence that Barry Kevin had been suffering insomnia and taking sleeping pills. May have influenced his driving, especially had he taken a drink. The public should be warned. It struck me as so cynical it was almost funny.

Death by accident.

Next column. Applause for numerous actor and actress friends of the deceased who had attended out of respect. Sympathy for beautiful sister-in-law, little more than a child, weeping continuously. Greater sympathy for wife, also beautiful, bravely not weeping at all. Murmur of sympathy sweeping the crowd as the sisters left together. Sympathy all over.

A special feature for women: What to wear when Death is among us. Little sister-in-law had been clad in a simple frock of stark dramatic black, relieved only by a silver angel on the left breast. Bereaved wife wore a very dark blue—not only permissible but by its reticence showing very perfect taste. It was doubted that either would wear a veil at the funeral. Veils had recently enjoyed a brief vogue, but were out again.

The funeral, day after tomorrow, would be at the Fulfillment Chapel of the Happy Voyager, Tranquil Leas.

"Not a guitar, darling," Fay said. "That's a harpischord. Something like a piano. Mr. Bach wrote this one entirely for strings. Strings are violins and cellos and violas."

I said, "Shouldn't he be in bed?"

"Certainly." She promptly put the child to the floor. "Upstairs, Johnny, and clean your teeth. Directly upstairs, Johnny. Not via the cookie jar in the kitchen."

He grinned at her and ran from the room, not glancing in my direction. Fay pushed the automatic stop on the record player, and the machine hiccuped and clicked and fell silent. She looked at me.

"What?" I asked.

"What sort of father are you? You haven't spoken to him since you got in. He's six. If you don't get his love before he's seven, you'll never get it."

"You want me to smother him with kisses?"

"Yes. Anything. I thought you came from New York to visit him."

"I did. It's turned out different to what I imagined. I thought I could take up a normal life again when I quit drinking. It seems I can't. Let's drop the subject."

"No. You're worried over this Barry Kevin business. It's a pity but not a tragedy, not for you at least. You've got enough money for a few years if you go carefully, so why don't you take Johnny off somewhere for a holiday? Just the two of you."

"Trying to throw us together? This is a new tack. What changed the wind?"

"I was thinking about it today. Johnny's all you've got, and we've no right to take him from you. Chet and I have each other. Now don't get any wrong ideas. I don't want him taken away without proper arrangements, living in a bachelor apartment with some stinking old bitch of a daily maid. Isn't there any chance of your getting married again?"

"I'll think about it. What will Chester say when he finds you're with the enemy?"

"Don't pick on him again." She lifted her head at the sound of an approaching car. She didn't know it, but added happiness came into her face. She said, "He's here now. Change the subject. No need to break it to him too abruptly."

The car slowed down, pulled up, but did not enter the garage. Doors slammed loud in the quiet night, footsteps approached on the garden path, the front bell rang. "Not him," Fay said. "Answer it, will you? Don't buy any encyclopedias. I have to go aloft and tend your child."

I went into the hall and switched on the light. A noise from the far side of the dining room indicated that Johnny had gone to the kitchen despite instructions. I opened the front door.

The shorter of the two men stood to the front. Light fell on his face, and I saw that he was young, dark-eyed, wore dark clothes and was short only in comparison with his companion. Back in the shadows the other man looked like a barn door.

"Mr. Alan Dufferin live here?" The voice was soft, confident and Irish.

I said, "That's me."

"Could we talk to you a little?"

"About what?"

I was expecting it. He reached in his pocket and flashed a police badge. "About Barry Kevin," he said. "About a document he gave you. You still have it?"

"In my pocket."

He nodded and stepped back a couple of paces, turning sideways. He said over his shoulder, "Or would you prefer that we came in?"

"No." I stepped out after them, feeling almost relieved. I said, "Are you Los Olmos cops?"

"Hollywood. We're going down to headquarters for a statement."

"I'll drive behind you."

We were in the garden. A large hand gripped my arm, and the other man loomed beside me like a pyramid. He had a disproportionately small head and reminded me of a badly made snowman. He used perfume. The Irishman said, "No, we'd hate you to run away, Jiggs. And it's not a long walk back if we can't bring you."

The big hand was propelling me to the street. I said, "I'll tell them in the house where I'm going."

"No need, you won't be long," he said, and took my other arm.

There was a large black Buick parked by the trees on the other side of the road. We stopped beside it, but no one opened a door. The street was silent. The shorter man said, "Let's consider this, Jiggs. We'll make a deal. Give us the paper, tell us what you have to say and maybe there's no need to go to headquarters."

The smell of trees was overpowered by the scent on the big man. I looked at the lights across the way. I said, "I'll make an official statement."

"Tomorrow. We know what you're going to say. You saw Barry Kevin yesterday and made some sort of dirty deal with him, and he gave you a document to keep."

I said nothing.

"Now you're going to give it to us."

"It's in a bank."

"What a terrible liar you are." He smiled. His hand flicked, and a gun stuck in my ribs. "The document, bully boy. I mean now."

"In the house," I said. "I'll get it..."

"That sounds like a ruse. A nasty twisty devious device to deceive honest men." He nodded to the giant, and my arm shot up my back. I started to struggle, and the arm nearly broke. I bent nearly double, and then I was being run off the sidewalk and into the trees.

The other big hand came around and damped my throat. I went up on my toes and kicked back. Twigs plucked me. I was half carried farther into darkness. My arm was released, the fingers tightened at my neck, and I was slammed against a tree. Tiny expressionless features peered down at me. The shorter man said, far off, "Soften him."

A fist sank into my stomach, and I stopped breathing. The big man shifted his stance, moved his clamping hand from throat to chin and held me a moment almost delicately; then he swung his other hand wide open and hit me on the side of the neck. It was very professional I dropped to the ground like a lead weight.

Irish stooped beside me. "Dufferin, lad, where's the darling document?" he whispered. "Come now, you're not as bad hurt as all that. My chum was only playing."

I was only dying. I tried to reach for my pocket, and the giant fell like an elephant and knelt on my arm. "Naughty," Irish said. "He thought you was after reaching for a gun." His hand went to my pocket and found the cast list. "This it?"

I made a sound.

"Because if it isn't, we shall be back to visit you. And meantime you'll not talk about this because, you see, we're *secret* police." He laughed lightly at his joke. He said, "Know what will happen if you do talk? Like this."

He jerked his head. The giant moved again and put one knee on my chest. It was like being overlaid by a tank. The shorter man stretched nonchalantly and put a hand tight over my mouth, and the big man pulled a blackjack from his pocket and spat on it. Then, with the precision of a machine, he began beating at my thighs.

"If it was your face," Irish murmured. I was fading fast. From the garden over the road Fay called, "Johnny, where are you? Johnny! Have you gone out?"

The blackjack stopped.

The shorter man got lightly to his feet, the gun already in his hand. He said softly, "Stand still!" and moved like a cat. He said, "Why hello, little sonny boy, and what are you doing out at this time of night with your mother calling you? Off with you now. Scat!"

He looked back, then hissed, "We blow."

The weight lifted from me, and I fought for breath. I heard the car go. I summoned all my strength, moved my head and saw my son a short distance away, like something from the forest, looking down at me, his eyes glinting bright in the dimness.

Then he was gone.

Fay said, "There you are, you wretch. What new game is this? Inside with you." Her footsteps retreated. Silence fell. Another car came up the road.

It drove into the garage. Chester called, "Home, Fay." I grasped the bole of a tree and pulled upright. I hurt like the devil. I smelled the leaves and the lingering cheap scent, and I waited for the night to stop revolving. I staggered back across to the house.

They were in the kitchen. Fay was taking a warmed-over supper from the stove, and Chester had the child in the air, throwing him to the ceiling, catching him. They were all laughing. Fay put the plate on the table, looked up and went pale. Chester swung the boy to the floor. Fay said, "Jeepers, Al, what's the matter with you?"

"Johnny," I said. "Johnny, why didn't you tell them where I was?"

He looked at Fay, at Chester, at the floor. He put his tongue on his lower lip, raised his head, glanced around for encouragement and blurted, "Uncle Chet, the men were smacking him."

"Smacking who, son?"

"Him."

"Who?"

"Him." His lip quivered, and he started to cry.

I said, "Fay, get him out of here."

"Yes."

She whisked him from the room. I waited till her footsteps sounded overhead, with Chester staring at me. He said, "What's this, Al?" and he was frightened. "Was someone really beating you up?"

"You heard what the kid said. Where are you going?"

"Call the cops."

"Stay where you are."

"Al, we must. It's all right. I got a lot of friends down there."

"I'll bet," I said, and looked out at the night. "You got a gun?"

"Yes. I belong to—"

"Give it to me."

"Al, I can't do that. It's licensed under my name."

"Let me have it."

"Al, I'm sorry, but—!'

I left the room.

Upstairs I packed a small suitcase, then went along to the bathroom. Fay was soaping the kid's back. I said, "Sis, I'm moving."

"Where to?"

"I'll let you know."

"Wait!" She stood up and followed me. She said, "He's been telling me. You have to realize he can't act like an adult. He's only just six."

I said, "Get back there before he drowns. And try to keep your husband's mouth shut."

I went.

ELEVEN

I did not register at a hotel. It would make me too easy to trace if anyone came looking for me again. On a back street I found a building called the Ellesmere Apartments. The name was its only elegance.

The hall needed sweeping, and there was no desk. The handwritten sign on the wall telling inquirers to knock at Apartment One and ask for Mr. Rowton was flyspecked and yellowing. Mr. Rowton himself was a part of the whole. He came to the door in undershirt and suspenders, a short fat watery-eyed man with a kindly, sloppy face and a smell of beer.

He didn't like being disturbed. I told him my name was Kingston and paid him a month in advance. After that the disturbance lost its importance, and he didn't care if my name was Khrushchev.

There was no elevator. The apartment was third-floor front, with two rooms, a kitchen, a bathroom and a wall telephone dating back to Theda Bara. The cooking stove in the kitchen was greasy, and the look of the bed decided me not to inspect the mattress. The sitting room furnishings were a frayed armchair, two other chairs and a table containing two ashtrays advertising radio tubes. From the opposite side of the street the neon sign of a bar flashed red and green into the apartment whether the lights were on or off. There was a frowsty smell of old fat and bed fluff over everything.

Mr. Rowton approved of me. He twanged his suspenders and invited me down to his place for a beer. I said that I had to go out again, that I had a lot to do. When he had gone I sat in the frayed armchair and wondered what I could do. You can't make a tackle in any game until you know who's holding the ball.

My legs ached from the blackjack. I was depressed enough already, so I didn't look at them. I sat and watched my hands change color as the sign flashed from across the way. I got up and opened a window. The opposite bar was full of customers. A juke box was playing, and I needed a drink. I went into the bathroom, doused my face and looked at myself in the cracked mirror.

There was a mark on either side of my throat, but otherwise I was passable. I took a long drink of water, then went out and looked at the phone book. It was two years old, but Leo Holst had not been listed even then.

I called Los Olmos. Fay answered.

"Yes, I'm all right," I said. "Fay, I talked pretty mean there this evening. How's Johnny?"

"Still awake. Sobbing his heart out. Chester's with him."

"Oh," I said. "Fay, if anyone calls, you don't know where I am. Say I've left Hollywood."

"I already did. A man phoned half an hour ago."

"Any name?"

"No, but he sounded like an Irishman. I don't think he believed me when I said you'd gone. He left a message. Are you ready? You can't get away with it. He's coming back for what you didn't give him. Al, I'm scared stiff. What is it?"

"Nothing important. Nothing to concern you."

"Anything to do with Barry Kevin?"

"Listen," I said, "don't try to be astute. Keep your nose clean. Tell Chester under no circumstances to talk to his cop friends. I'll call you again in the morning."

I hung up, took another drink of water and went out.

In the bar across the way, the juke box was silent but the drunks were singing. I left Hollywood by way of the back streets and headed for Beverly Hills. It was a nice night, the time going on for eleven. I thought of the paper that the Irishman hadn't got. What paper? I had to make a move of some sort.

I parked the car in the shadow of a tree beyond the white stucco walls of the garden, turned off the lights and walked back. The wrought-iron gates were locked. I looked around me. Nothing was moving. I went up the gate, hooked my jacket a moment at the top and dropped to the other side, onto the gravel path. I felt a numb pain in my legs, but it went away when I rubbed them.

The big house was in darkness. I used the overgrown lawn, to avoid making footfalls, but I had to cross the gravel parking space in the end to get to the front door. Also locked. I did not ring the bell. I got up on my toes again and gritted round to the side of the house.

The French door yielded under first pressure.

I stood inside, waiting for the parrot to scream. I stood for what seemed a long time and wished I had brought a flashlight. I felt for my cigarette lighter. I would start with the bedroom.

I took one step forward, and the light came on.

Karen Kevin was on the brown leather sofa, one hand holding a glass, the other on the lamp switch. She wore a plain dark blue dress that fitted the description of the one she had worn at the inquest. Her mouth was slack, and her eyes were blurred. She had taken sleeping pills and then drink. She was plastered.

"You," she said slowly, and finished the contents of the glass. "I thought it was another reporter. What do you want?"

She spoke as though speech was something new she had just stumbled on.

I said, "I came to offer condolences."

"Very welcome, if not a lie." She got teetering to her feet and went to the bar.

She said, "What does it matter so long as you're not a reporter or a souvenir hunter? Have a drink. I find I rather like it."

She tilted the bottle and poured half the contents on the bar. It made her giggle. She put the bottle down carefully, weaved back and sat again on the sofa. She said, "You pour them. Make them large. I'm going to get drunk."

She was already. I thought I knew from experience what she was going through, and I was sorry for her. I handed the glass into her nerveless hand. I said, "You shouldn't sit in the dark, even to avoid reporters. They'll find you."

"Finding me is all right," she said carefully. "The wearying part is that they expect me to put on a show, like rending my hair and beating my breast. Why the hell should I when I'm not suffering at all?" She chewed her lower lip and began noiselessly to cry. I sat beside her.

"Oh, do go away. I've had enough sympathy for one day." I stood up again. She said with sudden boozy dignity, "Would you mind, Mr. Dufferin, filling this just once more?"

I did as she asked. It was not a commendable action, but I had to get her talking. I said, "You shouldn't have been left alone, Mrs. Kevin. Where's your sister?"

No answer.

"She could have stayed away from Frascatti for one day."

"Frascatti." Her lips curled. She showed beautiful white teeth like an angry dog. "That pimp!"

"Is he?"

"Trying to tell me he's in love with her. I've been through it all before. I married the other little egotist because of her. Now she's mixed up with someone even worse. Well, I'll tell you—I've finished with her. I've locked the gate. She's not coming back except on my terms. He won't want her when he finds she can't get the money until she's twenty-one. She'll be back."

"Of course."

"The trouble is I love her so." Tears appeared in Mrs. Kevin's eyes. I knew now what she was suffering about. It was not Barry Kevin.

I sat beside her and poured more drink in her glass. I said, "I heard your husband used to go in search of money. I didn't know he tried to batten on women."

"On anyone. Anything to finance his comeback. He'd have married Gloria and then found a legal way of getting the money in advance. He was capable of it. He thought I was going to be even easier, but I fooled him. Oh, what a married life we had."

She stopped abruptly and frowned at me. She said indignantly, "But all this is none of your damned business, Mr. Dufferin. Go away. No, I don't want more to drink. What are you doing here?"

"Offering sympathy. I phoned earlier today, but you weren't speaking to anyone."

She raised and lowered her eyelids with distinct effort. She said, "I don't believe you. You're a liar. You must have climbed over the gate."

"I also want to find out if you know anything about the picture your husband was going to make."

"Another lie. What picture? There wasn't one. He'd have been preening and primping and squawking all over town about it. He was finished. He knew it. He had no money and no friends."

"He had influence with Leo Holst."

"I've never heard of Leo Holst." She raised and lowered her eyelids again. The glass slipped from her hand and hit the floor with a bump. The carpet drank her whisky. She said, "What's your game, Mr. Dufferin?"

"Did your husband have any special papers? He may have kept them in a safe somewhere, or in a locked drawer."

"I'll tell you what he did keep." She stood up and steadied herself with one hand on the arm of the sofa. "He kept a gun," she said. "If you don't get out of here, I'll use it on you. Get out! Now!"

I stood up with her. Then I saw the parrot. It was lying over in a corner with its neck wrung. Mrs. Kevin made a staggering run toward the bedroom, and I made for the French door. In her condition she was capable of anything.

I went down the gravel driveway, not worrying about footfalls, and over the gate. I had to go on a little way to find a place to turn the car. I came back slowly, and Karen Kevin had managed to get down the driveway. She was opening the gates, staggering as she swung them wide, her head lolling.

I did not wait to see whether she was all right but drove on and down through Hollywood. The time was a little before midnight. I parked the car out of the way and arrived at the Top Hat on foot.

The doorman did not recognize me, and the hatcheck girl pretended she did. The place was fuller tonight, livelier, with most of the people in evening dress. The TV star was back again, drunk again; she may have been a lush, but who was I to judge her? The bartender recognized me, but did not greet me.

Half an hour passed.

I was forced to drink two drinks for appearances' sake. Frascatti did not show, and neither did Gloria Mason. While the barman was busy with a flurry of newly arrived drunks, I went over quick to the office door and knocked.

No answer. I turned the handle. Locked.

"Mr. Frascatti's not in tonight."

A waiter was behind me. He looked hard, but not tough, and was merely giving information. He said, "Mr. Frascatti is off this night every week. The under-manager will be back in a while, if you'd like to wait."

I shook my head and left.

From downtown I phoned Ted Wilson's paper. He would be in in the morning, which meant he had his job back. I drove some more, parked the car again at a good distance and walked the rest of the way to the apartment block where Bertha lived.

The lights in the vestibule were on, but the big main entrance was locked, because of the time of night. There was no apartment index outside, and only one buzzer. I leaned on it.

A tail-coated man came from the office. He was not Mr. Tribblestitch but may have been his twin brother. He glided across the vestibule and slid open a grill in the big main glass panel of the door. He said politely, "Yes?"

"Miss Bertha Tweedy."

"She cannot be disturbed, sir."

"Tell her it's Alan Dufferin."

"Very sorry, sir, but she left explicit orders."

"Then give me her phone number."

"I regret, sir, but that above all is forbidden."

"Good night," I said.

He nodded pleasantly, closed the grill and glided off again to his office. I crossed the street, lit a cigarette and looked up at the light in Bertha's window. I was sucking down smoke, trying to think, when a big husky guy came along on the opposite sidewalk, ran up the steps and pushed the apartment house buzzer.

He was Bertha's employee, Hymie. He talked through the grill to the twin brother. I couldn't hear his words, but he was protesting; I knew by the sound. Finally, convinced that he could not enter, he went away. I finished my cigarette and returned to the Ellesmere Apartments.

I worried about where to leave the car; I did not want to post a sign for anyone seeking me. I settled for another back street, went up to the apartment, sat in the dark in the frayed chair and watched the room turn alternately green and red.

The neon sign quit flashing at half past three in the morning.

TWELVE

I awoke late, shaved, showered and examined the bruises on my thighs. They were dark and wide, but more tender than hurting. They did not affect my perambulation. I could still run if anyone chased me. While I was dressing I caught myself whistling.

I called my sister.

"We're just fine." Her morning brightness sounded forced. "Johnny went off to school happy as a bee. You?"

"I'm downtown."

"You're staying on then. You're not going back East."

I said, "All right. What happened?"

"Nothing."

"Tell me."

"Two men came looking for you last night. I think one was the Irishman who phoned beforehand. They wouldn't believe you'd gone. They tried to force their way into the house. Chester got his gun, and they went away. He threatened to call the police."

"And did he?"

"No, you asked him not to. What's it all about, Al?"

"Nothing I can't handle."

Fay said, "Barry Kevin's wife phoned this morning. No message. She said it wasn't important."

"I'll call you later," I said.

I stood a minute or two with the receiver in my hand, then got through to Bertha's office.

Lona Forman, the redhead on the switchboard, was delighted to hear me. We had a chat. She varied her range so much it was like an audition for several different voices. I almost recommended her to try radio. I was sorry I had no influence to use for her.

I said, "Bertha?"

"Make it quick, Al. I've someone here."

"I tried to visit you yesterday."

"I heard. It was too late. Only residents get in at that hour. Look, I'll contact you later. Where are you at?"

"I'll come to your office at lunchtime."

"Okay," she said. "See you."

I put on my jacket, locked the apartment, went out and up the street to the nearest drugstore for a counter breakfast. I was the only customer, and the clerk stared at me. The eggs tasted of soap, the bread was blotting paper, but the coffee was all right. I finished my second cup, went into the booth and called Ted Wilson's office.

"Pardon my breath if you can smell it from there." He was croaking with hangover. "I'll talk to you if it's urgent. If not, go away."

"It's urgent," I said. "Information. You claim to know everyone in town. Who is, and where can I find, a professional mug? He's around five-ten, one-eighty, dark clothes, twenty-five to thirty and talks phony Irish soft without moving his teeth much."

"Never heard of him. I'll look around."

"He has a pal. Six-six, three hundred or more, uses perfume, has a—"

"Pinhead Johnson," Ted said. "A muscle man. If his brains were Klieg lights they wouldn't brighten a matchbox. He's been around so long he's a fixture. He's worked for everyone in his time, but they all had to let him go. He's just not bright."

"Who's he working for now? Where do I find him?"

"I'll check. You have me interested. Anything more?"

"A young guy named Frankie Frascatti," I said. "He runs the Top Hat."

"And a very interesting case. It is rumored that he suffers from satyriasis. Mere propaganda for his occupation. I shall be delicate. You earn a living with your pen; he, if you follow my meaning, earns it with his pencil. A hired stallion for elderly mares, very discreet about it, but there are no secrets in this town. Three months ago he blossomed forth as the alleged owner of the Top Hat."

"Alleged?.."

"That's how I figure it. The meat boys get gifts, not ready cash. The lady friends don't want them to be too independent. He's persuaded one of his more stricken old crones that the Top Hat is good business. She'll be backing him."

"Does he have any young girl friends?"

"He wouldn't dare to. His sponsor would whip the Top Hat from under his feet like an old carpet. Again, that's only how I figure it. Anything else?"

"The connection between Barry Kevin and Leo Holst."

"None. You asked me before. The only connection with Holst now is by indirect prayer. He's God."

"What time do you finish tonight?"

"Don't know yet. Call me back."

"We'll go somewhere for a drink."

"Fine. There's a guy here claims it helps if you brush your tongue with fresh water. Not your teeth, your tongue. Any truth in it?"

"Could be. See you."

I went out to the counter, changed a bill from the staring clerk, then got back in the booth. Karen Kevin herself answered.

"Hello." She was trying to be pleasant but sounded as hard as usual. She said, "I woke this morning with a vague feeling that I owe you an apology. What happened last night?"

"You threw me out."

"Why? Were you making passes at me?"

"You were talking a lot. You got a sudden idea that you'd talked too much."

"And had I? What was I saying?"

"Where are you from, Mrs. Kevin?"

"Cleveland."

"Well, you were saying that your husband was once in Ohio trying to whip up backing for an independent film. Starring himself. He met your sister Gloria. The Mason girls had money, maybe enough to finance his comeback, and Gloria was film-struck, which made her an easy mark. She was underage, but that presented no great difficulty. He decided to marry her. He would have managed it, but you made promises and he married you instead. The promises were not kept. He didn't get a nickel. Life was painful, and your late husband is neither lamented nor a loss. That was about all."

She said, "Yes. You're nearly right, Mr. Dufferin. My name was not Mason, because Gloria is my half sister. I'm her legal guardian. I promised my mother to look after her."

"You love her a great deal."

"I do."

"You threw her out, too, last night, over Frankie Frascatti. But you unlocked the gates for her to come back again. You're making a mistake, Mrs. Kevin. You can't stop a spirited girl when she's in love."

"Perhaps you are right. But I can stop Frascatti. I have a private detective working on him. Thank you for telling me what I said, Mr. Dufferin; it was my only reason for calling you. Are you going to sell the information to the papers?"

"They wouldn't use it," I said. "I'm not broke. I dislike papers only a little less than I dislike cops. But I would like some information. Can I come out and see you?"

"I'm too busy. What was it you wished to know?"

"Anything about the film your husband intended to make."

"There was no film. He was finished. That was why I asked if anyone had sent you to him."

"What was his relationship with Leo Holst, head of Super Studios?"

"None, so far as I know. Super is television, isn't it? My husband was against television. It would have made him act his age. He still thought of himself as a youth."

I said, "Did he ever mention my wife?"

"Isn't she dead?"

"Did he mention her?"

"No. Why should he?"

"I might get an answer to that if I could look at his private papers. Did he have any?"

"I don't think so. You asked me that last night. Or did I imagine it?"

"I asked and you waved a gun at me. I'd like your permission to come out and take a look around."

"I've already refused it. I don't want you here. I don't want anyone. It's bad enough with—"

She stopped, then said, "You broke in here last night."

"You could stay with me while I searched. You could do the searching yourself."

"How very generous. What are you looking for?"

"I don't know."

She said, "Mr. Dufferin, there is an odor about you. I might call the police."

"And I might talk to the newspapers."

She paused, then said, "I was expecting something like that. Tell them that I maintained my husband from the day I married him. Tell them that I must even pay for the funeral."

She rang off.

I went back to the counter and had another cup of coffee. Halfway through it the soda jerk said, "Ain't you in TV?"

I shook my head.

"I seen you somewhere." He kept on staring and said, "Dufferin. Husband of that babe who committed suicide or something."

Then he blushed.

A week before I'd have hit him. Now I only paid him. I went out and down to the back street where I had left the car, got in and drove away in the direction of Super Studios.

I was going to try and see God.

THIRTEEN

There was a line-up at the studio gate. The people in front of me took turns at wheedling, cajoling and insulting, but none of them got in. A car swished up containing a superior blonde and the big gates opened; then the guy in the line-up that had formed behind me tried to sneak past with the exhaust fumes. The gate guards strong-armed him out, and the gates shut again.

My turn.

"I've come to see Mr. Leo Holst."

The desk guard was walled off from lesser people. He spoke through a device set in a sheet of solid glass. He had a derisive eye, a genial sneer and was lofty but compassionate like a minor deity. His job made him that way. He said, "I like to see a man aim high. Got an appointment?"

"No."

"Beat it!"

"He'll see me. Tell him Dufferin."

"Sure. You got influence. You're Mr. Holst's cousin. Beat it!"

The guy immediately behind me tried to get in good by giggling. The guard needed no encouragement. He was appreciating himself. He smiled broadly, gave a little flick of his head and leaned forward, his eyes narrowing slightly. "What name was it?"

"Dufferin."

"I'll see."

He picked up the phone beside him and started to speak. The ingratiating smile on his face indicated he was addressing a superior. I did not hear what he said. He had switched off the apparatus in the panel.

He nodded. He gave me an amiable smile, put down the phone, took up a pencil and wrote out a chit. He switched on the gimmick again, then leaned forward and slid me the paper under the panel like a banker giving me a million dollars. "Yes sir, Mr. Dufferin. Mr. Bannion will meet you, sir. Pass through the door, please."

The door was alongside the panel, and it looked as though it would lead into the guard's office. I turned the handle. I pushed. Nothing happened. There was a click as the guard pressed the release button, and then I was in a long bare artificially-lighted corridor with another door at the far end. Studios like to protect themselves.

The only thing lacking was a man to frisk me. Maybe someone was watching for suspicious bulges from a hidden slot. I went the length of the corridor; there was another click, and the far door opened. I stepped back into the sunlight.

Mr. Bannion was waiting. He had been very quick. Perhaps he had come on his scooter.

He was an impeccably dressed dainty little man with a pale face, a large thin beak, enormous cowed eyes and a tic. He was around thirty-five and the artistic type. His air of nervous fear fitted as neatly as his suit. He was afraid because he was a Yes man. The day was coming when he would be expected to say No, would say Yes through habit and get fired. He knew that. It probably haunted his days and nights. I said, "Mr. Bannion?"

"Mr. Dufferin?" He held out a small manicured hand. "Such a pleasure to meet you. I've always so much admired your work. *Love Veil* was wonderful."

"It had a good director."

"No, the dialogue, the way you built the tension. And the *construction!* Absolutely superb! All the studios must be simply hounding you."

He stopped pumping my hand and frowned. "You want to see Mr. Holst. I'm not sure that's quite possible. Shall we see?"

"Let's."

He hopped along beside me like a small gay tropical bird. We went past the fountains and the landscaped gardening, along an alley between the sound stages and past the line of one-roomed offices where they lock up the writers for the day. An unmounted posse of cowboys drifted by. Two babes in beads were talking to a group of Confederate soldiers. I said, "Making lots of movies, Mr. Bannion?"

"Well, mostly TV, actually. We have only one theater movie in production at present. *Blood of the Ghoul.*"

"Frightening."

He looked to see how I meant that. He took me by the elbow and steered me around a corner, past another fountain and into a building, standing alone, that might have been designed by a Corbusier gone mental. "One moment," he said, and left me standing. He disappeared through a door.

I looked around. I remained standing because there was no place to sit down. The room was large, circular, black-tiled and lined with classical statuary. The father in the Laocoön waved frantically at a sophisticated Nike; Apollo Belvedere modestly averted his eyes from the Venus de Milo. She was in no condition to wave. I went over to the Laocoön and tried to figure out, not for the first time, which way those snakes were going.

Bannion appeared, beckoning, at his door.

"In a good temper today," he whispered. "Busy, but he'll give you a few minutes. You realize this is a great privilege."

"Indeed yes."

He had me by the elbow again, whisking me through a powder-blue-carpeted office containing a clean, shiny desk and a thousand books under glass. He tapped on a door. Something grunted on the other side. He opened the door, ushered me in and piped, "Mr. Dufferin, sir."

After the two anterooms the place struck me as a broom closet. Sunshine poured through the window onto litter. About five hundred dog-eared scripts lay everywhere. There was a wastebasket, a spittoon, a desk piled with mountains of paper. Behind the desk, filling the chair and the whole room, was Leo Holst.

He looked as big as a small house, a massive man in the middle-European manner. He was smoking a cigar. His skull was flat, hairless and brown, and his big mouth split his face like a cut in a melon. His nostrils were as big and as wide-open as his little mud-colored eyes.

He studied me without speaking. The four circles of eyes and nostrils made me think of a hippopotamus emerging from a tropical river. He was in no way pretty, but power radiated from him like heat from a furnace.

"Sit down."

I sat down, feeling cramped, the sunlight in my face making it impossible now for me to see him properly. He yawned cavernously. I half expected Bannion to hop into the maw like an attendant bird and pick the brown teeth with his beak. "Yaaagh," Holst went. He smacked his lips, put his cigar back in position and talked to me through the smoke.

"Busy man, Dufferin. Let's get down to it."

"Thanks for seeing me."

"I always see a man of talent."

He burrowed into the heap on his desk and came up with a small sheet of paper. "Report from New York. Man of mine seed a TV show you done there— *The Granulated Egg.* Movie stuff, he says. Grade B, but it'll play the art houses and make dough in Europe."

I said, "That was six months ago. Why didn't your man contact me?"

"He contacted me first. Everybody contacts me first. You're contacting me. Okay. I'll offer fifteen thousand clams for the rights on this thing."

I said, "I'm not interested."

There was a pause. Bannion fluttered behind my chair. "Mr. Dufferin," he said reprovingly. "Fifteen thousand is a very good price for a B."

"Shut up." The cigar dropped, sizzling, into the spittoon. Holst spat on it. "Twenty thousand."

"It was strictly small screen. You couldn't blow it up without killing it dead."

"What's that to you if you get the dough?"

"I don't want to sell."

Silence. The muddy little eyes studied the ceiling. Holst ran a tongue like a shoe sole around his upper teeth. "The good Christ save me from guys with the artistic conscience," he said. "Okay, you don't want to hurt your reputation. I respect that. A guy with talent got to be respected. What work you doing?"

"None."

He said, "You wouldn't win no popularity poll in this town, but that makes no difference to me. You got talent, experience and integrity. I can use a guy with integrity. How'd you like to come back to the stable? Six months with option."

"For how much?"

The hesitation was fractional. "Two thousand a week." He lit another cigar.

"It's not bad," I said. "What would I do for it?"

"You're asking me? You know that end of the racket better than I do. Sit in your office, write, polish, adapt, anything that comes up."

"Bannion tells me there's only one theater movie in production."

"So what? You know TV as good as movies."

"I prefer movies."

"I wish the public did."

He grinned. It put leather creases in his cheeks from the corners of his mouth to his ears. He said, "I get it. You're trying to peddle a private movie script of your own. What you got?"

"An epic. Four hours of action, spectacle, Cinerama and technicolor. It'll make *Ten Commandments* and *Gone With the Wind* look like comic strips."

"Well?"

"Benvenuto Cellini."

"Cellini." He blew out a long blue plume of smoke. "I'll tell you something, Dufferin. I've threw out more cold scripts on Cellini than you've had cold Martinis. Forget it. The subject's a turkey."

"Not in my script."

"In any script."

"You haven't seen mine. I've a cast lined up with a special part written for everyone. I had the star role slanted for Barry Kevin, but you know what happened to him."

"Got killed," Holst said. "You got nothing else to do, Bannion?"

"Yes, sir."

I moved the chair to get the sunlight out of my eyes. The door closed as Bannion went out. Holst dropped his second cigar in the spittoon, spat again and leaned forward with both hands flat on the desk.

"Something you want to tell me?"

"Ask you," I said. "Why did you see me? Why was the guard told to expect me?"

He was big enough to lean almost right across the desk. I could see the open pores in his seamy brown skin. He said softly, "A word in your ear, Dufferin. Nobody shakes me down. I'm too big. If I lift a phone or clap a hand or wink an eye, you won't be around any more. I won't even have to send flowers to the funeral."

I grinned. I said, "You great big tough man. You couldn't buy me, so now you try scaring me. To me it's just wind from a big fat bag."

He leaned clear across the desk, swung a fist and knocked me off the chair.

I sat a moment, then got up from the floor, stood straight and brushed myself down. I said, "Didn't your mother ever tell you that temper will get you nowhere? Let's settle down to a quiet conversation. Item one. I have the document."

He was on his feet at the other side of the desk, less impressive standing because his legs were short. He was crimson in the face. I expected him to shout, but he whispered. "You ain't got the document. I don't care what you told Kevin or Kevin told you. I don't care if you read it. You can't do nothing when you ain't got it."

He started coming round the desk at me. I said, "Seen my wife lately?"

He stopped, put a clenched fist on the desk and said evenly, "I'm gonna call a couple of guards, you sonofabitch. I'm gonna see you when they've finished."

We stared at one another a moment longer. I turned around and went out through the door.

"Reached an agreement so quickly?" Bannion fluttered out from behind his desk. *"I am* so glad. There are legends about Mr. Holst as about all great men, but you see for yourself he can be wonderfully reasonable if you catch him in the right mood. You've been lucky, Mr. Dufferin. I have a job keeping people away."

I said, "Is your name Gabriel?"

"Adrian. *Why* do you ask?"

"Bannion!" the voice roared from the other side of the door.

"Yes, sir." The little man blanched several shades whiter and fled.

FOURTEEN

The electric lock clicked, and I was inside the gate in the sunshine again. The guard looked up, nodded pleasantly, winked and returned to the girl who was pestering him.

She said insistently, "I must talk to Mr. Holst. If he's not listed in the phone book and I can't speak to him here, how do I reach him? Tell him it's very urgent."

"It always is, girlie. Go away. Stop bothering me. And like I told you yesterday, don't come back tomorrow."

"Beast," she said, and turned from him, biting her lower lip. She was dressed in a green frock with gold bits on it, and she looked springlike and even younger than usual. She did not look as though she had attended an inquest yesterday or was going to a funeral tomorrow. I said, "Hello, Miss Mason."

She released the lip and the frown disappeared. Her candid eyes shone with pleasure. "Alan, how lovely to see you. Did you really just come out of that closed door?"

"Yes," I said.

"Can you get me in? Oh, please get me in. I've been trying for two days now. This awful man just sneers."

"It's his job. What do you want in for?"

"Well obviously, you silly. If I could only see the right people and get a screen test—"

"You know who the right people are," I said. "Asking for Holst."

"Isn't he the very top? I don't talk to underlings."

"Your daddy must have been very rich."

"He was. Fat lot of good it does me." She shrugged. "Well, tomorrow is another day. If I come back often enough, I'll erode a way into the studio. Shall we go?"

We walked down the line of cars. The Ford was wedged between a Plymouth and her smart-looking gray Jaguar.

She said, "Will you drop me somewhere downtown? I came by bus. I have to do some shopping."

We got in.

She lay back against the seat, her head almost on my shoulder, her clear cognac eyes gazing dreamily through the windshield at nothing. She said, "You going back to work in movies?"

"Not in the foreseeable future."

"What were you doing at the studios?"

"Listening to an offer of work. I turned it down."

"Oh," she sighed, "to be in a position where one can accept or refuse as the whim takes one. Oh, to be important and famous. People don't like you because they think you killed your wife, but they still want you. I don't blame them. I love your films."

"Thanks. What other scriptwriters do you favor?"

"Oh, all sorts."

"Hemingway and Faulkner?"

"They're a good team. They've made some good movies." Her head drooped slowly to one side and touched my shoulder. "Couldn't you use your influence to get me a part? I don't care how small. Just get me in the studios."

"No."

She was silent a moment. "I shouldn't have mentioned your wife," she said. "I was only repeating what I heard, but it was tactless. Forgive me."

"Did you ever see her?"

"Your wife? Once. In a movie. A lousy little B about gangsters. Just between us, Alan, she was terrible. I've got heaps more talent than she would ever have had. Why did the studio decide to build her up?"

I made no answer. In a while I said, "Didn't your brother-in-law ever try to help you?"

"Him," she said. "That drip. He couldn't even help himself. He was washed up."

"He had a picture in view."

"You said that before. Who told you?"

"Your brother-in-law."

"Wishful thinking."

More silence. I said, "I heard you were fond of him at one time."

"You've got it the wrong way around. He wanted to marry me, the silly old ham. I wouldn't even consider it. He married my sister instead. I warned her, but she was infatuated."

She stretched herself luxuriously, like a small golden kitten. She said, "I shouldn't talk like this when he's to be buried tomorrow. I suppose there'll be thousands of people there. I shall weep again. It's my natural reaction to a dramatic situation."

I said, "Some of the people may be from studios. It'll be as good as a screen test."

"I thought that at the inquest. Did you read my press notices? Wouldn't it be wonderful if someone did take me up tomorrow?"

"Wonderful." I pulled over to the curb. We were in the shopping area. "This do you?"

"Already? I'll stay with you a while. Buy me a Coke."

"Sorry." I leaned across her and opened the door. "I have business."

"I'll sit in the car and wait for you. I won't be a nuisance."

"I've something else to do than try and find you film work," I said, and gave her a little push out on to the sidewalk. "Visit Frankie Frascatti. He's more entertaining than I."

She said earnestly, "No one is more entertaining than you. And I'm finished with Frankie Franscatti. I never want to hear of him again."

"Your sister will be pleased. Good-by."

"Can't I see you later?"

"I have another date later. Good-by." I unsealed her hand from the side of the car and drove away.

Two blocks on I looked back. She was getting into a cab. I turned a couple of corners, parked and went on to Bertha's office.

The Brando boy was there again, and the same number of girls. They may have been the same girls. It's hard to tell in Hollywood. Lona Forman lifted her lovely red head on the other side of the barrier and gave me a dazzling smile. Hymie only looked to check me, then looked away again.

"Mr. Dufferin, what a pity. Miss Tweedy waited for you all morning. I had express orders to show you right in no matter who was with her. Now she's out. She left just five minutes ago."

"For where?"

"I don't know. Lunch, maybe."

"Bertha never goes to lunch," I said, and walked through the swing gate and opened the door.

The desk was covered with unopened food cartons, the office was empty. I turned back. "Sorry, Miss Forman."

"Perfectly all right, sir." She fluttered pitchblende eyelashes. "After the reception I gave you last time I don't blame you. Are you going to wait?"

"When will she be back?"

"She didn't say."

"I'll call later."

"But wouldn't you like to leave an address or a number?"

I shook my head and went back through the swing gate. The Brando boy had lounged into position.

He had seen all the Kazan movies. Lee Strasberg would have loved him. He put his chin in his collarbone, writhed his lips and said in a whining mutter, "See all y' pitchers, Mr. Duffn. Great stuff. Lotta punch. Was gonna call studios t' see ya. How's I buy ya drink?"

"Not thirsty," I said. "You got the right name but the wrong man. I'm nobody. Why don't you go home, son?"

One of the waiting girls laughed shrilly. The boy's eyes blurted tears. I left.

It was getting on in the afternoon, and I felt hungry. I parked the car on the same back street as the night before, went into a nearby restaurant and ate a big meal. I brooded over my coffee. Getting nowhere.

Back in my seedy apartment I called Ted Wilson. He was not at the office, he had left a message to meet him at the Ivory at nine. I called my sister. Everything was fine. She had fetched the kid for lunch and taken him back to school again. She did not fetch him in the afternoons because he always came home with some older, bigger boys.

Yes, I said, I was fine too. No, I would not visit them for a couple of days. I hung up and went and sat in the armchair for more brooding. I had not slept well for a couple of nights, and I put my head back. Then I slept.

FIFTEEN

I awoke to darkness. The neon light across the way was switched on, and someone was pounding on my door. "Who is it?" I said, and sprang upright. My legs were so stiff I nearly fell over.

"Help me!" Her voice through the door was desperate. "Help me, Alan! I can't stand any more. Let me in. Please, let me in."

I slid the catch.

She was wearing the same green dress, but there was nothing of springtime about her now. Her hair had fallen over her face, her eyes were wild and her mouth hung open in terror. She shut the door quickly and leaned against it with her hands limp at her sides. She made a stumbling step forward, put out her arms and molded herself to me from breast to knee.

She sobbed. She smelled nice. I held her away from me, and her head swayed from side to side like a flower in a breeze. She gasped, "Help me." She gave a moan and clutched again.

"All right," I said, "You're safe here. Sit down over there. What's it all about?"

The moaning ceased. She looked at me clearly for a moment; then a shudder rattled her body. "So sorry." She closed her eyes. "So terribly sorry. Do you have a bathroom? Can I use it?"

I took her. She went in and closed the door.

Minutes passed. The light flashed red and green. I called, "Are you all right?" No answer. I sat in the armchair.

The juke box across the way began a samba. I said, "Gloria!" The bathroom door opened. She stepped out, smiling.

I said, "Now go back and put your clothes on."

She came across the room at me, her hair hanging over one eye clear to her shoulder, emphasizing the whiteness of her skin. She looked like a pearl. She was more beautiful than a pearl. Her belly was flat, her breasts were globes of white with insolent pink tips, and when she smiled her tongue showed pink, too, through the white of her teeth.

She stood in front of me, made a pirouette and fell into my lap. She said, "I fooled you. You thought I was really in trouble. Am I or am I not a great actress?" She took my hand and held it to her breast.

"I really love you," she said.

I stood up and toppled her to the floor. I said, "Go and get dressed."

She rolled over and gazed up at me, resting on her hands, wondering which scene to play next. She pouted and lowered her long eyelashes. She said, "You do not find me attractive, Alan?"

"Yes, but not desirable. And drop the phony foreign accent." I reached out and pulled her to her feet. She immediately tried to close again. I pushed her down into the armchair, and she tilted her head back and looked up at me, still grinning, from under her lids.

"I'm bothering you," she said triumphantly.

"You're acting like a tramp. How did you find me?"

"Followed you. First in a taxi to Bertha Tweedy's office, then to the restaurant. I saw you begin eating and figured you'd be there at least half an hour. I went back and got my own car. When you finished eating I followed you again. I've been watching this building for hours, waiting for you to come out.

Finally I guessed you lived here. Mr. Rowton at Apartment One didn't know what I was talking about till I described you. Then he said you were Mr. Kingston. I came up."

"Why?"

She got to her feet again, all mockery fled from her face, a serious young nymph who merited a better glade. "You're going to think I'm still acting," she said gravely. "You're not going to believe me. I'm in love with you."

"All right, you warned yourself in advance. I don't believe you. Now get dressed."

"I love you. It happened the other night, the moment I set eyes on you. It went *boom!* like an H-bomb going off. It's why I've said good-by to Frankie. There can never be another man the way I feel about you."

I said, "Your feelings are in error. I've got no more influence in films than Frascatti has."

She took a small step forward, her arms half raised in appeal. "Alan darling, I'm not lying. Please believe me." There were sudden tears in her eyes. "Don't you think me beautiful? Can you stand there unmoved? Don't you want me?"

"Yes, no and yes. That's why I'll be waiting in the bar over there. Get your clothes on."

I made a quick exit before I changed my mind.

I didn't want a drink, I needed one. A girl who wanted that much to get into movies was not the type to commence with. I'd never be rid of her. In the bar across the way I downed the first one quick and asked for another. I was feeling pretty noble.

The juke box was playing a tango when she entered. She undulated down the room in time to the accordions and sat on the stool next to me. "Rum and Coke," she said. The bartender and five customers gaped with interest. "Not a very nice bar, is it?" Then she leaned close and whispered, "Fool! You only have to say the word. Don't you like women?"

I did not speak until she had gotten her drink. It gave me time to cool down. I said, "You're overestimating this influence of mine. In Hollywood you're overestimating your own value in bed. This is a bordel. There are thousands of girls here, as young as you are, as pretty and probably a lot more experienced. For a crack at the movies they're all willing to stretch out on the nearest bed. You'll either have to think of a new line, or find someone more important to rope with it."

"I could make you love me. Let me try. Let's get a bottle of something and go back to your apartment."

"Go home," I said. "I've more important things to do."

I got off the stool.

"You wouldn't abandon me in a joint like this."

"Watch me."

She believed it when I paid the bartender. She followed me outside and stood a moment with the neon flashing red and green on the hurt and bewildered young face, which was her latest role. She put a hand flat to the side of her face as though her temple ached. She said simply, "Then, Alan, this is good-by."

"Good-by," I said. "Sweet sorrow and sad now, but we've known from the start, haven't we? that it just could not be. We must live with our memories. I think I shall always remember you as you were that afternoon under the new green leaves, with the sunlight dappling your sweet face and the flowers sending messages of—"

"You're making fun."

"Aren't you?"

She emitted a little sob and ran. She ran about fifty yards, then stopped, opened her handbag, unlocked her Jaguar, got in and drove away. I returned to the bar.

I had two more drinks. A glow spread and felt pleasant, and I wanted to continue drinking. I got the strength of mind from somewhere to quit, pay up and go out into the night. Some of the glow left me. I went flat. I remembered a specific night when I had been drunk and fought Clare, and for a flash in the middle of the street I had a one-second nightmare.

I chewed my lips. I turned into the dim back street where the car was. I opened the door and was about to get in when a man stepped out of the shadows.

He said, "You!"

SIXTEEN

"Hello, Chester."

Ill at ease, my brother-in-law was peering at me, shifting his weight from one foot to the other. "I was looking for you," he said.

"You found me."

He came closer. "Have you been drinking again, Al?"

I said, "And how did you find me?"

"It wasn't me, it was the cops. One of the Los Olmos boys contacted the Hollywood boys to be on the lookout for your car. They phoned an hour ago. I've been waiting."

"I told you to keep cops out of it. Thanks."

He moistened his lips. "Why do you take that tone with me, Al? You always try to bully me. Why is it? Don't you like me?"

"Why did you want to see me? Something the matter?"

"Fay's worried," he said. "So am I, in fact—you know with those guys calling at the house and everything. They looked tough, Al. They looked like hoods. I don't want my wife and—and the kid mixed up with those sort of people. I had to tell the Los Olmos boys to keep an eye on the house. They're a good gang, Al, friends of mine. Some of them are fellow members at the Pistolero

Club. We go bowling together and that sort of thing."

"Get to the point, Chester."

"Just I don't want trouble."

"You have none."

"No," he said.

"But what?"

"Al, I don't know how to put it exactly. You got any work prospects in Hollywood?"

"Not yet."

"Weren't you doing pretty good in New York with TV?"

I said, "You want me to march off again. You want me to leave you in peace and quiet. You want Johnny. You'll feel more secure about him with me three thousand miles away. All this other talk about hoods and trouble is phony."

"You think so?" He looked as tough as he could ever look, and his mouth tightened. He said, "You got any idea what Fay and I went through two years ago on your account, with first that trial and then Clare? There was a whole week when Fay never stirred out of the house. She couldn't face the neighbors. What do you think I had to put up with at the office? Now they know you're back and it's starting all over again. They make jokes. They ask if I've picked you out of any gutters lately. There's something worse than that, too. Johnny's been talking to the kids at school. He came home the other day and asked Fay if—"

"Go on. He asked Fay if his father was a drunk who had driven his mother to suicide."

"All right. Yes."

"You were pretty fond of Clare," I said. "It was nice to brag around that same office about the famous relation who was going to be a big star."

"What's that got to do with it? I didn't come to quarrel."

"You came to tell me to go. You're very anxious to get rid of me, Chester. I'll go in my own good time and take Johnny with me when I do."

He said, "You got no moral right to him. What sort of upbringing would he get with his father always in a bar? The kid's got enough to put up with now."

I said, "He looks like Clare. Do you want him around because you were fond of her?"

He looked at me with contempt.

I said, "You haven't seen Clare lately, have you?"

"You drunken bastard." He turned sharply and walked away.

I watched him out of sight, then got in the car. The clock on the dashboard said nine-fifteen. I went to meet Ted Wilson.

The Ivory was past its heyday. Back in the thirties it had enjoyed a brief chic as a small rendezvous of high-paid stars. The encouraged owner enlarged his premises and, as a consequence, lost his atmosphere and the biggest part of his clientele along with it. The place had changed hands several times since then, going down the scale every time. It was now a resort for out-of-work bit players who wanted to maintain the illusion of being in the swim and of writers who, being writers, didn't care about social scales and didn't earn enough for swankier places even if they did care.

Ted Wilson was alone at a corner table.

"Scotch," I said.

I had three. Chester and the kid and Clare began to fade.

Ted was wearing one of those clever drunks where he felt confident and omniscient and wanted to bang my arm. He was talking loud about the features he had written on Barry Kevin. People glanced with mild interest but no condemnation. As a hang-out for writers and actors, the place was accustomed to drunks.

My own tongue was thickening. I said, "Find anything out today?"

"The eyes and ears of Hollywood," Ted said, and put his hand above his eyes and made cranking movements like the man on the old Paramount Sound News. "Think I'm drunk, eh? The guy has the good old Irish name of Kolanski. Five-ten, a hundred and eighty and older than you thought—thirty-five. Babe Kolanski, a Chicago boy, a graduate of the Royal Revue tavern. Auto theft, so far, armed robbery and two years post-graduate in Joliet. Then he got smart. He came West. The local cops claim to have lost sight, and there is nothing known against him. Nobody knows where he lives. Only rumor says what he's doing. I found this out with difficulty because the man has friends."

"What friends?"

"That's something nobody finds out. It checks with the rumor. He runs a professional mugging agency. He's on call whenever a guy with money wants another guy beaten up or scared or put out of the way. He demands high fees. He has a reputation for a closed mouth and reliability. He can be trusted. That sort of man can make all sorts of friends in Hollywood, the sort whose names you only mention in church when you're crossing yourself."

"Holst."

"You see, you whispered it. In answer to your further question, there was no connection whatever between Holst and Barry Kevin. As far as I can make out, and I make out good, they never even met."

"Did he meet Clare. Did Holst meet Clare?" Ted went almost sober. "What's this?"

"Did he?"

"It'll take longer to find out," he said. "Maybe. They were the same studio. Before the amalgamation with Splendid, she was Super and so was he. He made his last big production for Super. *Elijah*. Cost eight million and has made thirty so far. That's perhaps what gave him his big step-up. Another drink?"

"No."

"Me, yes." He snapped his fingers at the waiter. He said, suddenly very quiet, "And if you're gunning for Holst, Al, count me in. What do you want?"

"Anything. Everything."

He said, "Even if he had an affair with Clare? And don't get tough."

"I won't."

"Because it could be, you know. There had to be some reason for building her to stardom. It wasn't her talent. She didn't have any. It wasn't her looks. In this quarter you can get girls as pretty as that for ten cigar bands. Stop me when your feelings start to hurt."

"I'm surviving."

"Prepare yourself. You never know what might turn up."

He took his drink from the waiter, sipped it, looked at me steadily and said, "There's a guy been staring at you for the past five minutes. Bald. Over by the mirror."

I nodded, picked up my own empty glass and turned my head slightly. The man across the room was leaning well back in his chair, a drink in his hand, the back of his head to the wall. He was big, well-dressed, about forty-five and blond in what was left of his hair. He stared back at me unabashedly.

I turned back to Ted. "Don't know him. A hack trying to dream up a plot. Anything on Frascatti?"

"Yeah, and not too complicated. Until recently he hired out his equipment to half the crumbling old ducks of Hollywood. He was probably checking the field for someone stupid enough to finance him in the Top Hat. I imagine he found her, though maybe she wasn't so stupid. The deal was fixed by New York lawyers. The Top Hat has been floated as a company, and Frascatti is just the manager. One more small item. He has been glimpsed in his car on lonely roads at the dark of night with young girls. Frascatti is a Chicago boy, like me. You can't keep us down."

I said, "Kolanski is Chicago. Phil Greco was Chicago."

Ted rolled his eyes, then shook his head. "No. There's nothing to chase. I'll prove it to you. Until four years ago Phil Greco was—"

He stopped. He said, "Your buddy's coming over. I'd like the load that he's got on."

The bald man had lifted from his chair and was weaving toward us, maintaining his balance with his arms out like flippers. He fetched up with a bump against the table and put his hands down to steady himself. He looked at me with codfish eyes.

"You Dufferin?"

"Yes," I said.

"Then you're a God-damned stinking rotten rat."

All conversation stopped in the vicinity.

Ted said cheerfully, "Sit down, pal. Have a drink."

"I wouldn't drink with this guy. I wouldn't lay in the same graveyard with him after the way he treated that sweet, pretty girl." The man's voice was thick, but ringing. The heads turned; he had everyone's attention, and he made the most of it. "His wife was an angel," he said. "I met her, and she was an angel. I saw her the night she killed that bastard to defend herself, when she needed a man to protect and comfort her. And where was her God-damned husband?"

Ted said, "Getting as drunk as you are now."

"I may be. I wouldn't be if I had a beautiful little girl like that and a lovely little child. I wouldn't drive any woman to kill herself the way this—"

I stood up. Ted said, "Al, if you hit him, it'll be in the papers. That wouldn't be nice. Sit down buddy, old pal. We'll finish the night together. I liked her, too. So long, Al."

"So long," I said.

Somehow I got out. I walked two blocks, entered another bar and stayed a long time.

SEVENTEEN

I went weaving back across town. Another night the cops would have picked me up. Things might have turned out differently if, instead of going back to the apartment, I had spent the night in jail on a drunk-driving rap.

I parked the car on the back street and staggered along the sidewalk. I fell through the entrance of the Ellesmere and almost knocked down a young boy who was coming out. I think he had been talking to the landlord. Rowton was at the open door of Apartment One with a cheerful grin on his kindly frog face.

"Mr. Kingston. Like to join me in a beer?"

I would. I followed him inside.

He was in undershirt and suspenders again. His apartment had the same slack, sloppy air of noncaring comfort as he had. Faded prints of prize fighters hung around the walls, and a cheap alarm clock ticked loudly in an open cupboard. A plastic-covered table was covered with empty beer bottles, and three wooden crates stood stacked against the wall.

He got a fresh bottle, opened it and took a clean glass for me from a shelf under the ticking clock. He poured a beer without much head. He said, "Knew you were a drinking man like myself. Here's to it. Down the hatch!"

We drank.

He said, "No offense. I don't mean you're a drunk. Neither am I. It's whisky and gin makes a guy an alky. No one ever went drunk on beer."

"Thousands did," I said. "They put their first foot forward when they started claiming beer was harmless."

"That right? Then here's to ruin." He topped up both glasses.

He asked, "Didn't I see you somewhere before, Mr. Kingston?" and frowned artistically. "Where you from?"

"New York."

"Coulda sworn. Guess you look like somebody else I see somewhere. I see lots of 'em, keeping a place like this. You know how it is—they come, they go. Shall we fill 'em up again?"

"I don't want any more." I didn't. I put my hand over my glass.

"You didn't even sit down yet. We ain't started."

I said, "I don't want any more."

We looked at one another. It was curious. His smile faded and died. The alarm clock ticked loudly in the cupboard, and I could faintly hear the juke box in the bar across the street. I said, "Were you waiting for me, Mr. Rowton?"

"Yeah, as a matter of fact." The smile came back, broader. He sat down. "Message for you," he said, and put his hand to his hip pocket and pulled out a letter. "Take a chair. Read it. Have another beer. It's probably from the babe I sent up this afternoon. Was she ever some chick! How'd you make out?"

I took the envelope. It was plain and white, and had MR. KINGSTON written on it in block capitals. Nothing else. I said, "Did she bring it herself?"

"Just a gag, Mr. Kingston. It's probably a bill. That boy brought it a few minutes ago. That's why I was at the door. Take a load off your dogs. Have some beer."

I remained standing, opened the envelope and took out the single sheet of paper. The handwriting covered one side only. It said:

My dear Alan:

I wish to make a statement which will be a true account of what happened on the night of the party that made me famous. We arrived at eight-thirty when you were already in your customary state of drunkenness. About an hour and a half passed, during which I myself took one drink and conversed with various people, who have already given their evidence at the trial. Around ten-forty-five you became unconscious from drink and were sent home in a taxi. I continued conversing and had one more drink.

I did not speak to Mr. Phil Greco either then or ever. I never met him.

A little after eleven o'clock I was called into a small private room by Mr. Foxwell, the assistant producer, who seemed agitated.

That was all it said. The handwriting was Clare's.

"Does she want another date?" Rowton asked, on his feet again with a man-to-man leer. He came and stood at my shoulder. "What she say?"

I put the paper back into the envelope and tucked it in my pocket. "You were right. It's a bill."

"Must be a big one. You look sick. What you need is some more beer."

"What I need is sleep," I said. "I'm going up."

He gripped my arm with surprising strength. "Gee, Mr. Kingston, I hate drinking alone."

I unclasped him.

"Wait!"

I turned from the door.

He stared at me with a face gone miserable. Then he shrugged. "What's it to me, anyways? If you don't want to drink, you don't want to drink. Good night, Mr. Kingston."

I nodded and went out.

I had started to shake. I thought of going out to the bar across the street. I needed a drink now more than ever in my life, and not beer. But I also wanted to be alone when I read the letter again. I went up the stairs.

The building was quiet. I went along the landing, opened the door with my key and stepped into a room gone red. I flicked the light switch. I thought a fuse had blown. The room turned green, I flicked twice more, something rammed into my back and the door closed.

"Now don't move now, Mr. Kingston," the soft Irish voice said. "Just the hands above the head and no shenanigans. Come out, Genius. Put the bulb back in."

I smelled perfume. The huge shape lumbered out of the kitchen, and Pinhead Johnson stood on the armchair and screwed the fitting back into the ceiling lamp. The light came on. He got down from the chair and looked at me without interest.

The voice behind me said, "All right, laddo. Turn around."

I turned.

He said, "Jesus, it's you again!"

He stood and blinked rapidly. Astonishment flickered across his face, and he took a swift pace back, the better to cover me with the gun, and stood regaining his composure.

"Hello, Kolanski," I said.

"Hello, yourself. Hello. So you learned my name."

"I learned everything," I said. "Right back past Joliet to the Royal Revue. I've informed the cops. You've had a good run, but this is the end. They're on to you."

He lifted his free hand and waved a finger. "Overreaching yourself," he said. "The local cops are nice boys. It's you they'll be after if I care to pass along the word." He was completely recovered now, his face split in a charming grin. "What a puzzler you are, Mr. Dufferin-Kingston. You must be in the paper business, you have so many. Where would it be this time?"

"Drop the phony Abbey Theater. Where would what be?"

"The little document I come for."

"You got it out at Los Olmos."

"That's a naughty lie. I sometimes wonder to myself if there's a middling honest man left in all the world." He jerked the gun. "Genius. Search him."

"Hold it."

"For what? Procrastination, Mr. Kingston. We want the document. You've got it. We've searched here without result and make the logical deduction that it is on you."

"I've a message for Leo Holst."

"And who might that be? Move, Genius!"

I moved too, but not quick enough, because a ton-weight hand gripped the back of my neck. I resisted. My knees cracked, and I started to bend. With no drink in me I would not have tried what I did. It was just that—a try. I reached behind me, grabbed the wrist, pulled hard and suddenly collapsed.

Pinhead Johnson fell on top of me like a perfumed mountain.

He was too big. He couldn't move fast. I wriggled from under him and sank a shoe in his belly. He squealed, took a slam at me and missed. Kolanski gad-flyed around us, trying to get in a crack with the gun. I butted the big man in the face, and then it was over. He was on his knees with his arm clamped right around me.

I dug in my feet and strained. It was like dragging an ox to breakfast. I fell backward, with him on top of me. We hit the armchair, it went over, the table went over, the ashtrays shattered on the floor. I was finished. He put both hands at my throat and began banging my head on the floor. I wondered vaguely whether I would be killed as Barry Kevin had been killed. I wanted to be unconscious.

The big man heaved up and lifted on to tiptoe by what used to be my throat. My eyes closed, and a sack of wet cement fell on my head. Hands went over me, and the letter was taken from my pocket, and red and green lights ripped inside my head as though the neon sign across the way had been violently stepped up. I opened my eyes to check. A mistake. Pinhead Johnson gave a grunt of fury, took one of the hands from my throat and let fly.

I tried to dodge, but the truck hit the side of my head. I fell to the floor with my eyes rolled up and lay still, while the sign blazed a constant red and someone began a symphony with triphammers. I was not breathing.

"It's here," Kolanski said far away. Another smaller hammer started. He said in a light, friendly voice, "Who is it? Yeah?"

Even farther away the landlord said, "Rowton. Open up."

More voices. A door opening. Rowton said, scared, "What's all the racket? You'll wake the other tenants."

A pause. A whine. "I thought you only wanted to search the place. I tried to keep him downstairs. What you done to the guy?"

"You got your fifty bucks, what do you care? What did you see us do?"

"Nothing. Nothing at all. I never even see you come in."

"So? We blow."

The door shut.

The hammers moved to a steel foundry. I wondered whether, after all, I could breathe, and I decided to try. I drew a great whooping breath and went clean out.

Next thing, I don't know how long after, the telephone was ringing. I opened my eyes, found the light out and lay watching the interesting patterns made on the ceiling by the red and green flashes. The telephone stopped. That was immaterial, because there was no one in the world I wanted to talk to. I put a hand to my throat, wondered if I would ever talk to anyone again, thought I was now breathing fairly well and went off to sleep.

When I awoke the second time my head was clear in an aching sort of way, but someone had inflated it with an air pump. I got to my feet, floated, slipped in vomit and knew why I was not drunk any more. I went to the kitchen, took a long painful drink of water, shrunk my head under the tap to something like normal, then went to the bathroom mirror to examine the marks on my neck.

They were bad. I looked awful. I washed my face, combed my hair and felt a bit better, though by no means euphoric. I mooned around in a half dream, and then suddenly the panic hit me.

Kolanski and his pal would be back. I knew they would. I ran to the bedroom, made a quick change of shirt, packed my suitcase and headed for the door.

The phone rang again.

I got into the passage. The door was almost shut, and the phone was still ringing. I went back into the room with the suitcase still in my hand, picked up the phone and said, "Hello?"

"Alan?"

A woman's voice. I said, "Who is it?"

"Did you get my letter?"

My hand tightened. It was either that or drop the phone. "Who is it?" I said.

"Clare. Your wife."

I only stood there. It was a part of the dream.

She was silent. The juke box played, and the wire hummed in my ear. She said, "Did you get the letter?"

"I got part of a letter."

"Did you find it interesting?"

"Yes. I'd like to read the rest of it."

"Any time you wish, if you swear to secrecy. Do you swear?"

"Yes," I said.

"Say it."

"I swear."

"Shall I visit you tonight?"

I said, "I'd like that, but I won't be here. I'm checking out. I'm moving to the Piers Hotel."

She hung up. So did I.

On the stairs the light was dim. I went down so fast I stumbled. I reached the entrance, looked back and saw the crack of light under the door of Apartment One. There was something that I had to do.

I put my suitcase on the floor, went back across the hall and tapped.
A clink of bottles. Footsteps approaching. "Yeah?" he asked.
I tapped again.
"Who is it?"
And again.
He opened the door.
His jaw dropped; then his face stretched in a large rubber smile. "Mr. Kingston," he said genially, and stepped back an inviting pace. "Come back for that beer?"
I mustered everything I had and hit him. He made a fast backward run, hit the table and fell to the floor with empty beer bottles bouncing off him. He lay still.
There was a lot of money in his pants pocket. He was entitled to the month in advance because I was leaving without notice. I took only the fifty dollar bribe.
I left.
I was down the street, standing in a doorway, for twenty-five minutes before Kolanski and Johnson came back. I waited until they were inside, ran around to the back street, got the car and drove to the Piers.
If they could find me in a back-street apartment, they'd find me anywhere. The Piers is a nice hotel, one of the biggest in Hollywood, and a big hotel would afford me more protection. A figure in a corner armchair looked up as I entered. Hotel detective. It afforded me some comfort. The desk clerk looked up too, oddly, and more oddly after I signed my name, because he knew who I was. I left a call for ten o'clock.
Upstairs I had a shower and examined myself. I looked in the toilet cabinet, found some aspirins and took six. Then I went to bed.
I slept.

EIGHTEEN

I had breakfast in the room while my suit was being sponged and pressed. It was a good big breakfast and, with the prices I was paying, should have been. The man brought the suit back and took away the tray, and I smoked a cigarette. I called Ted Wilson's office.
Not in yet. Expecting him any minute.
I rang Fay.
"Al, a man just phoned. He wants to get in touch with you urgently. I told him you weren't here."
"He leave a name?"
"No."
"Tell anyone else I'm at the Piers."

"Swanky," she said nervously.

I said, "How's Chester?"

"Fine. Why do you ask?"

He had not mentioned our conversation of the night before. I said, "No reason," and we chatted about nothing a few minutes more and hung up.

Ted still wasn't at the office.

I smoked another cigarette, lay back on the bed and waited. Nobody called. There was a bad taste in my mouth, so I went to the bathroom and cleaned my tongue with a toothbrush and fresh water, as Ted had said. It worked. It would have worked better done the night before. I went back to the bed again, picked up the phone and asked for Super.

"Inquiries, please."

"Sir?"

"Max Holman here from New York. I want to get in touch with Mr. Foxwell. It's urgent."

"Can you give me his first name?"

"No," I said.

"I'm afraid we never—"

"Listen, what is this? I didn't come all the way from New York to get a standoff. Foxwell. He was assistant producer around two years ago."

"Mr. Cecil Foxwell," she snapped, annoyed, as I should have been, because I had shouted at her. She said tartly, "Well, I cannot put you in touch with him, sir, because as it happens he is away on location, sir, in Salamanca, Spain. Mr. Foxwell is a full producer now. Good morning, sir."

Another cigarette and more waiting. I could do nothing until they came to me. Another cigarette.

The phone rang.

"Dufferin," I said.

"Yes, I know, Mr. Dufferin." It was a best-grade Eastern university voice. "How do you do."

"Didn't take you long to find me."

"We would find you, Mr. Dufferin, in a gopher hole, which is neither here nor there. I am calling to discuss business on behalf of a client. You have apparently something in your possession that he would prefer in his."

"A sheet of paper."

"Several sheets of paper, as I understand it. My client, Mr. Dufferin, is a reasonable person up to a certain point and would like to know your asking price."

"A direct question merits a direct answer," I said. "Two hundred thousand dollars."

He surprised me. He did not laugh outright. He said, "No, we don't stretch to that. You will have to come down a bit."

"And if I don't?"

"Well now, Mr. Dufferin, you had the first visit last night, I believe. The next time they might not be so gentle."

"They still wouldn't find the papers," I said. "I don't have them. I never had them."

"Please. You have disproved that. What were you doing last night with one paper if you do not have the rest? We shall save a lot of unpleasantness if you can treat this as pure business. Are you willing?"

"I'd like time to think. Can I contact your client later?"

"Not too much time," he said, "and you cannot be sure who my client is. We shall find a way of contacting you."

"All right. But meantime lay off me. Any more rough stuff and I blow the whole thing. I've taken precautions. The deal gets automatic publicity if anything happens to me."

"My client has been constantly aware of that possibility. He wishes only to reach an agreement. I can safely promise that you will not be further interfered with. But please, Mr. Dufferin, don't be too long making up your mind. My client is a nervous type. He is apt to become angry. Good-by for now."

Click.

I waited again. No Clare.

I went and took a long hot bath, which is what I used to do when I wanted to think up plots. I soaked for half an hour, shaved, dressed and went downstairs. I sought out the house detective.

He had a little office in the corner of the lobby behind the cigar counter. He was sitting behind a desk that filled most of the room and was smoking a cigarette that stood upright in one of those fancy holders favored by Marshal Tito. The carved wooden plate on his desk said Mr. Tovey. The name meant nothing to me, but the thin face, the cold gray eyes were familiar. He waited for me to say something without greeting me.

"Dufferin," I said. "Room Five-eighty-four."

The little pipe waggled in his mouth. He said, "I know."

"I'd like you to keep an eye on my room. There may be guys try to visit me while I'm out. They may sit around in the lobby waiting for me."

"Anybody special?"

"A man named Kolanski and a big sidekick called Pinhead Johnson, if that means anything to you."

"I've heard of Johnson."

"Then you'll have no trouble."

"No," he said calmly. "And, if you're expecting any, you'd better check out. I don't want you here."

He took the holder from his mouth and examined it. It had a buffalo head on the bowl.

I said, "How would it be if I reported you for insolence?"

"You could try. I figure if they have to choose the management will pick me. I've been here since I retired. I give, as they say, every satisfaction. Me and the management get on."

I said, "We've met before."

"You wouldn't remember it."

"Where?"

"Me and my buddy were the cops who found you drunk the morning after your wife was killed. Is there anything else?"

"Nothing." I walked out.

I bought a newspaper at the cigar counter. Barry Kevin was to be buried that afternoon and still held the front page. I sat in the car, reading. Nothing new. The feature writers had run out of material and were rehashing all that had gone before from an On With The Motley angle.

I tossed the paper at a trashcan and drove to the Public Library to see some older editions.

The girl was obliging. I stayed nearly two hours and scanned everything from the banner headlines on the morning after Phil Greco was killed to the banner headlines that covered Clare's funeral. I was really reading them clearly for the first time. I began to understand why some quarters regarded me as they did. I had not cut a pretty public figure.

The papers, without exception, had implied—openly stated in one case—that I had been more or less responsible for Clare's death. The verdict of accident had not quieted them. They had been outraged. Going through the reports again I was not surprised at the outrage, the way I had been written up. I felt sick.

I searched. No paper at any time mentioned a Mr. Foxwell. I went to the nearest phone.

Ted Wilson had been in and out again. They did not know when he would be back. I returned to the car and drove to Bertha's office.

Brando wasn't there today. The girls were. Someone had passed word of my importance, and I got a great big smile from everyone. Lona Forman smiled. Hymie smiled. The redhead said, "Go right in, Mr. Dufferin, she's alone. She was hoping you'd call."

I went in.

"Hello, elusive," I said.

Bertha put down the contract she was reading and gave me a not very warm smile. "Nice to see you," she said. "Always nice when you don't catch me with my pants down."

"Sorry about the other morning," I said, and thought she was sorrier. I guess that at her age you can't whoop it up without paying a price. She looked haggard.

"Forget it," she said. "What do you want this time?"

"Questions."

"Go ahead. What questions?"

"Who is Cecil Foxwell?"

"A producer on the film side of the Super-Splendid combination. He's on a big deal at the moment, shooting *The Conquistador* in Spain. Using three of my clients. They go afterwards to finish the job in Mexico."

I said, "He was at the party where Clare killed Phil Greco."

"Was he? What about it?"

"He didn't appear in court. His name wasn't in the newspapers."

"Influence," she said. "There was a whole bunch of guests dodged the publicity. They couldn't have helped as witnesses, in any event. Clare was alone with Greco when it happened."

She suddenly frowned at me. She said, "How do you know Foxwell was there?"

"I've seen a statement written by Clare."

"You surprise me. The Hollywood cops usually keep that sort of thing private."

"Bertha," I said. "You were Clare's friend. You were about her only friend. Didn't she ever talk to you about the party?"

"Not that I remember. She seemed to want to forget it. I respected that; the girl had had enough. What about this statement? Have you got it?"

"I think I know where I can get it."

Bertha said, "It'll be nice for you to have. A sort of memento."

"A sort of blackmail weapon," I said. "Someone this morning offered me a lot of money for it."

"Who?" she asked.

"I think it was Leo Holst."

A worried expression came over her face, and she sank deep into her chair. She said gently, "And what has Leo Holst to do with it?"

"Can anyone hear from the other office?"

"No," she said. "Al, why haven't you mentioned this statement before?"

"I only heard about it recently. Maybe you can help make sense of it. I came back to Hollywood to see my kid. I had no idea of staying, no idea of working, but Barry Kevin contacted me. I went to see him. That was the day I first visited you. He offered me money he didn't have. He told me the film was to be Benvenuto Cellini, that he would star, direct and produce and that Leo Holst would co-produce. You get that? Leo Holst as a co-producer. Kevin gave me a cast list of people to build parts for. The list contained the biggest names in Hollywood. It was in Clare's handwriting."

Bertha said quietly, "You're nuts."

"Her handwriting. Without doubt. Which poses a few questions. One—why did Clare, who figured she was about to be the biggest thing in Hollywood, write a cast list for a movie that, no matter how you fixed it, would have only one star part, and that a male? Clare was too stuck on herself. Two—how did she know two years ago or more that Kevin would get a whim to play Cellini? He claimed he never met her. So far as I know, that's true. Three—how did Kevin get hold of the list?"

"Four," Bertha said. "Why have you started drinking again, Al? There are places like Bellevue in California, too."

"Maybe, but you're wrong, Bertha. I'd have asked Kevin the questions had I recognized the handwriting immediately. I didn't. And when next I saw him, later that evening, he was in his wardrobe beaten to death. Somebody shoved him over the mountain afterwards."

"I'm wrong and you're nuts," she said. "You're making this up."

"I swear to it."

"Been to the police?"

"No, I've had enough police for one lifetime. I didn't want to be involved. I knew how it would look. Kevin apparently died in the same way as Clare."

Bertha said, "But really he was murdered. Who murdered him?"

"I'm not sure. Maybe a couple of professional mugs called Kolanski and Johnson."

"And why would they do that?"

"Kevin had Clare's statement."

"You told me just now the cops showed it to you. Al, can you slow down a minute? What's in this statement that everyone wants it so much?"

"I can only guess. Someone is protecting this Foxwell guy."

"Al," Bertha said. "Al. Foxwell is not worth protecting. He's second-rate. The company could replace him any time they wanted. If it was a question of protection, they would have got him away long ago. He went to Spain last week. It's his first movie abroad."

"I need more information. Ted Wilson is doing spadework for me. I was hoping you could help."

"I'd like to." She took out a cigarette, lit it and slowly blew smoke down through her wide nostrils. "Al, do you believe what you're telling me?"

"I'm not here to exercise my jaw."

"Then I'll give you some advice," she said. "Go to the cops. If not, leave well alone. Forget the whole business. You're tilting at people with millions of dollars and an army of men behind them. You're also talking like a screwball, and *you've* got Bellevue behind *you*. Got any proof for all this stuff?"

"Nothing."

"Go back to New York. You were doing all right there."

"My brother-in-law says the same. You should form a committee."

"He's got sense. Why don't you blow?"

"I'm staying."

"You know best," she said. "Let's get back to it. Who has this statement?"

"I don't know. Barry Kevin's household had the best opportunity. Karen Kevin the widow, little sister Gloria and Frankie Frascatti, little sister's boy friend. He's a possibility, too."

"An actor?"

"A good-looking punk who runs the Top Hat. He'd caused a rift between the sisters. There may be more in it than I can see."

"He's carrying on with both of them?"

"Another possibility, but he's pitching for the younger at the moment. She claims he'd do anything for her. That may have included murdering her brother-in-law."

"What about these other two you mentioned? I'm listening very carefully. Are there no more questions?"

"One," I said. "Why did Barry Kevin wait for two frustrated years before he put on the screws about Foxwell? Why did he declare me in on the deal?"

"You really want an honest opinion?"

"Go ahead."

"Either you're suffering from overstrain, coming back for the first time to where Clare was, or someone's playing a joke on you. The whole thing is too crazy for credibility."

I said, "It was a pretty heavy joke to involve beating Barry Kevin to death. I saw the body in his house before he went for his ride in the mountains."

"You were alone with him? Did you search him for the statement?"

"I didn't know about it then. But yes, I searched him. I found nothing. Someone had beat me to it. I cleared out and went to a bar. That's where I met Ted Wilson."

"Then what? No more secrets?"

I got to my feet. "Sorry to have bothered you, Bertha. The hell with you."

"Al, don't get that way, Al. I'll help any way I can. If there's anything I can do in the way of business—"

"Thanks, Bertha. Be seeing you."

She said, "Al, you need treatment. Good-by."

I shut the door.

In the street I headed for the nearest phone and called the Kevin house. A strange woman answered. She told me in hushed tones that neither Mrs. Kevin nor Miss Mason were available at the moment. They were preparing for the funeral.

I went and had lunch.

NINETEEN

The funeral was authentic Hollywood, a combination of interment, picnic and premiere. I arrived early. Ten thousand people had arrived earlier and were waiting in an atmosphere of sunshine, flowers and expectancy. Admission to the Fulfilment Chapel was by ticket only. There was no hope of getting in. The carpeted walk from gate to chapel entrance was roped off with plush and guarded by two files of neatly uniformed Tranquil Leas attendants.

The waiting minister came repeatedly to the door to smile up at newsreel and TV cameras.

The main attraction had not yet begun to arrive. The crowd filled in the interim as best it could. Families sat on tombstones and finished box lunches. Those with less foresight paid inflation prices for nuts and popcorn from opportunists with trays. A Good Humor man arrived and was deluged with children. Three other men with mournful faces hawked black-edged photographs of Barry Kevin in period costume—hand raised in gay farewell—superimposed on pictures of the chapel.

The various Ladies in Black were sprinkled through the crowd and weeping severally. The public-address speakers hung around the church alternated between *Valse Triste* and the slow movement of Dvorak's *New World Symphony*, played sadly on the mighty Wurlitzer.

I took up position with my back to the iron-palinged fence that separated graveyard from street and stretched my neck in search of someone I knew. No one.

We passed the scheduled hour. Adults became impatient and children fretful. We had come on account of the living, not the dead. A little girl screamed loudly because the crowd was too thick for her to jump rope, and two little boys created a diversion by falling together into a fountain.

The cars began to arrive.

An impressive black limousine with chauffeur. The couple who alighted were nonentities, and had confessed it by arriving first. The crowd rippled, groaned critically and subsided. They wanted bigger game. It came. An open yellow-and-cream convertible screamed to a halt, and a man leaped out.

He stood nearly seven feet tall, had a chest like Kong and no hips. He was star of a TV Western series, had come direct from the studios and was still wearing make-up and costume, complete to spurs. We understood immediately that not even pressure of work could keep a decent man from paying his respects. We loved him for it. A cheer went up, his spurs chinked and he waved his sombrero.

It was too much for one woman. She screamed in sudden ecstasy, triggering the crowd. They surged forward and ran up each other's backs, and the guard of honor was forced to lock arms. Cameras whirred, *Valse Triste* increased in volume and people around me were scaling the palings for a better view. It was a great emotional experience.

After that the excitement was unremitting.

Nobody of first firmament stature arrived, but we were in hysterically good temper. There was a feeling in the air of genuine carnival, and everyone got a cheer, including the oldies who had worked with Barry Kevin back in the forties. We cheered even the technicians, cameramen and studio executives. We wanted to maintain the expectancy until the appearance of the widow.

She came.

She arrived in a professional mourning-wagon, a severe black chauffeur-driven Rolls with white-walled tires. A woman yelled, "There she is!" and there she was, on the sidewalk, cool in her dark clothes, her head up, her eyes hating the crowd. They sensed it. Near silence fell, and anticlimax swept in. Gloria Mason saved the day by milking the situation for everything it had.

She got out of the car with an apparently accidental cheesecake that demonstrated everything but her navel. She wore a tight-waisted, flaring-skirted charcoal dress and a widow-peaked hat with a small veil that brushed her forehead. She stood a moment on the sidewalk, swaying, lifting a distraught hand to her brow. The crowd's near-silence became reverent. She clutched her sister's arm, leaned heavily and went tottering off down the carpeted walk to the church like Ophelia on her way to the river. She overdid it.

An argument broke out near me. Which one had been the wife? The choir through the speakers struck up with *There Is a Brighter Land We All Shall Go To*, the Tranquil Leas Funeral Hymn. Those who had been before joined in the singing. Everyone else went back to general conversation. More popcorn was sold.

The oration began.

"Brethren, friends, co-workers-one-with-another, no matter what our capacity in this great and famous city, we were gathered here today to bid farewell to our illustrious friend as he sets out on that last joyous road that leads to the House of the Big Feature. Those of us who knew intimately his noble soul—"

A hand came through the railings behind me and plucked my sleeve. A voice said, "Dufferin."

I opened my elbows, pushed hard, managed to turn and was squashed hard against the fence. Frankie Frascatti's face was two inches away.

He looked very young, very sleek and very composed except for his eyes, which were half mad. He spoke with lips barely moving. "I got to talk to you. My car's down at the corner. I'll wait for you."

I said, "I can't move."

There was sweat on his upper lip, and his mouth twitched a grimace right across his face. He said, "I phoned your house this morning. Some dame claimed she didn't know where you was. She said she was your sister."

"She is," I said. "What's the panic?"

His eyes flicked all around for eavesdroppers. He needn't have bothered with all the racket going on, but he leaned loser. He said, "You got that thing of your wife's."

The man on the speaker was talking now of the mission of Hollywood, of the dedicated men who altruistically spread the American way of life throughout the world entire. None had been more devoted in the cause, none a greater exponent, than Barry Kevin.

I said, "Leo Holst send you?"

His mouth twitched again. "What you talking about?"

"What are you talking about? What thing of my wife's?"

"Don't stall," he said. "You got it."

"How do you know?"

He said, "She told me."

He leaned so close his nose came through the railings. "You were there after the guy was killed," he said. "You took it from him. Listen, I'll cut you in any way you like. I'll give you five thousand now, in cash."

I said, "Depends on the rest of the cut. We'll discuss it. Go to the Piers Hotel. I'll be there as soon as I can get out of here."

The corner of his mouth was twitching now like an electric cutout. His eyes flicked. "We can't be seen together," he said. "I don't want to take chances. Come out to the Top Hat before we open. I'll leave the back door open. Seven o'clock."

The man in the church was reaching his final peroration. Background music was being faded in on the Wurlizter. Frascatti said, "Is Gloria here?"

"Yes."

"I haven't been able to contact her," he said, and he was suddenly just a boy with eyes full of anguish and misery. He said, "I thought she was ill, or something. If you see her afterwards—"

Then he stopped. He said, "At seven," jerked his head and eased back through the people who surrounded him. I elbowed again and faced the church. The peroration reached its climax.

There was a closing song: *Adios, Happy Traveler, Adios.* The crowd jockeyed for position. Those who had been before and knew the routine dragged their children and streaked over the hill toward the Corner of the Stars, last resting place of all Tranquil Leas clients who had appeared in A's. The organ strains of *Saints Go Marching In* boomed over the graveyard. The coffin appeared, with the six bearers trying to get into step.

A sigh from the crowd. The guard broke ranks and formed a phalanx to force a passage. The sisters emerged, arms locked, and the sigh became a sympathetic murmuring like the noise of a swarm of hornets. Then the cowboy appeared. His make-up glistened in the sun, and his teeth flashed from side to side. A forest of autograph books shot into the air, the murmur became a sustained scream of adoration and everyone surged.

Chaos took over.

I gave a heave, turned my back and clung to the railings. It was the only way to breathe. The crowd swayed away and was forced back, my ribs were glued to the fence and the screams took on an edge of panic. A man shouted to mind his wife. Children were howling. The cameras whirred, the TV commentator on his truck rose to race-meeting fever-pitch, and the Saints went right on Marching In.

Police reinforcements arrived. Then ambulances.

Ten minutes later the main entrance was still impassable. There was enough space around me to make a running jump. I gripped the fence, heaved upward and dropped into the street on the other side.

Going to the car I got a look at myself in a store window. I was a mess. I felt unclean. I had no other suit at the hotel.

I got in the car and drove out to Los Olmos to change.

TWENTY

It was Fay's afternoon for bridge. There was no one home, but she had left the back door open for when Johnny came. I helped myself to pie and milk from the icebox, played some nice clean Bach to wash away the funeral, then went upstairs and had a shower and changed.

I had been doing some thinking. Among other things, I had decided that I would not be coming back here to live, that Chester would not allow it if I wanted it. I packed the rest of my luggage and took it down to the car.

A woman was watching from an upstairs window of the house next door. When I looked up she turned away and pretended she hadn't seen me.

It was getting late by now. The boy should be home. I went back inside and sat a while with the idea of waiting for him, just to get a look at him and see how he was. Then, although he was only six and my son, I could not face him. Not yet. I switched off the record player, went out to the car again and drove down to the Piers.

There were no messages, and no one had called. I left the luggage at the desk for the bellboy to take up, looked around the lobby but saw no familiar faces. I went to the cocktail bar.

It was full of people just out after work, all talking together. No one was alone, and no one looked as though he might be waiting for me. I sat on a stool at the bar and had a Coke.

Tovey, the house detective, must have had a buzz from the desk. He appeared within a minute and sat at a table just inside the door and watched me. I watched him back by his reflection in the bar mirror. I'm beginning to think that's what bar mirrors are for. When I turned around he did not bother to look away, but went right on staring at me with dislike in his face. After reading the newspapers at the library that morning I understood his feelings. I had another Coke.

The dock above the bar showed six-thirty. I got down off the stool. I passed Tovey with a nod, which was not returned, and went out to the car.

Evening traffic filled the streets. Swarms of cars jerked from light to light like crazy beetles, and their exhausts thickened the slowly descending smog. Neons were coming on. I thought I was going to be late, so I nudged out of the main line into a side street that led to the highway and stood on the gas. There was no special reason for it, but I felt eager. I caught myself whistling again.

There were no lighted neons at the Top Hat, and the place looked dismal.

There is nothing in the world so dismal as an unlighted neon. I drove up the approach and parked under the trees instead of going to the car park. I got out of the car and looked at my watch, and it was five minutes before seven; I was early after all. I tried the front entrance first.

It was locked. I walked around to the side, to the back, and found three doors, wide apart. The middle one was open, so I entered. I went through a locker room with waiters' clothes hanging on pegs, and then on into the main room. There were no lights there, either, and it was very dim. The air had been sprayed with scented disinfectant, but I could still smell sweet stale liquor and last night's cigarette smoke.

I went across the creaking sprung dance floor and up the single step to the office. I waited a second, then knocked.

No answer, no movement and no light under the door. A pulse thumped in my throat. If this was a trap, I might have difficulty getting out. I knocked again, turned the handle, walked in and brushed my hand down the wall.

I hit the light switch.

There was no window and a smell in the air like spent firecrackers. The office was larger than I had imagined. It had thick carpets, a drink cabinet, files, easy chairs, two small tables and a desk. Frankie Frascatti was behind the desk, fallen forward, his eyes and mouth open, his cheek resting in a pool of blood.

I would not have been able to talk to him had I arrived a lot earlier. The blood was thickening. He was shot through the head, and had been dead an hour or more.

There was no sign of a weapon.

TWENTY-ONE

I walked around the desk. He was on the edge of the chair with his hands dangling almost to the floor, needing only a touch to topple him. I couldn't search him. Neither could I open the desk drawer. He was up against it.

I took out my handkerchief, wrapped it around my right hand and went to the files. They were locked. I went over to the door and rubbed first the handle and then the light switch. The light went off and I stood there in darkness, not able to see Frascatti any more, wondering what to do.

Out in the main room someone moved.

He was walking soft, but not soft enough, because the dance floor creaked as he stepped on it. Then silence. I got out of the office without touching the door and flattened against the wall. His outline was perfectly still on the edge of the floor near the bar. I waited for him to move again.

He said, "Where are you, Al?"

I got away from the wall then and walked toward him. I said, "What do you want, Chester? What are you doing here?"

"The place isn't open yet."

"I know it," I said, and took his arm and got him out as fast as I could, through the locker room and around the side of the building to the car.

I was holding him tight, but he neither spoke nor protested. I said, "You come on foot?"

"No, I left the car down on the highway." He pointed. The car was there.

I said, "Visiting Frascatti?"

"Who's that?"

I pulled him dose. In the twilight his face was yellow. "What do you want?"

"Johnny," he mumbled. "I thought you had Johnny. I was following you to get him back."

"Isn't he home?"

"I don't think so."

"What makes you think I've got him?"

He said, "Well, I told the next-door neighbor to phone me at the office if she noticed anything funny happening around the house. She saw you carrying out some suitcases—"

"She knows I'm Fay's brother."

"Yes," he said. "She does."

I waited.

He said, "All right, I told her to call if you ever came around. What of it? Fay doesn't tell me anything since you turned her funny on me."

"The only funny thing here is the story you're telling."

"It's the truth. She phoned me about the time Johnny gets back from school. I drove home as soon as I could. He wasn't there, and neither was your luggage. I couldn't find him. I thought you had him. I came looking for you at the Piers and you were driving away. I couldn't see if you had him with you, so I followed. I got held up is the traffic awhile. I saw your car in here—"

He broke off. "Don't you have him?'

"No."

"Where is he?"

"Did you check Fay's bridge school?"

"I don't know what house they're at this afternoon."

"Did you check any house?"

"No."

I said, "It's getting thinner. How many times have you been at the Top Hat before?"

"Never."

"You found your way around to the back door."

"I knew you were in there. I tried all the doors."

"Did you try the office door?"

He just looked yellow.

I said, "You may or may not know it. Either way, you'll keep quiet for Fay's sake. There's a guy named Frascatti sitting behind a desk in there. He's been shot through the head. I didn't shoot him, but you may have."

My brother-in-law took a great gasping breath, as though he had just surfaced from spearfishing, but he said not a word. I released his arm and got in the car. I wanted out. He stood there a moment, gaping at me through the windshield. He spun on his heel and, fat as he was, he ran like a hare to where he had left his car on the road.

He didn't wait to turn on the lights. The motor roared, and he was doing fifty in ten seconds. He was probably running for the police. I had to run faster.

TWENTY-TWO

The gates of the Kevin residence were wide open. That surprised me. I drove straight in, parked on the gravel next to the Buick and rang the bell of the front door.

It was answered almost immediately. The stone-faced middle-aged woman in black called me "sir" and I recognized her voice as the one I had spoken with on the phone. Calling me "sir" did not prevent her shutting the door in my face while she went to see if I was admissible.

I was, apparently. The look on her face said only just. She let me in as though I were a leper.

I was starting for the room where I had seen Barry Kevin. She said, "This way, sir," led me across the hall to what looked like a blank wall, pushed one of the panels and I was in a new room with the door shut behind me. It was a nice room, all cream and green. Karen Kevin, out of mourning, was dressed to match in a tight cream sweater and a tighter pair of matador pants that showed her handsome legs. She sat on a davenport with an open leather folder of drawings in her hand. Her brow was furrowed, and she was smoking. The ashtray beside her suggested she had furrowed and smoked for some hours.

She said, "Good evening. Have you come to blackmail me?"

I tried to smile. "Not yet."

"Sit down. Do you want a drink?"

I sat. "No thanks. I'd be afraid of disturbing the maid."

"Hetty?" Mrs. Kevin's voice was just making conversation. It sounded boneless and defeated and dead. She played with the drawings, not looking at me. She said, "Hetty's all right. We had her for years back in Cleveland. She flew in yesterday to help me. She's been invaluable."

"Pity you had to let her go in the first place."

"My husband couldn't stand her."

"I don't think she can stand me."

"Oh, she thought you were another souvenir hunter. We've been rather pestered."

"I can guess. I'm surprised you left the gates open."

"That." She still didn't look at me. "It hasn't been as bad as that. People think we've gone. I made a statement to the press that we were leaving for Cleveland directly after the funeral."

"You changed your mind?"

She leafed through the folder.

"Did you have a special reason for visiting me, Mr. Dufferin, or was it only to offer sympathy again?"

"You probably need it," I said. "I was at the funeral this afternoon. You were suffering."

"It was revolting." She held a pen-and-ink sketch at arm's length and studied the two horses on it with narrowed eyes. She said, "My husband had no secret cache of papers, Mr. Dufferin. Hetty spent the day packing in preparation for our departure. She went right through the house. There was nothing."

"Hetty did not go to the funeral?"

"Hetty in her turn could not stand my husband. What sort of papers were you expecting?"

I said, "I guess I will have that drink."

She didn't have to ring for the maid. She got a bottle of Scotch from a little cubbyhole in the wall and poured one glass—nothing for herself. While she was doing it I picked up the folder of drawings so that she would have nothing behind which to hide. They were very good drawings, all of them pen-and-ink. I said, "Did you do these, Mrs. Kevin?"

"My sister." She handed me the glass and sat down. "She does beautiful water colors. She has had that sort of talent since she was about five. My mother sent her to art school, but she was too good for the teachers. I had hoped she would return to it now and study privately with an artist friend of ours in Cleveland."

I said, "But she's not interested."

"She does not want to leave Hollywood. Somebody has been filling her head with a lot of silly nonsense. You, Mr. Dufferin. I appeal to your sense of decency. Ask her to change her mind. She will listen to no one else."

"What gives you that idea?"

"She has talked of no one but you since yesterday. You are going to write a part for her and make her a star. She didn't go to bed at all last night, according to Hetty. She spent the entire night prowling the house. She's just a stupid, affected little girl, Mr. Dufferin, and it's wrong of you to take advantage of her."

"It would be," I said. "Could you call me Alan?"

"I'll stick to Mr. Dufferin."

I finished the drink and put the glass on a small green table. I said, "Is Gloria home?"

"Not at the moment."

"Maybe it's not films. She could want to stay in Hollywood for the sake of Frascatti."

I got a quick look, nothing else.

"When are you expecting her home?" I asked.

"Any time."

I said, "Mrs. Kevin, I don't believe you. You told the press you were going back to Cleveland. You say you've packed up in preparation. Despite souvenir hunters, you've left the main gate open. For your sister. You don't know where she is. If you tell me what's happened, I might be able to help."

Mrs. Kevin said in a dead tired voice, "Gloria has run away with Frascatti."

It was one of those times when I badly needed another drink. I said, "Are you sure?"

"He came here before the funeral. Gloria pretended she didn't want to see him, and Hetty refused him admission. I suppose Gloria was trying to throw me off the scent. Fifteen minutes later she took a phone call. That was when they must have made the arrangements. After we returned from the funeral she said she wanted to lie down. We all wanted to lie down. I heard her car start up, looked from the bedroom window and saw her disappearing through the gates."

"She may have gone shopping. She may be on a drunk."

"She's taken a suitcase of clothes with her. Why, if she wasn't going with that hoodlum?"

Mrs. Kevin reached over and took the folder from me. She said bitterly, "I thought I'd stopped him. I had a private detective investigating him. Yesterday I got the names and addresses of three of the women who have supported him at one time or another. I phoned them. I told each one that he was carrying on with Gloria."

"You phoned anonymously," I said. "That wasn't nice."

"I'd do anything to protect my sister."

"Who were the women?"

"It would be less nice if I told you."

"I'm trying to help."

"What does it matter?" she said, and gave me the names.

I knew them. A sixty-year-old female art director, a studio dress designer and an actress who always played Dear Old Mom because she was past everything else. I had the names, and I had a motive for Frascatti's murder that had nothing to do with Clare, a statement or me. Mrs. Kevin may have given it accidentally. Maybe not.

I got to my feet. I said, "I'm going back to Hollywood. If your sister comes back or telephones, tell her to get in touch with me at once at the Piers Hotel. If she hasn't contacted you by midnight, call the police."

"That's out of the question." She stood up. "We're supposed to be on our way to Cleveland. The papers would make a wonderful scandal so soon after the funeral."

"All the same, call the police. Don't mention my name or I'll deny speaking to you."

She said haughtily, "I don't think I need you to tell me what is best for my family, Mr. Dufferin."

"As you wish. Can I use your phone?"

Without thawing, she led me to the hall. She stood at a polite distance while I called the Piers. There was one message.

Ted Wilson had been knocked down by a hit-and-run driver, and was in the Samaritan hospital. He was asking to see me.

TWENTY-THREE

The nurse looked and acted like a middle-aged iguana. She kept opening the door of the room, rolling her eyes around the corridor to see if I was still waiting, then disappearing with a lizardy flick. I had not spoken to her since the first time that she said I could not possibly see Ted. It would have annoyed her and increased her resistance.

I smoked another cigarette. The doctor emerged alone, a short gray-headed man with a good-humored face. I stood up as he came over. He said, "Glad to see Wilson has one friend. Nobody else inquired except his office."

"He's a widower," I said. "No family. Will he live?"

"Live? He didn't even lose consciousness. There must be something in what they say about angels looking after children and drunks. He was so pickled we could have got by without an anesthetic. He's sober now, though. The pain fixed it."

"Can I see him?"

"No. He was lucky—I think he bounced. All the same he has a fractured femur, a broken wrist, a mass of abrasions and a high temperature. He's suffering from shock. He'll be here long enough for you to visit him in the morning. Come when the police make their inquiries. Desk will tell you the time."

"Good night," I said.

"Doctor." The nurse flicked out of the room. "Doctor, the patient insists on seeing this man. He threatens to get out of bed and walk home."

"Let him try. What's his temperature?"

"A hundred and four."

"Five minutes," the doctor said to me.

"Thanks." I went to the door with the nurse behind me. I said, "Alone?" He shrugged and nodded. I shut the door in her face.

Ted Wilson was flat on a pillowless bed, his arm in a splint and one of those igloos over his legs. He turned his head and whispered, "Thank God. You brought a drink?"

"Didn't think of it," I said, and sat on the bedside chair.

"Silly bastard, you might have known. Only reason I wanted to see you." He grinned weakly. "Don't look worried, Al, I'm insured up to the eyelashes. I've needed a vacation for a long time. This would be one way of curing the drink habit if I wanted it cured. I don't. Maybe I'll lay hands on some rubbing alcohol."

I said, "How did it happen?"

"Deliberately," he said, and stopped grinning. He took a long shallow breath. "They knew I was in Paco's. They were waiting for me. I was tanked up, but I'm never too tanked to cross a road. My consciousness goes an hour before my legs. This black car was up the street. I came out, started across, the engine roared and I jumped. Next thing I was lying in the gutter waiting for the ambulance."

"Who?" I said.

"It's a good question. I did some thinking while that doctor was throwing me around. I hate the guts of a lot of people in this world, but I'll tell you something. Nobody hates me. In my ex-job I presented the world with a bunch of egotistical bad bastards as though they were lovable human beings. I did it well. I was liked for it. I made no enemies. On the *Gazette* I've been just a harmless drunk."

I waited.

He said, "The guy I probably hate most is Leo Holst. That's why I'm concentrating on him. After the amalgamation, he threw me out of a comfortable well-paid job where I had prestige and position. I've got reason to hate him. I'd like my own back. I thought it last night in the Ivory after what you said to me. Something I heard later decided me to go on a hunt. I spent this morning making discreet inquiries, people I know who work with Super-Splendid. I thought they were discreet. They must have reached him."

"What inquiries?" I said. "What could you find out from public knowledge that would force his hand?"

"Nothing. If he didn't already have something on his conscience."

Ted moved his head from side to side and winced.

"God damn this arm. Funny, it hurts near the shoulder, not the wrist." Then he said, "You should have stuck around last night. That bald guy, the drunk, we did some boozing together. He was talkative. He admired Clare. He did meet her once, like he said. It was at that party."

My insides jolted.

"He was telling me about it. Clare appeared all pale and shaken and said there'd been an accident with Phil Greco. Baldy did something he's been ashamed of ever since. He cut and run to avoid the publicity."

"A lot of them did."

"I know. One of them was Leo Holst."

The door opened, and the nurse said, "Time's up, Mr. Dufferin."

"Get out, you cow," Ted hissed. "Go and bury your hatchet face before I—"

"How dare you, Mr. Wilson. I shall call the doctor immediately."

She disappeared.

"Holst," I said.

"Yeah. He particularly couldn't stand the publicity. He was in the middle of *Elijah,* his major epic. Police inquiries might have held him up and wrecked the film. A religious film. The simple publicity might have hurt. Remember? They wouldn't let Jennifer Jones get a divorce till *Bernadette* had raked off?"

I said, "Holst met Clare."

"If so, just that once. Which is strange. They were the same studio, he was high up, they began building her. It's like they stayed out of one another's way. Unless some of my people were lying this morning."

"Several people were lying before," I said. "His name wasn't mentioned in court."

"Nor other names. The case was cut and dried before the public heard of it. Influence at work."

I said, "Who's Cecil Foxwell?"

"Assistant producer on *Elijah.* Was he at the party? It's likely."

"He's a full producer now."

"It means something?" Ted closed his eyes, half opened them again and squinted at me. "What else?"

"A connection between Holst and Frascatti. "

"New. A new idea. Tell me."

"We won't immediately phone any newspapers," I said. "Frascatti was murdered this afternoon."

"Oh." Ted almost sat up. "Oh," he said, soft and long drawn. "Now you have to tell me."

"I would if I knew. Frascatti made an appointment with me. I kept it. He didn't. He was dead."

I thought of Fay and the boy. I said, "I'm the only one who knows about it."

"You and now me," Ted said. "I don't like this pairing off. Frascatti and me. We both got the chop on the same day." He winced and touched his arm. He said, "Al, we've been on this for some time and I've worked in the dark. I might be more help finding answers if you started from the beginning."

The door opened again.

The nurse whisked in, then the doctor. The nurse looked like a justified Nemesis, and the doctor had lost his good humor. He jerked a thumb. "Out!"

I went. I couldn't do anything else.

TWENTY-FOUR

In the hotel lobby I bought an evening paper and went over to the desk. The night man idling by the cigar stand straightened up, turned away, but continued watching me from the corner of his eye. Day-man Tovey had warned him about me.

I said, "Any messages?"

"Mr. Dufferin. Why, yes. Four telephone calls, sir, from the same number. I've made a note. You're to call back as soon as you come in."

I took the slip. Fay's number in Los Olmos. I crossed to the elevator feeling the clerk watch me, seeing the night detective swivel gently to keep me in sight. I went up.

There was a party in a suite along the corridor. The door was open. A mass of glass-holding people were jammed shoulder to shoulder and filling the air with loud talk and thick smoke. I was feeling for my key when a pretty little blonde of about seventeen staggered into the corridor in a state of advanced décolletage and near coma. The man with her could have been her grandfather, but there was nothing grandpaternal in his leer.

He took her arm and led her half-supported into a room farther down. They would discuss privately how he could help her career in films. In the morning, when the shock had passed, she would think it hadn't worked with him, but might with someone else. She would try again. Mary Astor, who knows her Hollywood, has called it Hell.

I thought of Gloria Mason, wondered where she was and went into my room.

I searched the newspaper. Long descriptions of Barry Kevin's funeral, how beautiful it had been, how touching the last heartfelt tribute of his thousands of faithful fans gathered reverently to bid him farewell. Pictures. Great stars never pass away. The widow had gone to Cleveland. Nothing of Frankie Frascatti.

The time element, maybe. He'd possibly appear in a later special edition. Unless someone had moved him as Barry Kevin had been moved. A cascade of bodies going over the mountain. One of them Clare's.

I thought of Chester.

He had talked or not talked. Four phone calls from Los Olmos were ominous, but less ominous than one visit from the police. I listened to the noises of the party up the way and boiled my brains. Finally I went over to the phone.

It rang on me.

"Dufferin," I said.

Silence from the other end. Then low and muffled: "Alan, this is Clare."

"Hello," I said. "How are you? Where are you?"

Silence.

I said, "Not in Heaven."

"You don't sound surprised to hear me, Alan."

"I got over the first shock last night. Sorry we didn't get a chance to talk. I was hoping you would contact me this morning. You didn't, did you?"

"No," she said. "Did anyone else?"

"All sorts of people."

"I was afraid of that. Who were they?"

"No," I said. "First things first. You've called about the letter. The part of the letter you sent me. One page."

She said, "You didn't expect me to send it all, did you? We have to make a deal first."

"I'm listening."

"Well—" She lingered doubtfully on the word. Then, in a sudden confident burst, "You recognized the handwriting."

"Yes," I said, "it was clever. But you made one or two mistakes. Clare never called me Alan in her life. I was Al, as with the rest of the family. She would not have called me 'my dear' even in a letter. The wording was strange, too, sort of formal, not the style of a letter, more like a statement. And you don't begin any letter with My Dear Alan, then go on formally and nastily about my customary state of drunkenness. The intimate opening is canceled out by what follows."

"I see what you mean. I suppose you notice those things, being a writer. Maybe that's why I admire your work."

"You told me before. Thank you."

She said, "My impersonation was good, though."

"Very."

"I couldn't resist trying."

"That's because you're an actress," I said.

"Yes, did you see me at the funeral? I was good, I think. I could convince anyone of anything."

I said, "Not everything, Gloria. You struck one false note from the start. You knew all about my films. You didn't know the name of another scriptwriter. For future reference, Hemingway and Faulkner were never a script-writing team; they only won the Nobel Prize. Your ignorance was natural in a little girl who wanted to be an actress. You all think that actors and actresses are the only important things in films. But you knew about me even before you met me. It was out of character. It showed an interest in me personally. Your brother-in-law had it, too, which made me think that maybe you had talked it over between you. You didn't, by the way, kill him, did you?"

"No," she said, shocked. "As if I would do a thing like that. He had it all arranged for me to play the part of Lucrezia Borgia."

"Fit you like a glove," I said. "Who did kill him?"

"Didn't you?"

"Not this time."

"Then it was either Frankie or my sister. She hated him enough. But does it really matter now that everyone thinks he died in a car accident?"

She was talking with an ingenuousness that chilled me. She said, "I still want to play Lucrezia. A period picture affords one such great opportunities, don't you think? I have a sense of history, a feeling for the age. I wouldn't wander around those big historical sets like most actresses, like tourists in an art museum. I could lend dignity to the part."

"You could," I said. "And I could still write the same film. Building up Lucrezia to the star part."

"Would you?"

"Isn't that why you called. To make a deal?"

"Well, yes. I suppose I could do it alone, now I know the statement is really in your wife's handwriting, but you know the ropes better. It's quite exciting, isn't it? You'll be able to study me and build the part to fit my talent. You'll make millions of dollars, Alan."

"And I'll be able to get in and see Holst, which you can't," I said. "Since we're going to be partners, Gloria, we'd better stop beating about the bush. I'll wait here in my room. Come up as soon as you can."

"But that's quite impossible, Alan. This is a long distance call. I'm hundreds of miles away. I daren't come back to Hollywood now."

"Why not?"

"Someone might try to take the document off me. I'm only a girl."

I said, "Where do we meet?"

She thought about it, then said, "I'm going farther. It's glorious driving by night. Romantic. It releases me somehow. I tell you what would be exciting. I've never been to Tia Juana. Let's meet there. There's a place I've heard about called El Robo, where people smoke marijuana and everything. I'd like to see it. An actress needs those sort of experiences. Shall we say at five tomorrow afternoon?"

"Wait. Don't go."

"I must."

"We're partners," I said. "I'm the man about to do all the work. I want cooperation on your part."

"For instance?"

I said, "What's in the rest of the statement?"

"You don't know," she cried. "I knew you didn't. I'm not telling you till I see you. I'm not sure yet that I can trust you."

"All right, tell me when you got the statement."

"Ten days ago."

"From whom?"

"Never mind."

"Gloria, from whom?"

"If you must know, Frankie Frascatti."

"How did he get it?"

"Alan, that's not important now."

I said, "Listen. I have money. I make a good fat living at TV in New York. I can get along without you and your deals, but you can't get along without me. Answer questions or you'll be trying to contact me in New York. I want to know it all from the beginning. With details."

"You," she said, "you're just stinking mean. I don't know if I want to deal with you any more." Then she brightened. She was going to present herself in what she thought was a favorable light. She said, "It was Frankie. He's never been in films, but he knows every bit of gossip about them. A little while ago in the Top Hat he heard someone saying you were back in town. They were talking about how you drove your wife to suicide and how she killed Phil Greco. That was when Frankie said—"

She stopped abruptly. She laughed. "I nearly forgot myself. I nearly told you what you want to know. I shan't. Not till tomorrow in Tia Juana. Frankie told me about your wife. He said he could prove it with a statement she'd made. He didn't want me to see it at first, but I said I didn't believe him, that he didn't love me. He does love me. He's crazy about me. He'll do about anything I ask."

I said, "You saw the statement. You realized it could be used. You asked Frascatti to give it to you—"

"Lend it."

"You didn't know enough to go about using it yourself, so you called in your brother-in-law."

"Poor old Barry," she said. "He thought it was a joke to begin with. But he was desperate. Anything to get back in films. He decided to check. He called you in and thought you recognized the handwriting on the cast list I wrote. That convinced him."

"He was trying to buy me," I said. "And then?"

"I thought you guessed about the statement and came back the same evening and killed him for it. I knew he called Holst. I saw your car go in and thought you were from the studios. I was parked up the road, waiting. I sneaked in to listen and you were leaning over Barry's body, searching him."

"The parrot screeched and you ran back into the hall."

"Yes," she said. "And after you'd gone I went in and found the statement under Barry's girdle. I guess you didn't look there."

"No," I said.

She said, "I didn't know what to do. I was going to tell Frankie, but when I got to the Top Hat you were there, too. I didn't know what to think then. I changed my mind about telling him. He's not very brave, anyway. Nice in a wet sort of way, but not very brave. He got frightened the next day and wanted the statement back. I had to tell him that I'd shown it to Barry. First off, I said it must have been in Barry's pocket when he was killed. Then, because nothing came in the papers, he said someone else must have it. He kept on about it. Finally I told him you must have it, that you killed Barry for it."

"Why did you tell him that?"

"Well, if he knew I had the statement, he'd have wanted it back."

I said, "And when did you tell him?"

"This morning. I wouldn't have done, but he tried to force his way into the house. I had to tell him something. I spoke to him on the phone."

"He contacted me," I said.

"Was he troublesome?"

"No," I said. "Gloria. Tell me one thing. Where did Frascatti get the statement in the first place?"

"I don't know. Honest. He wouldn't tell me. Maybe he was afraid to."

I said, "I'm leaving for New York tonight."

"I tell you I don't know. I wasn't really interested once I had my hands on it."

I said, "You think Holst will play ball with us?"

"Does he have an alternative?" she asked in a hard little voice. "I'd like to have a photostat taken and show him that first. It might be dangerous. I mean, the photographer would have to see it. Can you make photostats?"

"No."

"We could learn. It can't be very difficult."

"All right," I said. "Gloria. One thing. About my wife. She's dead, isn't she?"

"Yes, of course. I never heard anything different." I hung up.

I didn't want to hang up, but the noise of the party along the corridor had suddenly surged louder. I turned to my open door. The man standing there was a stranger to me.

TWENTY-FIVE

He was tall, intelligent and prosperous-looking, with a collar-ad face that betrayed nothing of what was going on behind it. He was a gray-flannel-suit type, though out of deference to the time of evening he was wearing a dark pin stripe and a Homburg hat. There was a briefcase under his arm. He was smiling with a shiny white set of teeth that may have been jacketed, and he said in the Eastern college voice that had spoken to me over the phone, "Good evening, Mr. Dufferin."

"Good evening," I said. "Been listening long?"

"Trying to." He came in, took off his hat and shut the door. "Couldn't hear a thing. Too much racket from the party up the way."

He looked around. He went into the bathroom, came back, glanced beneath the bed, opened drawers, felt under the table and under the two chairs and ran a professional eye over the walls. "No tape recorder," he said, and sat down. "Amiable. Sorry I didn't ask them to announce me, but you'll understand that.

Shall we call for drinks?"

"No."

"Perhaps you're right. A clear head is better. Let's to business."

He laid the briefcase on his knees, put his hands on it and appraised me silently for a few seconds. His eyes were knowing, good-humored and hard. No one had fooled him since he left high school. He said, "Did you ever hear of a studio writer getting a twelve-year contract?"

"Once."

"They're rare. The man who gets one has to be a writer of wide experience and exceptional talent. Some people think you are that man. Having seen some of your films, I agree. Mr. Dufferin, I have such a contract in this briefcase. It needs only your signature. Three thousand a week. Three thousand a week for twelve years."

"Nice money. And in return?"

"You write, of course. What did you think?" He was too well-bred to raise his eyebrows at me, so he achieved the effect with his voice. He said, "Hard work, at both TV and films. On top of that you'll be a consultant writer, passing judgment on the work of other people, giving the last word, reading novels in search of suitable properties. No sinecure, believe me. But the prestige will be enormous."

"Like the money," I said. "It's neat. Holst buys me off without taking a nickel from his own pocket. The studio pays. The shareholders foot the bill."

"The only part I understand is about the shareholders. I think they're getting a good deal. They need a man like you. Or haven't you enough self-confidence?"

"Enough to know I can make a living as a free-lance. I don't need to tie myself up."

"The contract can be modified in any way you wish." He paused. "There is also seventy-five thousand in cash."

"It gets better," I said. "And if I don't?"

"Why wouldn't you? I really fail to understand your reluctance. Let's forget all about my client and speak clearly, as one businessman to another. You have your wife's statement. How you got hold of it is no longer important. Now you either publish the statement or make other use of it. You have not published it so far, and, frankly, I see no reason why you should ever do so. I'm sure you have no wish to avenge Phil Greco."

"I never met him," I said.

"In that you were lucky. A dirty, cheap, blackmailing little racketeer." The eyes studied me again, no longer humorous. The man said, "Your wife is dead. Publicity would soil her memory. You have a child. Children must be protected. What have we left? Nothing but sign the contract, collect the money and let me have the statement."

I said, "You know what the statement contains?"

"Naturally, or I should not have taken on the job. There is no risk. My clients trust me. I make around two hundred thousand a year, Mr. Dufferin. I have a large house, four cars, two gardeners, a chauffeur and even a butler. All earned through the trust of other people. I never betray it. Now." He rippled fingers on the briefcase. "Do you agree to a deal?"

"What if I don't?"

"We'd have to think about that. You've been beaten up once."

"Once?"

"Once," he said. "The next time they might kill you."

I said, "Suppose I tell you I don't have the statement."

"You will not be believed. A page of it was taken from you last night in the apartment where you were masquerading under the name of Kingston. I confess, Dufferin, that it came as a surprise to find your wife had addressed the thing to you. I understood she didn't like you."

"Did you expect her to address it to someone else?"

"No. Unless it were a person who witnessed the statement."

"For instance?"

He was suddenly irritated. He said, "If you'll explain your game to me, Dufferin, I'll try and play it with you."

"No game."

"Then let's finish this." He started to undo the briefcase.

I said, "I need twenty-four hours. The papers are stowed in a safe place, and I need a day to get them."

He stood up abruptly, tucked the briefcase under his arm and put his hat on. "More games," he said. "My client has been patient and generous. He might not continue so."

"What else can he do?"

The man suddenly smiled at me again. He touched the brim of his hat to see that it was set right. "Good night," he said, went out and shut the door behind him.

I ran to the phone.

The girl on the switchboard was busy, but yes sir she'd try and check where my last incoming call was from. I hung up again, sat down and waited. I had to call Fay, but I was afraid to use the phone again until the operator called me. Then I was more afraid. I thought that she or someone else might have been listening in when I talked to Gloria Mason about Barry Kevin. In which case, I could expect the police.

I smoked one and a half cigarettes. The party along the way was dying down. The phone rang.

"Dufferin?" Her voice was different.

"Thank you, miss. Did you find out?"

A silence from the other end. She said in a curious, flat, muffled, impersonal sort of way, "You're making a mistake, Dufferin. I'm not apparently who you think I am. I've called with a message for you. You're to go out tonight to Compostella Canyon. It'll take about an hour. Bring your wife's papers with you. Get there at three in the morning when there's no other traffic, and come alone. Don't try any tricks. We can see you coming from five miles off. We know your car. There'll be a girl waiting for you."

"You," I said. "Who are you?"

"Three o'clock on the dot. Bring the papers."

"Or what?"

"Or we kill the kid," she said. "And that's no joke."

I sucked in a breath. All my pores yawned and the sweat filmed my forehead and damped my wrists. My shirt was glued to my back. I said, "I don't have the papers."

"We know you do. Three o'clock. Compostella Canyon. Call the cops and the kid dies anyway."

She hung up.

I stood there a long time. Someone was hammering on the door. I put up the phone and crossed the room.

The beefy man outside had an unlighted cigar in his face. The night detective. I thought vaguely that he had listened in on the call with Gloria Mason. It didn't matter. I stood and stared at him.

"Mr. Dufferin?" He took the cigar from his mouth and gave a friendly smile. "I figured you'd like me to come up and tell you personally. Girl downstairs checked that call. It came in from a public phone in San Bernadino. We can't do anything this end, but I got friends down there. If you want to contact anyone in particular, why, I don't say the chances are strong—but, if you'd like to give me the name and maybe a description, we'll do all we can."

"Thanks," I said. "It's not important."

He said, "You sick, Mr. Dufferin?"

"I'm fine."

He smiled again. "You professional guys must get a lot of tension when you make big deals."

"Yes," I said.

"Known Mr. Wilde long?"

"Mr. Wilde?"

His mouth met his eye in a wink. "Secret, huh? I guessed something like that when he didn't have himself announced. I came up at the same time. Just my rounds. I saw him come to your room. Very smart man, Mr. Wilde."

"Yes," I said. "Known him long?"

"Don't know him at all. My sister pointed him out once. He was attorney for a family where she used to work looking after the kids."

The phone rang.

I shut the door in his face.

I said, "Yes?"

"I've finally caught you in," my sister said, fury in her voice. "I hope you're damned well ashamed of yourself, pulling a trick like that, telling Chester to his face you didn't have him. Okay, you're entitled to him, but after all we've done for you you could at least have warned us. Chester's nearly out of his mind. He's going to sue you for custody."

She broke off. There was a scuffling murmur at the other end, and my brother-in-law shouted, "You no-good drunken bastard, I don't care what scandal it causes. Bring that kid back or I call the boys about Frascatti. You hear me?"

I said, "I'll be right out."

TWENTY-SIX

I parked in the quiet street. The coppice was dark, but no one waited there. They had no need to. I had to go to them now. I ran up the front pathway.

Fay had heard the car coming. She opened the door and said, "Where is he?" I passed her and went inside, and Chester came out of the sitting room with his eyes gone small and his face swollen. We froze at one another. Fay closed the door, and Chester said, "Where is he?"

"I don't have him."

He flung himself at me and swung a fist, hitting my shoulder and knocking me up against the banister of the stairs. Fay shouted, "Stop it!" and ran between us, her face flaming. "Stop it, you pigs. You're not going to brawl in my house. Act your age, Chester. Al is the boy's father. He's entitled to do what he wants with him."

"That's right, you go on his side." Chester made another movement, and heaved him away. He shouted, "The sonofabitch is not fit to have charge of a dog, let alone a kid. He's a drunk. He killed Clare. There's not a judge in the country will give him custody—"

"Shut up!" Fay snapped. "Where are you going?"

"To phone the boys," he said. "I've kept my mouth shut long enough. You may not know it, but your precious brother's mixed up in that Frascatti killing we heard on the radio. When he's in jail Johnny will have to come back here."

I said, "Call the cops and he'll never come back. I don't have him."

Fay said, "Al, what does that mean?"

There was a small tense silence. Fay said, "What are you saying, Al?"

"Johnny's been kidnapped."

Chester made another movement, then stood petrified. The color drained from him, and he whispered, "Kidnapped?" and moved again.

"Leave it, Chester. Call the cops and they'll kill him."

He said hoarsely, "You have to call the cops at a time like this."

"You'd be entitled to if he were your son. He's not."

Chester nodded. He gave a sob, his face crumpling to nothing, and lowered his head. My sister said faintly, "Al, this wouldn't be a joke?"

I said, "Are you sure he's gone? You've checked everywhere?"

"We've checked nowhere. We thought he was with you. No one would keep him till this time of night."

"They'd have phoned," Chester said in a dead voice. "And he's not lost. I take him when I go to the Pistoleros Club. The boys down at headquarters know him. They'd have brought him home by now."

I said, "Go into the sitting room, both of you."

I went to the phone.

There were four attorneys named Wilde in the book. One was listed with a suite of offices downtown and a house in the Hills. I called the house. The man who answered had an imitation English accent. He may have been the butler Wilde bragged about.

He said, "I'm very sorry, sir, but the master is about to retire. He cannot be disturbed."

"Tell him it's Dufferin. Important. He'll want to be disturbed."

"I'll see, sir."

In the other room Fay and Chester were not talking, and the house was filled with gluey silence. I waited for what seemed a long time. Then Wilde came.

"Hello, Dufferin. I won't dissimulate and pretend I don't know you. How did you find out? Follow me?"

"I want to talk to Holst. Give me his number."

"Who is Holst?"

'Perhaps the cops will know. I'm off to headquarters."

"Wait now, Dufferin, wait," he said. "Think clearly. What policeman within a hundred miles radius will act on your word without first checking with Mr. Holst himself?"

"They'll act on the statement," I said. "There are newspapers. Ted Wilson can help. You didn't manage to kill him this evening."

"Please tell me what you are talking about."

"I'm at Los Olmos. The number is two, five-nine-three-four. Tell Holst he has five minutes."

I hung up.

They were sitting motionless, like wax models, in the other room. They looked up at me expectantly, not speaking, but I had nothing to say to them. I lowered myself to a chair and sat with my hands on my knees.

Five long minutes passed.

Chester got up, went to the kitchen and came back with three glasses of Scotch on a tray. His hands trembled. Five minutes more.

The phone rang.

I snatched up the receiver. "Dufferin."

He said in a guarded voice, "You wanted to talk to me?"

"Yes. Listen. You get my little boy back here in fifteen minutes or I blow the whole works."

"What little boy?" he said. "What's the matter with him?"

"Don't stall with me, you sonofabitch, or the whole world knows tomorrow morning that you killed Phil Greco." He made a grunting noise. Then silence. I shouted, "Holst!"

"Yes, yes, wait a minute. This kid of yours. You mean he's been kidnapped?"

"You know it."

"I don't know it, boy." Silence again. He said, "But I can do something about it for you, and don't you worry. I can have every cop in California looking for him. Every cop and every citizen. I'll organize radio and TV. I'll have a photograph of him projected every hour in every movie house in the state. Any idea who snatched him?"

"You," I said.

"Act smart, Dufferin, I'm trying to help. I'll do everything in my power. I guarantee as far as possible to get the boy back."

He sounded sincere and kindly. He said, "All I want in return is that you give me the papers."

I said, "I get it. It boils down to the same thing. You kidnapped the kid for the papers. You'll return him for the papers. The only difference is I don't have to make the trip to Compostella Canyon. Holst, I'm calling your bluff. I'm publicizing the statement. On top of murder you'll face a kidnapping rap."

"Kidnapping?" Suddenly he was screaming. "What're you talking about? How many times I got to tell you I don't know nothing about it?"

The phone went dead.

"Holst!" I shouted. "Holst!"

"Stop acting like a madman." Wilde's voice on the phone was calm. "Don't yell. At times like this we must all remain calm and reasonable. I got here quickly. I'm glad I did. Listen, Dufferin, and try to get it into your head. We have had no hand in whatever has happened to your child. I promised that nothing would be done against you until agreement was reached, and I have kept my word. If the boy is missing, someone else has him. Mr. Holst can help get him back. You still get the contract and the cash settlement. All we want is the papers. But now. Before we do anything."

"I don't have them."

"Liar," he said coldly.

"I never had them. They're with Gloria Mason, Barry Kevin's sister-in-law. I don't know where she is. You think I'd fool around with my kid in danger? I have to make a deal with the kidnappers in three hours."

"Oh," he said. "Oh. Then perhaps you don't have them."

"I'll get them for you tomorrow night."

He said, "Then we shall have to talk again tomorrow night. It would not be sensible for us to move now. We might stir up a hornets' nest, going to the police while the document is still at large. Who knows—we might yet have to make a deal with this other party you mention. I'm sorry, Dufferin. A client must be protected, you understand. I don't suggest that you go to the police either, except perhaps about the kidnapping. No one will believe anything else you say without the documentary evidence. Call me tomorrow at my office if anything new comes up. Good night, now. Good luck."

He rang off.

I stood choking, then returned to the other room. Chester had poured another drink apiece, and he handed me the glass.

He asked, "What's happening," and he looked like death. He said, "Has he really been kidnapped?"

"Yes."

"We have to go to the police."

"No," I said.

"Is it mixed up with this Frascatti? I don't care if you did kill him. I won't mention it to anybody ever. Unless we have to, to get Johnny back."

"No police," I said. "They might find out. They might kill him."

Fay said, "Who?"

"I don't know, I don't know." I wanted to throw back my head and howl. "Not Holst," I said. "Not Wilde. Not Gloria Mason—she doesn't need him. Not Barry Kevin's wife and not Ted Wilson." I looked at Chester. "And not you."

"I'll call the police."

"I have to find him myself."

"How can you?" Fay said. "They'll have taken him somewhere far away and quiet."

"Yes," I said, and took a drink. I tried to put the glass back on the table and missed. It fell to the floor and broke. I said, "Fay, what did you say?"

"You must call the police. You can't find him yourself."

"The other thing."

"They'll have taken him somewhere far away and quiet."

I watched a serpentine trickle of whisky wriggle over the floor. I said, "Yes." They stared at me.

In a minute I said, "Yes. I might know where he is. I might be wrong. Chester, you have to help."

"Anything."

"You know Compostella Canyon?"

"It's about thirty miles from here. We go there some Sunday mornings to practice shooting with the Pistoleros."

"Take my car. Arrive there at three o'clock. A woman will be waiting, expecting me. She wants some papers that I don't have. Tell her anything, any story you like. Use force on her if you have to. She may know where Johnny is. She may have a crowd of hoods with her. It'll be dangerous, in any case, so take your gun."

"But you said you know where he is."

"I said I might be wrong. We need double insurance."

"I want to go where the kid is. If there's any chance of him getting hurt—"

"You'll do as I say."

"I'm going with you, where the kid is."

"Chester! Chester!" Fay said, and leaned forward and put her face in her hands and began to weep.

TWENTY-SEVEN

I got lost. I traced my way back to a dirt highway that ran among the pine trees above the sands and, after a while, distantly through the open window, I heard voices shouting to one another. I parked Chester's car and got out to ask directions. There was no other car in sight, and I figured the people must live somewhere near and would know the locality.

It was a dark night with no moon and only a few stars. I located the party by sound. They were right across the sand, nearly at the surf line—six of them, four men and two girls, all young and having a midnight bathing spree. All naked.

No one seemed embarrassed or surprised to see me. Perhaps because they were very drunk. Or it may have been marijuana.

I had trouble making sense of them at first. They asked me to join them. I said there were already two men too many, and that made them laugh at a private joke. I accepted the drink. They said there was only one more house anywhere near, a log cabin five miles farther on, standing back from the shore on a slope covered with pines. I might have trouble finding it.

I thanked them. One of the men walked a little way back across the sands with me and made a pass, but he wasn't insistent. I got to the car and drove on.

The dirt highway got worse, and soon degenerated into a rutted track. I didn't want to announce my coming and I didn't know how right the people had been about the distance, so I let only four miles tick off on the meter, pulled over to the side as much as I could and parked again. I jumped down from the track to the sands, much narrower here. Little waves broke a short distance away and scalloped to my feet, and my shoes sank in the wetness. I made no sound.

It was twenty minutes before two. No smog out here. The sea hissed gently, and the air was soft with brine and tree smells. It would have been nice to take off my clothes for a swim. I needed a wash. I was crusted with sweat from the fear of my own thoughts. Afraid that I had guessed wrongly about where the boy was, more afraid that I had guessed rightly about everything else.

I was unarmed. I needed a gun. Anything.

The dark trees on my right merged with the sky. At first the distant light, high on the slope, seemed to be hanging in mid-air like a star. I looked at it for half a minute. If I entered the wrong place, there might be trouble, police, the end of the night. The end of Johnny. Anyone else but the person I anticipated and I would pretend to be inquiring the way. I started up through the trees.

I made as little noise as possible. It still seemed too much. I could find no track. The trees were close together with their lower branches sometimes interlaced, and the bracken underfoot went off like fireworks. I made slow progress. I tried to run across a small clearing and fell over on my hands.

A bird hooted.

I stayed crouched. The sound was coming from somewhere up near the cabin, a sort of long unearthly wail of pain. Then it was not a bird, but a whimpering dog. Then it was not a dog. My heart burst. I flung upright and hurled forward.

Branches lashed, wood snapped, I probably sounded like a herd of elephants. The noise was no longer important. I burst into the other large clearing where the cabin stood and ran up the steps to the porch. The front door was open. I halted inside the cabin.

It was a nice cabin, large, adapted to the slope, well furnished. Skins hung on the walls, the floor and furniture were of pine and there was a big mantled fireplace with logs blazing in it. There were two other doors in the main room, both open, a bed through one and a kitchen through the other. Beyond the kitchen a third open door led to the back porch.

Wearing a kimono, she was sitting among cushions on a sofa in front of the fire, a drink in her hand, her legs stretched comfortably. She said, "Al. Surprise. And what brings you here?"

I went straight to the bedroom. Nothing. Not under the bed, nor in either of the cupboards. I returned to the sitting room, looked around and went through to the kitchen. She watched me with eyebrows raised, not saying anything more. Nothing in the kitchen either. I stood and listened. I turned to enter again and saw the big black box over in the shadow against the wall.

I went over to it, kicked it and tried to open it. The lid would lift only a fraction of an inch. It was fastened with a big padlock.

She called, "Come and have a drink."

She had not moved. She waved a hand at bottle and glasses on the table. "What are you wandering around for?" she asked. "I won't say I'm pleased to see you, but—"

"What's in the box out there, Bertha?"

"Which? Oh, the big box? Tools. The local handyman is going to build me an extension when he gets around to it. You know what people are in this neck of the woods."

"The box is locked. Where's the key?"

"I wouldn't know. The man probably has it himself. Don't tell me you want to build yourself something. Pour yourself a drink."

I said, "I want my kid."

She moved then, nervous all of a sudden. The fat rolled under her kimono.

A trick of the firelight, her ragged hair, gave her for an instant the hard look of an elderly man. She started to plump a cushion behind her, but changed her mind and held it on her knees instead, as though to protect herself. She said, "You're on another jag, Al. Be a good boy. Give yourself a stiff one and then beat it."

"No, Bertha. That angle was worked to death in your office this morning. It has to be you."

"I'm flattered." She managed a grin. "But not tonight, son. This may be a love nest, but right now I'm expecting someone else."

"Not Frascatti."

"Who's he?"

I lied. I said, "You can't dodge it. You've been seen together. You both covered your tracks, but I found out who financed him in the Top Hat. Films may be failing. You've been doing all right with your new flat and your genuine paintings on the wall. You had money to spend on your friend. I guess you loved him. It would explain why you shot him this afternoon after I said he was carrying on with Barry Kevin's sister-in-law. You'd be especially angry because you knew by then that he'd stolen Clare's document from you. He couldn't return it."

She twitched the cushion on her lap, and I looked into the barrel of a small gun. She said calmly, "Al, you're dangerous. I'm going to call the cops. You know how they'll treat you."

"That won't work either. You sent them after me the afternoon I went to Barry Kevin's. It had to be you. You were the only one who knew where I was. You tried hard yourself to scare me off. You never stopped."

"You should have gone," she said. "You'll find the cops always co-operate with me."

"Not this time. There's too much stacked against you."

I moved.

She said, "Stand still, Al. I'll drill you."

I changed direction. I went to the table and poured myself a drink. "You won't," I said. "Not till you know where you can lay hands on Clare's papers. Give me the kid and I'll let you have them."

She sat regarding me blandly and said, "This is all very strange. Tell me what you think you're talking about."

"I will," I said. "But remember all the time that none of it means anything to me. I don't care what happened in the past, neither what you did nor what anyone else did. Clare didn't kill Phil Greco. All right. Holst did. He picked a bad time. He was in the middle of a big movie that would have cost millions if held up. He and Foxwell between them persuaded Clare to take the blame. In return, Foxwell was made a producer and Clare was promised stardom. It was enough for her. She'd have pawned her immortal soul for half the chance. So she went on trial, was acquitted and the process began. We can only guess what she'd have done had she been convicted."

"Squawked her head off," Bertha said. "But there was no chance of conviction. Whoever handled the studio publicity was a genius. He made her a heroine."

I said, "She was your client and friend. I still don't understand why she told you what had happened and gave you the statement. She wasn't the type to share confidences."

"No, but she was a greedy little bitch and Holst was stingy. He gave her a contract. She wanted more money. She told me as her agent to put more pressure on him. I tried, and it didn't work. After a while she told me what sort of pressure to put. I was the one who persuaded her to make the statement. It was in my files when she was killed."

I said, "You've been blackmailing Holst."

"Who wouldn't?"

I said, "Frascatti knew about the statement. You loved him well enough to give him the run of your files. Or he found out while snooping. Or maybe it's the sort of thing that a woman like you whispers as a love secret in the middle of the night."

"You underestimate me," she said. "I'm pretty good when I get going."

"So was Frascatti, professionally and otherwise. When he fell in love out of business hours, he really went overboard. His girl friend was another film-struck doll. He used to thrill her with Hollywood gossip. He probably got it from you. He didn't tell her about you, though, because he was afraid of losing her. But he told her about me. And he told her about Clare's statement."

Berths said, "Then Kevin got hold of it through his sister-in-law."

I said, "She didn't know enough to handle it herself. She had to call him in. It was the chance he'd waited for. He could use Holst to get back into pictures on his own terms. First he had to make sure it wasn't a gag, that Frascatti wasn't playing big just to impress little Gloria. He called me in to check the handwriting. He seemed to think I recognized it. The deal was on. He contacted Holst and applied the screws."

"He showed you the statement?" Berths asked.

"He showed me a cast list, a forgery, a good one, done by Gloria Mason. She's been clever with a pen since she was five. I came to your apartment next morning to tell you about it. You probably thought I meant the statement. You waited all day for me to come back, and when I didn't you sent Kolanski and Pinhead Johnson to Los Olmos. I didn't have the statement."

"You always had it," she said. "That pair gets no more work from me. They're not as efficient as they're cracked up to be."

"You'd have done better to hire them the night before when you thought Barry Kevin had the statement. They're professional. They'd have persuaded Kevin to talk without beating him right to death. They'd have found the papers under his rubber girdle."

"My God," Bertha said. "No wonder Hymie couldn't find them. Hand them over, Al. I'll tell you where the kid is."

I said, "Why did you collect Barry Kevin's body?"

"I hate unnecessary investigations. I avoid trouble whenever possible."

"Over the mountainside in flames," I said. "Near where Clare had established the precedent."

"Papers," she said.

There was no bright light, no buzzing in my ears, no sense of revelation. I said, "You killed Clare."

"Al, the papers."

"You killed Clare for the statement."

"It was of more value to me than to her. Where is it?"

Then I was frightened; I had talked too much. My palate went dry with fear. I said, "I don't have it."

She shook her head. "Frascatti told me. He was a coward. He was in no mental condition this afternoon to tell lies."

"He believed what he was saying," I said. "He was wrong. I don't have it. Tell me where the kid is and I'll get it for you within twenty-four hours."

"From where?"

"You'll be able to go after it as easy as I if I tell you."

She stood up, with the gun trained on me, and said, "Maybe I won't go after it at all, Al. I've made my pile. Maybe I'd be smart to have nothing more to do with it." She stood a moment. She nodded. "That's about right. It's nothing to me if the thing is published. I can't be touched. I won't even be mentioned. Why should I be? Holst will be the one to suffer, and what's that to me?"

She moved away and put her back upright against the wall. She looked at me curiously. She said, "You've got no weapon against me, Al. Nothing to say that will interest me. You've already said everything. My only worry is that you'll go away and say it to someone else."

I had to swallow before I could speak. I said, "What about the boy?"

"We'll think of him when we've taken care of you," she said, and turned her head in the direction of the back door without taking her eyes off me.

She called, "You can come in now."

I thought he had fooled me. He came in by the front door with a gun in his hand.

Chester.

TWENTY-EIGHT

She turned and saw him, and both guns went off at the same time. A bullet plucked a hole in a pelt on the wall beside Chester's head. Bertha screamed. The gun jumped from her hand and into the fire, and she clutched her shattered wrist. She pitched sideways, hung for a moment and gave a funny sort of roll, then fell in the fire herself.

I didn't move.

She screamed. She was alight. Her voice went screechingly high and then stopped. Chester ran across the room ramming the gun in his pocket, his eyes wide and staring as though he saw nothing. He grabbed her kimono, snatched her from the fire and started to beat out the flames on her back. He shouted, "Look out, Al!" and fell to the floor beside her. She was still burning.

The weapon on the fire went off like a bomb, and the room whined with metal.

A window shattered, and there was a reek of cordite. I moved. I tore off my jacket, flung it over Bertha and beat at her with my hands. The flames went out. I removed the jacket. She was inert, like a dead pig. I took her chin and put her face in profile on the floor so she could breathe. Her shoulders were badly scorched, and all the hair was singed from the back of her head. Her mouth was wide open and she was snoring with shock.

Chester whispered, "Get a doctor."

He was sitting on the floor with his legs crossed, hand to his face. Blood was trickling through his fingers where a piece of flying metal had gouged his cheek. He looked on the point of being sick. His voice returned hysterically high-pitched. "I sent cops to the canyon. I had to. I followed you."

I said, "Glad you did," and started to help him to his feet.

"Where's Johnny?"

"Somewhere. I heard him."

"I couldn't come in before. There was a guy outside by the window. I hit him on the head. I had to wait till she was looking the other way. I heard what she said."

"What guy?"

"I don't know."

I ran through the kitchen. Too late.

The big box on the porch was open.

Hymie heard me coming. He whirled. He was paralyzed with fear, and the whites of his eyes were showing. He had a gun in his hand, but he didn't point it at me. His left arm was tight against Johnny's chest, clutching the dangling child to him. The boy's mouth was gagged with a woman's stocking, and his hands were tied at his back. The gun barrel was jammed tight into his stomach.

I said, "Hymie, put him down. You'll choke him. I've got nothing against you. You can go any time you like."

We stood unmoving. He croaked hoarsely, "He's coming with me. Then I'll be sure."

The boy's eyes looked almost calm.

I said, "Be good, Johnny. Don't struggle. Don't try to make a noise. I'm going to take you home tonight."

I heard Chester behind me. I waited, and then the boy nodded.

Hymie said, choking, "If you try to follow, he gets it. I'll hear if you follow. I'll hear. I'm going now."

He walked slowly backwards, then faded into the darkness around the side of the cabin.

Silence.

"No, Chester!" I grabbed his arm. "We can't take chances."

"I can't stand here and—"

I darted past him and into the cabin. I turned out the lights, and there was only the flicker of the fire and Bertha snoring motionless on the floor. I said, "He killed Barry Kevin. He's got nothing to lose. He's liable to pull the trigger through fear." I crossed the room and edged myself flat against the wall by the front door. Chester didn't move. I waited again. Silence. There was a crackle as Hymie entered the underbrush.

"Out!" I said, and we were on the front porch with the door shut.

He was crashing down the wooded slope directly in front of us, heading for the sea. With the noise he was making he maybe wouldn't hear us. I hoped not. I gripped Chester's arm and I said, "To the right. Fast. Stop when he stops. We'll close in on him at the bottom."

I gave him a push and ran to the left.

I went sideways, like a crab. I was getting pretty scratched up. I could hear Hymie ahead of me, off to the right. He had a start but wasn't making good time because of Johnny, and I was gaining on him. He stopped. I stopped.

I thought at first he had reached the road, but there had not been time. Then I thought he was doing things to Johnny, killing him, and I wanted to run for them. I daren't. The crackling started again.

I ran, fell over, picked myself up and ran on. I was level with him and then ahead and then at the road. An automobile gleamed in the darkness off to the left. It was not mine and not Chester's. Hymie would have to pass me to get to it. I stood in the trees and looked along the dirt highway, and he came bursting out with the boy hugged to him with both arms.

He poised a moment. He heard Chester coming. He jumped from the road down to the sands and dragged the boy with him. I couldn't see either of them any more.

Chester was a fool. He had not made a wide enough circuit. He had moved too far to his left and was coming down the exact track that Hymie had taken. I shouted, "Chester, he's got cover. He's down on the sands. Watch yourself."

The crackling footsteps came on.

They moved slowly, steadily and with too much noise. He was heralding his coming as though he were blowing a trumpet. "Chester!" I shouted. He was going to emerge right in front of where Hymie was waiting. "Chester!" The footsteps stopped and started again. "Chester! Look out!"

The figure appeared at the edge of the wood.

Hymie's gun spat flame.

I jumped the road and down to the sand and sprinted. The figure came out of the trees and staggered in a dance. It was Bertha. She put her arms straight above her head and shrieked *"Aaaaaah,"* all the time I was running. *"Aaaaaah. Aaaaaah. Aaaaaah!"* Then she fell over. Hymie was on his feet, scampering backward at the sea, his left arm clamped across Johnny's throat, the boy dangling before him.

He saw me.

The gun spat again, I felt a pain and my left arm caught fire. I ran at him in the sea. He fired once more, and the bullet whistled past me. I stood still. Then the other gun spat orange beyond him and he stood still. Unconsciously I began to walk backwards.

He dropped the gun first. He put the boy down as tenderly as though he loved him. He took three steps to the rear, stopped again and knelt down slowly in the water. It came to his waist. Then to his chest. Then to his mouth, and he rolled and he went under. He stayed under.

I touched my arm and gave at the knees, and I sat down. The boy had not fallen. I watched him come out of the water.

He was very good. Despite his tied hands he slipped only once. Chester came along the sand from the other side, still holding his gun, and stood apart from me. The boy emerged clear.

Chester said, "Johnny. Go to your daddy, son. Go to your dad."

He came to me.

I remember untying the bonds of his hands and taking the gag from his mouth. Then I fainted.

The doctor at police headquarters fixed up my arm. A flesh wound, a nicked bone, but nothing from which I wouldn't recover by morning. The two bodies were brought in. By that time Fay had come and taken Johnny home. I stayed the rest of the night answering questions. Chester stayed with me.

The cops were pretty nice. I think at first it was because they all took a shine to Johnny. I mentioned Holst, and they became nice and respectful as well. I was pretty cautious, and so was Chester. He was a help. Some of his fellow Pistoleros were present. A marksman's club. After the beach I was glad about that.

A call was put out for Gloria Mason.

TWENTY-NINE

It was a nice day outside. The sunlight came in the window of Holst's office, skated over his unlovely bright skull and wandered among the dust on his hundreds of scripts. He gobbed into the spittoon. He lit a cigar and smiled at me through the smoke like a suave and genial alligator. He was feeling good about something. I could not understand it. He was going to be up to his eyelashes when the cops found Gloria Mason.

I said, "Bertha take much off you?"

"Too much." He thickened his lips. "I made her presents. I used all her clients. Some of them were punk."

"When did she start the pressure?"

"Two weeks after your wife was killed. She showed me the second page of the confession. It was enough."

He paused a moment, then said, "Tell you something, Dufferin. I wasn't exactly heartbroken when your wife went over the mountain. She didn't have an ounce of talent. What would I have done with her?"

I said, "Bertha killed her."

He blinked once. "Is that right? Well, this is a hard racket we're in. The Tweedy agency was on the skids. I guess Bertha wanted a weapon to fight her way to the top again, and the confession must have looked like the answer. She did very well out of it. That's why she wouldn't admit to me that she'd lost it."

I said, "That aspect confused me for a while."

"You?" he said. "What about me? Kevin phones to say he has it. We're going to make a Cellini movie. You're going to write the script. It's going to cost ten million, flop, make havoc among the shareholders and put me out on my ear. I call Bertha. She says it's all a gag, and she still has the confession. When Barry Kevin dies the same night it looks like she's speaking the truth."

"He was murdered," I said.

"I figured it wasn't a coincidence. Who was I to worry?"

I said, "She sent her boy Hymie to get the papers back. Kevin got killed in the process, but Bertha didn't get the papers. I spoke to her next morning. She thought I had them. She sent two professionals to get them from me."

"I knew nothing about it. I thought the position was the same as always. Two days later you turned up. I left word for you to be admitted because Kevin had mentioned you. I wanted to see how much you knew. You seemed to know everything. You said you had the confession."

"I didn't."

"I know it now. I didn't know then if I was on my ass or my elbow. I had you followed. I sent for Bertha to get here right away."

"I went to her office right away. She was out. That was rare."

He said, "She couldn't show me the confession. She had to admit then someone else had it. She said she didn't know who. I thought I did. The boy who followed you found you registered at some dump under the name of Kingston. I sent a couple of collectors."

"The same two Bertha sent. They were surprised."

"I was surprised when they only got one sheet of the confession, and it was in the form of a letter to you. I decided you were too smart to fall into traps. I set my lawyer on you. He's smarter."

I said, "He couldn't do a thing when Bertha set herself on my kid. You'd have both been smarter to tell me from the beginning that she was the original blackmailer. It would have saved trouble."

Holst smiled. "A crazy move," he said. "In a racket like this you always protect yourself by saying nothing. Always."

"You might have saved Frascatti's life," I said. "You might have saved Ted Wilson from being run down. I told Bertha he was digging for me. She probably thought he would discover that you were employing all her clients."

"Wilson? I remember him. A drunk. I fired him." Holst dropped his cigar in the spittoon and lit another. Apparently he only liked the first inch. He said amiably, "I'll still buy that B movie from you. Ten thousand. A six-month contract with option. Seven-fifty a week."

"Prices have come down."

"Now I don't have to," he said.

I said, "Stuff the ten along with the contract."

"You're missing an opportunity."

"No," I said.

"As you like." He blew out smoke, merry as a grig. "Okay, no business and nothing more to say. It's been interesting, but I'm a busy man. On your way."

I stood up. "Just for interest. Why did you kill Greco, apart from quick temper?"

"Just for your interest," he said. "It's not in my interest to answer."

"Something from back in Chicago? Blackmail?"

"On your way, Dufferin. I don't want to have you put out, you with a bandaged arm and me feeling good this morning."

"What did you do with that first page of the letter?"

"Burned it."

"It won't help," I said. "It was a forgery. Like the cast list Barry Kevin gave me."

Holst said, "Gloria Mason. A clever and pretty little girl."

"You won't think so when the police find her."

"And what can the police do?" he asked kindly. "They caught the office girl of Bertha's in Compostella Canyon, and she said she was taking a midnight drive. She had a license for her gun. They held her for a day and had to let her go."

"Did you have a hand in that?"

He ignored the question and said, "What can they do with Gloria Mason?"

"Get the original confession from her."

He laughed and said, "Sit down a minute."

He pressed a button. The door opened behind me, and Bannion's voice said, "Oh yes, sir," and the door closed again. Five minutes passed. Holst blew smoke rings that mushroomed like A-bombs.

She came in with Bannion. She was wearing a period gown and studio makeup, and her eyes glowed as though she had glimpsed heaven. She sat pertly on the corner of Holst's desk and smiled down on him. She paid me no heed. He looked back at her as though she were a heifer and he a farmer. He said, "Well, honey?"

"It was wonderful, Mr. Holst."

"How did it go, Bannion?"

"Well, actually fairly well, sir. Yes, sir. Something will have to be done about her voice, but, after all, sir, we do have people for that."

"Gloria," I said.

She turned. "Hello."

"Where's the statement?"

"What statement?"

"The one you wanted me to help you with, even to seducing me. The one you kept phoning about."

She fluttered her long false eyelashes and smiled all around. "What's he talking about?"

"Don't you know, honey?"

"No idea whatever."

I said, "You made a deal."

"Deal?" Holst said. "What's this? I get a buzz this beautiful little girl is down near the border. She has talent. This studio is on the lookout for talent. New talent is the lifeblood of the industry. So I send a scout after her. She starts small, but—"

I said, "What did you sell it for, Gloria?"

"I have money," she answered proudly. "I don't have to quibble."

"Two-fifty a week for six months, then out on your fanny."

"Not with my talent."

I said, "Wait till you have to use it on the police."

"But the police are utterly charming." She did the business with her eyelashes again, liking it. She said, "I spoke to one of them down at the border. He was lovely."

I looked at Holst. He was grinning again. I said, "How does she wriggle away from Frascatti?"

"Nothing to do with her, Dufferin. A cheap gangster killing. Nightclub stuff. She hadn't seen him for days."

"And the statement?"

His little eyes filled with a sudden cold glee. "Burned," he said. "There never was any statement. It never existed. We're all going to forget what we imagined about it. Because if you try to remember in public I'll ruin you, Dufferin. Here and in New York and in every place between. I'll slap a slander suit on you that'll keep you in debt until you're eighty. That clear?"

"Crystal," I said, and turned to Bannion. "Give me an honest answer. Does she have any talent at all?"

He looked at Holst, then said, "Well no, actually. She's awful."

"A consolation," I said, and walked out, through the other office, past the statues and into the fresh air. I took a big deep breath.

The sun was bright. There was no smog, birds sang, the atmosphere felt green. I went through the sealed corridor, out at the other end, got a fond smile from the gate-guard and a look of envy from the people in the line-up. I went over to the car.

Karen Kevin was standing there, talking to Johnny. She turned her bitter face as I came up and tried to smile. "Nice little boy," she said.

"Yes, I like him."

"I phoned your sister's house. She told me you were here. I'm looking for Gloria."

"She's inside."

"In the studios, you mean? Mr. Dufferin, you shouldn't have filled her head with so much nonsense—"

"She's made the grade," I said. "She's got a contract. She's going to be the biggest thing in films."

"Is that really true?" The crease disappeared slowly from Mrs. Kevin's brow. She seemed to be awakening from something. She said, "Of course, Gloria has all sorts of talent, I've never doubted that. Only she's so young and innocent. She doesn't know how to look after herself. Hadn't I better go in and see she's all right?"

"Yes," I said. "Just speak to the man in that desk over there."

She nodded, forgetting me already. She walked straight to the head of the line-up and began to talk. She spoke softly. Then her voice raised and she began to argue.

I got in the car.

We drove down through Hollywood. I was still shy, but the boy was smiling and chattering and generally being what boys are. He said, "Where we going, Dad?"

"Home to pack," I said. "Then down to Mexico for a few weeks for some fishing and swimming. Think you'll like it?"

"Gee!" he said. "I'll help you with the suitcases because of your arm."

He did, the small ones, sweating and grunting like a furniture mover. Fay and Chester waved us good-by from the porch, and I discovered how funny kids can be. I had to remind Johnny to turn and wave back. He did, but only briefly. Chester waved until we were out of sight. I could see him in the rear-view mirror.

All along the highway the billboards said that movies are getting better.

THE END

www.ingramcontent.com/pod-product-compliance
Lightning Source LLC
LaVergne TN
LVHW021701060526
838200LV00050B/2451